USA TODAY bestselling, RITA®-nominated and critically acclaimed author **Caitlin Crews** has written more than one hundred books and counting. She has a Master's and a PhD in English Literature, thinks everyone should read more category romance, and is always available to discuss her beloved alpha heroes. Just ask! She lives in the Pacific Northwest with her comic book artist husband, she is always planning her next trip, and she will never, ever, read all the books in her 'to-be-read' pile. Thank goodness.

Jennifer Hayward has been a fan of romance since filching her sister's novels to escape her teenage angst. Her career in journalism and PR, including years of working alongside powerful, charismatic CEOs and travelling the world, has provided perfect fodder for the fast-paced, sexy stories she likes to write—always with a touch of humour. A native of Canada's East Coast, Jennifer lives in picturesque Nova Scotia with her Viking husband and teenage Viking-in-training.

Also by Caitlin Crews

A Secret Heir to Secure His Throne
What Her Sicilian Husband Desires

Innocent Stolen Brides miniseries

The Desert King's Kidnapped Virgin

The Outrageous Accardi Brothers miniseries

The Christmas He Claimed the Secretary
The Accidental Accardi Heir

Also by Jennifer Hayward

A Deal for the Di Sione Ring
A Debt Paid in the Marriage Bed
Salazar's One-Night Heir

The Powerful Di Fiore Tycoons miniseries

Christmas at the Tycoon's Command
His Million-Dollar Marriage Proposal
Married for His One-Night Heir

Discover more at millsandboon.co.uk.

THE SPANIARD'S LAST-MINUTE WIFE

CAITLIN CREWS

HOW THE ITALIAN CLAIMED HER

JENNIFER HAYWARD

MILLS & BOON

First published in Great Britain 2023
by Mills & Boon, an imprint of HarperCollins*Publishers* Ltd,
1 London Bridge Street, London, SE1 9GF

www.harpercollins.co.uk

HarperCollins*Publishers*, Macken House, 39/40 Mayor Street Upper,
Dublin 1, D01 C9W8, Ireland

The Spaniard's Last-Minute Wife © 2023 Caitlin Crews

How the Italian Claimed Her © 2023 Jennifer Drogell

ISBN: 978-0-263-30693-4

09/23

MIX
Paper | Supporting
responsible forestry
FSC™ C007454

This book is produced from independently certified FSC™ paper
to ensure responsible forest management.
For more information visit: www.harpercollins.co.uk/green.

Printed and Bound in the UK using 100% Renewable Electricity
at CPI Group (UK) Ltd, Croydon, CR0 4YY

THE SPANIARD'S LAST-MINUTE WIFE

CAITLIN CREWS

MILLS & BOON

CHAPTER ONE

GERALDINE GERTRUDE CASEY didn't mean to laugh.

Truly, she didn't.

One moment she was sitting with an appropriately poker-faced expression, as suited the occasion, and the next...well. She let out what could only be termed a cackle.

A rather loud cackle, she could admit.

It was involuntary.

Really, it was—though it was also true that she'd had some or other vague notion that she might slip in her objections to the wedding today, assuming that priests here in Italy actually asked if anyone harbored any. Geraldine wasn't certain if they did or didn't and more, harbored no particular certainty that she would understand such a question even if it was asked, as she did not speak Italian.

But another, more salient truth was that she was delirious from flying all the way here on a remarkably uncomfortable overnight flight from Minneapolis via Chicago. She had been crammed into the back of the alarmingly oversize jumbo jet in the middle of a row of tiny, uncomfortable seats with limited recline. Her mother and she had been pressed up against each other from knee to shoulder as they'd passed the unamused baby back and forth between them while pretending that the peace between the two of them wasn't *quite* so precarious in the wake of Geraldine's decision to travel to Italy in the first place.

And while Geraldine and her mother were close, and had always been close, she was fairly sure that the last time she had been that physically close to her mother had been in the womb.

Geraldine had not been all that keen on landing so early in the morning, having slept a total of five minutes, only to have to sort herself out sufficiently to drive her mother and a screaming child from the airport outside Milan all the way to Lake Como, locate the overpriced yet aggressively bland hotel room she'd managed to secure a mere two days before, and then *not* collapse on one of the narrow, monastic beds waiting there. She'd left that to Mama and little Jules, who had been headed into her fifteenth tantrum that morning. Geraldine had changed into a dress, because she was crashing a wedding after all, and had set off to traipse about in the bright heat until she could find her way to this wedding chapel.

What had pleased her was that she'd found it.

Despite the fact there had been no specific information about it anywhere, which had required some next-level sleuthing skills.

Geraldine had expected some kind of security. Quite a lot of security, actually. She had assumed, the groom being the sort of nightmarishly rich billionaire that he was and the bride an heiress in her own right, that she'd be stopped well before she made it to the door of this place and would be required to argue her way inside.

She might even have been looking forward to that argument. A cross she had long been forced to bear—and had thus made it into a weapon—was that no one could ever imagine that a woman who did nothing to enhance her appearance and, in fact, was happy to wear clothing considered "dowdy" so long as it was comfortable, could ever truly be up to no good.

Even if it took a bit of effort to cross the language barrier, Geraldine had been sure that she could brown-hen her way in.

But no brown-henning had been required. There had been only a few people milling about on the narrow road that was really more of a path outside the chapel, looking only vaguely security-like, and none of them had paid her any mind. Perhaps it was because she had a certain way of marching forth, head held high, that went a long way toward convincing anyone who might look that she belonged.

Or perhaps it's actually because you look like someone's maiden aunt, she told herself dryly. *Emphasis on maiden and aunt.*

Then again, she did that on purpose. What wasn't on purpose was the fact that she'd made a bit of a racket coming inside the ancient building. Also, the Italian breeze had caught the door behind her, wrenched it from her grip, and slammed it shut.

Loudly.

But what Geraldine had noticed immediately wasn't who was or was not glaring at her for causing a commotion. Instead, she was quite surprised to find that the bride was not only walking herself down the aisle, she was already about halfway done with the entire exercise.

And though the bride had stopped and looked back over her shoulder, all dressed in white and eyes solemn, Geraldine hadn't seized the moment the way she should have.

The bride turned around again and had started for the altar once more.

Leaving Geraldine to slink into the last pew much more quietly than she'd entered, her mind racing.

She had shoved her glasses up her nose as she'd sat, a nervous habit she preferred to deny she possessed. Usually she wore her contacts, but she'd been sure they would dry out her eyes on that flight and she hadn't had time to pop them back in while changing in that tiny hotel room, her mother muttering *I told you so* beneath her breath and little Jules in mid-tantrum.

And your contact lenses have nothing to do with anything, she had snapped at herself.

She'd reminded herself then, rather severely, that it wouldn't do her any good to have come all this way if she wasn't prepared to jump in as planned at any given opportunity.

Like the one she'd squandered just then.

And so she had been drumming up her courage to leap to her feet and stop the proceedings—and she'd required that courage not because she was in any doubt that her cause was just, and certainly not because she was any sort of shy or retiring mouse, but because she was Midwestern born and bred and, deep within her, had an inbred horror of causing a scene of any kind no matter the reason—when the door to the chapel had slammed wide open again.

Louder this time.

And as it did, a ferocious-looking man came striding in, dressed in black and seeming also to *exude* a matching black fury as he came.

He did not take the first available seat, as Geraldine had.

Instead, he'd helped himself to the bride.

He'd found her in the aisle, tossed her over his shoulder without a word, and then strode right on out again.

And Geraldine had always taken pride in her practical, rational nature—so much so that she even dressed so that said nature was what was noticed about her, first and foremost. She was a woman who had always enjoyed the company of facts and the books where those facts were so often housed. The cool, leather-bound intellect of a library was the happiest place she could imagine, and she would be back in hers right now if it weren't for poor motherless baby Jules.

But she couldn't claim that she was thinking about Jules after the door slammed shut behind the man and the kidnapped bride, leaving the few people left in this chapel to stare at each other blankly.

Maybe she wasn't thinking at all.

Because she let out that cackle. And once she'd laughed, she hadn't seen any particularly compelling reason to *stop* laughing.

Geraldine was still laughing, in fact.

With a little more sleep, or really *any* sleep, she was certain she might have controlled herself—because didn't she always control herself?—but then again, perhaps she wouldn't have bothered.

Because it was a certain kind of funny, wasn't it? She had pulled together a shocking amount of money to come all this way to stop a wedding that hadn't needed stopping after all.

If only someone had thought to mention that the bride would be abducted before the vows were spoken, Geraldine thought, and set herself off again.

She was rummaging around in her bag for the tissues she always kept close to hand—because her eyes were watering the more she laughed, another likely consequence of that endless flight—and she was making that cackling sound again, which only made her laugh more. But eventually she found a tissue. She dabbed at her eyes, like the sort of lady who didn't go around hooting and hollering at the abortive wedding ceremonies of total strangers.

Only after she'd calmed herself slightly did she become aware of a kind of shadow that fell over her. A strange sort of shadow that made every last cell in her entire body seem to tighten of its own accord.

Only then did she look up.

And up.

And still farther up.

To find the would-be groom standing above her, a thunderous look upon his face.

This close to him, Geraldine made the entirely unwelcome discovery that he was significantly more attractive in person than she had imagined.

She had researched this man exhaustively. She had therefore spent a lot of time imagining not only him, but what she would do and say should she encounter him as she'd planned to do. She had any number of lectures in her back pocket, but the sight of him in real life was…

Unexpected, somehow.

And he was *glowering* at her.

The *he* in question was Lionel Asensio, born to a revolting amount of wealth in Spain somewhere. He was the result of generations of affluence, the very notion of which sent a bolt of dismay straight to Geraldine's deeply understated Midwestern soul.

Lionel himself had come of age more serious by far than the family playboys and international Lotharios who had preceded him. He had spent rather longer in educational pursuits than at least the three previous generations had done. He'd gotten a double first at Cambridge, no easy task, no matter how well-connected the student. And it was with a coveted graduate degree in business from Harvard that he had marched, grim-faced if the pictures were any indication, into the sad little family business that was likely no more than a tax shelter and turned it into a vibrant multinational corporation that some spectators claimed must have tripled his inherited wealth within ten years.

In other words, he was mind-numbingly, incomprehensibly wealthy, and yet that was not her objection to him.

It was not even his excess of male beauty, which she had expected to be harsh and off-putting. Every picture she'd seen of him had featured him glowering about just as he was now, either at the people he was with or straight into the camera itself.

She'd thought he looked surprisingly pugilistic, if not downright mean, for a man who could have no battles to fight.

It was true, she saw. He still did.

But in person there was a magnetism to this man that no picture could possibly convey. She felt her whole body shiver into a shock of awareness, as if she had no choice but to sit up straighter. As if the force of his regard commanded her flesh to respond.

Worse, it seemed primed to do his bidding.

Geraldine had always taken pride in her height, inherited from any number of her possibly Viking ancestresses, because she enjoyed that she stood taller than many women in her bare feet.

But the way this man looked down at her, she felt tiny. Somehow *delightfully* fragile. As if he could snap her in two with no effort whatsoever and more alarming, that she might like that. Or better still, tuck her away in one of his pockets.

She had the stray, treacherous thought that he could not possibly be the man she thought he was because there was something deep in her own bones that told her otherwise, that *knew b*etter—

But it didn't matter what *her bones* said, she told herself sharply. What mattered was what her poor, lost cousin Seanna had told her before she died—that there had been only one name she had ever uttered. And that Geraldine had come all the way to Italy to make certain that there would be justice for her cousin and her cousin's daughter, one way or another.

Even if it meant going toe-to-toe with a man who made her *want* to quiver.

To *quiver*, of all things.

He rattled off some sort of dark demand in what she thought was Italian, given where they were, though it may well have been Spanish for all she understood either language. And she meant to reply, she really did, but Geraldine's body did not seem to be interested in obeying her commands.

It was him.

It was the way he *looked* at her. He was dressed in his fine and elegant clothes that should have made him look fussy, but did not. Instead, it was as if they couldn't quite contain him. As if this chapel itself was too small.

As if he carried a brooding force within him, rough and sensual, that her body recognized instinctively.

Whatever the reason, she couldn't say a word.

"Let me guess, you speak only English," he said in the face of her ongoing silence, in a voice that seemed to cut straight into her, sounding both faintly British and undoubtedly Spanish at once.

And also dripping with disdain.

"I have conversational French and can read German," Geraldine retorted, stung by the disdain and the inference that she was one of *those people*, forever barging around the world, expecting everyone to speak her language. She'd read all about them. *She* would never be so conceited. "I'm also working on my Japanese. Since you asked."

"Perhaps you will share, then—in any of those languages—what it is you find so amusing."

"Humor is very subjective," she demurred, spurred by a sudden sense of self-preservation she wasn't sure she had ever felt before. It had something to do with his eyes, the color of coffee too bitter to drink. It was something about all the harshly elegant lines of his face, like old sculptures that had never been meant for the menial gaze of the peasants. It was that last notion that infuriated her enough to keep talking. "I doubt you would find it as funny as I do. What with all the cultural differences and whatnot."

"Try me."

It was not request.

And Geraldine found that she had to remind herself,

sharply, that she was not here for this man's entertainment. She was not here for him to command her in any way.

She was not here for *him* at all. This was about Seanna. This was about the daughter her cousin had left behind.

Despite her body's worrying reactions to Lionel Asensio in all his considerable state, she forced herself to get to her feet. Right then, to *prove* she was unaffected.

But she found that it had not been a trick of the Italian pew where she'd been sitting. It was no optical illusion. Lionel Asensio really did tower over her.

Even when she was standing tall.

"It's not every day that you see a bride carried off from a groom who does not seem to mind a bit," she pointed out.

As she stood there in her ill-fitting dress in this Italian chapel filled with incense and sunlight and this glowering, appallingly handsome man.

Not *quite* quivering.

And really, Geraldine had just thrown that last bit out there to be provoking. But as she said it, she could see that it was true. For one thing, the man was standing here, talking to her about jokes and languages. He wasn't racing out of the chapel himself. He wasn't ordering the people around him, all his minions if she had to guess by their deferential expressions, to chase after his bride for him. Neither he nor they were calling in the authorities.

"Who are you?" he asked her, instead of addressing what she would have assumed was the more glaring issue of his missing bride.

Yet it did not occur to her to disobey him by not answering the question. "My name is Geraldine Gertrude Casey, not that I expect that to mean anything to you."

He did not quite incline his head. Though there was what appeared to be an infinitesimal gesture in that direction. Almost. "It does not."

And then he infuriated her all the more by subjecting her to what could only be called an overtly thorough head-to-toe *examination* that was in no possible way appropriate, much less polite. That too-dark, too-intense gaze of his traveled from the top of her admittedly frazzled head all the way down to her sturdy travel shoes, then made its slow way up again, taking care to linger over her deliberately frumpy dress.

It was *deliberate,* she reminded herself as the urge to flush in some kind of heretofore unknown embarrassment nearly took her over. *If you cared in the slightest about how dresses look upon your frame, you would have bought one that fit it.*

She then told herself that when she did flush, and all over, it was from fury.

Geraldine was well used to not exactly bewitching men with her charms. Though she had many gifts in this life, and was proud of all of them, that particular skill had never been one of them. It had been her poor cousin who had possessed that talent, and nothing in Seanna's short and largely troubled life had convinced Geraldine that she ought to think she'd missed out. She didn't.

But it had also been a long while, possibly since she'd been in those dreadful middle school years, since anyone had dared look at her the way this man did now.

As if he was sizing her up and finding her wanting—*as a woman*, clearly—in every possible way.

It almost made her laugh all over again.

She was certain that mad heat bubbling up within her was *laughter.*

"You do not look married," he said, and there was a note in that silk-and-steel voice of his that she could not say she liked.

The insinuation was all too obvious. He did not have to ask, *Who would marry the likes of you?*—and yet the question hung over the old stone floor as if it was smokier by far than the burning incense.

It got right up her nose.

Normally she would have found hilarious the very idea that some hulking billionaire found a librarian from Minnesota not to his taste.

I should hope not, she might have said with a peal of laughter. *Or I would assume I'd lived the whole of my life entirely wrong.*

But today Geraldine was overly tired. So tired she felt pale straight through. And she did not like being looked at and analyzed with so much *derision*, as if she was a bit of spoiled produce in a bargain bin set out in front of the sort of down-market grocery store that she, personally, did not frequent.

"I cannot imagine what it is you think *married* looks like," she shot back at him, a bit recklessly. Maybe more than *a bit*, given that she was on her own here in this chapel while *he* had brought a selection of minions with him. "Though I would imagine that anyone married to *you* would likely look desperate for escape. If your previous almost-bride is any indication."

"I will take that as a no, you are not married," he replied, with a certain languid note in that voice of his that was even more insulting. *Because how could you be?* was the next question that he didn't actually need to put into words for it to hang there between them.

Smoky and rude.

"I'm not sure that's the issue I would be harping on if I was in your shoes," she retorted. "I'm pretty sure we saw *your* bride fail entirely to put up any kind of fight at all while being carried away from you and this wedding, friend."

And she thought she saw a flicker of *something* in his dark gaze at that. But before she could press him any further, or dig her own grave any deeper, more like, he silenced her simply enough—by placing his hand on her upper arm and thereby urging her to walk with him back up the aisle.

Ushering her along as if she was the one being forcibly removed from the premises, with exactly as little actual *force* as the previous bride had experienced on her way out.

Only they were headed in the opposite direction, not that she had it in her to care too much about that.

It was that hand, Geraldine told herself through the strange haze that descended. It was *his* hand, or more precisely, that she could feel the wild heat of it. Not only where it gripped her upper arm, but all through her body.

As if the hold he had on her was nothing more than an ignition point, and everything else was ablaze.

She could feel the flames dance through her, licking this way and that along her arms and then all through the rest of her, finding every secret part of her body and setting it alight. One after the next, as if every step she took was from one bonfire to the next.

Her breasts felt heavy. And deep between her legs, something began to ache.

Then, before she knew it, Geraldine was standing at the head of the chapel's surprisingly long aisle, staring at the priest who stood there—though she couldn't seem to make sense of anything.

Not the priest as he began to speak in what she was certain was Italian this time. Not the rumbling sounds that seemed to come as much from the man beside her as *through her*, too, as if he was nothing short of an earthquake.

Except she was so *hot* when she had always imagined that, should she find herself confronted with the earth itself heaving about beneath her feet, she would be cold to the core, iced over with fear.

There were words exchanged, which she could understand even if she didn't speak the language. And she was certain she *tried* to object, but she couldn't seem to make her mouth—or any other part of herself—act properly.

Especially when Lionel Asensio, that impossible creature, turned to face her and while he did, pulled her hands into his.

Then held them there while out of the corners of her eyes, the chapel seemed to spin a little drunkenly.

Geraldine tried not to pay attention, which was her usual policy with actual drunks, too.

That was just as well, because all she really *could* manage to do was gaze stupidly at him, because his hands were on hers and she couldn't seem to *breathe*, while he spoke rapidly. Almost carelessly, she might have thought, except the look in his eyes was intense.

Particularly when he slid two rings onto her finger, one

after the next, then gazed at her when the priest spoke in his turn.

"You must reply," Lionel said gravely, in English when the priest was finished. And the silence seemed to billow between them like still more smoke.

"But I..." she began. Her tongue felt too large. Her jaw too small. "I really don't..."

"All you must say is *yes*," he told her, again in that deeply serious manner.

And then, as she stared at him, fire dancing where it liked inside of her, one of his dark brows rose.

As if he was daring her.

And Geraldine was not a *daring* sort of person. The only thing she had done in the whole of her life that could be described as anything approaching *daring* was the fact that she'd come here, determined to make this very man take responsibility for what he'd done to her cousin.

Surely that alone should have had her stepping back and shaking her hands free of his, reclaiming herself from...whatever spell this was.

But his eyes were bittersweet chocolate, dark and rich. He gleamed like gold, though he was in no way blond. As if he, himself, was liquid gold from within. And that dark, aristocratic eyebrow felt like a call to arms.

She did not have it in her to do anything but whisper, *"yes."*

Like the obedient soul she had always, secretly, imagined she was not.

And then everything seemed to speed up again. The priest was going on in Italian, Lionel was responding. Geraldine was beginning to frown as she stared down at her hand that no longer looked like her own—because there was now a great honking stone plunked down on her ring finger with another band, all heavy diamonds, next to it. It looked ridiculous in and of itself, a finger bedecked and bejeweled like that, given she had the sort of hands that were meant to dig fields rather than loaf about in Italian chapels.

But then the man beside her was turning her to face him, his hands on her shoulders.

Her breath vacated the premises entirely.

Because his head was descending and she almost felt as if she was dreaming, because Lionel Asensio—*Lionel Asensio*—was pressing his mouth to hers.

Everything inside Geraldine simply…stopped.

His lips were warm, and stern.

They pressed against hers in unmistakable command.

And everything that Geraldine was or ever had been disappeared, melting away in the face of a roaring fire unlike any she had ever known.

It was too bright.

It was too *hot*.

It was all too—

Everything spun around and around, and not just in her peripheral vision.

A strange sort of languor melded with the heat, invading her limbs, making her hotter by the second.

And she was so tired and it must have been the jet lag and there was too much incense everywhere and surely she hadn't married this preposterously dark creature, so demanding and daring and—

But then everything went mercifully blank.

CHAPTER TWO

LIONEL ASENSIO WAS well used to causing a commotion in the female population, whenever and however he encountered them. His staff liked to whisper, where they imagined he could not hear them, that he could barely walk down a street without women clinging to his every limb.

That was an exaggeration.

But not much of an exaggeration.

And yet despite all that, he was quite certain that he had never made a woman *faint* before.

Then again, he had never married one, either.

It was hard not to conclude that the two were somehow related.

He caught her, of course. Like it or not, the tryingly named *Geraldine Gertrude Casey* was his wife now, and Lionel hoped he was not the kind of man who let a woman under his protection crash to the ground no matter the circumstances.

Today was not the day to change the whole of his character, despite the fact he had gone ahead and changed his life over the course of a short ceremony. No matter that he intended there to be precious few ramifications from that decision, there would be *some*, and yet he had still done it.

He caught her long before she hit the floor. He swept her up into his arms, lifting his chin at his assistant in the first pew as he turned. The man leaped to his feet and headed for the door at once, and Lionel knew that meant that his car would be brought around so that, hopefully, he could leave this place without the ever-lurking paparazzi any the wiser that he been here in the first place. Much less that he had gone ahead and gotten married to a literal nonentity, as far as he could tell at a glance. Not to mention that said nonentity had been so overset with sheer joy at the sudden dramatic shift in her circumstances that she had literally swooned in his arms.

Something in him chose to remind him that it had not been *joy* he had seen all over the woman's face, but he pushed that aside. Because it should have been joy. She should have been prostrate with gratitude.

Perhaps this was her version of precisely that.

His second assistant approached. "I will need to know who this woman is, obviously," Lionel said, keeping his voice low in case anyone not in his employ was lurking about in the shadows. "I will need to know everything she has eaten for breakfast over the past ten years, at a minimum, and anything else you can turn up. She said her name was *Geraldine Gertrude Casey*, of all things, and I cannot think why an American tourist should turn up in the middle of a private ceremony the way she did, then laugh with so little attempt to conceal it when the wedding ended so precipitously. Find out why, please."

His second assistant nodded, then stepped back, typing away on her device.

He ordered his third and fourth assistants to assemble his legal team, for there would need to be contracts drawn up, replacing the name of the Cartwright heiress with Geraldine's. There might also have to be some creativity involved in the documents for today's events, but he had discovered that there was precious little in the world that could not be altered to suit him. All it took was money. And as he considered the woman he had almost married, he beckoned yet another assistant close.

"We will need to ascertain what has become of the previous bride, please. And whether she requires assistance." He felt a slight pang at that, but Hope Cartwright had known exactly what he was about. And that he had needed a bride today, come hell or high water. As theirs had been an entirely cold-blooded business venture that had never trafficked in or near any emotional terrain, Lionel assumed that his near-wife would understand that he could not do anything but what he had done here, not that he intended to consult her about it. But that didn't mean he couldn't put his men on the case to determine what had actually happened to her today.

It is literally the least you can do, came a voice inside that sounded suspiciously like the conscience his grandmother had been at such pains to instill in him all his life.

Only when all of these instructions had been fired off left and right and his people were hurrying about with tasks to perform did Lionel finally take a moment to look down at the woman he had held in his arms all the while.

His initial impression of her was that she was, decidedly, what he knew was called a *frump.* Dowdy almost beyond comprehension. He had seen her when she'd come in, thanks to the racket she'd made, and had wondered in passing what dreary organization had set its church mouse free to crash weddings in Italy.

But then she had laughed when no one else in the chapel had dared.

When everyone else had been frozen into place, and silent, awaiting his reaction.

And then on top of this she had been, if not openly defiant, markedly and noticeably unimpressed with Lionel himself.

He was...not used to such reactions.

Not unless said reactions were themselves a bit of play-acting by those hoping to differentiate themselves from the crowd, but that was not the impression he'd gotten from this woman.

Something had shifted again when she'd stood and proved herself not to be a tiny, frail little thing. She was tall enough, not an unusual circumstance in his circles, but she was not a whittled-down figurine all gaunt bones in the vague shape of a woman. She was not emaciated—fashionably or otherwise—as so many women were these days, as if starving themselves was a bit of sport and they wanted a medal.

He would have said instead that she looked...well. Tired and frumpy, certainly, but there was a smoothness to her shape. A pleasing hint of an actual figure, somewhere beneath that tent-like monstrosity of a dress.

Now she was in his arms, her eyes closed behind the unduly large glasses she wore. Shut, her eyelids covered the unusual green of her gaze and the way she'd stared at him so owlishly, with that intensity of regard that had called him to a kind of attention he did not quite understand.

Lionel did not wish to understand it. He dismissed the

notion that he should. Because this close, he was aware of a great many things about the woman he'd just married.

Whether he wanted to be aware of her or not.

Her skin was extraordinary. She seemed to *glow*, somehow, and not simply because the flush he'd seen all over her earlier had left some marks. Lionel would have said that no woman alive in these greedy and calculated times still blushed, but this one had proved him wrong.

Yet now the deepness of that flush had receded like the tide and all he could see was softness and that impossible *glow*.

Her hair was dark and was twisted back in one of those hideous claw devices that looked like nothing so much as the return of the Inquisition to him, and not in a manner he would ever dream of calling *artful*. Lionel felt certain that she had thrown it back to get it out of her way and had likely thought no more about it.

He could not account for why he could not seem to do the same. It had something to do with the fact that he could smell the shampoo she'd used, a bright pop of coconut and papaya, of all things. She smelled of the fruity, frothy cocktails he would never drink and there was no reason at all he should find that appealing.

Particularly when she was clad from neck to ankles in her entirely shapeless dress that appeared to be covered in some kind of indefinable floral element. The hint of flowers, though their shape gave him no clue what precisely they were supposed to be. The garment made her look like nothing so much as a rather dreadful couch.

Yet the woman in his arms was not shapeless. He could feel it. She was soft and warm and worse by far, he could feel her curves.

Lionel did not wish to feel anything. His father and his grandfather before him had been men of great passion, by their reckoning and according to their excuses. Lionel thought of them as men made of greed, for anything that caught their fancy. Or any passing whim. They had been heedless, reckless in every respect, and had waved it all away by claiming that it was their enormity of feeling that made them act as they did. That they could not be expected to rein themselves in, for they were men of great appetites and needed to feed.

To Lionel, the pair of them had been nothing but vampires. He had vowed that he would never let his feelings dictate his behavior in that way.

Or in any way.

His grandmother had taken a similarly dim view of the man she had married and the one she had raised, and it was her influence that had saved him from following in their footsteps.

He was grateful to his *abuelita* every day.

And yet this woman in his arms smelled like the tropics while looking like a library.

Lionel knew he had never kissed a mouth as plain as Geraldine's. He could not account for why the experience still reverberated through him, as if this woman was a fault line, and having tripped over her, everything was now far more precarious.

He was Lionel Asensio. He did not *do* precarious.

But none of that mattered, because the deed was done. She had married him, not that he had allowed him any doubt that she might balk once he had decided that she might as well take the Cartwright heiress's place. And

Lionel was not one to spend too much time looking backward. There was nothing to be done now but to move on.

Into what came next.

He was already steeling himself for it.

Lionel carried her from the chapel, already working out what his next steps would need to be, when he felt the woman, his *wife*, stir in his arms. He paused on the steps outside, looking down at her as those surprisingly dark lashes moved against the bright skin of her face.

He had no idea why he found the sight so captivating.

And then, once more, he found himself pinned by that solemn green regard.

He expected her to react badly and braced himself, but though he could feel a new tension invade her form, she only held his gaze. She blinked.

Once.

"Why are you carrying me?" she asked, very calmly. And quite reasonably enough, to his mind.

"You were overcome," he told her with the matter-of-factness he was known for. "Had I had not caught you, you would have fainted dead away on the ancient stones and would no doubt have a bruised head besides. You may consider this my first gift to you as your husband."

Another long, slow blink that somehow seemed to roll through her. All through her body, so that even the ghastly shoes she wore seemed a part of it, and then it all seemed to roll through him, too. Lionel could not imagine why he felt the urge to stand taller.

"Impossible," she said in that same calm, collected manner. And now the way she was looking at him seemed to brand him a liar, of all things. "I have never fainted in my life."

"Then I congratulate you, Geraldine." And that odd name felt like one of those silly drinks in his mouth. "For it seems today is a day of a great many firsts for you."

He was certain that what he saw ignite in her gaze then was temper. Lionel did not do temper, and so he set her down on her feet. And pretended not to notice when she shook off the hand he kept on her, to make sure she remained steady.

"I don't know what happened," she told him, in that same brisk manner that also seemed to suggest that she thought he was at fault nonetheless. "But I can assure you, I do not make a habit of *losing consciousness* at the slightest provocation."

"Perhaps, for you, the provocation was not so slight." He lifted his shoulder when her brows drew together. "Have you ever been kissed before?"

The frown she gave him then was ferocious. "What kind of question is *that*?"

"I will tell you," he continued, fully aware that the way she'd answered him was a confession all its own, "that I suspect you never have."

"You are mistaken." Her voice was frosty.

"Your reactions suggest otherwise." He eyed her. "Among other things."

Her eyes blazed. "I am devastated that you find me so lacking in so many areas. No one else has ever complained."

"Somehow, that does not surprise me," Lionel said, which was true. As he doubted there was anyone *to* complain.

But when his car pulled up in front of the chapel, he ushered her down the steps and she walked along with him gamely enough. He was intrigued, despite himself, that for all the many ways she seemed determined to defy him, all he needed to do was put his hand on her and she would follow him wherever he liked.

Or perhaps *intrigued* was not the right word.

This time they were both sitting in the back seat of the car and driving away from the chapel before she seemed able to collect herself and look around.

Or collect herself as much as a woman could while her face had come over red again.

Another blush when he had thought one odd enough.

Remarkable, he found himself thinking. When the only remarkable part of any of this was the lengths that he, Lionel Asensio, who was feared and admired the world over, should go to please his grandmother.

"I am staying in a hotel," Geraldine told him. Rather crossly. "And I don't think it is in this direction."

"Only tell me which hotel it is and I will have my men gather your things and cancel your reservation," he said, and he thought he sounded rather magnanimous, all things considered.

He did not expect her to glare at him the way she did. "Why would I do that?"

Lionel stopped worrying about how he was going to sort out the mess this wedding had become and focused on her. "Perhaps your fainting spell has made you confused."

"I don't think I'm the only one in that position," Geraldine replied, in a tart sort of way that did not sound as if *confusion* was much of a concern here. He told himself he was grateful. He should have been grateful. "In case you've already forgotten, you had a very different bride walking down the aisle toward you not long ago. You're supposed to be married to an entirely different woman. And I'm not sure that you're actually married to me. I wasn't in my right mind. Clearly."

He could not say that he cared for the way she said that last word.

"The priest asked you to state your vows and you did." Lionel let his mouth curve in what was likely not much of a smile, given the way she looked at him. "I am afraid it is done now. We are married whether either one of us likes it or not."

"None of this makes sense." She shook her head, looking out the car window and then back at him. "You're not even Italian."

This was the most reasonable thing she'd said so far. Or at least the most familiar thing. "You seem very certain. Almost as if you know who I am. I am flattered."

"You're a famously rich man," Geraldine said flatly, which was not the way people normally referred to his consequence or position. "I'm sure people recognize you all the time."

"I will tell you now that I do not much care if they do or do not," Lionel told her, honestly. "So if that was the reason you came to the chapel today, I suspect you will find the next few years of your life a great trial."

She only glared at him. "But what I don't understand is why you, a Spanish billionaire, were marrying an Englishwoman here, in Italy."

"Perhaps, in addition to never having been kissed, you are also unfamiliar with the concept of a destination wedding," Lionel suggested. When her eyes flashed anew, he had the wholly uncharacteristic urge to laugh. When he prided himself on his stern and sober steadiness, in all things.

He had no idea what it was about this woman, who was unlike any other woman he had ever been linked to in any way, that made him feel so unlike himself.

If he could have, he would have let her out of the car and never thought of her again. But that was not possible now.

"You are quite right," Geraldine said, her voice so sardonic that it should have left marks. There was a part of him that wanted to check. "I have never heard of such a thing as a destination wedding. And obviously, because I wear glasses, I am untouched. Entirely. Your perception is truly astounding."

But he could tell that she was lying about the *untouched* part. It was the way she lapsed off into the ether every time he touched her. It was the way she flushed so charmingly, then seemed to go off into some kind of a daze.

And it was the fact that she had brought it up again.

As if the notion that he had thought such a thing of her stung her, and why should it if it was untrue? If someone suggested to Lionel that *he* was untouched, he thought he really would laugh.

And so Lionel did not choose to tell her what he could so easily discern. Just as he did not tell her that this wedding had taken place here in Italy because it was the sort of place his grandmother might believe he would choose to get married without it being close enough to the family estates in Andalusia that she might feel moved to attend. So when he presented her with the bride—the very bride she had been demanding for years now—he could explain precisely why she had not been invited to attend at all.

I was thinking only of your comfort, Abuelita, he would assure her.

His grandmother would not believe him, of course, but that was another day's problem.

He pushed those things away and settled back in his seat. His phone was in his pocket and he checked it, reading the message his man had sent him.

Bride number one boarded a helicopter with her abductor. Under her own steam and with no apparent distress. There did not appear to be any force applied.

Lionel tucked the phone away again. If Hope Cartwright had found herself a better option, who was he to complain? No contracts had been signed. Hope and he had come to an agreement, but all signatures had been saved for after the ceremony, when the both of them had taken the final step.

He had fully expected that Hope Cartwright would make him a perfectly fine wife.

But he could admit, sitting in the car while Geraldine Casey gazed at him with her green eyes nothing short of baleful, that he had never found the Cartwright heiress's company even remotely so interesting.

He was not at all sure what that might say about him.

"Where you taking me?" Geraldine asked, and now that he had returned his phone to his pocket, and was no longer standing in a wedding ceremony without a bride, he took his time studying her. He had no idea why a woman would drape herself in the sort of garment she wore, but it did nothing to hide the shockingly elegant line of her neck or the hollow there, where he could see her pulse fluttering.

As if he interested her too, loathe as she seemed to be to admit it.

Though he acknowledged there was a possible other reason. "I do not wish to do you any harm, if that is what you mean."

"You married a perfect stranger who you happened to find in the back of a wedding chapel," Geraldine pointed out and this time, she sounded somewhat less calm. "And not just any stranger. *I* don't like you."

"Impossible," he said, much the way she'd said it before. "All women like me. Or, I should say, I have never met one who does not."

Geraldine sat very straight beside him. She turned her body in the bucket seat so that she could look at him fully, and took her time pushing her glasses up the length of her nose. Making certain to broadcast her disapproval all the while.

"I know you to be the worst kind of man," she said, very distinctly, and kept her gaze trained on him while she said it. "A monster in every respect."

And it should not have mattered in the least what a woman he did not know, a woman he had not exactly thought highly of in the mere hour of their acquaintance, thought of him. It should not have mattered, yet Lionel found he did not care for the way she said that.

And he cared even less for *how little* he liked it.

Especially when she continued. "You hide behind this notion that you are somehow a creature of propriety," she told him in that same stern, certain manner that felt a great deal like a ringing conviction. "When the truth is, you are at least as licentious as anyone else. And a great deal more than some."

And Lionel found that he could not be offended at such an absurdity. It was exactly as he'd imagined he might react if she'd gone the other way and proclaimed he was a virgin. Laughable and little else—except, perhaps, intrigued about how she had managed to come to such an odd conclusion about his character.

It hardly seemed to matter that it was completely and utterly false. That was how ludicrous it was.

"I will give you this, Geraldine," he said, and he sounded as close to laughter as he had in some while. He couldn't remember the last time he'd strayed into the vicinity. "I have never before been accused of such a thing. Rather its opposite."

"It says nothing about a person when they only interact with those who are as powerful as they are," Geraldine said in that same way, as if she was laying out evidence before him and all of it led to his guilt. It was nothing short of extraordinary. "What matters is how a person with power treats someone who has none. What matters is preying upon a vulnerable woman, convincing her that it is the deepest sort of love only to abandon her when she's pregnant."

"I beg your pardon." Lionel frowned at her. "Are you suggesting that I got a girl pregnant and cast her aside?"

Geraldine's green gaze was direct. "I know you did."

And he did not understand why there was a part of him that wanted to argue. And more, wanted to make her take back such lies against him when he should not care—when were there not rumors and lies circulating about him? It came with his name and the way he'd chosen to live his life.

Instead, Lionel sighed. "That is ridiculous for any number of reasons, but let me tell you the foremost reason. You know who I am. You know that I have tremendous wealth and power at my fingertips. What do you imagine could compel me to marry like this?" When Geraldine didn't answer, he continued, impatiently. "So quickly, almost furtively, and to a woman I do not know at all. What could account for such a thing?"

She blinked, but her gaze did not become any less baleful. "Rich men are very strange. It is one of their most well-known characteristics, though we are all encouraged to consider it *eccentricity* and nothing more."

"My father and my grandfather before him were sometimes entertaining at a party, but were otherwise largely useless," Lionel told her, and restrained himself from asking if she had as many *rich men* in her life as she did lovers. "This is not a matter of opinion, so much as it is inarguable fact. The only family I have left, and the only one worth a damn, is my grandmother. And she wants nothing more than a grandchild."

"I'm sure you think that makes you relatable," Geraldine began hotly, "but I don't really see why—"

"It is statistically improbable that I could impregnate a woman with the precautions I always take," he interrupted her, "but not impossible. What *is* impossible is that a woman might tell me that she carried my child, prove this to be true, and then watch me walk away from her. This would never happen. It never did happen."

"But it did," she insisted.

"On the contrary, Geraldine," he said, and there was

something about her name. Something about the taste of it—but he kept his attention on that grave green gaze of hers. "I would rejoice. My grandmother's dearest wish would be fulfilled at last and with ease. I would marry any girl who was pregnant with my child, sing a round of hosannas, and call it a day."

Geraldine only stared back at him, frowning, and not as if she thought she was confused. It was clear that she thought he was.

"That's not at all what happened." And she leaned in closer then, so he could see that there was not one part of her that did not believe what she was telling him. She was totally and completely sure that she was speaking the truth—he could see that all over her as easily as he'd seen her blush. "My cousin died in childbirth. Alone and with your name in her mouth."

"I cannot account for that," Lionel told her in the same grave manner. "But the child cannot be mine."

"I have the baby with me," Geraldine said, ignoring him. Another thing that did not usually happen to him in the presence of women. Or anyone else. "Her name is Jules, she is wonderful, and I intend to make certain you take responsibility for her at last, Lionel. Whether I am married to you or not."

CHAPTER THREE

GERALDINE WAS PROUD of the ringing tones she used then and the way her voice filled the car, as if there was no difference whatsoever in their positions. As if she commanded the same authority he did—because she did, back home in her library.

And also because, she kept telling herself with what might possibly be some small bit of desperation, there were no differences between them that she did not allow. He had more money and more unearned power because of it, certainly, but otherwise she need not feel the least bit cowed by this man unless she *wished* to feel cowed, which she did not.

Of course, there was also the confusing part where she'd accidentally *married* the man in what could not possibly have been a real ceremony—though that priest had certainly seemed real enough—

I refuse to be cowed by anyone, Geraldine told herself stoutly, cutting off that unhelpful line of internal wittering. *Especially a man who treated poor Seanna so shabbily.*

She did not like the voice inside that suggested that, perhaps, the person who had treated Seanna the shabbiest might well have been Seanna.

Geraldine told herself, as she always did, that thinking such a thing was unfair. Seanna had been young and impressionable. It hadn't been her fault that she'd been too naive to see what was happening to her until it was too late. Or if it had been, well, there were others far *more* at fault.

Like this man.

Lionel Asensio, who had treated her cousin the way he had and who Geraldine had somehow let *kiss* her—and even if it was a part of that so-called wedding ceremony, there was no excuse.

Lionel Asensio, who looked wholly unscathed to Geraldine's eye, which was an injustice in one profoundly male form.

Lionel Asensio, who was looking at her now as if she'd sprouted an extra head when she'd fainted.

Not that Geraldine could get her head around *that*, either. She was no wilting flower. She had never *swooned* before.

She was sure that was his fault, too. Somehow.

And she was certainly not planning to dwell on the way it had felt to come awake in his arms, warm against his chest, as if the whole of the world and all she would ever be or want to be was…him. That harsh, aristocratic face, tipped toward hers. That gleam in his dark gaze, as if he could and would hold her forever.

As if he really was her husband.

She'd had the strange and yet comforting notion that, at last, she was precisely where she belonged.

Odious thought, she told herself now. *You must have hit your head, despite what he told you. There will no doubt be a bump to make sense of all this later.*

As for right now, she told herself she was *sitting in her power*. She had made it perfectly clear that she meant what she said and whether he believed it or not, Geraldine was prepared to do whatever was necessary to make sure that Jules was taken care of as she deserved. As Seanna had deserved, too. The confusion of this strangest of days was nothing compared with her mission here.

And she felt something inside her ease, almost, because she was finally doing the thing she'd promised Seanna she would. Again and again in those last days, when she hadn't known if her cousin could even hear her any longer.

"I can see that you have nothing to say for yourself," she said a few moments later, when all Lionel did was gaze back at her with that faintly bemused expression on his supremely arrogant face. "I'm not surprised. I know it is often difficult to face the consequences of one's actions."

Or so she had heard and witnessed. *She* had personally never left anyone pregnant by the side of the metaphoric road, so *she* was not an expert on these matters. Only their terribly sad and unjust consequences.

Which, apparently, Lionel Asensio had avoided until now. It had astonished Geraldine that no matter how deep her digging on him had gone, she had found no other illegitimate children knocking about. When she'd expected to find several battalions' worth, at the least.

"Mi querida esposa," he murmured, seeming to *expand* somehow, there in the back seat of the car as it bumped its way along ancient Italian roads she might have found beautiful at any other time. To say nothing of that famously beautiful lake gleaming in the distance.

"My dear wife, you seem to have me confused with some-one else."

"I know exactly who you are," Geraldine told him, and shoved her glasses back up her nose. Perhaps more vig-orously than necessary. "Yours is the name my cousin spoke again and again on her deathbed. And just to be certain, I spent months researching you after she passed."

"I do not doubt these things, necessarily," he said, though there was a certain sheen in his dark-coffee gaze that made her suspect that he did, in fact, harbor more than a little doubt. But if so, it did not appear to upset him overmuch. All he did was relax back into the seat, managing to look somehow indolent and stern at once. Geraldine had no earthly idea why a simple shift of his body should seem to run straight through her like some-thing electric. She assured itself it was further evidence of his guilt. "However, a few words from a woman in some distress—no matter her circumstances—and whatever it is you call research do not add up to proof, I am afraid. That would require blood tests."

The *audacity*. Geraldine bristled. "I'm not at all sur-prised you have found a way to excuse yourself. Isn't that just like a man? Always willing to shirk responsibility at the faintest indication—"

"I have never shirked responsibility in my life and do not intend to start now," Lionel told her with a certain intensity in his voice, so that when he cut her off it did not quite occur to her to continue. Especially when she could see a matching blaze in his eyes. "This is a point-less conversation to have in the absence of any tests and the cool comfort such scientific fact inevitably provides,

Geraldine. But I will ask you this. Who exactly is this cousin of yours that you believe I treated so shabbily?"

And then, because he actually looked as if he wanted to know, Geraldine found herself wishing that was a simpler question. Or one that even now, all these months later, long after Seanna had finally gone to her rest, she could actually answer with some authority.

She told herself she wasn't entirely sure she even *wanted* to open up Seanna's wounds to this man, when he'd already proved he could not be trusted to take care of them. Or her.

On the other hand, she had gone to all this trouble to find him. And was now married to the man, if he was to be believed. That she did not intend to honor any part of a ceremony she still couldn't quite believe had taken place did not make her any less married. Not if it was real. That was a curveball she hadn't seen coming.

She was beginning to deeply regret that she had charged into this whole situation so thoughtlessly. There had been no need to disrupt that wedding. She could have made an appointment with this man or one of his minions, as her mother had suggested repeatedly on the plane. But Geraldine had decided that the situation called for *a little bit* of drama. Surely the man deserved it after what he'd done.

I hope you're happy now, she told herself, in a voice that sounded uncannily like her mother's.

Because she really did know best, it seemed. Entirely too much of the time. No wonder she was Geraldine's favorite person.

Still, Geraldine had never been any sort of shrinking violet and it wasn't as if she could rewind and start the day anew. What was done was done and now all there was left to do was make the best of things.

She fully intended to do just that, no matter what it took.

Geraldine had promised Seanna she would, and *she* was a woman who kept her promises. So she squared her shoulders, adjusted her glasses once more for good luck and courage, and forced herself to meet his gaze as directly as ever.

Maybe more, because he clearly hadn't *seen* Seanna before. He'd seen only what she'd become, Geraldine assumed. Only what the life she'd chosen had done to her.

But she wanted him to know the person her cousin had been beneath all that. The person who should have lived long enough to raise her own baby.

The person who deserved far more than his callous abandonment.

"Seanna was a magical child," Geraldine told him fiercely, though she was mindful that men dismissed any hint of emotion should they hear it—so she forced herself to keep that fierceness at as even a keel as possible. "I was nine when she was born. And though my family has never been particularly close, it was as if she had been created for me alone. I treated her like a living, breathing doll at first. Then as a miniature version of me. We only became closer as she grew. She told me things she would never dare to tell her parents. She told me of all the dreams she had that didn't seem to fit. All the fantasies she had of a life that was bright and happy and far less cold than her parents' house, which, it has to be said, makes the whole of Minnesota seem like a sunny beach by comparison."

She expected a man of such intense self-importance to betray his impatience as she told this tale. To hurry her along, or snap at her, or bite her head off in some other way as she laid out Seanna's story in the way she'd been practicing for weeks now, but Lionel did none of those things. He remained where he was, in that same confusing position in the seat beside her. His long, hard body in its finery exhibited some level of indolence, surely, yet everything about the way he looked at her was taut. Intense.

As if he listened the way it was rumored he did everything else.

With every part of himself.

Geraldine had the stray thought that no one in her entire life had ever paid such close attention to her. Not ever.

And she was not entirely sure she knew what to *do* in the face of it. She had the unworthy urge to laugh. Or simply close her eyes and tip herself toward him, as if that might *do something*—

It was obvious that the jet lag was messing with her once again.

She forced herself to carry on anyway, hoping that this time, *fainting* wasn't on the table and if it was, that he would leave her to it in her perfectly comfortable seat. "Seanna was a remarkably pretty girl. And I don't mean that she was simply cute, as so many little girls are. Most if not all little girls, in my opinion. But Seanna was so pretty that strangers would stop her in the streets to marvel at her looks." Geraldine smiled slightly, remembering the commotion her cousin had caused wherever she went. At five. Seven. Nine. To her mother's enduring horror, as if the attention Seanna drew to her so effortlessly was something she was *doing*, deliberately, to spite her. "She was so pretty that my aunt would often see people taking pictures of her on the sly, and not in a creepy way, but as if she was a piece of art. By the time she was a teenager, it was quite clear that she wasn't simply *pretty* any longer. Most of us hit those years and devolve into trolls of one variety or another, but not my cousin. She was already pretty, and then she became astonishingly beautiful, seemingly overnight. And it was more than the simple sum of her features. She had…something else. A kind of magnetism. I don't know how else to explain it. There was something about her that made whoever looked at her want to keep looking."

It amazed Geraldine how much it hurt to talk about her cousin, even when she'd truly thought that she'd put so much of this to rest. Because she had tried and tried. She'd read every book on grief and mourning she could get her hands on. Then she'd tried out the advice in each and every one of them.

Even before Seanna had died, Geraldine had been trying to come to terms with what had happened to her shooting star of a cousin.

Sometimes she wondered if watching the price of all that prettiness had left more of a mark on her than she liked to think.

Because now, face-to-face with the man she'd considered the bogeyman for so long, she felt that same old hitch inside of her. That same urge to collapse into the tears that threatened yet again, when she'd thought she'd left the sobs behind her.

It was talking about those early days, she thought. It was remembering what it had been like when Seanna was still such an innocent and had shined so brightly that the whole world had always seemed to hold its breath around her.

She really had been magic.

But Geraldine refused to give this man the satisfaction of seeing her cry about the things he'd helped do to her cousin.

She *refused*.

"When she was fourteen, she caught the attention of a talent scout on the streets of Minneapolis," she said instead, forcing herself to keep telling this story. Because she already knew no one else would, and that could not stand. She would not let it stand. "My aunt and uncle had no interest in letting their daughter get sucked into that sort of world. They have a very particular, very rigid sort of morality and certainly no imagination to speak of. They didn't think their daughter needed pictures taken of her, much less by strange people in far-off cities. The talent scout who found Seanna on the street gave her a card and my aunt not only ripped into pieces, she threw it into the fire." She sighed a little. "So maybe she has more imagination than I'm giving her credit for."

Geraldine studied Lionel's face for a moment then, as the car bumped along. She wondered why it was that neither sunlight nor shadows seemed to affect him. He didn't change at all. Worse, neither state was more or less revealing.

It was as if he was as enduring as stone.

There was no reason that idea should have made her shudder a little bit, but it did.

"But Seanna quite liked the idea of modeling." Geraldine smiled. "Or, if I know my cousin, she liked the idea of the attention. Because she was used to it, you see. That was the sort of beautiful she was. She was *used to* turning heads. She was used to fusses being made over her, wherever she went and whatever she did. Some people would shy away from that kind of thing, because it isn't about who a person is, is it? It's about what other people imagine a person might be. But Seanna wanted more. So she went ahead and tracked down the scout on her own, flew to New York when her parents thought she was on a school trip to Chicago, and the next time she spoke to her parents about modeling she did it with a lucrative contract in hand."

Geraldine blew out a breath then. She hated this part. Because it felt too much like selling out her family to a man who didn't deserve to know a single thing about them. And more, to a man who could not possibly understand the sorts of trials regular people faced. But there was nothing for it. This was the story, and she was telling it.

Besides. She had long since decided that simply being blood related to people did not mean that she was required to pretend they weren't problematic when they were. "My aunt and uncle weren't on board with their daughter getting swept up in something as squalid and showy as *modeling*, but there was a lot of money on the table. And they lived very modestly after my uncle was laid off. You might not understand this, but the sort of money that men like you might scoff at could change everything for regular people. And it did."

Geraldine laced her fingers together in her lap. Across the back seat that they shared, Lionel remained still. But there was still that intensity in the way he looked at her.

She should have found that a barrier. She should have felt self-conscious, surely, but instead the seriousness of his expression made it easier to carry on.

"There was no warm-up, no testing of the waters," Geraldine told him. "Seanna became an instant sensation. She flew all over the world. She appeared in the pages of every magazine you can think of and a great many more I had certainly never heard of before. There were catwalks by the dozens. By the time she was eighteen she had worked with top designers and legendary photographers in Paris, Milan, New York, and anywhere else you can imagine. She was a stalwart at the fashion shows. In terms of a modeling career, she was an enormous success by any measure—if already worried about getting old. But her personal life was a disaster."

The man beside her said nothing. He certainly didn't issue any accusations, and yet Geraldine still felt her own guilt crash over her in some kind of heavy wave. There was an undertow there that she knew might sweep her under if she let it—

But she hadn't let it in some time. Today was no time to backtrack.

"It was very obvious that she wasn't well," Geraldine managed to say quietly. "It wasn't only that her appearance deteriorated so alarmingly—in person, I mean. Never in photographs. It was more concerning that she just...wasn't herself. She stopped her weekly calls home. She even stopped her daily calls to *me*. If we wanted to keep up with her we had to track her in the tabloids, where it became very clear that she'd learned how to party and was spending most of her time doing so in the company of very rich, very famous men who never seemed to care much for her. I used to ask her about the men she was linked with and every time it seemed to hurt her a little more. So I stopped asking. I regret that."

Lionel caught her gaze and held it one beat, then another.

Until Geraldine almost felt the need to rub that sensation away, as if he had actually reached out and made her heart pump with his own hand. A ridiculous notion by any measure and one she should have found alarming.

But she...didn't.

She felt a bit more severe as she pushed on. "Then, finally, she came home. Quite obviously unwell. Her mother and father, I regret to say, disowned her entirely within a day because of the substances she had become dependent on. All while claiming a certain moral high ground they certainly had not dithered over while taking her money. I took care of her myself."

"As you had when she was young," Lionel said in a low voice.

And it was shocking, somehow, to hear his voice just then. Much less to hear him tie such a neat bow around feelings that were still so raw. Geraldine felt shaken.

"I nursed her as best I could through her pregnancy, but she was very ill." She looked down at her fingers clenched in her lap, and swallowed. Hard. "There were concerns for the baby. Seanna did not get better. To be honest, I don't think she wanted to get better. And in the end, despite the doctors' best efforts, her poor heart gave out while she was giving birth. Her daughter was mercifully unharmed, though she did have some more issues in the first few months of her life than a baby should." She blew out a breath. "I took care of her, too."

"And did your cousin appreciate your martyrdom while she lived?"

It was a soft, almost silken question, and Geraldine took offense to it immediately.

"I think you mean to be unkind," she said, staring him down while her cheeks warmed with the force of what she told herself was temper. Not the embarrassment of hearing him say that word that her aunt and uncle had used to bludgeon her with. And that even her mother had been known to suggest might apply, more than once. "But I did not martyr myself to my cousin. I loved her. I was able to take a leave of absence from my job to care for her, because I wanted to. Because she had no one else. And because she trusted me. Unlike the rest of our family, I did not judge her. I still don't."

Lionel still did not seem to move a single muscle. He reminded her of a statue—somehow capturing a great predator in a stillness that made the viewer think only of the coming attack. "And how is it you have remained so free of the judgment that so many others seem immersed in, I wonder?"

"Because I read widely," she shot back at him. "It is impossible to read as many books as I have and remain narrow-minded. It's the very purpose of reading, I would even say." And when he only gazed back at her, almost as if he pitied her in some way, she felt strongly that he was not understanding the situation at all. "I'm a research librarian. It is literally my job to gather information without emotion or agenda, collate it, and present it. All facts, no feelings."

"But in this case, it would seem that feelings were at the forefront. Not facts." He lifted a distractingly well-shaped shoulder in that way of his that she had already grown to dislike. "I am familiar with a number of beautiful women, some of them models. This I have never denied, nor would I. But that does not make me father to the child of a teenage junkie, Geraldine."

She felt something inside her then, different from before. It was much colder. Much darker. And beneath it, something else too—the faintest hint of a kind of...disappointment?

But that made no sense. She had come here expecting this man to be the villain he was. To be far more appalling than he seemed, in fact. She had been absolutely certain that she could dress him down as he deserved. Shame him if necessary. She was very good at both, and more, was never afraid to charge heedlessly toward the right thing no matter what.

She would get Jules the justice both she and her mother deserved, no matter what. Geraldine was resolved.

Yet Lionel was not acting in accordance with the script in her head. How was it possible to be disappointed that he was...exactly who she'd expected him to be?

The words *teenage junkie* swam about in her head, oddly specific.

"So," she said softly. "You do know her."

"Not in the way you imagine," Lionel replied, and for the first time, sounded slightly less than entirely calm. "One of my investments involves a rather famous couture house in Milan. I met your cousin. I can assure you, I'm not in the habit of sleeping with children. Or addicts, for that matter. It was...abundantly clear that she was unwell."

"And yet, of all the names she could have dropped, it

was only yours she ever spoke to me." Geraldine scowled at him. "Why would that be? Why, even when she knew that her life was slipping away, would you be the only person she mentioned? Make that make sense."

"I cannot," he said.

But she didn't believe him.

It was something about the way his gaze shifted. That intensity diluted itself as she watched.

Lionel turned his attention to the streets around them, and away from her.

She didn't believe him, and a hard little knot seemed to form inside her, tying itself tight around that hint of disappointment, making it lead to something else entirely.

"I suppose the science will prove it one way or the other, then," she said, perhaps too forcefully. Funny, but she no longer cared. "I'm assuming you will have no objection to taking the necessary tests. To prove that what you say is true. A man like you should have no trouble having an answer to illuminate us all by the end of the day."

But when Lionel looked back at her, his expression had changed once again.

There was nothing there but stone and steel, and something implacable that was far more unyielding than either.

She had the strangest urge to hold her breath.

"I have no objection to a paternity test, Geraldine," he told her quietly enough, but there was nothing soft in it. And nothing soft in him, either, as far she could see. "But before we do any of that, you and I will have to come to an agreement about this marriage."

"I didn't agree to this marriage in the first place. Why would you think that I would do anything at all but divorce you at the first opportunity?" Geraldine sniffed. "In case I haven't made this clear, I don't think highly of you. I doubt very much that will change. Whether you are proved to be Jules's father or not."

But something she would not call a smile moved over his hard face then. The kind of curve that only made it clear that he was far more dangerous and significantly less indolent than she might have imagined so far.

And if she was perfectly honest with herself, she'd imagined a lot.

"I do not require your affection, Geraldine," he told her, quietly. Very, very quietly—which was in no way the same thing as *soft*. "In fact, I would prefer there be nothing of the kind between us. What I need is a wife. If that wife comes with a child in tow, all the better. I am perfectly prepared to make your life, and the child's life, remarkably easy."

That intensity was back in his gaze then, and it seemed to pierce straight through her, so that she really was holding her breath.

"I don't think—" she began, feeling as if things wanted to start spinning once again.

But Lionel Asensio only let that curve in his mouth deepen. "Nothing comes without a price, Geraldine. I have certain requirements." Again, that shrug that was not a shrug at all. "And I will insist that they are met before I subject myself to any test, much less contribute to the raising of any child, no matter whose she is."

CHAPTER FOUR

LIONEL COULD TELL at once that Geraldine had not expected him to bargain with her.

This suggested to him that her research into him had not been as comprehensive as she claimed. For whatever else he was, he was known far and wide for his cold-blooded negotiations and his nonchalance in moments where other men crumbled.

Lionel did not crumble. He doubted he was capable of such a thing, and this should have been no different. He certainly shouldn't have found himself reaching for an uncharacteristic explanation, simply because...her green eyes widened in dismay.

He did not offer one, of course. But he was shocked that he even possessed the urge.

Since when had he tolerated the intrusion of someone else's feelings into the way he handled his business or himself?

But, of course, he knew the answer to that. The only person whose feelings he considered in any sort of on-going fashion was his *abuelita*, because she had earned that consideration by making herself the only steadying influence in the whole of his life.

He had buried his interest in other people's inner workings and outer emotional performances with his father. And he had never looked back.

Green eyes should not have registered with him one way or the other.

He waited as the car pulled into the small, private airfield where his jet stood ready for takeoff. His man came to the door and opened it wide once the car rolled to a stop. Lionel thought that Geraldine would refuse to get out, but she didn't. Instead, she turned toward the door, looking more confused than anything else, and let the man help her climb from the vehicle.

But that confusion seemed to have fled her entirely when Lionel exited from the other side of the car and rounded it to stand by her side once more.

"Why are we at an airport?" she asked him, in what was not the friendliest of tones.

Lionel did not think she was in any particular mood to discuss the differences between proper airports in private airfield, so all he did was beckon toward the sleek little jet that waited there for them.

"We will return to Spain," he told her. "Tomorrow is my *abuelita*'s eightieth birthday, and you are her present."

Geraldine's mouth dropped open and he found himself unaccountably transfixed by it. The memory of that kiss upon the altar seemed to flash through him, though he could not have said why. It had hardly been a kiss at all. It should not have registered. It had been a simple press of his mouth to hers and yet here he was, consumed with a hunger he was certain he had never felt before.

He would remember something like this, cluttering up his head and making him begin to wonder if he might start living his life according to the dictates of his sex,

like his father had done to such an extent that it was rumored his mother had deliberately infected herself with
that virus to escape the shame of having married such a
base philanderer.

Lionel had never believed that it had been deliberate,
because he'd known his mother all too well. If from a
distance, as he had been all of twelve when she died and
she had been nothing if not careless with herself as well
as with everything else. His father had lived some ten
years longer, but that had only given him more time and
space to wreck everything he touched.

All of these things he had lived through, these histrionic
lives and deaths, and he was standing here in an Italian
afternoon, obsessing over a plain woman's mediocre kiss.

He told himself it was because of the novelty, nothing
more. She was not like the sort of women he had dal-
lied with in the past. He had *married* her, for the love of
God. He had never kissed a *wife* before. And certainly
not *his wife*.

Perhaps a second thought—or five—was only to be
expected.

"I can't have heard you correctly," she said, when he
was certain she had heard him with perfect clarity. "You
cannot mean to suggest… Why on earth would your
grandmother want *me* as a present?"

"I have already told you this." He commended himself
for his patience. "What my grandmother wishes is for me
to be married and en route to producing the grandchild of
her dreams. This has now been accomplished. Tomorrow
I shall present you to her and all you will need to do is
follow the appropriate script when that happens. Nothing could be easier."

And somehow, when that chin of hers rose, he was not surprised that she wished to defy him in this. "I'm not an actor. I'm not much for *scripts*."

He should have wanted to crush her, here and now, so that he might know he could depend on her tomorrow. He wanted to bend her to his will, as he did everyone and everything, many times without even having to try.

But then, of course, he would. Eventually, he knew he would.

There was no other outcome that he would allow.

And perhaps it was nothing so simple as defiance with this woman, who imagined herself on some kind of crusade. "Geraldine. You are not seeing the full picture."

"I believe I'm the only one standing here who is actually aware of the full picture. As I have just been at pains to share with you."

"You have no bargaining chips," he told her, softly enough. "This should be obvious to you. Look where we are."

He watched a small frown increase in the space between her eyes as she did as requested, which felt perhaps too much like a victory. "I told you, I have a hotel on the outskirts of town. I don't know why you brought me here."

"I brought you here because it doesn't matter what you tell me." And he was proud of how he sounded then. Very nearly *gentle*, a word that anyone who had ever attempted to negotiate with him would have laughed at. Bitterly. "I have told you how it will be, and I assure you, that *is* how it will be. What you have to decide is how you wish the inevitable to take place."

She turned that frown toward him, and intensified it. "Inevitable?"

He could see the challenge in the way she asked that. And more, the clear inference that she believed that she was the one holding the cards here. That she thought she had some power over him.

And he almost admired that. He really did. Lionel couldn't recall the last time that he had ever had any kind of encounter with someone who didn't know precisely how much power he wielded, and more importantly, the vast power differential between him and them.

Once again, the novelty of this woman caught him off guard.

"We are already married," he told her patiently. Or close enough. "I understand you do not wish this to be true, but that does not make it any less so. Another truth you may find unpalatable is that we will be landing in Spain later this afternoon. I would prefer it if you boarded the plane of your own volition, but that is not required."

Her green eyes widened. "Is that a threat?"

"It is reality, Geraldine. This is what I'm trying to express to you." It was getting more difficult to maintain that patient tone with her, but he tried. He really did try. He reminded himself that while this might have been an unorthodox contract negotiation, that was still what was happening here. These things did not all have to happen in tedious boardrooms. "You have few choices here, so I would use the ones that you do have wisely."

"That sounds a whole lot like a threat, no matter how you try to dress it up."

"I do not have to dress it up. I would not bother to try." He shook his head, as if he felt sorry for her. He might have—had he not elevated her far above what must be deeply humble beginnings indeed. And yet asked so little in return. "I need a wife to present to my grandmother. This presentation will occur tomorrow. If you do as I ask, I will be only too happy to take whatever tests you like. And no matter what their result, I will make certain that this child is provided for in perpetuity."

He did not see how she could refuse or why she would wish to.

Yet the look on her face was not one of joy and acquiescence. Not by a long shot. "And if I do not play this bizarre game for you, a small child suffers. Is that what you mean to say?"

"That is a matter that is entirely under your control," he reminded her softly. "If you do not do as I ask, I will have to do what I can to convince my grandmother that our marriage is the sort she has long imagined for me, but without your input. I will tell her you are indisposed. She will ask, at once, if that means you are pregnant. And I will have no choice but to tell her that you are. What that means for you is that you will need to become so. Immediately."

When he had discussed something similar with the Cartwright heiress, it had been a far more arid conversation. He had not considered for a moment that any such necessary pregnancies would occur outside of a doctor's office.

It was odd that this woman made him wonder if, perhaps, it might be better to try things the old-fashioned way.

"You do realize that everything you're saying makes you sound like a raving madman, don't you?" she was demanding.

And what was funny was that her saying that felt a bit like a relief.

"I cannot deny it," Lionel said, aware that he sounded something bordering on *cheerful*, whatever that was. "These are the lengths that I am willing to go to please my grandmother and I will tell you, I do not really care if you think it mad."

Geraldine folded her arms in front of her and the way she looked at him took on a flinty sort of cast. "You have had many relationships with women."

Lionel blinked at that unexpected shift in the conversation. He tried to recall the last time anyone had surprised him so much, or at all, and failed. "I would say I have had a reasonable amount of relationships for a man of my age."

"What I mean is, you're known for always actually having relationships. Not merely strutting about like a rock star teeming with groupies." She made that sound a bit too much like *lice* for his comfort. And she was still talking. "That said, they are always quiet, these relationships of yours. Perhaps you'll allow a photo to be snapped at this or that high-profile event, but you do not run around making headlines regularly."

He considered her for a moment. "Certainly not. I prefer my personal life to be private."

Because it was impossible to do the kinds of business deals he did if everyone at the bargaining table knew every last lurid detail of his assignations. Lionel had always wondered why that wasn't more obvious to his peers.

Assuming, that was, that he, Lionel Asensio himself, could be said to *have* any peers.

"There are many men in your position who litter the trail behind them with one-night stands," Geraldine proclaimed, apparently answering that question herself. "You not only don't do that, ever, but the women you have these relationships with never take to the press when you're done with them."

"Perhaps," Lionel suggested lazily, "they are the ones who finish with me and therefore see no reason to discuss it with anyone."

And he could not have said why it pleased him that she laughed at that. "I don't think so."

"Dare I ask why we are delving so deeply into my romantic history?" When she didn't respond at once, he lifted a brow. "Could it be that you wish to fully inhabit your role as my wife? What an unexpected left turn, indeed."

Her frown deepened, but was undercut entirely by the way that flush betrayed her, yet again.

Something else he liked far more than he should.

"What I am trying to understand is why, if you were so desperate for a wife, you didn't marry one of your girlfriends," Geraldine said, sensibly enough. "Perhaps no one told you, given the rarefied circles you inhabit, but that's actually the typical way of things."

"Is it indeed?" He leaned back against the car, never shifting his gaze from her upturned face. "And you are conversant on this topic because of the numerous husbands you have married and then discarded, I take it?"

She ignored that, though he saw her stand a little straighter. "I'm sure that you could have called up any one of them, indicated you had the slightest interest in them again, and they would have come running. You could have had a perfectly easy wedding to a woman who would not require threats to do your bidding... But maybe

I'm missing something. Maybe all of these relationships were terrible, fraught with insurmountable minefields."

That hit a little too close to home, Lionel could admit.

The truth was, he was not well-suited to relationships, something he always told the women he dated before they embarked on one. But no matter how many times he explained that he did not believe in love and would not succumb to it, the same tired refrain played itself out in the same way. Each and every one of the women became more and more emotional, which he could not abide. And every time he finished with them because of this, they had professed their love and accused him of all manner of sins, most of which boiled down to the very thing he told them at the start. That he was unfeeling, uncaring. Heartless.

They were correct, he would always remind them. He had told them so himself.

How could anything else be expected from him? His father's emotions had resulted in trashed hotels from Barcelona to Fiji and back again. It had been operatic, the way the man had made the whole of the world a stage upon which anything and everything could be a fainting couch for his affairs, his schemes, his over-the-topic shamelessness in all things.

Lionel had closed himself off from all such emotional traps before he reached the age of eighteen.

"I do not wish to have discussions about my marriage," he told Geraldine instead of any of those things, because he could not see that psychoanalyzing himself was at all useful here. "And I do not wish there to be any doubt about who is in control of it."

She blinked at that, then blinked again, as if he'd told

some kind of joke. "It is my understanding that there are many women who would sign up for that today. Happily."

"Relationships are always tricky." And Lionel couldn't seem to help himself. His brow lifted of its own accord. "As, naturally, you are well aware, given your vast breadth and depth of experience. It is very easy to promise things at the beginning, only to feel quite differently about them as time goes on. The beauty of a business arrangement is that feelings become carefully thought-out clauses, and squabbles are settled in advance with the power of a signature."

"I think that is a fiction that businesspeople like to tell themselves," Geraldine countered. "But corporations, business deals, and even contracts—these are all the work of human hands. It's just *people* wandering around pretending that they can take the human out of it."

Lionel did not quite smile at this odd hen of a woman lecturing him on business affairs. "I prefer to think of it as managing expectations."

The Italian sun beat down, warm for a fall afternoon, and he could feel his phone buzzing repeatedly in his pocket. It was alerting him to all the various fires that were no doubt being set right and left across his empire, because there were always fires and he was the only one who ever seemed able to take those blazes and lower them to a more manageable simmer.

The truth was, he enjoyed it.

But still he stood here on this airfield, carrying on this pointless conversation with a green-eyed woman in the ugliest dress he'd ever seen, when he knew—as she must—that all he needed to do was to lift the faintest finger and his security detail would sweep her onto his plane despite any objections she might have. He could do it himself, for that matter. She already knew that he was perfectly capable of lifting her up and toting her about.

Yet, looking at her now, she seemed to be under the impression that she was the one in control of this interaction.

And Lionel had been fascinated by power and authority for the whole of his life. That was what happened with a father like his had been, so decidedly unequal to the task. If not actively engaged in squandering whatever measure of either he had ever had, because he could.

Because he knew no one could stop him. Not his wife. Not his son. Not even his otherwise formidable mother.

Lionel's father had reveled in the things he could not be told not to do.

Perhaps it was unsurprising that Lionel himself had felt, from a very young age, that he had to earn what power he had. That he had to work hard so that he spoke with true authority and could not simply throw money at the problems he made, like his father and grandfather had always done.

That was wealth. And it was not the same thing as real power, no matter how it might look from the outside. No matter how many people tried to pretend otherwise because it was all they had.

But he found himself fascinated all the same by this woman who did not appear to notice that she possessed no power here, even less authority, and had not even the faintest hint of wealth to make it worth ignoring her lack.

If he was not mistaken, Geraldine Gertrude Casey seemed to think that whatever power she possessed was... innate.

How extraordinary.

"The hour is growing late," he told her then, instead of continuing to discuss her thoughts on the humanity of the corporate world he doubted she had ever experienced. "We are rapidly approaching the point of no return. And I regret to inform you, *mi querida esposa*, that if you force me into a position where I must flex my muscles here... I will."

And Lionel was something a little more than simply fascinated by how wholly unimpressed she looked at that statement. Because he could feel it. Everywhere.

"Here's the situation as I see it," Geraldine told him in that forthright way of hers. "For whatever reason, likely that you're entirely too rich for your own good, you have a lot of strange ideas. That would be your business, but you've made it mine. Luckily, my aims are simple. I've already told you why I am here, what I want, and what I intend to make sure I get out of this. You should also know that I'm not a complete moron."

"I do not recall suggesting otherwise."

"Haven't you? Still, you should know that my mother is aware of exactly what I was doing and where I was headed today. If I don't make it back to our hotel room, she will sound the alarm. And loudly."

If she expected a reaction, she was to be disappointed. "A pity, then, that when that alarm sounds you will be in Spain."

It took him a moment to place the sort of look she gave him then. He realized he had never seen such an expression on anyone's face, save one. His grandmother's.

For this woman he had married today was looking at him as if her patience was sorely tried. *Her* patience. With *him*. "That you still feel compelled to threaten me to take part in this ruined wedding of yours speaks volumes," she said, and even shook her head. "It seems to me that a person who could not hold on to his first bride might treat the second a bit more carefully. Imagine the conversation we could be having right now if you had laid out your objectives, allowed me to do the same, and we'd found a way to meet in the middle."

Her temerity was unmatched.

"This from the woman who was under the impression that I preyed upon an unwell teenager, then cast her aside when I was done with her." Lionel tried his best to keep his temper locked away, where it belonged. "Where, precisely, do you imagine the middle to be between that position and mine?"

"Does your grandmother have her hands on the purse strings? Is that why you feel the need to go to such theatrical lengths for her?"

"My grandmother is none of your concern."

Geraldine laughed. It sounded faintly triumphant. "Then I can't imagine why you'd want me to play this elaborate game of pretend to deceive her."

That was the moment that Lionel realized a great many things.

First, and most surprising, was that they had somehow...gotten close. He wanted to think it was her doing, but he was quite certain that she was in the exact same position, standing there with her arms crossed over the front of that floral monstrosity, glaring up at him. That meant that he must have been the one to move closer, so that he stood there above her, looking down, entirely too close—

As if, at any moment, he might reach out his hands and wrap them around her upper arms, and then—

And then...what? he asked himself.

That was when the second thing occurred to him. Namely, that they were standing out here in public. He had only seen his own men here, but that didn't mean there couldn't be others nearby. Because while it was true that he did not spend a lot of his time in the headlines, there were always paparazzi lurking about, hoping to sneak in a shot that might change things.

He could not recall a single time in his entire life that he had ever lost sight of that.

That he had ever forgot, for even one moment, who he was and what he represented to those who might use him for their own ends. Or even just his name.

Next thing you know, you will be cavorting about on appalling yachts in the Mediterranean, awash in C-list actresses and models past their prime, he told himself scathingly. *Is that what you want? To become the parody of your useless grandfather that your father was? To remind the entire world how and why the Asensio name became associated with everything tawdry for far too long before you?*

Lionel wanted no such thing. Not when his entire life had been an attempt to emulate the kind of quiet command of the family name and assets that his grandmother had always embodied so well.

He had no intention of letting that change now. No matter the strange pull this woman seemed to exert on him.

He signaled his men, then looked back at Geraldine. "If you are planning to make a choice that does not involve me throwing you over my shoulder and carrying you on board the plane myself, now is the moment."

"I will pass on Neanderthal displays, thank you," Geraldine said. Stiffly, he thought. She sniffed, then unfolded her arms at last—but only so she could shove her glasses back up her nose.

A gesture he told himself he found deeply irritating. That was surely the reason he couldn't seem to look away while she did it.

"Wonderful," he said smoothly, as if he had heard nothing insulting at all. "As I mentioned earlier, there are certain scripts that we will need to follow—"

"Listen to me," Geraldine said then, cutting him off. Another moment so outside his experience that he could only stare back at her, too astonished to otherwise react. "Jules is what matters to me. Not your grandmother. Not even really you, though I think you should have to pay for what you did. There is the issue of responsibility, but there's also another issue, of restitution. That's why I'm here. And the only reason I'm even considering playing ridiculous games with you is because that sounds a great deal like the fastest way to get Jules what she deserves. Do you understand me?"

Lionel gazed down at her for what felt to him like a long, long while. "Do I seem to you to be...deficient in understanding?"

She only glared. Again. He had never known a woman to glare much at all in his presence, unless she was related to him. Even then it had never been so often.

"I will need you to say it, please," she told him.

As if she did not find what he had said already sufficient because she found him untrustworthy in some way. As if she, a nobody from nowhere—and that was being generous—needed more. From him.

From *him*.

And that was the moment, Lionel realized. The moment that everything shifted, little as he might have wished it to.

He knew too many things then that he wished he did not.

Too many things he would have taken back, if he could.

"I understand completely, Geraldine," he said, from between his teeth.

And he watched as she inclined her head, like royalty, and then actually beckoned for him to precede her to his own damn plane so she could trail along after him, as if this entire situation was hers to command.

She was wrong about that, of course.

But it was that moment that Lionel kept returning to. As the plane took off, and Geraldine stopped scowling at him only long enough to fall asleep before the plane completed its climb into the sky.

It was that moment he thought about over and over as he studied the circles beneath her eyes that suggested she really was tired, and not simply narcoleptic. Or simply trying out a new form of defiance as best she could.

He kept studying her, noting that in sleep her glasses slid down even farther, so that they nearly reached the tip of her nose and then, when she shifted in her seat, fell to her chin. Where they hung from her ears and should have made her look ridiculous. Perhaps she did. But Lionel found himself cataloging, instead, what appeared to be mounting evidence that he had somehow stumbled upon a diamond in the rough.

He already knew that she was not as shapeless as she seemed to wish she was. He had discovered that first-hand. But now he could see that she had the potential to be quite beautiful, in her own way. Now that she was not glaring and scowling, rolling her eyes, or making those disapproving faces of hers.

She did not look as if she had ever cared very much for her hair, save that shampoo she used that smelled like beachside holidays. But it was a more interesting shade of brown than some and if he wasn't mistaken, had a bit of a natural wave to it as well. There were stylists who could do wonders with such a canvas. Especially when her skin was smooth and her nose was straight. Her lips, as he had discovered, were firm and not overly thin. Her teeth had looked straight enough. She might even have a nice smile, not that he would know, as she had not aimed one in his direction.

Lionel could work with this. He could make her over into a woman resembling the sort his grandmother would expect him to have married—because convincing her was what mattered. There was no way that his sharp-eyed *abuelita* would believe, for even one moment, that he had accidentally become besotted with a woman who wore sofas as dresses and went about *scowling* at people through dark-framed glasses that made her face look misshapen.

Geraldine possessed the one thing he knew his grandmother wanted for him above all else. Lionel was so certain that he would bet the Asensio name and the whole of his fortune on the fact that she was completely innocent. His grandmother would approve of that, he knew.

But she would not believe for one moment that it was a real marriage—the kind she had lectured him extensively that she wanted for him—if he brought Geraldine to her looking like this.

My marriage to your grandfather was arranged, she had told him on his last three birthdays. *As was your mother's to your father. I would call neither a success. You must do better,* mi nieto. *I want something real for you.*

What you want, Abuelita, is less scandal attached to the family name, Lionel had replied each time.

The older woman had eyed him, amused. *I am not opposed to your happiness, child. I simply cannot trust you to find it yourself.*

Lionel shot off the necessary messages to his assistants, so they might have the appropriate people in place when the plane landed in the Asensio estate in the hills of Andalusia. Tucked between the olive orchards and the vineyards, gorges in one direction and white hilltop villages in the other, the estate had stood for far longer than the reputation of two late and largely unlamented men who had done their best to dismantle what their ancestors had built.

The selfishness. The waste. The complete inability to think of anything beyond self-gratification, no matter the cost—

But he ordered himself to shut that off. It was the past.

And he would not do the same as they had done. He would use this strange woman he had married as the weapon she needed to be to achieve his aims.

It started with the transformation he wished Geraldine to undergo before tomorrow, so that his grandmother could live out the rest of her life in ease and comfort—insofar as she allowed herself such weaknesses—and pay far less attention to her only grandson's personal affairs.

But when that was done, he returned again to that same moment, there beside a car in Italy.

Because that was when he'd known.

That despite his best intentions—and whether she took to her transformation or did not—this marriage was not going to be any kind of business arrangement, after all.

Because Lionel intended to have Geraldine beneath him, in every way a man could, and soon.

CHAPTER FIVE

IF GERALDINE HAD known what Lionel had planned, she thought crossly some hours later, she would have flatly refused to help him.

She'd woken up as the plane started its descent into Spain. She stared out at white buildings clinging to hillsides that gleamed in the September sun. As the plane got lower and lower, there were rolling fields, vineyards and olive orchards, and then a grand sort of Spanish-style house that took over the better part of a valley hidden away between two rolling, unspoiled hills.

It was so beautiful that it actually made her chest hurt.

If she was more fanciful, she might have allowed herself to brood on the notion that it felt like coming home— but she wasn't. So she didn't.

"I have to let my mother know where I am," Geraldine informed Lionel once the plane's wheels hit the ground. When really, she just wanted to know if the baby was okay. It wasn't that she didn't think her mother could care for Jules, because of course she did. It was just that she liked doing the caring herself. "Otherwise, as I said—"

"Yes, yes. Alarms will sound, and so on." He did that thing with his hand that was somehow an invitation even while it was dismissive. Maybe aristocratic sorts learned such things while ordering the nursery staff about from their cradles. "By all means, call whoever you like."

And then made it clear that he had no intention of giving her any privacy to do so.

"What you mean you've gone off to *Spain*?" Her mother had sounded astonished by that news when she picked up the call. And fair enough. Geraldine could hear Jules babbling to herself in the background, sounding sunny and happy, and had to close her eyes against the piercing sort of longing that washed over her. Especially because her mother was still talking. "I thought we came here for a very specific purpose. Not a sudden Grand Tour when we've barely landed."

"Wonderful," Geraldine had said brightly. "I let you know when I'll be back just as soon as I can."

And then she'd finished the call, feeling guilty that she'd abandoned both her mother *and* the baby.

"I prefer business arrangements," Lionel had said in that dark, stirring manner of his, as if he was not only aware of all the little fires that kicked up inside of her at the sound of his voice, but intended to light them with his own hands. As if he knew every last contour of the things she felt, when as far as she could tell, he was made of ice. "As I said."

She made herself smile. "Once again, you seem to be missing the part where this is something humans do. Having relationships are what life is supposed to be about."

"Alternatively, you could arrange your life to serve you," Lionel had replied. "This is what I choose to do."

And then he had shown her what he meant.

She had walked down the folding stairs that served as the plane's Jetway to find herself on yet another private airfield, this one even more remote than the one they'd stood on back in Italy. And she may or may not have dreamed about being that close to him, hardly aware of the words that were coming out of her mouth because she was too busy gazing up at him, wondering what it would feel like to surge up a little higher and press her mouth to his—

But she had very little time to reflect on the difference between Italian and Spanish private airfields, because she was swept up into a noisy crowd almost immediately.

They all spoke too quickly, and not to her. They were all dressed in black, and despite Geraldine's talk about human behavior, they appeared to be treating her as if she was something like cattle.

Her hair was let down by someone, while another held strands between his fingers, letting out a stream of remarks that she did not have to speak Spanish to know were not exactly admiring. Worse, another man staggered back and clasped a hand to his chest in what appeared to be not entirely feigned shock at the sight of her dress. So dramatically that he had to be propped up by the woman beside him, who spoke rapidly to him, as if attempting to convince him to continue breathing long enough to fix the situation.

It did not take long to understand that there was indeed a situation, and the situation was her.

"If I wanted a makeover," Geraldine snapped over the din, finding Lionel's slightly too amused gaze as he climbed into a separate, clearly far quieter car beside hers, "I would give myself one."

"No need," he told her smoothly. "We will meet for dinner, after my people determine whether or not miracles can be performed. And then we will go from there, you and I."

She had felt rather more let down than she should have when he'd actually got into his vehicle and drove off into the spectacular countryside that surrounded them.

Geraldine was forced to acknowledge that she was a little more focused on Lionel Asensio than she should have been. When she knew full well what kind of man he really was. And worse, what he was capable of doing. Or not doing.

"Do any of you speak English?" she asked once she'd been packed into her own car, where the horde descended upon her once again.

"Of course we all speak English," said the woman nearest her, not bothering to look up as she inspected Geraldine's nails. "But until we have something nice to say, we will speak Spanish."

And she was as good as her word.

Geraldine found herself carted off to some kind of small cottage. Though it could only be called such a thing—small or cottage—when considered next to that sprawling house she had seen on the flight in. It had more rooms than her tidy little two-bedroom house that she'd been so pleased to buy a few years ago, so she could feel like an adult at last.

It had taken Jules to make her realize that there was so much more to feeling like an adult than the little house, if that was what she wanted. Geraldine had always thought that she didn't want those things. That a life of books and friends, quiet joys, and the pleasure of her own company were enough. They had been enough.

Certainly the fast, loud, high life that Seanna had led had never appealed.

But then Geraldine had taken Jules into her arms at the very moment of her birth, and had held on to her tight ever since.

Her aunt and uncle had refused to get involved in what they called Seanna's catastrophically bad choices. Even after Seanna died, they could not be swayed to take the slightest notice of their grandchild. They'd advocated for Seanna's child to be given up for adoption, so that no one in the family would be forced to remember any of the unpleasantness unless they wanted to. Geraldine and her mother had tried as best they could to make them see reason, but they could not be swayed. And in the end, Geraldine had prevailed.

Because she had held that wriggling little creature against her neck. She had breathed in her first cries. And she'd understood, in a terrible and wonderful wave, that she would do anything and everything—always—to keep that little girl safe.

She could admit to herself that it was also possible that taking care of Jules allowed her to do it all over. To do it better this time, as she wasn't a nine-year-old. And sometimes, late at night, she would stare at her ceiling after putting the baby down and wonder if one of the things that made caring for Jules such a no-brainer for her was that it allowed her to feel a great deal like the savior she hadn't been able to play for her cousin.

Or even the big sister she'd always wanted to be, though her parents had tried. They hadn't been able to have any other children, so when Seanna had come along, Geraldine had adopted her as her very own.

And the truth was, she knew only too well that people couldn't save each other. They could only save themselves, and help those who asked for it. *If* they asked for it.

But she felt nothing like a savior today. If anything, Geraldine felt like a child herself. Or a mannequin. The scrum of stylists took her over. She was marched into a bathroom suite and her hair was washed. She was given a manicure and a pedicure at the same time that one of the stylists fussed over her hair with scissors, a comb, and the light of battle in his gaze.

In the next room, she could hear the rest of them discussing her, but she wasn't allowed to even look at herself when her hair was done. Too busy were they marching her behind a screen, demanding that she remove her dress to put on a flimsy little robe before hauling her back out from behind the screen and making her stand on the little platform.

Once again, a tide of rapid Spanish threatened to sweep her away.

"It is not so bad," said the original woman who had spoken to her in the car, smiling slightly. "Everyone is pleased that it is only the dress that made you look so terrible."

"I like that dress," Geraldine protested. "It's comfortable."

"*Comfortable* is another word for surrender," the man who had nearly fainted on the airfield chimed in then, also in English. "And if one must surrender, better to do it so stylishly, so elegantly, that in retrospect your surrender might look a little bit like a victory, after all."

And then no one spoke to her again as they worked.

There were no mirrors in the room, a kind of graceful

salon. Up on her little raised dais, Geraldine had a view out the windows. It was beautiful. The rolling hills, the incoming autumn season, the bright sky.

She had no idea why it made her want to cry. That was how peaceful it was.

They made her put on one thing, then another, and then debated among themselves as they made her turn this way, then that. There was a seamstress on hand who took whatever garments gained the approval of the crowd and tailored them on the spot, so that, in the end, everything that she was approved to wear fit her to exquisite perfection.

A notion that made her...uneasy.

"Do I get to look at your masterpiece?" she asked when a great many hours had passed, the sun was setting over the hills outside, and they had finally decided that they could take her to Lionel.

"There is no particular need," replied the man who led her through the cottage that was no cottage at all, with its rooms upon rooms, halls filled with whitewashed walls and art, and the hint of bookshelves heaving beneath the strain of too many volumes she itched to get her hands on. The man beside her sniffed. "You must know that your opinion has not been solicited, Señora Asensio."

But even as he called her that name that she could not accept was hers, he slowed as they walked into a sort of atrium and nodded his head toward the decorative mirror that took over the better part of one wall.

Where Geraldine saw, to her horror, that they had made her beautiful.

Inarguably so.

"Oh, no," she whispered. "This is a disaster."

"What did I tell you?" cried the man beside her. He clucked at her as if she had disappointed him, personally. "*Callate*, if you please. We are artists, you are our creation, and this has nothing to do with what *you* think. You would wear that dress before *la ilustrísima* señora Doña Eugenia Lourdes Rosario herself, and this we cannot have."

And then he ushered her with a rather ungentle hand on the small of her back, through the glassed-in atrium with orchids blooming madly and then outside, where Geraldine stopped dead.

Because there was a bit of a secret garden here, back behind this place. A walled-in, overgrown, glorious patch of paradise, where flowers bloomed everywhere she looked, the sweet air was scented with mysterious things she could not quite identify, and there were a thousand candles fighting off the dark.

And in the center of it all stood Lionel.

Looking at her with a certain *intent* that made the world seem to spin again.

Oh, no, Geraldine thought again.

And not because she worried that she might faint. More that she was afraid that…she wouldn't.

"I hope you're satisfied," she said, her voice sharper than planned.

She was too aware of…too much. The sultry Spanish night, flowing around her like the kind of caress she did not wish to think about in this man's presence. The scent of so many flowers, dancing on the evening breeze. The last of the sunset itself, a pageant of deep pinks, burnt oranges, and deep indigos that she would have watched like its own movie under any other circumstances.

But there was no looking away from Lionel.

Just as there was no pretending that there was some other reason for the sudden breathlessness she felt while she did.

"*Satisfied* is not the word I would choose," he said, the low heat of his voice a counterpoint to that dark blaze in his eyes. They looked less like the color of dark coffee in the evening light, with so many candles flickering everywhere, and more like something significantly less prosaic. Very old whiskey, for example. Smoky and dangerous.

Geraldine remembered, then, that she had stopped dead in her tracks.

It was harder than it should have been to force herself to walk toward him, when it felt so much like walking to the edge of a very steep cliff and hoping against hope that she could balance there.

She became suddenly and shockingly aware of the clothes she was wearing. It was as if she hadn't been present in that room as all those people had swirled around her, dressing and undressing her as if she really was nothing more than a canvas. She'd sighed when they'd let this particular dress float over her shoulders, then had sewn her into it. And it had been the particular fit of the garment that caught her eye first when she'd actually seen her reflection.

That had been bad enough.

But this was worse. Much worse.

Because she understood with every step that Lionel's reaction was catastrophic.

He was not looking at her the way he had before, as if she was a very faintly amusing novelty that he could use to his own ends. He was not looking at her in that pitying way, the way she was sure he had been when she'd found herself in his arms. He was not looking at her with that scowl that had demanded, before he'd said a word, that she think better of her own temerity in laughing at his misfortune.

The look on his face now was something else altogether.

And she hated that it had nothing to do with her, and everything to do with her appearance. An appearance that had required an entire team to create.

"I do not understand." And there was a hoarse note in Lionel's voice as she came to stand before him, there where a small table had been set, with crystal glassware reflecting the candlelight. "That hideous garment you wore today makes no sense. I do not understand what would make you do such a thing. When you could look like this."

Geraldine glared at him. "Because that hideous garment is comfortable." She waved a hand down the length of her body, too aware of the way his gaze tracked the movement. "Does it look to you as if this is comfortable?"

The dress was a column of vibrant color that clung to her figure. And Geraldine had no illusions about herself or her charms. She had grown up with Seanna. She knew only too well that her own form was not fashionable in the least. Her proportions were much too generous. She had accepted that long ago. Happily enough.

But she was fully aware that on any occasion she mistakenly wore something that presented her figure so all could see, there were…reactions.

Too many reactions.

And she knew what followed on from such reactions. Her cousin's entire life was a cautionary tale.

Besides, Geraldine had never wanted to shine like that. She'd wanted to be smart and capable, thank you, and back in the horror of adolescence it had seemed very clear to her that she had to choose. One or the other.

So she had.

It didn't help that tonight they had done whatever they'd done to her hair, so that it seemed glossier and softer. It swirled around her shoulders, making her look as sultry as the Spanish night all around them, when she would far prefer to forget about it and twist it up and out of her way. It was irritating when it heated against the back of her neck.

Nor did it help that they had taken care of all the little details she found too annoying to ever do herself. The manicure that made her hands look somehow less capable than before. The pedicure that had made her feet feel overly soft and fragile. The high-heeled sandals with delicate straps that were suitable for walking extremely short distances, if that.

There was nothing practical about a single thing she was wearing. Including the necklace they'd clasped around her neck with a single diamond solitaire set to sparkle just there, above the place where the dress ended, so that it was impossible not to look at the thrust of her breasts and the hollow between them. Not to mention her entirely bare shoulders, which someone had dusted with a powder that had made her gleam in that hallway, and likely made her outright sparkle here in the candlelight.

She knew, too, that they had taken shocking liberties with her face. Left to her own devices, Geraldine did not wear color on her lips. It only called attention to them, making them seem plumper and glossier than they ought to have been. She had never been one to take such care with her eyes, elongating her lashes, rubbing on creams and shadows, and adding layers of mystery and shadow so that her green eyes were far more inviting than necessary. When they were already *green*, for God's sake.

There's no way around it. This was a disaster.

If he was looking at her like this, if this was all he saw, how could she force him to face what he'd done? That required fortitude, not fashion. She was sure of it.

"Comfortable," Lionel was saying, echoing the word she'd used as if he had never heard it before. He said it again, managing to sound even more baffled. "Surely you realize that comfort is for those who could not achieve what you have naturally, yes? It is a trap at best."

"It is a necessity if a person lives through winters in Minnesota," Geraldine retorted. "I can assure you that I have very little call to go prancing around dressed like this when the weather is below zero, my car won't start unless it's hooked to a heating block, and layers upon layers of cold-weather gear are required to step outside."

"Those are no longer your concerns," he told her, in the silken sort of way that made all the hairs all over her body seem to stand on end in warning. It was a *warning*, she told herself. "For you are now the wife of an Asensio, and there will be no more scrabbling about in cold winters, concerning yourself with such menial tasks."

"If that's the sales pitch you think you should be leading with, I have some news for you," Geraldine replied with admirable calm, she thought, given the state of her pulse. "You've read this situation wrong. Why would I have the slightest interest in the kind of superficial glamour that killed my cousin? Or the man who helped engineer it?"

She had sense that something in him hardened, but all he did was study her for a moment, then step back and indicate that she should take her seat at the table.

Geraldine felt like a trap was closing around her. As if she'd stuck her arm into a terrifying set of steel jaws and the only way out might be to gnaw the whole thing off—

Then again, she thought, repressively, *it could be that you're simply hungry, since the last thing you ate was a selection of stale nuts on that plane.*

"Perhaps it would be better if we hold off on accusations and character assassinations, *mi querida esposa,*" Lionel said as she pulled herself together and took her seat. As he stood there and helped her into it when she needed no such aid, then held the back of the chair to slide it into the table, so that she felt him all around her. As if he was touching her when he was not. "After all, I would not wish you to feel embarrassed when the results prove my innocence."

He looked entirely too sure of himself for her peace of mind when he rounded the small table and took the seat opposite hers.

"Even if the results do come back and prove that you're Jules's father, I won't feel embarrassed," she declared then, though she wasn't really sure that was true. But what mattered was that she *sounded* sure, she told herself. "I told you the reasons why I sought you out. They remain valid. If you are named incorrectly, that only means that I will have some follow-up questions for you."

"Geraldine," he said, a different note in his voice—

or maybe it was just the way he said her name, making it a lilting thing. A scrap of a song, much the way his own name sounded in his language, three lovely syllables instead of something that rhymed with *vinyl*. "This all sounds like a great many words and attempted diversions to cover the fact that you are quite beautiful. And that you have clearly gone to great lengths to hide it."

It was only now, sitting at the table, that she realized what she should have noticed immediately. They had taken her glasses away at some point while washing her hair and had never given them back. The realization was a relief, she found. *No wonder* she found everything so sultry, so atmospheric.

Not that it helped her now. She couldn't see details well in the distance, but now that she was sitting with only this table between her and Lionel, she could, regrettably, see that he looked even better up close.

Not better, she lectured herself. *More dangerous. Everything about him is a calculated seduction, and you know where it ends.*

But she was dismayed to find that knowing such things did not set her straight as much as it should have. Because her body did not appear to be getting the message that she was not to find him attractive.

"I'm not beautiful," she told him matter-of-factly. "My cousin was beautiful."

"It is not all one thing or the other." Lionel leaned back in his chair and the way he looked at her seemed to happen from the inside out, making everything within her *hum*. "Is this what you meant when you spoke about shying away from beauty because it is only on the surface? Because it is not who you are?"

Geraldine barely remembered saying that, though it sounded very much like something she *would* say. She didn't understand that tightening in her chest then, as if the very idea that this man had actually paid that much attention to her while she was speaking made her…some kind of stranger to herself, as if the woman she could see reflected in his gaze was more *her* than she had ever been.

She did not care for that at all.

Or maybe she was worried that she did.

"True beauty is not something that can be hidden away with a pair of glasses and an unflattering dress," she said quietly. "That's a Hollywood movie. The reality is that I have a certain shape, that's all. I find that I very rarely like the attention that shape brings me. But then, unlike fancy billionaires and famous models, I do not find that I enjoy very much attention at all."

He seemed to look at her for a long while, and that humming inside her was turning into something more like a seismic episode, but still he kept on. And she wanted to break this moment apart before it broke her, but she couldn't seem to open her mouth. She couldn't seem to do anything at all but look back at him, the harsh beauty he wore so easily seeming even more magnetic, even more tempting, in the soft touch of the candlelight.

"Very well," he said at last, as if something had been decided.

He did something with one hand, and suddenly their private little garden was filled with two staff members who managed to make it seem as if there were at least triple of them. They bustled about and when they left, there was wine in the glasses, candles between them, and platters of food that smelled so good she had a moment where she thought she might actually weep.

"The food is a selection of local delicacies. Andalusia is known for its food, and my cook is the best," he told her, and not in a way that suggested he was exaggerating to compliment his chef. But in a way that suggested that it was a quantifiable fact. He inclined his head. "Eat, Geraldine."

And for a while, that was exactly what she did. The flavors were seductive. The dishes played with savory and sweet in different combinations, like a complicated dance. She only wished that her appetite was big enough to eat every last morsel on the table.

But Geraldine did not realize until some time had passed that she'd miscalculated. Because there was something too intimate about sitting in the candlelight, as the sky darkened above them and then gave itself over to the night. There was something about the way the candles danced in the little bit of breeze, the only music the soft touch of it as it went. And how the act of eating together, in silence, made whatever this was between them feel fraught. Deeper than it was. Almost as if—

But she could not allow herself to think these things. Not with this man who might very well be responsible for what had happened to her cousin. Not when Jules was her first and foremost responsibility these days—as she should be. The baby was the point of all of this, not whatever she felt on a night breeze in the company of this man.

She put down her fork when it occurred to her that she had started to think about it as if it might not be true. As if it might not be him.

As if she was tempted to believe him.

Lionel was lounging in the chair across from her, toying idly with a wineglass on the table before him, though his gaze remained trained on her.

"You seemed to have enjoyed the cuisine of my country," he said, after some while had passed. An eternity or two, to her mind, caught up like that in his dark, gleaming gaze. "I am glad."

And Geraldine had never felt like this before. As if there was something effervescent stuck in the pit of her stomach, like a kind of indigestion—only she knew that it was not the type that would make her sick. On the contrary, it felt a great deal more like joy.

She suddenly found that she had a great deal more sympathy toward her cousin's choices than she ever had before. She hadn't judged Seanna, that was true. But she hadn't understood her, either.

Suddenly, what had not made any sense to her before seemed clear.

And she wanted to lash out at him, because she felt precarious, as if despite the fact that she was sitting down with a table between her and him, she was still standing on that cliff she'd imagined before. Arms wheeling, legs shaking.

She didn't like it.

But she also couldn't quite bring herself to let the sharp edge of her tongue fly. "Every bite was exquisite," she said. Truthfully.

And that wasn't a compliment, she assured herself. It was the simple truth. And the fact that the simple act of eating with him seemed far too sensual, well. Perhaps that was something she needed to work on. Within herself.

"I am delighted to hear it," Lionel murmured.

And when he lifted his gaze just slightly, she found herself sitting up straighter, which in no way shifted that fizzy thing deep inside her. If anything, it made it grow. It was something about the way the candlelight caressed the harshly perfect lines of his face. It was the way he looked at her, pitiless and sure.

It made her want to giggle. Then melt.

"Now," Lionel said. "It is time you and I discuss exactly will happen tomorrow, exactly what you will do, and what penalties you might expect if you do not obey me."

Geraldine had never wanted to obey anyone. She had never considered herself *obedient* in any way.

But the way Lionel looked at her now, she was reconsidering her stance.

She had to shake herself slightly to make that wondrous aching and sparkling thing that was taking her over loosen its grip. Though she wasn't sure it worked.

"Tomorrow is my grandmother's birthday," Lionel was saying. "She was never shy or retiring in any way, but the advance of her years has made her even less discreet than she was. You must be prepared for this. She will ask you whatever she likes. She delights in being provocative. I expect that you will handle whatever she throws at you with humor and grace."

"This might come as a surprise to you," Geraldine replied, though it was harder to sound dry and amused than she would have liked, "but I have actually interacted with eighty-year-old women before."

"I doubt very much that the sweet pensioners you might have stumbled over in your library have anything in common with a woman some have called the unofficial queen of Spain," Lionel replied with a hint of amusement in his voice that made Geraldine feel something a little too much like foolish. "You may have a distaste for wealth, but you must not show it. In your American way, imagine yourself somehow equal to an aristocrat, but that is not a position my grandmother shares. Doña Eugenia Lourdes Rosario Asensio can trace herself and her bloodline back across untold centuries, and that means something to her. You will do well to remember that."

"So far she sounds like a gorgon." Geraldine only shrugged when that brow of his rose, signaling his disapproval. "Once again, I am forced to wonder why it is you are so determined to do her bidding."

"She is the only woman on earth whose bidding I will ever do," Lionel returned, and there was something about the way he said that. It was like some kind of premonition, or foreboding.

Geraldine told herself she was being absurd. "Then what I would like is practical, concrete advice on how I'm expected to behave tomorrow if I'd like you to take responsibility for the child you might have created." She told herself that she liked the way his eyes darkened at that. And that her growing certainty that she was being set up to disappoint him was a good thing, no foreboding premonitions necessary.

That's what you need, she lectured herself. *To be nothing he wants. To embarrass him. So you remember what's actually happening here. Not whatever it is you think you* feel *tonight.*

And so she only half listened as Lionel began to outline the sort of customs and expectations, manners and protocol that a woman like his grandmother would expect. The party was not going to be some intimate gathering, or visit in a care home, as she might have been imagining. *La ilustrísima* señora Doña Eugenia Lourdes Rosario liked to celebrate herself in style.

"You do not appear to be as overwhelmed by these things as I would expect," Lionel pointed out after he had talked for some while, and he did not sound pleased by that. "As would be perfectly appropriate for a person in your situation."

"I'm not worried," Geraldine replied, and tried a wave of her own hand to indiscernible effect. "I can assure you that I'm perfectly capable of picking up the correct fork a dinner party and managing myself decently enough that I do not embarrass anyone in my vicinity."

"Because of your vast experience at grand affairs of this nature?"

"Because, once again, I have read across a wide array of topics," Geraldine said lightly. Or perhaps not quite so lightly, because even she could hear the edge in her voice. "I have likely read a great many more books about customs and propriety than you."

"I admire your confidence," he replied in a way that made it clear that he did not.

And Geraldine couldn't seem to get a handle on all the sensations competing for her attention, deep inside, so she decided it was time she stopped trying. She pushed back from the table, standing up and smiling a little bit as she looked at him, as if she was the one in charge of this. "I will expect that by the end of this dinner party of yours, a fleet of doctors, scientists, whatever you like, will descend upon you and Jules. And that they will answer the question of whether or not you're her biological father once and for all. That's the only thing I'm interested in. If I have to make sparkling conversation with snooty aristocrats to make that happen, that seems a small price to pay indeed."

She was not prepared for the way Lionel rose, then. She'd miscalculated once again, she realized too late, because once he did they were suddenly standing entirely too close to each other.

Much too close, something in her seemed to cry out, its own alarm.

In a secret garden filled with candlelight and the scent of night-blooming flowers on the breeze.

"I assume I'm to stay here," she said, dismayed that her voice seemed to get higher and higher with every syllable. She cleared her throat. "I'm sure someone mentioned that this was the guest cottage. I assume you stay, awash in your magnificence, somewhere significantly more spectacular."

Lionel studied her in the candlelight, and it made everything inside her feel...fragile.

Except it was far too raw for that.

And somehow she knew exactly what he was going to say. Before he uttered a word.

"This is my home, Geraldine." She heard the words he said, but the way he looked at her made them *feel* like something else. "I am devastated that you do not find it up to your standards."

"I'm sure it will be fine." And she sounded more frigid than she might have wished, because her head was spinning. She didn't want to stay in the same place as this man. She didn't want to be anywhere near him—and she didn't particularly want to explore her reasons for that. Or how they might have changed since she'd walked into that chapel what felt like a lifetime ago. "A hotel or guest room, it's all the same to me."

And she knew, somehow, that just then they were both standing on the edge of that same precipice. They were both being rocked by the same wind, making their footing unsteady.

Just as she knew that left to his own devices, Lionel would jump.

Geraldine had no idea what part of her it was that rather thought she would like to do the same.

The night seemed closer. The candles danced. He had called her beautiful, and more, she thought he meant it.

She had never wanted to be beautiful before. She wasn't sure she liked how much she wanted it now.

Particularly here. With this man, of all men.

But every single buttery-hot sensation that moved through her then, she told herself harshly, was a betrayal. The way her breath caught. The sweet weight of her breasts, the way they moved against the soft fabric of her dress each time she breathed. That sparkling, melting part of her, deep in her belly and high between her legs.

She was betraying Seanna. And she hated herself for it.

Or she should.

Geraldine took one step back, then another. And she did her best to arrange her features into something scornful.

"I trust you will not make this difficult," she said, as sharply as she could.

And then, as she watched, his stern, stone face changed.

Because Lionel Asensio smiled.

In a way that made everything inside of her begin to burn, that humming nearly breaking out through her skin.

"Run along, my little innocent," he told her, every inch of him a wolf. Every beautiful, decidedly male inch. "And sleep well. There will be time enough for difficulties in the days to come. This I promise you, Geraldine."

And later, she would be ashamed that she did not turn and saunter away, effortless and unbothered.

But just then, with that particular gleam in his dark gaze making her body feel something like feverish, Geraldine did the only thing she could.

She kicked off her pointless shoes and ran.

CHAPTER SIX

LIONEL HAD SPENT the day immersed in the usual concerns of his various business enterprises, but he was uncomfortably aware that his attention kept wandering. When his attention was normally fixed and unshakable.

Worse, he found his mind returning again and again to last night.

To that moment when he had first seen Geraldine no longer hiding her beauty but honoring it. Making it clear that she was pure diamond, straight through.

Or later, when he had found himself more nearly undone by a single conversation with her than he had been in whole relationships with others.

And he was not sure that he would ever get over the sight of her in bare feet, racing across the flagstones before she disappeared into his house, her dark hair streaming behind her as she moved.

Making it clear that he was not the only one so close to undone.

His people kept him apprised of his new wife's doings throughout the day. She had woken late and had seemed disgruntled, according to the maids, because she had claimed—repeatedly—that she never slept like that, so deeply and so long. She seemed suspicious of the breakfast brought to her in her room, an Andalusian staple of olive oil pressed here at the estate on toast made from freshly baked bread, with a pinch of salt and *jamón serrano*. Even when encouraged to take it out on one of the terraces off her rooms that overlooked the Asensio state, the fields gleaming in the bright fall sun, she had seemed out of sorts until she'd had a fair bit of the *café con leche* that was typical for a Spanish breakfast.

"Perhaps," the maid who brought him this information had theorized, "she is suffering from the jet lag."

"Perhaps," Lionel had said, as if he agreed.

When he was not certain he did.

After her breakfast, his people had laid out dressing options for her—another thing not taken in entirely good grace, according to reports—and then Geraldine had taken herself on a self-guided tour of his home. She had lingered anywhere there was a book, running her fingers down the spines and leafing through the pages. And then she had spent hours in his library, where she had been served a traditional lunch running the gamut from breads and cured meats to gazpacho to a hearty stew and a green salad, with coffee to finish.

She had eaten heartily, then returned to her exploration of his books. And she had not been exactly thrilled when the team of stylists had taken her in hand again, but nor had she objected outright.

All of these things were reported to him, one by one, and with many colorful asides about the new mistress of the house—a term Lionel had not used and was not at all sure he planned to approve—so perhaps it was not very surprising that Lionel could not quite focus the way he would like.

And that evening Lionel found himself waiting for this woman he had married with every expectation of thinking little of her again. He stood ready in the entry hall of his own home so that he might take her hand and lead her into the great celebration that was the entire point of this farce. Because for as long as he had known her— and so therefore, as long as he had been alive—Lionel's iconic and widely revered grandmother had never done anything by half.

Her eightieth birthday party, meticulously plotted out and entirely conceived by Doña Eugenia herself, was certainly no exception to this rule. Lionel had assumed that he would approach this landmark feeling quite pleased with himself, given the trouble he had gone to for the occasion. Collecting a wife as ordered and all.

Yet celebrating the woman who had been the only family he had, and long after she was the only family he acknowledged, was the furthest thing from his mind tonight.

Because Geraldine appeared at the top of the stairs and Lionel could think of nothing and no one else.

For a full moment he was not certain that he was capable of speech. Perhaps it was a great many moments, he would never know. He made an immediate mental note to give all the staff who'd worked with her tonight a hefty raise for their trouble.

Because he was certain, at a glance, that she might very well set the whole of Andalusia alight.

For they had dressed her in a column of flame. Once again, the dress was a love letter to that figure of hers, from her wide hips to her tiny waist to the aching fullness of her breasts. Geraldine, who had looked like a piece of furniture in that chapel yesterday, was today nothing short of a dream come true.

A dream Lionel had not permitted himself to indulge in the night before, but there was nothing to be done about it now. Tonight she was pure sex on two feet.

Yet all he could think was that she was his.

His.

He watched as Geraldine made her way toward him, her green eyes wary, betraying her nerves as she fussed with the dress with every step she took in another pair of shoes that made her legs look like a fantasy come true.

"The more you fidget, the more you call attention to how uncomfortable you are," Lionel said, aware that he sounded not quite himself. It was that or swing her up into his arms, carry her to his bed, and hope his grandmother understood some weeks from now when he emerged, finally sated.

This was likely the first moment in his entire life that Lionel wasn't sure he cared what his grandmother thought at all.

And that was shocking enough that it cleared his head. A little.

Geraldine, naturally, took that opportunity to glare at him, but that hit differently when she was dressed like this. When her beauty was in no way hidden. "I'm not uncomfortable and I don't fidget. I'm nearsighted and I can't see as well as I would like, but they wouldn't let me wear my glasses after I pointed out that this dress is hardly appropriate for an eighty-year-old woman's birthday party."

Lionel moved toward her, then pulled her arm through his. It was an old, courtly sort of gesture, and it sat in him oddly. As if it carried some weight beyond simple expediency.

As if it mattered. Or she did.

He could not allow such thoughts to derail him. "As you will see when you meet my grandmother, *appropriateness* is not a concern. She would be the first to tell you that the only thing that matters in terms of a woman's attire is how glorious she feels while wearing the items in question. And if it can cause a head or two to turn, all the better."

"I think you're brushing past the fact that your people confiscated my glasses a little too quickly."

"You do not need to see," he told her. "Hold on to me and you will be fine."

She scowled at him. "That is not remotely comforting. I think you know that."

Instead of answering her, Lionel led her outside to the waiting Range Rover. Because it was a short walk over the fields to the main house, but tonight he had decided it made sense to take the drive that looped around the long way. Not so much to make certain that they would make an entrance, though he knew all eyes would be on them nonetheless, but also so that his brand-new wife could walk more easily in those shoes that made her legs look as if they would wrap around a man's back all too easily.

"You walk well in those heels," he said as they settled into the back of the vehicle.

Geraldine sighed. "I was a teenage girl once upon a time. I learned how to walk in all kinds of ridiculous shoes. The fact that I *can* walk in them doesn't mean I *want* to walk in them, but I was told in no uncertain terms that I was never going to see *my* shoes again."

"You are welcome," Lionel said, trying to sound more severe than he actually was. "They were an offense against all that is stylish."

And then he consulted the usual flood of messages on his mobile rather than chase up the things he heard her mutter, not quite beneath her breath. But he did not read a word. He was much too busy questioning why it was this woman who should have been overawed by him, yet was not, amused him.

He was not easily amused.

And was less amused by the moment as he wondered why Geraldine, of all women, should bring this out in him.

Moreover, he had not expected to get caught in traffic with half of Spain on the drive to the main house. Inching along meant he was stuck in this confined space with Geraldine, who he knew he could not touch.

Not now. Not *yet*. Not when she had been carefully crafted tonight to appeal to his grandmother as well as wow the crowd.

Lionel found to his surprise that he appeared to be ill-suited to this notion of *waiting* for the things he wanted. He assured himself that this was only because he had been planning to present a wife at this party since his grandmother had decreed she would be throwing it, some eighteen months ago.

It was this situation, he told himself. It wasn't *this woman*.

But he was happier than he thought he ought to be to get out of the Range Rover, all the same.

"There are so many people here," Geraldine said as they walked inside with the gathering crowd. She seemed to have left her scowls and glares back at his house, and

Lionel knew he should have been grateful for that. Yet, oddly enough, he was not. As if he liked her unpredictable. "I suppose that makes sense. Your grandmother must have met a great many in all her years."

"People have been invited to come and pay their respects whether they have met her or not," Lionel told her as they made it through the entryway and were caught up almost at once in the music and the chatter as the flood of guests were directed into the great ballroom. This house had been a part of the court of some-or-other duke who had once claimed these lands, but had then lost them.

Geraldine did not drop his arm as they wound their way through the throngs of well-wishers, and Lionel decided that was a victory of its own. She held on to him, but her eyes could not seem to stay in one place—and made him wonder exactly how blind she really was, hiding behind her glasses. Because tonight her gaze moved from well-known cinema stars to recognizably famous pieces of art on the walls, then seemed to widen at the quiet, understated magnificence of this place that had been the seat of his family for generations.

Despite himself and all the many ways he knew he really needed to treat this like the business venture it was, Lionel found that Geraldine made him...protective. Of her. Because she wasn't the Cartwright heiress—even now happy off in the desert with the man who had claimed her yesterday, according to all reports, and more power to her—who had cut her teeth on parties like this one. *She* had moved in the sorts of circles that would have prepared her for nights like this, like it or not.

Not so Geraldine.

But his many assistants had done their jobs well, and

Lionel had been presented with files stuffed full of all the details anyone could ever want about his new wife the night before. Long after she'd run from him, he had sipped at his brandy from Jerez there in his library where he often spent his evenings, and read everything there was to know about Geraldine Gertrude Casey.

Geraldine *Asensio* he corrected himself.

The files his people had compiled proved that she was exactly who she seemed to be, and there was something about that. It seemed to tug at him. It made his throat need clearing.

For the wife of the heir to the Asensio empire had been raised by two schoolteachers outside Minneapolis, which Lionel knew vaguely from his time at Harvard was somewhere in the American Midwest. He'd had to look it up on a map. Geraldine was an only child. She had done exceedingly well at school and had gone to Chicago for college, but had returned home to get her degree in library science, and then, later, her job.

She was enormously well-suited to that life, he thought.

Tonight, he felt very much as if was leading a lamb to the slaughter.

Though he supposed that the saving grace was how little Geraldine seemed to notice or care that she was the object of so much speculation that Lionel could actually *feel* the weight of so many stares as they walked through the ballroom.

Because it was known far and wide that even when Lionel was indulging in one of his relationships, he never brought a woman here. Not to this house.

Not when his grandmother was in residence.

He could see members of the Spanish nobility, who

he would never quite call *friends*, gossiping behind their hands as he walked Geraldine through the crowd. He saw the same assessment on the faces of politicians and celebrities. Yet he did not stop. He did not want to let anyone get their hooks into her.

Even though he knew that if anyone could handle herself, even in a place like this that better resembled a lion's den tonight, it was Geraldine.

Lionel did not stop no matter who caught his eye or waved him over. He kept going until he achieved his target.

"Behold," he intoned, with all due deference, inclining his head. "May I present *la ilustrísima* señora Doña Eugenia Lourdes Rosario Asensio." Geraldine inclined her head the way everyone else did when they approached his grandmother. "Grandmother, this is my Geraldine."

Geraldine blinked in astonishment at last, but Lionel thought that had more to do with the *my Geraldine* than anything else. She looked up at him for a beat too long, then followed his gaze.

To his grandmother, who sat in all her considerable state in what might as well have been a throne, set up on a dais at the far end of the room so she might cast an eye wherever she liked over the proceedings and see everything she would not if she was on the ground.

I am a tiny woman, she had told Lionel on one of their typical morning walks.

Only in physical stature, he had replied loyally.

She had tutted at him. *Obviously,* nene, she had said reproachfully. *I am otherwise grander than the sky, and don't you forget it.*

His *abuelita* sat so that everyone who came to greet

her was slightly below her eye level, like the queen she had always been in Lionel's estimation.

She had always been breathtaking, though she had long since left the sloe-eyed, mysteriously beautiful girl she'd been behind—the one who still claimed pride of place in a great many portraits painted by modern masters all over this house. But Doña Eugenia was not one to cling to her lost youth, freezing her brow or injecting questionable substances into her skin. She had settled into her years with grace and elegance and tonight her snow-white hair was arranged about her face in such a way as to suggest that she might just be wearing a crown. She wore a set of priceless emeralds around her neck, each the size of a small fist. And she clasped a cane before her that was topped by the bejeweled head of the serpent, with rubies for eyes.

Because, she had told Lionel when she'd showed the cane to him last week, *I do not wish to be* too *approachable.*

Even at your own party? he had asked.

Especially at my own party" she had declared.

"She's absolutely magnificent," Geraldine breathed.

No talk about how ferocious his grandmother was. No hint of intimidation.

Deep inside, Lionel felt something kick at him, hard.

But his grandmother was watching. She lifted one aristocratic finger and beckoned him close.

"I hope you're ready," Lionel murmured to Geraldine.

Then he brought forth the woman he had married to meet the only woman he had ever loved. And felt something twist in him that he could not possibly have explained if asked. As if this, here, was his true wedding. As if this was the only ceremony that mattered.

His grandmother waved the rest of her admirers away. They melted away at her command, because she wasn't the sort of woman that anyone dared disobey. As she was the first to say, she had been less formidable in her youth. *But the true power in this world is outliving everybody,* she liked to say with a laugh.

"Abuelita," Lionel said as he stepped up onto the dais and brought Geraldine with him, "I am certain that you have never been more beautiful than you are tonight."

"Whereas you used to be far better at flattery," his salty grandmother responded in her usual crisp manner, presenting her one cheek to be kissed, then the other.

"May I present to you the woman that I have made my wife," Lionel said, and in English. "Geraldine Gertrude Casey, who did me the great honor of taking my name only yesterday at Lake Como."

As he spoke, Geraldine stood beside him. She was not exactly relaxed, but she did not appear overly intense, either. This allowed him to pay closer attention to his grandmother. He watched different emotions chase across her usually inscrutable face. Shock. The faintest hint of temper. Then, at last, consideration.

"Have I already gone to meet my maker?" she asked Lionel. In Spanish, because she could not be told or led. "Is there reason that my only grandson saw fit to marry himself off outside of my presence? What can you be playing at, I wonder?"

"We were swept away by passion," Lionel told her, expressionless. "It was necessary that we marry as quickly as possible."

"Is that so?"

His grandmother turned that lively dark gaze of hers

to Geraldine, and studied her for a long moment. And Lionel did not know if Geraldine realized how critical it was that the way she appeared in this moment was nothing short of perfection. But he did.

"There are only two things that cause anyone to rush to an altar, as far as I am aware," Doña Eugenia said, this time in perfectly crisp English. "One is a feverish desire for consummation. The other is the fear of illegitimacy. And which was this clandestine ceremony, might I ask?"

Lionel could see the way his grandmother's gaze still moved all over Geraldine, no doubt cataloging flaws at every turn. She might have been the kindest and approachable of his family members. She might always have been his favorite.

This did not mean she was cuddly.

He should have prepared his new wife better for this. Had he spent less time trying his best not to think too much about her, he might have.

But next to him, Geraldine smiled. "There are some men who only value something if they are required to work for it," she told his grandmother, in a voice that somehow managed to be respectful and amused at once.

And then, as Lionel stood there feeling surplus to requirements for what was likely the first time in his life, the two women gazed at each other for a long moment. Then another one, as the band played old standards and the better part of fashionable Spain tried to eavesdrop without appearing to do so.

Until, to Lionel's great astonishment, his grandmother laughed. "Fair enough," she said, and did not precisely incline her head to Geraldine, though the notion seemed to hang between them anyway. Then she shifted her gaze to Lionel. "Now that you are here, the dancing can begin at last. Had I known you would go to such lengths to exclude me from your wedding ceremony, I might not have gone to the trouble of waiting for you."

"*Abuelita.* Come now. You know as well as I do that you no longer wish to travel. How many times have you told me that the world must come to you?" He indicated the still-growing crowd behind them. "And so they have."

"You are saying it was your new wife's choice to exclude me?" But she was still smiling, if more at Geraldine than Lionel. "How ungallant."

"I could have invited you. But I thought you might prefer it if I arrived here at the party with the best present you could possibly wish for." He nodded at Geraldine. "The Asensio line, assured at last."

"You will forgive me if I wait a bit longer to applaud you for acquitting yourself of those responsibilities, *nene*," his grandmother said dryly. "It isn't only the marrying that matters to the bloodline, as well you know."

Lionel sighed. "I have had a wife for only slightly more than twenty-four hours. Perhaps we could have a slight grace period before we decorate the nursery."

"What I can give you is the first dance," his grandmother told him instead, and rapped her cane against the floor.

Across the room, the musicians stopped playing. Then started again as the dance floor cleared.

And Lionel had absolutely no choice but to take Geraldine's hand in his. He bowed to his grandmother, as much a mockery of something genteel as anything else, but it made her laugh.

He had known it would.

Then he pulled his wife with him, off the dais and out into the center the dance floor. Once there, he pulled Geraldine into his arms and did not care for the sensation of something like *relief* that enveloped him. Nor did he wish to pursue it, or think what it might mean.

He thought instead of the fact that, even in those heels of hers, he was still taller than her in a way he liked. And in a way she liked too, if that shine in her green gaze was any indication. Lionel wrapped one hand around hers, then slid his other hand down, anchoring it in the small of her back.

"Do you know how to dance?" he asked her, aware of that husky note in his voice, but he did not wish to consider that too closely, either.

A kind of humor flitted through her eyes, making them gleam like emeralds all their own. "Not a single step."

"Then I suggest you simply let go and let me lead." He tipped his head slightly to one side. "Do you think this is something you can manage?"

And he understood that he'd said that precisely so that it would light that fire of battle in her gaze. "That will depend on how good you are at leading, I would imagine," she clipped back at him.

Lionel let himself smile. Then he pulled her closer, and began.

And with every step, the room around them retreated further and further away.

He could tell she was inexperienced, but she kept her gaze on his. And he found her fluid and lithe as they moved through the steps of the dance and knew it could only be because, somehow, the chemistry that he had felt last night had been no mirage. No attempt to make sense of the ruin of his plans, but a very real thread pulling them both together.

Because she might claim that he was untrustworthy, a despoiler of young girls, the kind of man who would toss not only a woman aside, but any baby she carried besides.

But her body told a different story.

And every time they turned, every time they moved, all Lionel could think was, *mine.*

Mine.

One number ended and another began, but Lionel did not let her go. Nor did he release her for the next song, or the one after that.

It was not until he heard that same rapping of his grandmother's cane that he finally stepped back and allowed space he didn't want between him and Geraldine.

Geraldine, who looked flushed and full of wonder. Geraldine, who was without question the most beautiful woman he had ever beheld. Especially when she looked at him this way, as if it was the sight of him alone that set her alight.

Geraldine, who had married him and who he intended to make his wife in every possible way, no matter what it cost him.

But first there was his grandmother, and this party.

Lionel brought her over to his grandmother again, and this time, there was a different sort of look in the canny old woman's eyes.

"I have decided I like you," she told Geraldine. "What have you to say to that?"

"I'm delighted," Geraldine replied, cheerfully enough. "But I cannot think it is me you like, as you don't know me at all. I must warn you, I can be a handful."

"That's all for the best," his grandmother said airily. She leaned forward, her hands propped up on that cane. "Lionel is a good man, but he has been raised to consider himself above all others."

"What man has not?" asked Geraldine.

And Lionel could not say that he particular cared for the way Geraldine and his grandmother both laughed at that, a wealth of understanding between them.

"I have always told him that I require an innocent," the older woman continued, her gaze moving from Geraldine to Lionel, then back again. Looking for evidence, Lionel rather thought. "And this is not simply because I am an ancient relic. It is because, in the fullness of time, I believe that a man is more likely to treasure something he knows has always and ever been his. They are so possessive, you see."

"I'm standing right here," Lionel reminded her.

Geraldine didn't even look at him. "Are they? That does not seem to be a universal experience. Besides, pledging one's troth to another until death seems to cover all the same bases without putting the weight of an entire marriage on one poor bride's virginity."

"My dear girl," his grandmother said mildly, though her gaze was intent, "I hate to be the bearer of bad news. But I think you will find that it is often the wife who carries the weight of a marriage, like it or not. Virginity has nothing to do with it."

"Does anyone possess enough purity to please the nearest priest?" Geraldine asked, lightly enough. "I'm not sure that's something to aspire to, if I'm honest."

Doña Eugenia leaned forward, then. "Purity is not for priests. Priests are but men. It is for the husbands who proclaim that they care little about such things, only to find themselves awake in the middle of the night, fretting over situations that can never be changed. You understand."

Geraldine looked as if she might. Lionel wished that he did—because all that made him do was replay what he knew of his grandparents' chilly marriage, wondering how it had ended up that way.

Another topic he did not care to explore.

"In the absence of a bloodstained sheet to wave about in front of the villagers," Geraldine said with what Lionel found to be admirable calm in the face of such provocation, "I suppose you will simply have to take my word for it that if your grandson is awake in the middle of the night, wracked with concern over my past, I will be more than happy to wake up and talk him through it."

Lionel fully expected his grandmother to take issue with that in the way she took issue with so much else, always. But once again, she surprised him. Because all she did was look at Geraldine for a long while, then laugh yet again.

"Marvelous," she said. "I wish you both every happiness in the world." And when Lionel found himself gazing back at her, in something like shock, she waved her hand toward the dance floor again. "Dance, *nene*. For soon enough, you will be sitting where I am and wishing that you had. While you still could."

And once again, Lionel obeyed her.

"I think that went well," Geraldine said as he took her in his arms again. "Though I suppose I wouldn't know."

"You would know," Lionel assured her.

But he did not wish to talk about his grandmother any longer.

Because Geraldine was in his arms, and he was certain that everyone who looked at them believed that they had spent many long, sleepless nights in his bed. How else could they move together the way they did, with such ease and grace?

When only the two of them knew the truth. That they had barely kissed.

Lionel spun her around and around. In between dances, when he had to put space between them or cause a scene, he took her about the room, on his arm. He introduced her to all of these bright and shining creatures he considered friends—though he would cut them all off in an instant if they tried to sharpen their favorite little knives against his bride.

And it was much, much later, so late that there were already the hints of the new day in the sky, when they finally made it back down to his house. He helped her from the car and they walked inside to find everything hushed and the lights down low.

Lionel was not certain that he could bear this. Or perhaps it was that he did not want to. That he did not know how anyone could.

"Tell me," he urged her in a low voice as he stood there, much closer to her than was necessary, now they were alone. And not dancing. Not in any sense of the term. "Tell me what you want, Geraldine."

Because he already knew what he wanted. He already knew exactly how he wished to kiss her first. How he longed to slide his hands all over the marvelous hourglass of her body. How he wanted to kneel somewhere, and this would do, so he might get his mouth between her legs at last.

Lionel already knew, beyond any doubt, exactly how he wished to learn her.

She was even more beautiful here, in this soft light. Or perhaps because he could hear the way she caught her breath, here in the space between them. Or because he alone could see the way her green eyes gleamed with a light he considered his own now, and her cheeks flushed, pinker by the second.

He reached over and traced a little bit of that flush with his fingers, marveling at the warm satin of her skin. And the way she quivered there before him as if the way that ran through him, electric and intense, was lighting her up inside, too.

"Tell me, *mi querida esposa*," he whispered, there the barest millimeter away from those lips of hers that haunted him already. "My Geraldine, only tell me what it is you want and I will make it yours."

Her eyes fluttered closed. She swayed on those impossible heels of hers.

And Lionel could not recall ever wanting anything the way he wanted this. The way he wanted *her*, so much that he was shoving aside the alarms that rang inside him, warning him that he was much too close to breaking each and every one of his own rules—

"I only want one thing, Lionel," she whispered, and for a moment, she pressed her cheek into his hand. He felt it like fire, but then she straightened. And Geraldine's green eyes were distressingly clear when she caught his gaze again. "A paternity test for Jules. Tonight."

CHAPTER SEVEN

GERALDINE WOULD NEVER know how she managed to get those words out, when they weren't at all what she wanted to say. They were what she *should* say, and so she had, but then she'd wished that somehow she could claw them back from where they hung in the air between them—

It was the look on Lionel's face, she thought. It was that expression of his, as close to shock and betrayal as she imagined a man like him ever got.

There was only an instant of it. Just that one little instant—but then he stepped away, his dark gaze shuttering.

And when he looked at her again, it was as if he had never touched her at all.

She told herself that was a good thing.

Especially when she woke up, late again, to find her mother being ushered into her bedroom with the baby in her arms.

The baby. *Her* baby. Her Jules. Geraldine was up before she knew it, crossing the floor of the bedchamber so she could take the laughing, cooing child into her arms. Then cover her sweet, beloved, damp little face with kisses.

"Geraldine Gertrude," her mother said in a voice so low and so appalled that it made Geraldine flinch. "What have you *done*?"

"What I must," Geraldine replied over the baby's head, seriously enough.

But it was only when she saw her mother's gaze widen, then focus on the rumpled bed behind her that she understood what her mother thought was going on here.

"I didn't sleep with the man we think is Jules's *father*," she said, with perhaps more righteous indignation than was strictly called for. Given she had kissed the man. And danced with him. And run from him two nights in a row, in one way or another. Still, she stood straighter and stared her mother straight in the eyes. "What do you take me for?"

"I don't like any of this," her mother said, which wasn't really an answer. "These aren't how regular people behave. All this gallivanting about from *Italy* to *Spain* on a lark. I don't like it."

"You used to tell me that life wasn't worth living without a few adventures thrown in to spice it up," Geraldine reminded her. "When did that change?"

Her mother blinked, and then, just for a moment, looked a little more like the woman who had always told her only daughter that the only limits she should ever set were the ones she chose, not ones that anyone else tried to press upon her.

"That was before," Lorna Casey said quietly. Her mother held her gaze, a bit hard. "I couldn't lose you the way we lost Seanna, Geraldine. I couldn't cope."

And hours later, Geraldine was still replaying that in her head.

It was long after the fleet of doctors came in, made the baby laugh, and ran their little tests. Her summons had come a mere quarter of an hour earlier in the form of her phalanx of stylists. They had all come whirling into the room, ignoring her mother and insisting that Geraldine get dressed according to their specifications.

Something she couldn't begin to explain to her mother, who had been wearing the same pair of jeans for the past thirty years, and so didn't try.

Geraldine went out of her way to avoid her mother's eyes when she left at last, dressed in what she suspected was supposed to pass for a casual outfit in this place. The sort of high-waisted, wide-leg trousers that she had only seen in magazines, though she had to admit that they felt like a caress against her legs as she walked. With a tight-fitting, high-necked sleeveless blouse that her favorite stylist, the man called Angel, had told her was for *that little kick of clever* to go along with *the classically chic.*

She wasn't thinking about clever or chic when she walked into the library to find Lionel waiting for her. His grandmother was there too, wearing an outfit not dissimilar to the one Geraldine was sporting, though Doña Eugenia was bedecked in far more gems and fine jewels.

What she couldn't decide was when or why, over the past two nights, she had become the sort of person who noticed such things.

"Your cousin's baby is a lovely little thing," Lionel said, every word measured. He tapped a set of papers sitting before him, and Geraldine was unreasonably pleased that she'd managed to keep her glasses for this. Because it felt like a bit of armor as she waited, her stomach heavy with what she refused to call *dread.* "But she is not mine. As I told you."

And Geraldine would never know what kept her from reacting to that news the way she wanted. Once his words arranged themselves into some kind of sense inside her. Once she fully understood what they meant.

Once she realized that what she felt was a kind of bone-deep, systemic relief that she had no intention of acknowledging, much less analyzing.

Just as she had no intention of collapsing into the nearest chair, either. Because it was no one's business but hers what the state of her knees were, so shivery beneath her just then.

"But how do I know that I can believe what you're telling me?" she made herself ask. "I'm certain that all those doctors that you managed to get to turn up here would happily say anything you want them to say."

"I had the very same thought," Lionel's grandmother said then, with a thump of her cane against the floor. And when Lionel raised a brow in her direction, she only smiled. "I love my grandson, dear. But it has not escaped my notice that he, regrettably, is a man. And even the best of them can act a fool. I had my personal doctor run the test again. But I am afraid it came back with same answer. And that is a pity. Because I quite fancy myself as a doting grandparent."

"Doting?" Lionel queried. "Are you certain that is within your capabilities, *Abuelita?*"

She said something in Spanish that made Lionel smile, then looked back at Geraldine. "Lionel tells me that you both agreed to take a honeymoon sometime in the future, but I must insist that you reconsider. It is my belief that the true beating heart of a marriage can only be heard at first during the honeymoon. I have always said so."

"You have never said such a thing in all your days," Lionel said darkly.

His grandmother waved her hand languidly. "And yet I know I am right."

"*That* you have said a great many times."

As if she had only needed confirmation from herself, and ignoring her grandson, the old woman angled herself up from the chair where she sat—with an agility that Geraldine found questionable. It was as if the cane was for show.

"It is settled. I shall find the finest nannies and nurses in the whole of Spain to make certain the child wants for nothing. And you and this grandson of mine will do what all newlyweds must do in the perfect privacy you deserve." Doña Eugenia shifted her gaze to Lionel, an obvious challenge even from where Geraldine stood. "The entire Asensio empire will not crumble without you over the course of a single little month, *nene*. Believe me."

"A month is entirely too long," Lionel said, certain tightness in his voice then. "The world is not as slow as you might recall it."

"Said no besotted new groom ever," replied his grandmother. And then matched his lifted brow with her own.

The family resemblance was astonishing, Geraldine thought. But she was glad they were too busy glaring at each other to pay any attention to what she was or wasn't doing. Currently, she was still trying not to *shake*. With that same relief coursing through her like its own kind of heat.

Lionel wasn't the father. *He wasn't the father.*

It took her a moment to realize it when they stopped staring each other down and turned to her instead.

"This is such a kind offer," she made herself say, somehow keeping her voice even. "But my mother is here."

She shrugged, as if her mother required a chaperone when Lorna Casey was nothing if not a great fan of her own company. Anywhere and everywhere.

"Nonsense," said Doña Eugenia grandly. "I feel certain that I can entertain your mother, my girl. My company has enchanted no less than kings and presidents in my day. I flatter myself that I can make anyone at all feel at home, should I wish it."

And then, as if she was considering being affronted, she swept from the room. Leaving Geraldine face-to-face with Lionel at last. This time, feeling dizzy for more than one reason.

Geraldine thought he might gloat, then. But all he did was slide the papers toward the edge of the table where he stood, then tap them again, his gaze an intensity that made her want to shake all the more.

"What I need you to know," he said, very intently, "is that what I have told you is true. Your cousin was too young for me. She was not well. But even if, somehow, those things had escaped me, I do not walk away from my responsibilities. I never have and I never will. Do we understand each other now, you and I?"

And Geraldine had the strangest urge to give in to the sob that seemed to be gathering there, right behind her ribs. Not because he had been telling her the truth. Not even because she needed to start the search for Jules's paternity all over again.

But because he wasn't looking at her the way he had been last night, with all of that longing and desire, and that molten gleam in his dark gaze.

The loss of it felt like more grief than she could bear.

"Lionel…" she began, but something bright and hot

seemed to arc between them, there in the library with only the books as witness.

"I like hearing my name in your mouth," he told her, dark as sin. "I intend to hear it often over the next month."

She swallowed, hard. "Because, naturally, you will not be telling your grandmother *no*."

His eyes were so dark and rich that it was as if she could feel them inside her. "I will not."

She felt that bright heat between them again, and wanted nothing more than to reach out and touch it. To close the distance between them, and—

And.

That was the trouble. There was so much on the other side of the word *and*.

Particularly because, she couldn't help but think, she didn't have to tear herself apart for harboring all these strangely overwhelming *feelings* for a man who'd abandoned her cousin.

"I suppose I'd better go tell my mother she's about to have her very own Spanish vacation," Geraldine said instead of leaning into all that *and*. Even though she was sure that the glint she saw in Lionel's gaze as she backed away from him was laughter. Possibly even mockery. *And, and, and*— She shoved her glasses into place. "With a new best friend to boot."

Then she turned and bolted for her rooms.

But Lorna declined the offer to stay in Spain for all that time. "What would I do?" she asked, shaking her head as she looked out the window at all the rolling hills and vineyards. It was all a far cry from the view out back of Geraldine's childhood home. "Besides, your father needs seeing to."

Geraldine imagined that somewhere in Minnetonka, Patrick Casey sat up straight at that, understanding he was being maligned from all the way across the planet. As he had never been the sort of man who needed his wife to do things for him that he could himself.

And Geraldine did not ask her mother to take Jules. Not only because she knew that her mother wouldn't do it. But because Jules was *hers*, and there was something in that acknowledgment that felt different, now. Because she had spent all this time thinking that finding the man who'd gotten Seanna pregnant meant that maybe, somewhere out there, there was a man who would be interested in stepping up to his responsibilities. Or paying for his disinterest. But it turned out that she still didn't know who that was. And in the meantime, a baby girl needed a parent.

Geraldine had been her mother all along.

Maybe it was time that she accepted that, then, as her own mother stepped away.

"And you married him?" Lorna asked, still not quite looking Geraldine in the eye. As if she feared the answer when she already knew it. "On purpose?"

There were so many things that Geraldine could have said to that, but she didn't. She held Jules. She pressed her lips to the baby's soft, warm head.

"I suppose I did," was all she said.

Her mother let out a sigh that was much too close to a sob.

"Then I will leave you to it," she murmured, as if she was keeping her voice low to hide the crack in it.

But somehow, the pain in that gave Geraldine the strength she hadn't quite understood she needed. *I couldn't lose you the way we lost Seanna, Geraldine,* her mother had said earlier. *I couldn't cope.*

So she left Lorna to fuss with her bag, as if it needed repacking when it plainly did not. Geraldine didn't argue with her. She made her way back out into the hall and down the stairs until she was in the main part of the house. Instead of walking out through the atrium again to find the garden, or out the front door to the grand foyer, she turned in the other direction and started down a different hall.

And she knew at once that she had entered Lionel's domain.

There was a subtle shift in the art on the wall, though it was not until she walked some ways down the hall that she realized the difference. The walls boasted canvases with bold lines and arresting colors while in the main part of the house, the art tended more toward Old Masters and pieces that became a part of the decor as a whole rather than making her want to stop and look more closely.

She didn't stop now, either. But she was aware that she wanted to. And she wasn't surprised that this hall did not lead to a warren of little rooms leading off it like the part of the house she was staying in, but instead opened up into a grand open space that felt both out of place in a house like this and entirely of it.

She understood at once that Lionel had fashioned himself a kind of loft space, here in this ancient place, when she would have expected something far more traditional. She let her gaze move over the exposed beams beneath the glass ceiling, the grand fireplace in one corner, the spare yet comfortable furnishings.

And then, at last, turned to find the man himself sitting

on one of the low leather sofas with stacks of documents piled to one side of him, his computer on his lap, and more documents before him on a low, wide coffee table.

"I would have thought you'd have an office for that," Geraldine said without thinking.

As if his office arrangements were the point of any of this. And as if that was what she'd come here to discuss with him.

One of his eyebrows rose, but he did not otherwise react. "I've a great many offices, Geraldine. And when I wish to go to one of them, I do. Other times I prefer to work at home. I know my grandmother thinks otherwise, but the Asensio empire does not exist simply because she thinks it should. It takes work, I am afraid."

His gaze moved from her to the baby she held, and she wasn't sure that she could quite define the look on his face then.

Or maybe it was that she wasn't sure she wanted to.

"My mother would prefer to go home," Geraldine told him. "And to be honest, I think it would be best she did."

"My grandmother is not used to her plans being up-ended." But Lionel did not sound as if he minded it happening, even so. "Perhaps it will be good for her to remember that the entire world does not revolve around her, despite all indications to the contrary."

Jules began to kick and wave her arms in the air, so Geraldine set her down in the center of the plush, richly colored rug that took over the middle of the big room. She watched the baby for a moment, knowing that it wouldn't be long now before Jules would turn that rocking into crawling, and then, shortly after that, toddling around on her feet.

You should be here for this, she thought, sending a message to her cousin the way she often did, inside.

Geraldine straightened to find that Lionel had stood, too. She moved toward him, telling herself that there was no reason for her heart to be beating like that in her chest. He was only *looking* at her. The baby was *right here.* Surely there was a limit to...whatever might come of this heat she wished she didn't feel.

"I think that I should go with her," Geraldine said, and was suddenly aware that the words she was choosing were like mines. And that the way his dark eyes gleamed meant she needed to watch her step. "I never meant to marry you, as you know. I only did because I thought you might be Jules's father. But you're not, so it seems to me we would be better off annulling the whole thing and going our separate ways."

"But this is impossible," he said softly, but it was the kind of *soft* that made the back of her neck prickle. "Did I not make this clear? My grandmother is to be happy. Your mother does not need to stay here to achieve this. But I am afraid you do."

"I think the fact that she wants us to take a honeymoon can work perfectly," Geraldine argued. "You can simply tell her at the end of the month that it didn't work out between us. That you thought it might, but were mistaken. These things happen all the time."

He shook his head as if he was sad, but she could see his expression. She could tell that he was nothing of the kind.

"These things do not happen here, Geraldine. Asensios do not divorce." He was closer then, and Geraldine felt the oddest sensation inside her. It was as if her heart was beating so hard that it might knock her back and then tip her over at any moment. "Certainly not as long as my grandmother is alive, at any rate."

"You can't possibly be suggesting that we carry on with this farce?" Geraldine was astonished. "For any number of years?"

"I'm not suggesting it." Lionel's voice was still soft, but the stone in it was unmistakable. "I'm insisting upon it."

Geraldine glanced over at the baby, still gurgling happily to herself as she lay on the floor, kicking out her little legs. Then she looked back at Lionel.

"And if I refuse?"

And later, perhaps, she would think about how strange it was that she had never sounded quite so calm in the whole of her life.

But then, his eyes had never seemed so dark. Or so *inside* her. "You can refuse all you like, *mi querida esposa*. It will change nothing."

She was still so oddly calm. "It will make all of this unpleasant, I would think."

"What if I have another idea?" he asked in that same soft, stone way.

Geraldine watched, feeling almost as if she was in some kind of dream, as he closed that last bit of distance between them. He reached out, running his hands down from her shoulders to grip her upper arms.

Then he pulled her closer to him, as if it was inevitable. As if they had always been destined to be right here, right now, her head tipped back to look up at him and his harshly beautiful face blocking out the sky she should have been able to see above him through the glass ceiling.

It was as if her whole life had been an arrow pointing here, to that place where her pulse beat wildly in her throat.

The place he already knew about, because Lionel leaned down and pressed his mouth directly upon it.

Then, both gently and not gently at all, he scraped his teeth along the surface of her skin.

Just a little.

Just enough.

Because everything she was seemed to *implode*. To melt and then reform again into one great, long, luxuriant shiver. A shimmering sort of comet that shot straight through her from the point of impact, reaching deep between her legs, where it burst apart anew.

She felt him laugh, there against her own body. And it was a low, flammable, glorious thing, scorching her where she stood.

Geraldine had the presence of mind to push him back. And then, more critically, to step away herself. Then keep right on backing up until she could scoop Jules up once more.

"We will remain married no matter what you choose," he told her quietly. And there was a promise there that she desperately wanted to call a threat.

And might have, if she hadn't been chasing fire with more fire herself.

When she had the distinct impression that all of it was the same sort of need and hunger within.

Later that night, long after she put Jules to bed and told his grandmother's staff that she would be doing so every night for as long as she stayed here, she found herself standing out on her own terrace as the night came in.

Missing her mother. Missing her cousin.

Missing the version of herself she'd been before she'd come here, so certain that everything was black-and-white and she could slay any dragon she encountered by force of will alone.

Missing the version of her that wouldn't have understood what she felt right now, because she'd never felt anything like it and—if she'd stayed in Minneapolis— never would have. She had built a life that would never lead to this or anything like it.

And besides, came a wise sort of voice from deep inside her, *you would never have met* him *there.*

Geraldine sighed. And she understood the layout of this house now, so she walked along the terrace until she could see around the corner and into Lionel's wing. And felt everything in her spin and whirl, because he was in there now.

There was no sign of his office work. Just him, sitting on that couch again, this time swirling a drink in one hand.

Looking brooding and implacable and delicious in ways she couldn't entirely admit to herself.

Geraldine told herself that he couldn't see her, because the lights were on where he was and she stood in the dark, but her body knew different. Every hair on her body seemed to be lost in those dances from last night, standing on end and swaying as if his hands were still all over her...

Maybe he couldn't see her, she thought when he shifted, but he knew she was here.

And she let out a breath, though it shook.

The terrible truth was that she wanted him.

Geraldine had never felt anything like this before in her life.

She did not deceive herself. He did not want a divorce, but he certainly didn't want her as his wife in any real way.

That should have been enough to send her packing and looking for escape routes.

But she *wanted* him.

And maybe she could have fought that, but it would necessitate leaving this place and leaving *him* and she wasn't quite sure how she would do that if he didn't allow it. She knew where she was on a map, but all the staff were loyal to him, she spoke only a few words of Spanish, and didn't have private jets at her disposal.

Yet even if she did, where would she go? Back to Minneapolis where she was certain Jules's father was not? If she had to start from scratch in that search, it seemed obvious to her that it would be a lot easier to do here, already in Europe.

If she thought about all that, it almost felt rational.

Geraldine knew that it wasn't.

She knew that the real reason she was even considering this had nothing to do with paternity tests, and everything to do with him. With Lionel himself. With the way they'd danced last night. She had surrendered herself to him, to the music, and it had felt like flying. Yet all the while she had been anchored to the earth and the way his hand pressed against her back. The way the other gripped her hand. The way he looked down at her, all gleaming dark eyes and the hint of a dangerous smile.

Tonight that spot on her neck still pulsed too hard from before. She could still feel the graze of his teeth against her flesh.

Surely, a voice inside her whispered dangerously, *you deserve to feel* something *for once. Maybe more than* something.

And Geraldine had always been distressingly practical. She understood, as she stared out across the Andalusian night into the windows where the most relentlessly masculine man she'd ever beheld sat waiting, that there was far more at risk here than the loss of a few years, her autonomy, or the respect of her family and friends.

There was her heart, already feeling precarious in her chest. Likely because she couldn't seem to separate what she knew intellectually was a physical reaction from her emotional response to the fact that Lionel Asensio was the only man who had ever made her feel like that.

Who had ever made her feel much of anything at all.

A smart woman would rejoice that she *could* feel and then run in the opposite direction, and Geraldine had always prided herself on being smart.

But instead she stood here, on the first night of her official honeymoon with this man she should never have met in the first place.

And she knew herself well enough to know that she'd already decided.

He wanted her. And she wanted to know what that meant. What that was.

What those promises in his dark gaze meant.

She would be his.

Whatever that looked like and for however long this lasted.

And she would worry about picking up the pieces later.

CHAPTER EIGHT

LIONEL LEARNED A GREAT many things about himself in the weeks that followed.

First, that he was not accustomed to delayed gratification. He found this a bit of a surprise, for he considered not being able to wait a deep flaw that he had witnessed entirely too many times from his father and grandfather. He had long considered himself made of sterner stuff.

And yet the fact remained that he was not used to wanting something he could not simply have. Certainly not when it came to women.

Second, and related, was that he found he had never truly experimented with the limits of his self-control before, and certainly not while enjoying such close proximity to the object of his desire.

The truth was, he had never imagined any of this to be a factor. It would not have occurred to him that it could be.

He was Lionel Asensio. He had never known a woman to spend much time in his presence before offering herself to him on the nearest silver platter. Some women did not require an introduction. Most women were drawn to him without him having to do more than...exist.

But Geraldine was like no other woman he had ever encountered.

It was almost as if she did it on purpose—but he knew too well that she did not. That what he saw was who she was, always. For a man who had always considered himself the soul of directness and forthrightness, despite his upbringing, Lionel found it nothing short of confronting that this woman had him beat in both of those areas.

If she didn't also tempt him beyond reason, he wasn't at all sure what he would make of her.

He had insisted that they eat their meals together. He had done so as a counterpoint to her demands when she had agreed to stay here with him for the honeymoon period his grandmother had demanded. All the things Geraldine had insisted upon involved the child. She refused to hand the baby off to nannies entirely. She refused to spend a month—or even a day—apart from little Jules.

A lesser man might have been displeased that he took second place to an infant.

But Lionel found the way she cared for a child that was not even of her own flesh made her seem to glow all the more for him.

And so it was that they sat there every morning in the part of his great room that was set aside for eating, and watched the way the new day moved over the fields beyond.

"I begin to understand the entire purpose of honeymoons," she told him one morning.

"I do not believe you do understand their purpose at all," he replied darkly, because his body understood. Only too well. His body wanted all kinds of things that he would have thought were the whole purpose of a honeymoon, of any description or length.

The kind of things he thought about late into the night, staring up at his ceiling and imagining she was with him...

Yet he was only too aware that this was not at all what Geraldine was talking about.

As she quickly made clear.

"It works no matter what type of marriage you've embarked upon," she said brightly, buttering her toast. "If it's some kind of arranged situation, like the one you had planned to have, well, then. You have a honeymoon to get to know the stranger you married. If it's a love match, you get to deepen your feelings. But really, I do think it's a bit ingenious that once upon a time, someone assumed that what couples needed most of all was to be locked away together if anything was to come of it."

"What was to come of it was a child," Lionel pointed out. "That would be the entire purpose. The phase of the moon to get a new wife pregnant, because that is, of course, the only purpose of a marriage in some eyes."

Geraldine, he had come to realize, was remarkably good at ignoring anything she did not wish to discuss. She only glanced at him today, a simple touch of that maddeningly cool green gaze. "Lucky for you, then, that there is already a child."

As if she didn't understand what he meant when he knew very well that she did.

But she had negotiated more time with Jules than Lionel had expected she would want. He could not recall his own mother insisting that she see to his bedtime. Or that she see him much at all. She had been a shadowy figure in Lionel's life. He had been raised by nannies, nurses, and tutors when his grandmother was unavailable, and had been presented to his father and grandfather infrequently.

Geraldine insisted on actually spending time with the baby. She had the child brought to her in the mornings after she'd been fed and clothed and was usually in a happy, sunny sort of mood.

If all babies were as delightful as this one, Lionel found himself thinking with no small amount of surprise, he might be predisposed to go ahead and have one before the five years he'd imagined he would wait were up.

"Is she always like this?" he asked on one such morning. They had finished their breakfast and the staff of nannies had brought Jules in. Geraldine didn't seem to care that her cadre of stylists dressed her exquisitely every morning for his pleasure, not hers, and he knew this because she had no qualms whatsoever throwing herself down on the floor with the child.

She looked up at him now, her lips curving. "She gets tired and cranky like anyone else, but she really is happy little girl. Just like her mother was."

Sometimes she spoke of her cousin lightly, but other times it was like this. With that weight.

"I never met her when she was happy," he found himself saying, though he could not have said why. "I only knew her when she was impaired."

"You must have met a great many women in various states of disrepair," Geraldine said, perhaps too carefully. Lionel eyed her, though she was concentrating on the baby. "I'm surprised you remember Seanna at all."

"She made an impression."

Her gaze was darker than usual, then. "As you did too, for her. She said your name when she came home. She said it a lot. That's the reason I assumed you were Jules's father."

Lionel set his paper aside and considered Geraldine instead, not at all sure she wanted to head down this road. And there must have been something on his face, because her expression changed.

"I'm not going to faint if you tell me something unpleasant about my cousin," she said quietly. "I was with her through far worse things than I think you can possibly imagine."

A birth, Lionel thought. And a death. And everything that had happened in between.

He could not recall a time he had ever wanted to reach back through time and change things, and not for himself, but so Geraldine did not have to carry that particularly shade of darkness in her gaze just then.

The notion disturbed him, for reasons he did not care to examine. "I met your cousin at the end of a shoot." He spoke quietly, but directly. He did not look away. "The pictures were good but she was a mess. The way others in the room spoke of her was not kind, but they are used to bright stars who rise quickly, then crash and burn. It is not a kind business."

Her eyes were overbright. "You don't have to preface it. You can just tell me."

"She knew who I was and she made overtures," Lionel said, still not moving his gaze from hers. "I declined."

"And what about you?" Geraldine's voice was so quiet then, so rough, he barely heard it over the baby's pleased little gurgles. "Were you cruel to her, too?"

"I was not." He watched as she looked down, then swallowed hard enough that he could see her throat move. "I told her that she deserved better, but that she would never find it if she did not first value herself."

Geraldine was looking at Jules, her expression fierce enough that Lionel suspected she was trying to keep her tears at bay. "I am not sure she took your advice."

"She had what I would describe as a moment of lucidity." Lionel remembered the way the girl had looked at him, her dull eyes too big in her face, her body far too thin. "And she told me that her value was set by the marketplace, and didn't I know? That was what it meant to be a commodity."

Geraldine flinched, but no tears marked her cheeks.

"And so I told her that she had mistaken the matter entirely," Lionel said, not gently. That would have seemed too easy. It would not have done the lost Seanna any justice—though he could not have explained why he felt such a thing. "That her value was inherent. That all she needed to do was believe it and she would find it."

He blew out a breath, not sure why a chance encounter some time ago got to him like this one did. It was tempting to think it was because he knew that she was Geraldine's cousin, but he hadn't known Geraldine existed back then and still, he remembered. He remembered the bruised look around the girl's eyes. The way she'd laughed after he'd said those things to her, and how that spark had changed her entirely. He had seen a glimpse of who she might have been, there for a moment, then gone.

I don't think that's where I'm going, she'd told him, with a wisdom—a knowledge—he had found chilling.

Lionel remembered asking after her, months later, and being told she had disappeared the way so many did.

These girls are disposable and replaceable, he had been told, dismissively. *Better not to ask what they get up to once they go, no?*

He did not share those things with Geraldine. And not only because he knew exactly how Seanna's story had ended. That she had been right about her trajectory.

"I think," Geraldine said, her voice sounding as if this was far more difficult for her than she wished him to know, "that you must have stood out. It's my impression that she did not otherwise encounter much kindness."

"The world is not usually kind, no," Lionel agreed. "We must find it ourselves, I think."

Geraldine twisted around to face him and there was something darker in her gaze, then. It seemed to punch into him. "That sounds a little too close to placing blame, doesn't it? We can talk about choices. Psychology. Mental health. Parenting." She handed the baby the toy she had just tossed aside with her usual infant glee. "But in the end, do any of us know why one life goes one way and another a different way?"

"Indeed we do," he replied darkly, as much because he felt as if she'd punched him as anything else. "Lives are like anything else. They're made up of choices. And ego. Do you make your choice for yourself or for something greater than yourself? I was raised by two generations of men who thought of nothing but their own pleasure. Ever. I do not make the same choices they did. On purpose."

"I don't think Seanna was overly concerned with pleasure." Geraldine took a heavy sort of breath. "I think she was trying to hide." Then she looked at him again, and her gaze was clear. He didn't think that made things any better. "But is that why you are so determined to do as your grandmother asks? To make up for your father and grandfather?"

"If I could make up for them, I would." Lionel didn't know why he was having this conversation, when it had seemed to slip so far beyond his control. Or why he could *feel* too many things jostling about inside of him. When he did not indulge *feelings*.

Just as he did not talk about lost girls he had failed to save or the bitter inheritance the men in his family had left him.

What was it about this woman that made him unlike himself? Why couldn't he view her with the same calm and distant regard he did everything else?

"I don't think any of us can make up for another person," Geraldine said softly, her gaze a little too intense for a moment before she shifted it once again to the child. "All we can do is be the best version of ourselves."

And he was not sorry that he had to take a call then, though he assured himself it was in no way a *relief.* Because he was Lionel Asensio and he did not look for ways to avoid uncomfortable conversations. He reveled in them.

Or he always had before.

Possibly because you have never had anything at stake, a voice inside him suggested.

He did not believe he had anything at stake now, he assured himself. And was perhaps even more inflexible in a negotiation than usual later that day, to prove it. Because he had nothing to prove. Because he felt nothing.

Because he had decided a long, long time ago that feelings were for the weak.

Yet soon enough, weak or not, the sun went down and he could once again sit across from Geraldine at their little table in the garden.

Lionel had never taken his meals out in this garden before her. He had lived in this house for years, preferring his own space to what privacy he could cobble together at the main house. But he had always viewed this as a place of duty. He was far happier moving between his various offices around the world than staying here too long, mired in memories of his childhood.

He could not recall the last time he'd spent so many consecutive days on the estate. And yet with Geraldine here, he found he did not think back to a great many of those memories as he'd always assumed he would. Lionel was far more concerned with her.

Because during the day she could ignore him. She could pretend she didn't understand the references he made to the way this honeymoon should have been progressing, if it was traditional.

Everything was different at night.

It was because of the food, perhaps, because Andalusian cuisine never failed to impress and his cook was a wonder. Perhaps it was the wine, sourced from the Asensio vineyards, and always the perfect accompaniment.

Perhaps it was these sultry fall nights themselves. Because in the depths of all the shadows, as the nights grew cooler, Lionel found he could see far different truths than were visible in the light of day.

Tonight there was something edgier than usual, there in the flickering candlelight between them.

Tonight everything seemed...a little bit brighter. A little bit hotter.

They had taken their time over the meal and were sitting there now it was done, speaking of everything and nothing. Lionel wasn't certain when this had become their habit.

He wasn't sure he had ever had *habits* where women were concerned. Not ones that involved anything outside the bedroom.

And if he was tempted to *feel* something about this strange turn of events, he reminded himself that he had never had a wife before, either.

He did not *feel* anything, he told himself. He simply wanted her, and so he stood—enjoying a little too much the way her eyes widened. The way whatever she had been telling him about the Spanish language course she had started taking on her mobile simply...stopped. Mid-sentence.

"Dance with me," he commanded her.

Or perhaps he was kidding himself. Perhaps it was an invitation, no command, just entreaty.

And he waited, when he had never waited. When he was so tired of waiting. When *waiting* was beginning to sit in his bones, making them ache.

Lionel's whole body tightened with that same bright fire, that same wild need that these days had only honed to an ever-sharpening hunger.

Geraldine gazed up at him from the table, her fine lips parting as if she could taste it too, this maddening *thirst*.

"Don't be silly," she said, but she hardly sounded like herself. Her voice was low and rough. "There is no music."

"There is always music, *mi media naranja*," he murmured. "If you listen hard enough, you will hear it."

Then he held out his hand.

And he did not pretend that he could not feel the heat between them, now. Or that this was precisely the sort of inflection point they had been talking about earlier.

A moment to choose.

Lives were choices, he had told her earlier with such great confidence.

Lionel could not pretend to be unaware that this was one. Right here. Right now.

And more, that he had already made his choice. That what remained was hers, whatever that might be.

He might have been known as a titan in the boardroom, but he always knew the answer to any question he asked where his business was concerned. He could not say the same about Geraldine.

Her eyes were whole worlds he had not explored, though he wanted to.

God, how he wanted to.

But it was as if the barriers between them, all the resistance that she had been attempting to put up for weeks, simply *shimmered* tonight. As if all the barriers between them were a bit thinner than usual.

She looked at his hand for too long, and then, very slowly, Geraldine lifted her fathomless green gaze to his face.

And something inside of him jolted, electric and intense.

Because Lionel knew. He knew, at last, that she would be his.

Finally, something in him roared, as much in triumph as heat.

Geraldine shifted in her chair. Then she reached out and slid her hand into his, and they both let out a sound at that.

As if neither of them could help it.

His was deeper, more of a growl. Hers sounded to him like some kind of gasp.

He wanted to taste it. He wanted to taste her, everywhere.

But first there was this. The touch of her skin to his. Her palm in his hand. The heat of her, that satin smoothness that already haunted him. That was deep in him, making his hunger near enough to overwhelming.

Lionel pulled her to him, or she stood and moved herself—but either way, she was in his arms.

At last, *at last*, she was in his arms again.

And he remembered, distantly, dancing with her at his grandmother's celebration. It seemed a lifetime ago now. It seemed to him that they had been different people entirely, strangers, nothing like who they were now.

Yet even then, he had felt this driving hunger for her. That he had wanted to clear the whole ballroom. Looking back, all he could recall was the two of them, spinning around and around, shining with all of this need and wonder.

He had felt too many things to name.

He had *felt*.

Because it was a mad burst of impossible light, filling both of them at once with the same fire, as if it had always been meant for them. Dancing had made it worse. Dancing had made it *obvious*.

That there was this thing between them, far more than mere heat. Far more complicated than anything that could be sorted out in a bed—

But Lionel didn't like that thought at all.

So instead of teaching her to dance to the music of the moon alone, and feeling whatever questionable emotions that might bring, he bent his head and took her mouth with his.

CHAPTER NINE

THIS KISS WAS nothing like the last one.

That was the last full thought Geraldine had, as Lionel's stern mouth opened over hers and he licked his way between her lips.

And then her whole life seemed to burst into flame.

As if there was *before* this moment and *after* this moment—this impossible kiss—but she was not the same. And never would be the same, ever again.

She had the idle notion that she should care about that, but it disappeared at the taste of him. That stunning hit that was part wine, part smoke, and all him.

Because she'd had no idea.

No earthly idea that it was possible that anything could ever taste like he did, or that she had been walking around all this time, all her life, having no idea that *this* was something people could just *do*.

That she could have been doing since the moment she'd met him.

He kissed her and he kissed her, angling his jaw, and pulling her body even closer to his, so that she was *pressed* up against him.

Geraldine had never known such heat. She had never

understood the spinning, lustrous, silken darkness of this, and the sheer glory of it, too.

He kissed her and introduced her to herself.

A version of her Geraldine had never known.

She learned that a kiss was not a finite thing. That it grew and changed, shifting as they did, taste and heat and fire. She learned that the ache in her breasts was to encourage her to press herself against the wide planes of his chest, the soft parts of her against the hard heat of him.

It was the only thing that made her feel better and then, immediately, she only wanted more.

More and then still more. More and more and *more*.

She understood her body in a new way, now, because all the different parts of her were filled with that same aching electricity, and seemed to match his.

Exactly.

Geraldine could even feel his arousal against her belly, and though she'd read about such things in too many books to count, she had never understood that it could *feel* like this.

As if the entire course of human history had led unerringly to this moment. To the two of them in this garden. To the things she learned about herself when she could melt into him and press herself against him, seeking that knife-edge relief that became longing almost in the same moment.

That she could want nothing more than to take him into her body, or rub herself against him, or do what she actually did—twine her arms around his neck as if she knew that was what he wanted most, then let him lift her straight off the ground.

She had known this would happen, hadn't she? She had

decided to stay. She had stood out in the dark, looking at him through the glass, and she had known.

That that decision to remain here meant that she was choosing this. That she had decided to allow this to happen.

That really, this was what she'd wanted all along.

But then she hadn't quite understood how a person went from *decisions* to *actions*, not in a case like this. All the research in the world, all the books and articles, couldn't help her read a stern, beautiful man. Much less tell her when and how he might decide to *do something* about that gleaming thing she had seen in his gaze all along.

So she had waited. And she had meant it when she'd told him that she understood the function of a honeymoon period, even if it didn't involve the act most honeymoons were dominated by. She'd told herself, nightly, that she was enjoying the opportunity to get to know Lionel in a way she doubted anyone else did, not even his fearsome grandmother.

Then again, perhaps she'd known all along that it would take one touch.

One simple touch, and they would ignite.

And with that same deep wisdom, welling up from somewhere she couldn't access deep inside herself, Geraldine knew something else, too. There would be no returning from this. There would be no going back.

Maybe she had always suspected that would be true. Maybe she had wanted to hold on to what she knew, the odd domesticity that she and Lionel had created here over the course of the last few weeks.

Maybe she had been mourning the loss of what felt

very much like an ease between them, as unlikely as that should have been.

But what she understood now was that there wasn't a single part of her that wanted to go back. To undo this. To keep her hands to herself and take herself to her own bed, alone again.

Because she might not know what this night would bring, but she wanted every part of it. With every single thing that made her who she was, with every touch of his lips to hers, and every breath that made her breasts move against him yet again.

She wanted *everything*.

When Lionel lifted his mouth from hers, he was carrying her into that great room of his but he was not stopping in the great, glassed-in space. He strode through it, carrying her into a bedroom that was built on the same grand scale. Only this one was not made of glass. There were windows on one side and a vast bed that made her stomach feel funny inside her, but he carried her instead to the seating area arranged before an imposing fireplace, then laid her carefully upon the soft and cozy sheepskin rug that stretched before the dancing flames.

And better yet, followed her down.

"I feel as if I have waited for this for whole lifetimes," Lionel growled in her ear.

Geraldine felt the goose bumps prickling into life up and down her arms, but then he was pressing her back into the soft embrace of the sheepskin beneath her. And he was holding her face in his hands, kissing her and kissing her, then muttering things in that dark, evocative way of his—Spanish and English and other languages like lines of poetry that all wound around her and then deep into her.

He peeled back the bodice of her dress and found her breasts with his hands, making low, approving noises at their weight, their shape. Then he continued on, taking the dress with him, until he moved the faintly rough surface of his palms over just about every part of her that she could imagine and tossed the dress aside when he was done.

Lionel sat back, taking a moment to look down at her with an expression on his face that she'd never seen before.

It made her heart hurt as it beat too hard inside her. Because he looked possessive. Intent.

Mine, she thought, though she knew better than to say such a thing out loud.

Or even think it so he might suspect it lived inside her.

And the harsh lines of his face seemed somehow more sensual now, even though she supposed he should have looked something like scary, gripped as he was in that same heat that shook through her again and again.

Making her feel a delightful kind of feverish.

Geraldine sat up because she needed her hands on him, too, in a way that felt like an actual, physical necessity rather than some kind of longing.

She moved on her knees to kneel beside him and she thought she would die if she didn't tip forward and put her mouth to his neck. So she did and it was overwhelming and seductive and the taste of his skin moved in her like its own mad heat, making her fumble with the buttons of his shirt.

Not because she didn't know how to unbutton something, for God's sake, but because she never had from this angle. Not when the buttons that she was undoing were on the shirt of a man.

And not just any man, but this one.

This man. Lionel Asensio, who had been living in her head for much too long.

Geraldine had considered hers a *life of the mind* for a long, long while, but she already knew that she could never go back to it. Not now that she knew the sheer, sultry perfection of the line of a man's neck and where it met his shoulder. The rough-sweet taste. The scent of him, bold and all-consuming.

She pushed the shirt from his shoulders and made a little sound in the back of her throat because he was more beautiful than she could possibly have imagined, and she had done some extensive imagining lately. She let her fingers move over the dusting of hair she found before her until they dragged over his nipples, and she thought that it was an unbearable marvel that they should both have them. That they could match here, too. That touching him there made her own nipples tighten and point toward him, as if they knew things she didn't.

She trailed her fingers down his ridged wonder of an abdomen, and it was the same kind of wonder. Everywhere she touched him made that corresponding part of her...*bloom.*

And no one had told her. No one had explained that this was the reason why people went mad for each other in ways she had never understood. Why sex was an obsession. Why the most astonishing decisions seemed to be made in pursuit of it.

Because Geraldine already knew that she would do

anything to do this again. She could already tell that this was not enough. That it was possible—that it was *likely*—that nothing ever would be.

She took her time exploring him, aware that she could feel the lick of the flames as if they were leaping from the grate—but no. It was the fire they made between them. The tinder of her mouth against his skin, her fingers learning every inch of him.

But when she got down to the waist of his trousers, he stopped her.

"One night," he told her and his voice was deliciously rough, its own kind of caress as it moved over her, "I will tutor you in what, precisely, brings me pleasure. But that will not be tonight, *mi media naranja*. Tonight we have other things to consider."

"Like what?" Geraldine asked, her voice hoarse. Because she could see the outline of his sex, huge and hard, changing the shape of him as she looked down.

Between her legs, she felt herself grow slick and hot.

Ready, something in her pronounced.

"You are an innocent," he said. "A virgin. This is not so?"

His voice changed as he said that, so she sat up straighter. He had gone stern. His dark eyes glittered. And there was something about the way he looked at her, as if sizing her up, that made her shiver to attention. "I am."

"Why did you attempt to lie about this before?"

"Why did you think it was appropriate to ask?" she countered, but her voice was a bare scratch of sound.

She was breathing too heavily, she realized. As if she was running somewhere when all she was doing was kneeling before him, her breasts caught up in that lacy bra they'd put her in tonight. And still wearing the lacy panties they'd given her, too.

Geraldine did not have to ask him to understand that he knew, to the last millimeter of fabric, exactly what she wore. And exactly how the flush of desire, heat and hope, rolled over her.

He knew everything here, she understood.

And she liked that he did. It made her feel safe. Protected.

As if she might survive this fire between them after all.

"This is how it will be," he told her, very sternly, his words like cool stones against her heated flesh. "I want you pink and breathless. I'm going to make you come, Geraldine. Again and again. Until you beg me for things you cannot even imagine."

"I've done a great deal of studying—" she began.

But he reached over and traced her lips with his thumb, silencing her that easily.

"You will not speak again," he told her in that same deliberately stern way. "Unless you wish to say my name. You may cry it out. You may sob it. You may let it fall out in a sigh. But that is all I will allow. There will be no questions. There will be no unsolicited dissertations. Do you understand me?"

And she wondered if, at another time, she might question how she felt in this moment. But right now, Geraldine found she did understand.

More than that, she thought that the rules made everything feel easier.

"You will not focus on anything except what you feel," he told her in that same formidable way. And while he spoke he moved closer, so he could trace a lazy sort of pattern in that hollow between her breasts. "If I want you to do something, I will tell you not only what I wish you to do, but how to do it. You do not have to worry about anything except following my instructions. Do you understand?"

But even as she began to form a response, she saw that dark brow lift. Only his name, he had told her. And only in the ways he had laid out.

Geraldine swallowed hard. She had never taken direction like this in her life. She was not one for taking direction at all, if she was honest about it.

Yet nothing in all her years had ever felt as right as the way she held his gaze with hers and nodded. *Yes. I understand.*

Her reward was the curve of his hard mouth. *"Buena chica."*

Then he set himself to his work.

And Geraldine knew that she had no frame of reference here. No one had touched her like this. No one but her had ever looked at the whole of her body. No one had ever stripped her naked as he did, then laid her out before him.

No one had ever touched her the way he did then, taking his time. Making her flush and buck and moan.

She knew she didn't have the experience to put this into context, but she couldn't imagine that there was any other way this could have happened that would have allowed her to feel so...*free.*

Geraldine didn't think. She didn't question him.

He told her what to do and she did it.

"Turn over," he said at one point, his voice sheer gravel. And that was its own sort of wonder, as she'd pressed herself into the fluffy embrace of the rug below her with the heat of him at her back. His mouth and his hands finding new ways to make her sing.

The way she could feel that rampantly male part of him as he entertained himself, preview and promise all at once. The way other times he simply moved about, tasting her here, touching her there.

He flipped her over again and this time, explored her body as if it was entirely new because he was using his mouth.

Lazily, he made his way down the length of her torso. He took his time with each one of her breasts, introducing her to erogenous zones she hadn't known she possessed, like her navel. Like the soft skin behind her knees.

Only when she was shaking already did he settle himself between her legs.

"Lionel..." she managed to get out.

And when he looked up at her, there was a glint in those dark eyes—something like approval—and she felt that quake through her.

All that before he pulled her legs up higher, so that he was holding her thighs apart and letting her legs dangle down over his shoulders.

Geraldine didn't know if she was shocked or horrified, delighted or simply mad with need. All of the above, perhaps.

She was shaking and shaking. She was too *hot*.

Her hips were lifting of their own accord. Her eyes drifting shut. And she couldn't bear the intensity of this. She couldn't bear to look at him as he moved over her in this way, or as his fingers found their way into the core of her, into all her sleek and secret heat, and began to play her like some kind of instrument.

He made her into a melody she had never heard in her life, not like this, and it made her feel as if she was dancing.

It made her throw back her head and sing the only song she could.

His name.

Again and again, his name.

And that was how she found her first peak, then hurtled over it, still singing out that same song.

But she had no time to gather herself because he kept going, shifting even lower, so he could begin to lick his way all over the molten center of her need, teaching her things she could never have known otherwise.

How to melt and bloom into his mouth. How to grip his thick hair in fists.

How to ride him as he ate at her, as if her hips held a wisdom of experience she could only guess at.

And all the while, the need in her only grew.

This time, when she exploded, she screamed.

He took his time as she floated down from that, shifting their positions. Laying himself out beside her and kissing her again, so she could taste her own mysteries on his mouth while she could feel his hugeness, hard and rampant against her belly.

Lionel took her to the peak and beyond once more, this time plunging one finger and then another deep inside her, stretching her, readying her—

God, she thought, *I am so ready*—

And it was as if he could read her very thoughts. For only then did he move between her legs and settle himself there, the heavy weight of him pressing her down into the soft rug and the hard floor beneath it.

He reached down between them so he could take the thick head of his sex and begin to make his way inside her at last.

"Geraldine," he warned her when she moaned. "I have told you the rules."

That made her shudder all over again, but she whispered his name.

Then moaned it as he began working himself inside her.

It wasn't that it didn't hurt, because it did. But her sob was his name and every time she cried out it felt like a connection and her body surrendered just that little bit more.

Then just a little bit more than that.

And soon enough, she could feel him crowding inside of her, the very tip of him flush against a part of her that she had never felt before.

Geraldine was panting. She felt as if she couldn't pull in a full breath.

But he had told her that she had only one word at her disposal and it worked that same magic every time she used it.

So she cried out his name until she needed to move her hips, and that was how the first wave of impossible pleasure crashed into her. So wild and so intense, so *everything*, that she couldn't quite tell if she was arching her back because she wanted it to go on forever or if it was simply the most intense pleasure she had ever felt.

So she did it again.

And then again.

She kept doing it until Lionel laughed, gathering her against him and dropping his face to the side of her neck. Then he began to teach her all over again.

The thrust, the retreat. The friction. The heat.

And the peaks she'd reached before were hills, she saw that now. This was too big, too intense, to bear.

Geraldine wondered if she should have been afraid, but she wasn't.

There was nothing she wanted more than *this*. Than him.

She arched against him, meeting each thrust. She wrapped her legs around him, dug her nails into his back, and she used his name again and again. A song, a whisper. A moan, a sob.

Because it was bigger every time. It was everything. There was nothing in the world but the enormity of this thing that rushed for her then.

And the pace he'd maintained, ruthless and inexorable, broke. Lionel made a noise, animal and wild, and it took her a moment to understand that he was saying her name this time.

Then there was no rhythm at all.

There was only him inside her, there was only the endless sensation, and her certain knowledge that she would do anything at all to keep going. That nothing could possibly stop them.

That nothing would be worth stopping for—

She felt that mountain slam into her, then throw her—spinning and shimmering—straight out into space.

Until she became the stars.

She could feel the way he said her name edge itself into her, changing her, marking her forever.

She could feel the way he gripped her even tighter, and then scalded her so that her own wild pleasure started all over again.

Geraldine would never be the same. She had known that going in.

But she also knew, as he dropped his head to hers, that she was forever altered. That her heart beat with his and always would, now. That she had fallen recklessly and dreadfully in love, and there was no changing it.

More than that, she knew that she could never tell him. No matter what.

So she told him the only thing she could. Geraldine turned her face to his and though she felt the moisture on her face, she pressed the faintest kiss to his temple anyway. She whispered his name.

Again and again, until Lionel lifted his head, fixed her with a look she recognized now, and started all over again.

CHAPTER TEN

LIONEL HAD WANTED HER. He had intended to have her, and so he had.

Over and over again.

What he had not expected was that having her would become an obsession. That she was a kind of need that only deepened and sharpened as time went by.

That *she* was far more than he had anticipated, in every possible way.

He told himself it was because he'd waited, that was all. It was because of how unfamiliar it had been to find himself wanting something he hadn't been able to sample at once. Perhaps it was no more than a message, letting him know that he had become far too spoiled by his wealth and the privilege it accorded him to have his every need met instantly.

That was why weeks passed and he was still consumed with her, he assured himself. He was making up for that unexpected deficit.

With no end in sight.

The honeymoon period his grandmother had set for them ended, but nothing changed between them. Lionel found his interest in Geraldine intensified, if anything, which hardly made sense. Familiarity bred contempt.

Everyone knew this. It had always been his experience before—but Geraldine was different.

In every possible way, she was different.

For example, Lionel had never brought his women here to the estate, and some had begged him for the chance. But he had always refused, because he had never allowed the women he'd had relationships with access to his life like this.

Not to his childhood home. Not to the land that his family had held for so many generations. And never, ever into his grandmother's orbit.

When he had conceived of marrying to please his *abuelita*, he had imagined that after the birthday party, the wife he'd chosen would take herself off to one of his properties elsewhere. He hadn't minded which one. He had expected he would need to trot out the wife on special occasions, and would otherwise plead his busy life.

His grandmother would have seen through him, but that hadn't worried him. Doña Eugenia knew better than most why her grandson was the way he was. Lionel had been sure that when she saw how easily he planned to get along with the wife he bought—and he'd planned it that way, so he knew it would have been that way—she would come around.

He had not been prepared for the Cartwright heiress to be stolen out from under him or for Geraldine to laugh her way to the altar.

But then, Lionel also would have said that he had no interest in spending time with an infant. He'd never been all that interested in having babies, even though he was well aware that he was required to procreate to keep the fortune in the family.

That had always seemed to be a problem he could deal with far off in the future, if at all.

Now Geraldine was his wife. She lived in his house. She slept in his bed. And she would have spent every minute of every day with little Jules if she could, which meant he spent time with her too.

And somehow none of his rules seemed to apply to either one of them.

"Have you spoken to your mother?" Lionel found himself asking one evening, which was in and of itself astonishing.

He assumed that all the women he'd been involved with before had also been in possession of mothers, but he had never inquired. It had never occurred to him to wonder about people so wholly distant and unconnected to him. Yet here he was, the very picture of domesticity all of a sudden.

He was sitting in that great room of his, before the fire. He was gazing about warmly as if it had always been his dearest wish to spend his evenings with a woman he had already explored thoroughly and a happy baby that was not his own.

What he should have been, he kept telling himself, was outraged, for Geraldine had clearly cast some kind of spell on him.

But he could never quite work himself up into any kind of outrage, no matter how he tried. And if Geraldine thought the question about her mother was strange, she kept it to herself. "I speak to my mother all the time. At least three times a week."

That surprised him. Maybe that was the reason Geraldine was so firmly lodged beneath his skin—he never knew what she was going to say or do. She had never bored him yet.

"Even after she left here the way she did?" he asked.

Geraldine was sitting on the rug the way she liked to do, supervising Jules as she gurgled with delight and flung the toy she was holding as far as she could. Over and over again. Every time, with a patience that Lionel could only admire, Geraldine would pick up the toy, smile at the little girl, and hand it back to her.

And when he asked her that question, Geraldine laughed. "My mother and I have always had a peculiar relationship. It's almost as if neither one of us can bear how much we care for the other. We do better when we are simply discussing our lives with each other, not looking for support, just sharing the details. It's when there are expectations of particular emotional responses that we are less successful. But my aunt and my cousin never really got along at all, so believe me, I can tell the difference."

She smiled down at the baby with such joy that it made something in Lionel seem too tight. He found himself pressing the heel of his palm to his chest to dissipate it.

But Geraldine was still talking. "I think my aunt was always afraid of Seanna's beauty and what it would mean. And I suppose you could say she wasn't wrong, given how it ended up. She ended up blaming Seanna, as if she'd meant to be that beautiful and therefore meant everything else to happen too."

"My mother took it as a personal affront that she was ever expected to pay any attention to me," Lionel told her, and shrugged when she looked at him, her eyes wide. "She had already suffered through the pregnancy. And the indignity of a lifelong scar on her abdomen, forever ruining her figure."

"Lionel…"

"In truth, I was always grateful that she did not pretend otherwise. It was easier."

He meant that, but the words hung there in the room, seeming heavy next to the way Jules laughed and clapped. And Geraldine looked for a moment as if she might cry.

And this, Lionel told himself, was yet another reason he avoided feelings at all costs. He preferred that he always knew precisely what went on in the rooms he inhabited. That there were clear agendas to follow and obvious signs indicating what was happening and to whom.

Allow emotion in and there were undercurrents and uncertainties. There were *kind eyes* and overbright glances and too much he did not want to think about, like the mother who had excluded herself from consideration years ago.

"Some say she deliberately infected herself with the bacterial infection that killed her," Lionel found himself saying. "I doubt that, but she certainly did nothing to protect herself against it when she could have. It's not as if it was an easy thing to catch. What I do know is that all she cared about once she was ill was the planning of her funeral. She wanted to make sure that it was a grander function than any party my father might throw to celebrate himself, in life or death. That was their primary relationship, you understand. Base competition."

"Surely not." But she wasn't arguing, Lionel saw. She only *wanted* what he was saying not be true.

"She could have gotten treatment," Lionel said, and he didn't know why reciting these facts made his ribs ache.

"She knew she was ill. She might even have suspected what it was. Instead, she died within the week, though she did make certain to tell me that she was delighted she wouldn't have to pretend to care about any children I might have one day."

That sat even more heavily in the middle of the room, filling it up until he was surprised that the glass ceilings didn't crack and rain shards down upon them.

"My mother and I get along marvelously, really," Geraldine said softly, and the wideness in her eyes turned to a kindness that he did not wish to see. Or feel behind his ribs. "But she didn't want me to take care of Seanna either, if for different reasons. Everyone else in the family thought we should let Jules get adopted and pretend Seanna had just...gone off somewhere. My mother didn't think that, necessarily, but she was concerned at what nursing Seanna would do to me. Personally. And what taking on a child on my own might do to me, also personally. It's a critical distinction, you see."

Lionel did not see.

As if she could tell, Geraldine smiled, and that made that pressure in his chest worse. "I mean that she worries about me, not what people might say about her or our family. That's why she left. It might look like judgment, but it's not. It's that she can't bear to stay and watch me do things she worries might hurt me." It was her turn to shrug. "Love doesn't have to look the way you think it should, Lionel."

Later that night, when she came back from putting the baby to sleep and joined him for their usual dinner, he stripped her of the clothes she wore and laid her out on that very same rug, where the glass hadn't shattered and the room still felt too full.

And he did everything he could to make her scream.

Though he refused to ask himself what he thought he was proving. Or what he thought he meant by it.

Lionel kept waiting for the spell to be broken as the days passed. Fall rolled in, limning the fields with a deeper gold. The sky was a far more intense blue overhead. And the green of Geraldine's eyes seemed to grow more mysterious.

If anything, he felt more enchanted by her, not less.

Yet having taken that month that his grandmother had ordered, though he had worked despite her demands, he had to go back to his usual travels. And at first, he assumed that he would enjoy his visits to different offices around the globe the way he always had. The excitement of waking up in a new city. The challenge of walking into a different office.

But he did not find it all as thrilling as he had before.

Historically, no matter how much he enjoyed a relationship, Lionel had always been grateful for his work. Because he enjoyed that as well—and often far more, if he was honest. When he was in the office, he had always been perfectly capable of compartmentalizing. Not that he would have called it that.

He simply didn't think about the woman in his life until and unless he wanted to see her.

But he thought about Geraldine all the time.

In the middle of the tense negotiation in a boardroom in Singapore one evening, he found his mind wandering as he wondered what Geraldine was going to do with her morning with him away. And whether she missed him when he traveled—

When Lionel realized the direction of his thoughts, he sat back in his chair, so shocked he had to cough to cover the growl of dismay he was sure he'd made audibly.

For never, in all of his life, could he recall ever wondering—for even a moment—if anyone missed him.

He was Lionel Asensio.

On some level, he supposed, he had always rather thought that the lights dimmed when he quit a room.

When he came back from that trip, he found Geraldine fast asleep in the bed they now shared. Because he had insisted that she move into his rooms. *For the access,* he had assured himself. *For the convenience,* he had told her.

Tonight he stood there watching the moonlight play over her, for far too long. Fully clothed.

For far longer than he would have admitted if she'd woken up to see him at it.

Eventually, he talked himself out of whatever daze he was in. He'd showered off the mess in his head, then slipped into the bed beside her, waking her up in the best way he could imagine.

Every time he came home, it was the same. Whether she was asleep or awake, she always greeted him with the same obvious delight. The same sweetness, the same fire.

And every time he tasted her anew, he was certain that this would be the time that it failed to excite him as it had before. That she would fall short of the memories he tortured himself with when he was away.

It was possible he looked forward to that happening, but it never did.

Instead, every time, it was better.

Because he had taught her everything she knew and she was a clever student. He could do nothing but exult in the way she set about attempting to master each and every skill he'd introduced her to.

Until some nights, it was hard to remember who had taught who.

"I need something to do," she told him one day, when they had been together some while. They were walking outside along the fields, taking in the cooler air. "I'm not used to all this inactivity."

"You are an Asensio wife," he intoned, as if that was all that should matter to her.

There was a primitive part of him that thought it was, in fact, the only thing that should matter to her. But there was also a part of him that liked her more than he wanted to for saying such a thing, because *he* certainly wouldn't have liked sitting around, waiting to be dressed and living for her return.

The very idea was absurd.

And Geraldine clearly agreed, as she only rolled her eyes at him.

Lionel felt his mouth curve. "Many women in your position throw themselves into charity work. That is always an avenue that you could choose."

"It's not that I'm opposed to charity," she said after considering it a moment, worrying a stick she'd picked up with her fingers. "That seems so removed, doesn't it? I feel certain that if you or anyone else wants to hand out their money, they will. I'm not sure that I could even discuss such impossibly large sums without laughing."

"Not an ideal tactic in fundraising," Lionel agreed.

But later, when they had a dinner with his grandmother

in the private dining salon she used only for family, the *ilustrísima* señora waved two bejeweled hands. "I have been looking for someone I can trust to catalog the Asensio collection," she pronounced as if she had called Geraldine here to the estate for this purpose. "I was beginning to think it would never happen in my lifetime."

"You have a collection?" Geraldine asked, a note in her voice that he had never heard before. When he had heard it before, it had been in the voices of certain men when they discussed race cars. And in the voices of some women when they looked at jewelry. "As in, an actual *collection*, not simply an attic full of sentiment?"

"I am not sentimental," the old woman told her with a sniff. "I am disarmingly shrewd. Ask anyone."

"This is true," Lionel said when his grandmother lifted a brow in his direction. "It has been repeatedly confirmed throughout all the halls of Europe."

And so after dinner, Doña Eugenia herself led them to the grand library that claimed an entire wing of the old, rambling house.

"These are merely all the books that are considered readable," his grandmother said, turning in a circle as she looked up at the floor-to-ceiling shelves, all packed tight. Beside her, Geraldine actually quivered with delight. Lionel knew it when he saw it. "We do not have attics, but we do have any number of outbuildings filled with documents, a great many objects of historical interest, and, of course, any number of books. In all kinds of different languages, last I checked."

And Lionel watched as his wife tried her best not to twirl around herself, possibly letting out a squeal or two.

"It's like Christmas," Geraldine told him later. "My

second favorite holiday, but the best one as far as gifts are concerned."

She had a look on her lovely face that he had taken as a challenge, then. And he spent several hours showing her that he, too, could give her the kind of joy she had gotten from the very existence of piles of books. That he could provide whatever she craved.

But he was beginning to wonder if he was the one whose cravings were undoing him.

He had been gone for several days on his latest business trip—about which he remembered only that he'd caught the scent of her, coconut and papaya, on a crowded city street on the other side of the planet—when he walked into his house to find that it smelled like a feast.

"There you are," she said brightly when he found her in the semiformal dining room. She clapped her hands together, a lot like Jules did. Then she held them out over the table, which it took him long moments to realize held any number of dishes. "I have been in collusion with the kitchen and they prepared a proper Thanksgiving dinner for us." When he only stared at her, she tilted her head to one side. "You went to school in the States. I know you must have an idea of what Thanksgiving is."

"Of course I do," Lionel said gruffly. But he did not tell her that his memories of that North American holiday were some of his favorites. That he had loved the convivial notion of the holiday that was simply about gathering together and sharing a meal, something he dearly missed when he was not in Spain.

"Thanksgiving is my favorite holiday," Geraldine told him, as if she was sharing a secret.

Lionel sat with her, and the baby, who both laughed

too much. That was the trouble. There was all the *smiling*. Even the baby gurgled happily when he looked at her, as if she knew him.

As if you really are her father, something in him suggested.

And he already knew, didn't he, that the notion didn't horrify him as it should have. As he wanted it to.

As he told himself it would have if it weren't for Geraldine, who had gone to the trouble of making it clear she thought about him too much when he was gone. Who indicated, again and again, that she not only listened to the things he told her, she took them into account. She *considered* him.

Over and over again, she made it clear that he mattered to her.

Him. Lionel, the man.

Not the businessman, the billionaire, the heir to the Asensio wealth and power.

He told himself he was tired, that was all, or too full after their American feast, but he knew that it was more than that. Because he was getting too comfortable here. This was all entirely too comfortable. It would be easier if he could convince himself that she had set this whole thing up from the start. That this was all a game she was playing. That she was only pretending...

But he knew better.

He knew innocence when he tasted it. And Geraldine was the worst actress he'd ever encountered. There were some women who could pull off a fake like that, but she wasn't one of them. She never would be one of them.

That was the trouble with her in a nutshell.

Later that night, after she put Jules to bed, Geraldine

came and found him. She slipped her arms around him from behind as he stood at the glass windows of his favorite room and looked out into the dark.

Though what he saw was her reflection, superimposed over this land he'd been raised to believe was, truly, the whole of the world.

"Geraldine," he said, because his heart was pounding at him, and he refused to interpret that as anything but a warning. To disengage. To step away from her. To end this, whatever it was. He told himself it could mean nothing else, even if the thought of doing any of those things did not exactly fill him with happiness. *"Mi media naranja..."*

My other half. Why did he keep saying that? Had he made it so?

But she tugged on him so he turned to look down at her. And she smiled up at him, the heat in her gaze so bright that he found he could not resist.

That he did not *want* to resist.

"Tonight," she told him quietly, her green eyes dancing, "you will not speak at all, unless it is my name in your mouth. Do you understand?"

Everything inside him stilled. Then...hummed.

"You play a dangerous game—" he began.

"Lionel," she said, and shook her head as if saddened when still her eyes gleamed with laughter. "That is not my name."

And then, as he stood there, *undone*, she ran her hands down his chest. She took her time. Then her green eyes held his with a kind of solemnity as she knelt down before him.

Then, never looking away from him, she pulled him from his trousers, thick and ready. She wrapped her hands around the base of him, then leaned forward and sucked him in deep.

And she loved him like that, slow and hot, fire and need, undoing him with every low sound she made.

With every stroke of her tongue. With the suction, the heat.

She loved him past the place of no return. She ignored him when he said her name in warning.

And when he finished, despite himself, he shouted out her name.

While inside him, it felt like a song.

She sat back, looking up at him with a smile on her face and what looked like sheer, uncomplicated joy in those green eyes of hers.

And it was as if something in him broke open.

Lionel didn't know what it was. He didn't want to know.

He reached down and pulled her to her feet, then straight into his arms.

And he carried her into the bedroom. Once there, he laid her out on the bed and looked down at her, his heart setting up such a clatter inside his chest that once again, he had to press his own hand to it.

Because it felt as if it might break his ribs.

And for a moment, he could do nothing *but* stand there, his breath coming in too fast. The blood inside him too loud.

For once, he didn't know what he was meant to *do*.

Because Lionel did not feel. He did not *feel things* like this, with an overwhelming need so powerful and so enduring that he was beginning to suspect there was no amount of time spent with her that would ever be enough.

That he would always be caught up in this spell of hers.

But tonight, there was only one word that he could say. And perhaps there was a part of him that was grateful for that, because otherwise he could not trust that he would not say things that he knew he shouldn't.

That he had always vowed he *wouldn't*.

So he crawled up next to her, into her open arms, and then he set about making her his.

All over again.

He pressed his lips to every new swath of skin he uncovered as he removed her clothes. He loved every part of her, and then again.

And he could not tell her what he felt, because he had no vocabulary for such things. And because tonight, there was only her name.

"Geraldine," he whispered, making her name into whole songs.

When she was naked and pink and quivering, he slid his hands beneath her bottom and lifted her up like dessert. Then he sang his favorite song as he licked into her, deep, so it was her turn to scream and lose control completely.

And she was still shuddering when he crawled up the length of her body, still pressing kisses to that sweet, flushed, pink flesh.

He drew her onto his lap so that she knelt astride him, and he waited for her to look down and see where they were joined. Then to pull her lip between her teeth as she looked at him.

And then begin to smile, her eyes shining, as he let her take charge once again.

This time it was a slow, rolling explosion. She rocked

against him, wrapping her arms around his neck so she could kiss him as she moved. And there was little he could do but wrap his hands over her hips and enjoy the bright-hot fire between them.

She fanned the flames so they danced higher and higher.

And then, as they both spun out there on the edge, Geraldine pulled her mouth from his and looked down, smoothing her palms over his cheeks to frame his jaw.

Her eyes were darker then. Storm-tossed emeralds, and all his.

"Lionel," she whispered, and his name in her mouth made him thrust harder inside her, deeper and hotter, "I love you."

The words echoed inside him.

I love you.

The words were like a bomb, too huge and too—

But then she bore down, squeezing him tight.

And she sent them both tumbling over the edge, soaring out to all the galaxies they'd made here between them, as if she hadn't ruined everything.

CHAPTER ELEVEN

GERALDINE WOKE UP SLOWLY, found the sun in her face, and her first instinct was to smile.

But in the next moment she realized that if the sun was up, she must have missed Jules's usual morning wake-up routine and so she sat up, frowning, and shoved her hair out of her face.

Only then did she see Lionel sitting in a chair by the fire, staring at her with a dark and brooding sort of look that made him look more like stone than he had in a long while.

It took a moment for the night to come back to her. And then it did, hard, and she knew exactly what this was.

You knew better, she told herself.

"Did you mean it?" he asked, with no preamble.

Geraldine did not pretend she wasn't fully aware what he was asking.

"Te amo," she said, because she'd been practicing. She'd been taking advantage of all the nannies at her disposal and giving herself workdays. She spent hours in the libraries up at the house, arranging things in preparation for the cataloging that she would only begin in earnest once she learned more Spanish, so she could read everything she found. Lucky for her, Lionel's grandmother was

proving to be an excellent and devoted tutor. *"Te quiero. Te quiero con todo mi corazón."*

Because she did love him. With all of her heart.

"I don't understand why you would take this and ruin it in this way," he growled at her.

"What is ruined?" Geraldine asked lightly.

And then watched as Lionel stood and began to pace, which made her heart beat much more rapidly inside her.

Because this was Lionel Asensio. Cool, calm, controlled.

And he seemed to be precisely none of those things just now.

"I cannot have this," he seethed at her, sounding nothing like that stern man of stone she had first met in that Italian chapel. "It was enough that everything was so pleasant. Too pleasant, I grant you. But why couldn't you have left well enough alone?"

"Because I love you."

"You don't."

But Geraldine only smiled.

He made that growling noise again. "You must leave, of course. I have many properties and I'm sure we can find one that will suit you. There's a town house in Manhattan. We can tell my *abuelita* that you wished most fervently to be back in your country."

He scowled when all Geraldine did was shake her head. "I wish no such thing. And she will not believe it anyway. She knows how excited I am to dig into her collection."

"You will stay in Manhattan," he gritted out at her. "Until whatever sickness this is passes."

But something about that made her...almost giddy, she found.

"I'm not sick," she said cheerfully. "In fact, I'm not sure I've ever felt better."

"I should have made this clear." It was almost as if he was talking to himself then, pacing back and forth before the bank of windows with the cold fall morning stretching before him. "It is my fault that I failed to do so."

Geraldine sat up straighter then. She let the covers fall from her, since the fire warmed the room nicely. And then considered herself something close enough to virtuous that she did not smirk at all when his jaw tightened and his dark eyes glittered at the sight of her breasts.

"A long time ago, I had to make a choice," he rasped at her, gravelly and grim. "As we have discussed, my father and his father were wastes of human space. If they were here they would argue with that and say that they simply *followed their feelings* wherever those feelings took them. No matter how dark, how depraved. I made certain that I could never do the same."

"How did you make certain of it?" she asked, careful to keep her voice mild.

Inside, there was that giddiness, but there was something else—and she knew it, now.

It was the way she wanted to be near him, always.

It was the fact that she trusted him, implicitly.

He was the person she most wanted to see when she opened her eyes and the last person she liked to see before she went to sleep. She liked knowing that he was beside her in that enormous bed, wrapped all around her.

She liked his heat. His passion. His intensity in all its forms.

She loved his heart, even though he didn't think he had one.

She loved him.

It was that simple. It was the whole universe. It was her heart, and she was his.

"I am not capable of feeling the kinds of things you want me to feel," he threw at her.

And Geraldine felt too many things at once. A deep sadness for him that he believed this about himself. A kind of wonder that he did not understand that he was already turned inside out, or he would not have thundered at her the way he did.

And beneath all of that, tangled into it, that same wild, wondrous love that had made these weeks glow.

Even if she had wanted to take it back, she wouldn't. She couldn't.

"I don't recall asking you to feel anything for me," she said softly.

And strangely enough, she thought of her cousin. She thought of the ways Seanna had told her again and again that she had tried so hard to love the various men she become entangled with. *I always thought it wouldn't matter if they loved me back,* she had told Geraldine long ago. *That I could love them enough until they did.*

Geraldine could remember thinking that she couldn't understand that kind of math, when it was so clearly never going to add up to anything. And she still believed that.

But she also believed in Lionel.

She believed in all the things he couldn't say, and not because he didn't feel them. She saw the way he looked at her. And not only when they were here, in his bed. She thought of the way he took her hand when they walked.

She thought of the way he listened when she spoke, making her the total focus of his world, as if nothing else could ever exist, or ever would.

She thought of how much more often he smiled now. She had even made him laugh a time or two.

And then, wrapped all around these and threaded through it all, was the way he looked at Jules. Geraldine did not have to ask if this man had a great deal of experience with babies. She knew he didn't.

Yet these days it was perfectly natural for him to take Jules in his arms the way he had when he'd come home last night. One morning she'd had to rush out of the room for a moment to get Jules's favorite toy and when she come back, she had found Lionel down on his hands and knees, making the baby squeal with delight.

She had already known that she loved him then.

But it was that morning, that moment, that had made it inevitable that she would tell him so.

That and the way he had looked around at the Thanksgiving feast she'd plotted with the kitchens to prepare for him, then had smiled at her as if she'd personally climbed up into the night sky and fetched him the moon and a sprinkling of stars.

It was the fact that if she could, she would.

"I've spent a lot of time with your grandmother," she told him now, when all he did was glare at her. "She's helping me learn Spanish. But her favorite topic of conversation is you."

"I would strongly urge you not to put too much stock into what my *abuelita* says when it comes to me. She cannot be trusted to tell the truth when she could meddle instead."

"She says it's her fault," Geraldine said quietly, and Lionel looked as if she'd struck him.

There was a part of her that wanted to stop, because she knew that he wouldn't want to have this conversation. But she pushed on.

"That she grew tired of your grandfather and was disgusted with your father's excesses. She left you here, thinking that there was enough staff about and that you might be all right, because they cared for you better than your own mother did."

She had brought up Lionel's mother with the assumption that he was exaggerating, but had discovered, to her dismay, that he had been underselling it. *That woman was no good,* his grandmother had said quietly.

"Instead, when she returned, you had changed completely. You had been a loving, happy boy, and she'd thought that was simply your personality. That it wouldn't matter what your parents did or didn't do—but she was wrong."

"She has no idea what she's talking about," Lionel said, his voice rising—until he stopped himself. Geraldine thought he might stop talking altogether, but then he shoved his hands through his dark hair. "You don't understand what it was like. Everything was...this feeling or that feeling, as if feelings were facts. As if feelings were more important. As if any promise, or any hope of a promise kept, disappeared in the face of those feelings. It was like walking in quicksand and I decided when I was fourteen that I would do it no longer. There was only one way to find solid ground, and I found it."

He turned toward her then, staring at her with a look

on his face that she knew, somehow, he would hate to know he was even capable of making.

But she saw it. And she couldn't stop herself. She was upon her feet and crossing to him without knowing she meant to move.

And she didn't much care when he looked as if the last thing in the world he wanted was her to touch him. She went to him anyway, sliding her hands up his chest to loop around his neck, and then gazing up at him.

"My grandmother is trying to trick you," he told her stiffly. "She wants the bloodline secured into the next generation."

"I'm sure she does," Geraldine said. But gently. She tipped her head back. "But do you really think she's the sort of woman who cares *only* about bloodlines and family traditions? I've known her for less than a whole season, and I know better. That isn't why she wanted you married. It isn't why she thinks you should have children."

"You cannot possibly think that you know my grandmother better than I do." But his voice was a low scrape of anguish.

Geraldine pressed on. "She loves you. She wants you to know that you are loved. And more, that you *can* love."

But Lionel looked as if he was awash in nothing but misery. "My grandmother is many things, but never has she been mawkish and sentimental."

"She loves you," Geraldine said again. "And let me tell you something about love, Lionel. It's not selfishness dressed up in terms of endearment. It's not self-centered justifications for bad behavior. You've never told me a single story about your parents that made me think they ever loved anything but themselves. Neither has your grandmother, for that matter. But you aren't anything like them."

And she felt the shudder that went through him then, as if his bones themselves were quaking. She thought he tried to argue, but all that came out was her name.

Like a song he'd once sung, but he'd forgotten the melody.

So Geraldine would remind him. "You love your grandmother beyond reason. You love this land and the legacy of what has been created here, then maintained. You love the people who work for you, here and in all your offices. You treat them like humans, not faceless robots here to do your bidding. You listen with your *whole body*, Lionel. Do you have any idea how rare that is?" She laughed, then, and held him all the tighter. "You are demanding but never imperious, never rude. You simply expect that everyone should be the best version of themselves, including you."

The strong column of his neck worked. "That is simply good business."

"You love Jules," she said softly. "I've seen the way you look at her when you think I'm not paying attention. But I've seen it. And I know."

"Geraldine…" he gritted out.

She slid her palms down so she could press them into his chest. Then she moved one, just slightly, so she could make it clear that she was feeling the way his heart pounded.

And how it pounded even harder once she did it.

Geraldine smiled. "You pride yourself on being cold

and unreachable, but you're not. I've seen the way you look at me, too. Every time you look at me."

"I am warning you, Geraldine."

But her smile only widened. "Lionel, I don't know how to break this news to you. And I'm sorry you don't want to hear it. But I'm as certain as I can be that you're in love with me, too."

And it was like watching a hurricane.

The storm wrecked him and she watched it as it happened. She watched it play out in his gaze, in that anguish etched into his face.

She watched it tear him apart.

But then his hands were on her, pulling her closer and spearing his fingers into her hair so he could hold her right there before him.

Not that she wanted to be anywhere else.

"Don't you understand?" he demanded, as if the world was ending. As if, outside, the trees were bent in half beneath the howl of the wind instead of standing prettily beneath a perfectly blue sky. In here, in him, the storm raged. "*What if I do?* That can only mean that I will destroy you, too."

And for a moment the only sound of the storm was the way the two of them breathed, ragged and intense, as if they'd just climbed up something steep. For hours.

"You couldn't destroy me if you tried," she told him when she could speak again. When she could hold her gaze steady on his. When she could make certain he understood that she meant this. "I come from peasant stock, Lionel. I'm built to withstand far greater horrors than the love of a good husband." She leaned in then, sliding her arms around him and holding him close. The way he deserved to be held. "Bring it on, I say."

His arms moved, and she thought for a moment he might try to push her away—*try* being the operative word—but instead he wrapped them around her.

Not exactly gently.

He gazed down at her, stern as stone. "If I love you, Geraldine, there is no going back. There is no escape. There is not only no divorce, there is no separation. I don't like leaving you. Coming home to you is a joy, but I would far rather have you at my side, and I mean that. I mean everything I say and you should know—I am not a man who traffics in half measures. If I say I am in, I will never be out."

"I'm glad to hear it," she shot right back. "Because you do realize, don't you, that you haven't used even a hint of protection with me? That you never even asked?"

And as she watched, then, Lionel Asensio began to laugh.

He laughed, but he held her close until she was laughing, too. And somehow that became kissing, desperate and delighted. Then they were wrapped up in each other, rolling on the bed, and this was as it was supposed to be. This was right.

Geraldine said as much when he worked his way inside her, filling her completely, thrusting in deep. Then deeper still, and yet it was never deep enough.

"You are the only lie I have ever told myself," Lionel growled down at her as he braced himself above her, taking up the whole sky she should have been able to see beyond him. A better view, in her opinion. "Because this is the truth, Geraldine, and it always has been. I want you naked, just like this. I want to be inside you. I want nothing between us, ever. As many children as you wish to give me, I intend to raise. Right here, with you. I want you so much a part of me that it will be as if we are two sides of the same coin. And even that will never be enough."

"Good," Geraldine retorted fiercely. "Because I have been waiting my whole life to love you and I didn't even realize it. It will take me the whole rest of my life to revel in it, and several forevers after that, I would think, for it to sink in."

"Geraldine," he said as he began to move, that slick, hot, perfect rhythm that took everything they were and made it a sweet hot celebration that they could share, over and over again, "I love you. And I promise you, I will love you forever."

So she wrapped herself around him and she fixed her gaze to his. "For richer and for poorer," she told him, because the last vows they'd taken had been a blur, and then she'd fainted.

This felt much better.

"I promise you," he said at once. Then he smiled. "But I must assure you that there is very little possibility that you will ever be anything like poor, *mi media naranja*."

And then, together, they made the only vows that could ever matter.

Here in the chapel of the bed where they found each other, found their way back to each other, and found love wherever they looked.

Over and over again.

CHAPTER TWELVE

LIONEL ADOPTED BABY Jules before her first birthday

"How can she be anything less than mine?" he asked.

"That's how I have felt about her from the start," Geraldine told him, smiling in that way that made her eyes gloss over with emotion.

He would have hated that once, but he was learning.

The presence of an emotion did not mean that the kind of excesses his father was so fond of would follow. It did not mean that, like his grandfather, he would take it upon himself to blow something up—simply because he could.

Geraldine had their second child before Jules was two. A sturdy, green-eyed little boy, who was already so charming, his *abuelita* declared, that surely he would wrap the whole world around his chubby fist before he was five.

In the meantime, Lionel and his beautiful wife made their life together.

They spent time with her family, so that Geraldine's parents could feel easier about the choices she had made. And while they would always be suspicious of his wealth and power—something he grew to appreciate—he thought that over time, they came around.

Then again, that was likely just the grandchildren.

Geraldine learned Spanish at a surprising pace and threw herself into cataloging the Asensio collection, which did not remain a private concern. It was so large and so fascinating that, eventually, they built it a building all its own on the part of the estate that bordered public lands. Then they opened it to anyone who wished to come and view it, and Geraldine got to run the entire operation.

"You have become quite a mogul in your own way," he told her many years later as they arrived for one of the Biblioteca Asensio's grand events that called in scholars and academics, celebrities, and intellectuals from all over the world.

"The thing no one ever tells you," she said, smiling at him with all that laughter in her gorgeous green eyes that she still liked to hide behind her glasses when she was working—because she claimed she couldn't resist the stereotype, "is that moguling is so much *fun*."

"That is a secret," he admonished her, though he was smiling. "You must tell no one, Geraldine. We can't have that kind of thing getting out."

But the real secret, he knew, was love.

They loved each other. They loved their family. They added to it as the years passed. Another boy and then a little girl.

Who they got to watch Jules dote on the way Geraldine had doted on Jules's mother long ago.

They loved each other, and they loved their children, so they never lied to Jules about her parentage. They never kept where she came from a secret, from her or the other children. And they decided that she should be the one to seek out her birth father if she wished. If he could be found.

Though she never showed the slightest inclination to do so.

"All I'd have to say to him is thank you," Jules said when she was older. "He was so terrible, and treated poor Seanna so badly, that he accidentally made my life fantastic. I don't need a single thing from him."

"You," Lionel told her, "are a marvel of a child."

"I take after my mother," Jules told him, laying her head on his shoulder as they watched Geraldine out in the garden, playing with the younger children.

Love was the point of all of it, and that was what Lionel told his grandmother as he sat by her bed as her last days seemed to come much closer than they had before, though she'd made it to the hundredth birthday party she'd vowed she would throw for herself.

She had even made her grandsons dance with her.

"It was a marvelous party, *Abuelita,*" Lionel told her, holding her hand in his.

"I certainly hope so," she responded, with that same old satisfied grin. "Because how else should a life end if not with the celebration? That's the point, *nene.* Love is always the point."

And as the years passed, that was what Lionel remembered.

That life was meant to end, like it or not. And that being so, better that a life should be a celebration of love. Better that it should be marked with joy, and then remembered by those who lived on with laughter, with stories, and with love.

Always and ever love.

If there was a greater legacy than love, Lionel did not wish to know it.

"Aren't you lucky," Geraldine would say when she found him in their bed at night, whether it was at home in Andalusia or in one of their places around the world, where they would stay whenever Lionel needed to travel for work, "that I decided to fall in love with you all those years ago?"

And Lionel knew that he was the luckiest.

But he also knew how to handle his wife. "The lucky one is you, *mi media naranja*," he would tell her sternly. "And I will have you prove it tonight, I think. By saying only my name. Do you understand?"

She always smiled so wide, his Geraldine.

Then she would whisper his name, as commanded.

But what he heard was *love*, so that was what he gave her. And that was what he got.

And that was what they made, until it was a life, and then it bloomed on into forever.

* * * * *

HOW THE ITALIAN CLAIMED HER

JENNIFER HAYWARD

MILLS & BOON

This one is for you, Dottie Auletto.

No one could have been a bigger Modern fan
or loved books more than you did.

I'm heartbroken that you're gone.
I miss you so much.

But your love of romance and your amazing spirit
will always be with me as I write. xx

CHAPTER ONE

CRISTIANO VITALE HAD just consumed a fortifying, and more importantly eye-opening, sip of strong, dark espresso when his chief marketing officer appeared in his office, looking far more frazzled than the holder of such a position should be, just weeks out from the launch of the most important collection in Francesco Vitale's storied history.

Founded over a half century ago by his late grandfather, Francesco Vitale, the legendary Italian fashion house he commanded was on the verge of a massive rebirth, a do-or-die moment for the company he'd spent a decade rebuilding. What had necessitated a 4:00 a.m. start to the morning that he was presently attempting to wake up from. Putting out another fire before he'd even gotten to his emails wasn't how he particularly wanted to start the day. He was sure, however, from the frustration written across Antonio Braga's inordinately stressed face that he had no choice in the matter.

He sat back in his chair, hands wrapped around his coffee cup, and motioned his CMO into the chair opposite him. "You have five minutes before I'm due in a meeting with the lawyers. Make it quick."

Antonio ignored the chair he offered and paced to the window, where he stood, staring out at a magnificent view of Milan, every muscle in his perfectly groomed body tense, his shoulders practically up at his ears. "I need you to do me a favor."

Cristiano hiked a brow. An interesting way to start the conversation, given the power differential between the two, and given that his CMO knew the weight he was presently carrying. But as he'd never seen Antonio this out of sorts before, he elected to play along. "Which is?"

Antonio turned and leaned a hip against the windowsill, his handsome face haggard and lined with the strain he'd been carrying for months. "You are in London tonight?"

"Si." An in-and-out-in-a-night business trip he would prefer not to do, but one that was key. "Why?" he queried. "You need to tag along?"

"No." Antonio raked a hand through his short dark hair, looking as if that idea horrified him. "I have an ad campaign to finish and a television commercial to shoot, and no time to do either." A silence followed as he set his gaze on Cristiano. "It's Jensen Davis."

The hairs on the back of Cristiano's neck rose. The wild-child face of his brand, American supermodel Jensen Davis, had been causing havoc for him for weeks, racking up headlines faster than the millions he paid her. Scandalous, *salacious* headlines with the power to sully the FV legacy at a time when it could least afford it.

A dark current of frustration sizzled up his spine. "What has she done now?" he growled.

Antonio deposited the entertainment section of one of London's daily newspapers on his desk. Cristiano set his coffee cup down and pulled the newspaper toward him. The front page of the section featured a photo of the twenty-six-year-old Jensen stumbling out of a club, dressed in a jaw-dropping red dress, in what looked like the early hours of the morning.

Her luxurious chestnut-colored hair fell in a silken curtain over her shoulder; her stunning ebony eyes emphasized with dark, smoky makeup that made them look undeniably haunting, her sensational body encased in a body-hugging silk, she was the most unforgettably beautiful woman he'd ever set eyes on. The perfect canvas for the FV brand.

He scanned the text beneath the photograph, his trepidation mounting.

Catwalk Catfight!
Jensen Davis, the hottest model on the catwalk, continued her headline-grabbing behavior of late, engaging in a very public catfight with Princess Juliana Margues last night at Zoro. Rumored to be a disagreement over Davis's nude romp in an Italian fountain with Prince Alexandre of Santeval, the princess's on-again, off-again beau.

After the spirited exchange, which featured a shouting match and a drink Margues purportedly threw at Davis, the American supermodel made a quick exit with her entourage.

One can only wonder how far this will go before the palace steps in. Bets are it won't be too long.

Meanwhile, Davis is set to headline the Designer Extravaganza in support of the London Hospital Foundation this evening, the most coveted ticket in town.

Cristiano's blood heated in his veins. The fountain incident in Rome had been bad enough, given his family's close personal ties to the pope, and the resulting scandal that had followed. Now Davis was instigating a full royal PR response? There was a line, he breathed. A line to these antics of hers she couldn't cross, and she'd done it twice in the past few weeks. *Infuriating*, when he'd been reassured she'd left her irresponsible behavior behind. Promised she was a professional now.

He drew in a deep breath. Tempered the wave of dark heat scorching through him. "I told you to take care of this, Antonio. It is too much. *Troppo*."

"I've tried," his CMO defended hotly, a swath of color climbing his aristocratic cheekbones, "but she is a moving target. And her agent has been no help."

"Because she is out of control," Cristiano thundered, jabbing a long finger at the photograph. "Racking up thirty-thousand-euro bar tabs in Monaco on wild nights of partying... *Debasing* sacred fountains in Rome... Blowing off her FV responsibilities. Pascal is ready to lose his marbles," he said, referring to his brand-new star designer, set to take his grandfather's place as the creative head of the company. "He can't finish the collection without her. She is a *phantom*," he breathed, waving a hand in the air, "appearing only when she likes."

His CMO scrubbed a palm over his brow. "She's usually a complete professional when it comes to her work. I have no idea what's going on with her. How to deal with this."

Cristiano pushed the newspaper away, frustration singeing his fingertips. He'd been content to look the other way at some of Davis's attention-grabbing stunts, because they only tended to increase her popularity, and thus that of the FV brand. But these latest exploits? They had the potential to do real damage to both her own brand

and Francesco Vitale's if they continued. Not to mention the shirking of her FV responsibilities, something he would never tolerate.

"Need I remind you," he bit out, his gaze resting on his marketing chief, "that we have bet the bank on her, Antonio? That she is the centerpiece of *everything* we have created? That I went against Francesco's express wishes on this because of *your* recommendation, a decision that likely has him turning in his grave?"

"Which I stand firm on," his CMO replied staunchly. "Jensen Davis is the most important influencer on the face of the planet when it comes to the millennials we need to capture if this company is to survive. Young women aspire to *be* her, Cristiano. She is making our clothes aspirational again. Our brand relevancy scores have doubled since she came aboard."

"Which will plummet into the nether if she continues like this."

"I won't let that happen," Antonio assured him, his elegantly shaved square jaw flexing. "Yes, it's been a rough few weeks. But she will deliver. She always does."

Cristiano exhaled a deep breath. He had hired Davis, whom his grandfather had not approved of, the "it" girl of her generation, the most recognizable face in America from her days as a fashion-obsessed teenager on her Hollywood family's reality show, to make the Francesco Vitale brand relevant again. But it wasn't a decision he'd made lightly.

He had balked at the idea of hiring Davis when his marketing team first put her name forward, sure that with her wild-child history she'd be more trouble than she was worth. But he hadn't been able to deny the influence she'd held over the fashion world. Nor the power she wielded over the prevailing pop culture. He'd agreed to go see a shoot she was doing, sure he would talk himself out of it by the time he'd left the room. Instead, he'd found himself as beguiled as everyone else in attendance by her beauty. Fascinated by the untamed free spirit she'd been, a life she could breathe into the stagnating Francesco Vitale brand, which badly needed a jolt of fresh air. By the magic she'd created in front of the camera.

His gut had told him she was *it*—a battle he'd waged with his grandfather, who'd favored a traditional Italian model versus the wild card Jensen had represented, until his grandfather had reluctantly acquiesced. A decision he was now having to second-guess, given Davis's erratic behavior. Exasperating, because he didn't have *time* to be questioning any part of his ambitious plan. When he'd been promised Davis's behavior would not be an issue.

He pinned a look on Antonio, framed in the sunshine of a magnificent Milanese morning rapidly losing its rosy glow. "What is your plan? I assume you have one."

"Si." Antonio reached up to tug at his tie and loosen it, an uncharacteristically nervous gesture for his ultra-confident, brilliant marketing guru. "I thought you might attend the Designer Extravaganza tonight. Talk to Jensen. Impart on her the *importance* of the next few weeks for the company. Coming from you, I thought it would have more impact. Unless," he added hesitantly, casting a wary glance at Cristiano's smoldering expression, "you would like me to come with you and do it myself."

Cristiano rubbed a palm over the stubble on his jaw, a task he hadn't had five minutes to see to this morning. He did not have the *capacity* for this. He had three major crises raging on two different continents and an outdated supply chain making his life hell. A major investment deal he needed to land in order to make it all happen, which wasn't at all a sure thing at the moment, not to mention a dozen other minor fires he had waiting to put out. He didn't have time to *breathe*. But with everything resting on Pascal Ferrari's debut collection for FV, the first by his grandfather's successor, a campaign in which Davis sat squarely at the center of, he had no choice but to step in.

If neither his CMO nor Davis's agent could control his star asset, he would. Because with Jensen Davis at the heart of his plans to reinvent Francesco Vitale, failure was not an option.

He eyed Antonio across the desk, a steel-edged sense of purpose lancing through him. "Focus on the campaign. I will deal with Davis."

Jensen Davis absorbed the frantic backstage atmosphere at the historic, glamorous Guildhall in London with a brain so bleary with fatigue, it felt like it was stuffed with cotton wool. Usually, in these last few moments before a show, the electric anticipation of those adrenaline-packed few moments on stage provided her with the charge she needed for the patented high-energy performance she was known for, what had propelled her to the status of the world's top model. Tonight, however, she was operating on only four hours' sleep, half of what she required to feel vaguely human, so drained by the prior month's relentless schedule she was shocked she even knew what city she was in.

Registering her current location might have been easier on this particular occasion than others, if only for the fact that she'd had to fight her way through a crowd of paparazzi as she'd left her hotel, each of them demanding to know about last night's altercation with Princess Juliana, a scene she would prefer to forget.

Jensen, what do you have to say about Princess Juliana's claim you've stolen her fiancé?

What does it feel like to be a relationship-wrecker?

Are you having an affair with Prince Alex?

What does the palace think of all of this?

Baseball cap jammed on her head, sunglasses shading her eyes from the glare of the flashbulbs, she'd ignored them all and slid into the back seat of the waiting car. But she wasn't foolish enough to think it would end there. There would be months of tabloid headlines. Endless speculation. Ridiculous drama manufactured by a royal-obsessed press that couldn't seem to get enough of the story.

All because she'd given in to her mother's desperate plea for one last favor before her show, *Hollywood Divas,* went on hiatus. Her mother, a fading silver screen legend, divided her time between her infamous on-and off-screen exploits, perfect fodder for the wildly popular reality show she starred in each week along with a supporting cast of former A-list stars. Only now, since Jensen and her sisters had left the show, refusing to participate in the stunts her mother pulled as they each pursued their own careers and a life outside of television, the ratings for the decade-long-running show had plummeted, with the producers threatening to cancel the series unless a season finale stunt could provide a major boost to the numbers.

Jensen, determined to maintain her distance from the life she'd left behind, had flatly refused to even consider the whole fountain stunt, until her mother had broken down in tears, sobbing that she'd have nothing left if the show was gone, too. That she'd be flat broke. Which Jensen knew was true, since she'd been bankrolling her mother for the past eighteen months, her mother promising to *do better* each time, which never seemed to happen. Nor could she ask for help from her sisters, Ava and Scarlett, who had founded a fledgling design business and boutique in Manhattan, with no extra money to spare. Which meant all of this fell on her.

Which she might have been able to handle if she wasn't also dealing with the aftereffects of her mother's big end-of-season stunt. The *fountain episode,* which continued to haunt Jensen, even in her sleep.

What had started out as an innocent stunt involving a historic fountain in Rome and a midnight skinny-dipping episode with her good friend, Alex, had seemed harmless enough. Until he'd used it as a tactic to get his ex-fiancée back. Little had she known that Alex planned to leave her hanging in the wind amid rumors of an affair, refusing to correct the salacious headlines that had raged, in the hopes that Juliana would come running back to him. Which, judging from the princess's behavior the night before, she was about to do.

"I did you a favor," Alex had protested when she'd called to ask him to step in. To quell the rumors. "I saved the show." Which technically was true, with the ratings for the season finale the highest of any network television show this season, guaranteeing her mother yet another year on the air. But what about *her*? Her reputation? That professionalism she'd worked so hard to cultivate? She had not signed on for this. A tabloid firestorm that was burning out of control.

Jacob, her hairstylist, finished the last big curl of her Hollywood-inspired style and doused her with a cloud of hair spray. She closed her eyes in the briefest of respites. Really, she should have known better. The media always twisted the facts to fit whatever they were looking for; she a favorite target for their keyboards. Not to mention the fact that giving in to her mother was always an exercise in futility. It always created more problems than it solved.

At the end of the day, this was *her* fault.

"But really," Lucy Parker, a British model with a wicked wit, tossed at her as they were given the ten-minute warning by the showrunner. "What *is* going on between you and Alexandre? You can tell me. I won't say a thing. You can't possibly just be friends."

"We are," Jensen responded wearily, for what seemed like the hundredth time. "Why is that so hard to believe?"

"Because he's gorgeous… The heir to a fortune. And you were naked in that fountain together."

"We weren't naked. I had lingerie on." Something the press *hadn't* seen fit to print. "And it was just a lark." One she wished badly she could take back now.

"Who cares about Prince Alexandre?" Millie, one of the French models interrupted, arriving at their side in a swish of gossamer fabric. "Cristiano Vitale is here. *Mon Dieu*," she breathed, "he is the hottest man I have ever laid eyes on. Beautiful, but not so beautiful he's perfect. Beautiful in the *manly* sense. I met him once and I couldn't even look at him straight. He is so amazing. He's completely intimidating."

Jensen's stomach dropped to the floor. *Cristiano Vitale was here? Why?* FV didn't have a presence here tonight. Nor was it customary for the CEO of the company to attend these types of things. Her mind flew back to the salacious headlines of the past few weeks. The rather panicked text she'd received from her agent on the way over here tonight, a text she hadn't answered because she'd been running late.

CALL ME, was all it had said.

"You would have the scoop." Millie fixed an avaricious gaze on Jensen. "Is he here with anyone? What's his status?"

"I'm not sure." She hadn't seen Cristiano Vitale since her very first shoot for the company, at which he'd lorded over the proceedings like the king of England. She'd gotten the distinct impression he'd been there to make sure he hadn't blown his millions on a piece of reality show trash. She'd never gotten such an infuriatingly arrogant impression in her life.

"He's supposed to marry the beautiful socialite Alessandra Grasso," a Spanish model pointed out. "I wouldn't pin your hopes on that one."

"They are on-again, off-again," Millie tossed back. "And right now, they are *off*. He is fair game."

"I would give it a go," Lucy said, fanning herself with a handheld mirror. "I bet it would be worth every minute of the crash and burn."

Jensen was fairly sure it wouldn't be. Not with that overabundant arrogance reigning supreme. She ran damp palms down the skirt of her sleek silver dress, a movement that got her a frown from the showrunner. There were a million reasons Cristiano Vitale could be here, she reasoned. He could be in town on business. He might know someone in attendance. Except, she conceded, this appearance *was* out of the ordinary for him, because rumor had it, he was too busy making the sweeping behind-the-scenes changes at FV she'd quietly applauded if the brand she'd loved ever since she was a teenager were to survive.

The show manager gave them the two-minute warning. Jensen pulled in a steadying breath, attempting to mentally psyche herself up when her legs felt like lead. *Twenty minutes* and this would all be over. All she had to do was put one foot in front of the other until she'd finished her three wardrobe changes and the show was done. She'd give the after-party a ghostly quick visit, get out of here early and get some much-needed sleep before her flight to Paris.

She took her place at the entrance to the stage, the first in line to kick off the night. Absorbed the magnificent, soaring architecture of the gorgeous Gothic hall with its sweeping arches, atmospheric stained-glass windows and five-inch-thick stone walls, lit in purple and silver tonight. The blinding light and the intimate narrow runway, which made putting a foot out of place an inherently disastrous mistake. The packed, buzzing crowd.

"Do some reconnaissance," Lucy whispered in her ear. "Find out where he is."

She would prefer not to. In fact, practically swaying on her feet with exhaustion, she was just hoping to keep her feet on the runway, rather than end up in the crowd.

The music slowly increased in volume, and the lights went down. Adrenaline moved through her veins, transporting her to that magical place where it was just her and the runway ahead. Nothing else. And then, her cue came.

She stepped into the spotlight at the top of the runway. Waited for the crowd to register her appearance with a dramatic pause. Then, as the music reached its peak, she started down the stone walkway with her patented confident prowl, hips sashaying as her long stride ate up the distance, a feminine flourish to her walk her agent liked to call her secret power.

When she reached the end of the runway, she stopped to pose, focusing on showing off the gorgeous dress from every angle, every shimmer of the fabric revealing yet another carefully executed detail. Planted in the space for an extended moment as flashbulbs went off in a blinding cascade, she finally saw *him*.

Seated in the front row alongside the executive director of the show, she felt the full force of Cristiano Vitale's electric-blue gaze as it hit her like a sledgehammer. He moved it over her from tip to toe, taking in the exquisitely designed dress with an utterly unreadable look. But it was his eyes that revealed the barely banked emotion fueling him. He was *furious. Incensed.* She could feel it radiating from him like an invisible force. And suddenly, she knew it was no coincidence he was here. Not even a chance.

Her stomach plunged, a flurry of goose bumps unearthing themselves over the surface of her skin. She was in deep trouble. And all she could do was face the music. Literally.

Blowing a kiss to the crowd, she made her way back up the runway for her wardrobe change. Managed to somehow make it through the rest of the show under the force of that furious, cerulean-blue gaze that watched her unblinkingly from the front row. When someone passed her a message after the show that Cristiano Vitale wanted to see her, she wasn't surprised, although that didn't make her any less nervous. She felt a bit sick, actually.

She considered slipping out the back door and not dealing with it at all. But that would redefine the term *career-limiting move*. Could perhaps be a *career*-ending *move*.

Best to get it over with. She left her makeup on, because she felt less vulnerable with it, changed into the gauzy metallic olive-green dress the designer she was wearing tonight had chosen for her, and left her hair loose, falling down her back in a silken cloud. Surveying herself in the mirror, she cursed her unusual pallor before deciding it was the best she was going to do with Cristiano Vitale waiting. At least he couldn't see inside to the knots that were tying her stomach into a ball.

Picking up her clutch, she descended the stairs to the magnificent old crypts located directly beneath the Great Hall, where the after-party was being held.

Usually, this would be the time where she could relax and kick off the stress of the high-intensity evening, but tonight she couldn't seem to do it, her eyes scanning the crowd for a glimpse of Cristiano Vitale.

It didn't take long. If her gaze hadn't been drawn to him, she might simply have followed every other set of female eyes in the room to the man standing leaning against one of the thick pillars that swept up into a series of graceful arches that adorned the room. Dressed in a dark gray three-piece suit that bucked the trend of black in the room, the dove-white shirt he wore gleamed starkly against his swarthy skin, his silver-gray tie the epitome of elegant European style.

Which didn't end with the suit. It was there in the perfectly cut, raven-dark hair slicked back from the hard lines of his face. In the handmade gold cuff links at his wrists. The relaxed, indolent posture that screamed power from its very restraint. Hands thrust into his pockets, the fine material of his suit pulled taut across powerful muscle, he was the most virile, arresting man she'd ever encountered. Smoking hot in a way few women could resist.

JENNIFER HAYWARD 21

Okay, she admitted shakily, so Millie had been right. He was outrageously good-looking. The only explanation for the mind block she'd been suffering was that she'd blanked it all out at the shoot, because it had been the only way she could maintain her concentration in the face of his extremely distracting presence.

She forced herself to move toward him on legs that suddenly didn't seem to want to work, stopping when she was a mere few inches from him. "Cristiano," she greeted him.

"Jensen," he acknowledged with a dip of his head, the light rasp of his accent working its way under the layers of her skin. He bent his head to brush his mouth against her cheek in a typically Italian caress. Which didn't feel in any way typical to her. It felt nerve jarring and unsettling, in a way she'd never experienced before. She sucked in a breath as he did the same with her other cheek and stepped back. His sapphire gaze fixed on hers, penetrating and unyielding.

He moved it over her from head to foot, taking in the sexy semitransparent dress that revealed a daring amount of bare flesh. Her skin felt singed as he cataloged the deep vee of the provocative neckline and the clever cutouts designed to show off her curves, an involuntary sizzle rippling through her as he returned his gaze to her face, a dark glitter in his eyes. For a split second, she could almost imagine the fury she'd absorbed from him onstage was tinged with another emotion entirely—a pure, unadulterated chemistry that zigzagged between them, so potent it shook her to her toes as it reverberated through her.

Which she must have imagined, she thought shakily, as his long dark lashes swept down to veil his blue gaze, because she was sure anger was his predominant emotion. Which made her wish desperately the designer had chosen something a little more sedate for the evening. Less vamp and more...*sophisticated,* so she didn't feel so exposed. But it was too late for that now.

She straightened her shoulders and tipped her head back to look up at him, refusing to be intimidated. "I—I had no idea you would be here," she stammered, annoyed at herself for the nervous tip of her hand. "That anyone from FV would be here."

"I was in town on business for the day. Richard Worthington is a friend of mine." He took a sip of his drink, savoring the spirit before he leaned back against the wall, his eyes on her. "I also thought that, given the string of headlines you've managed to generate over the past few weeks, it might be a good idea if we chatted."

The ball of nerves in her stomach knotted itself tighter. There it was. The displeasure she'd known was coming. He wasn't wasting time getting to the point, but then again, he didn't strike her as the type of man who would. He was all business, all the time, from what she'd heard. And then, there was that air of combustive energy that seemed to surround him like a glove.

She swallowed past the sudden constriction in her throat. "The media like to blow things up into something they're not. I, unfortunately, seem to be one of their favorite targets."

"Because you make yourself one. You've built a career out of it."

"Well...yes." She sank her teeth into her lip, caught off guard by the scythe-sharp assessment. "That might be true of the past, but not so much of the present."

He arched a dark brow at her. "So you and your entourage didn't rack up a thirty-thousand-euro bar tab in Monaco on a wild night of partying in which hotel rooms were trashed? That was someone else and not you *nude* in the middle of the Trevi Fountain at midnight... A body double, perhaps? And clearly, the drink-throwing incident with the princess was simply a fabric of the press's imagination?"

Hot color doused her cheeks. The bar tab had been her mother's, but that wasn't something she could share, because her mother's drinking and gambling problem was a deep, dark Davis family secret she and her sisters had concealed for over a decade. Nor could she reveal that the fountain stunt had been a product of her mother's desperation, because the fact remained she'd done it. She had no excuse for her behavior. Nor could she deny the drink the princess had thrown at her, though it was hardly the catfight the press had reported it as. It had been more along the lines of Juliana hysterically shouting at her that she'd ruined her life and losing her entire rationality, before she'd thrown the cocktail at her. Which wasn't an impressive explanation either without the accompanying backstory.

Which left an apology her only viable option. "It was an error in judgment," she said quietly. "The past few weeks. You can expect nothing but professionalism from me from now on."

Once the firestorm faded.

Cristiano Vitale gave her a long look. "I think we've gotten to the point where I'm not willing to take your word for it, Ms. Davis. In case you weren't aware of it, I am in the middle of a massive transformation of the FV brand. A transformation which relies on the sanctity and reputation of FV's legacy—a legacy you are currently dragging through the mud."

Jensen blanched. "I wouldn't put it quite like that. Some would say any publicity is good publicity."

"Not in this case," he slung back, voice razor-sharp. "I was willing to overlook some of your usual antics, because I get that the buzz builds your influencer status and by default my own brand. But there is a line, Ms. Davis. Representatives of the FV brand *do not* drink themselves under the table. They do not indulge in excessively public affairs with royalty, nor do they *debase* national monuments in the country in which Francesco Vitale was founded."

Now he was the one embellishing the narrative. No one had drunk themselves under the table in Monaco, though she was fairly sure her mother had been a mere drink or two away from it. Why she'd felt compelled to drop everything and swoop in and clean up. Nor was she having an affair with Alexandre. In fact, right now she'd rather strangle him. But she was fairly certain, taking in Cristiano Vitale's glittering blue gaze, that providing explanations or arguing the point was likely to have little effect.

"Like I said," she said quietly, "it won't happen again."

"And then," he forged on, as if she hadn't spoken at all, "there are the FV responsibilities you have blown off over the past few weeks. Responsibilities that are written into your contract."

She frowned, confused. "I'm sorry…what responsibilities?"

"The American Music Awards after-party for one. An extremely important brand partnership for FV you've now damaged. Antonio was mortified. Then you blew off Pascal's fittings for the new collection. Which should have been your number one priority."

She bit her lip. *That* felt like a slap in the face, given how hard she'd worked for FV over the past year, killing herself to ensure its success. All the times she'd gone above and beyond her mandate to ensure a campaign received the visibility it needed to catch fire. But right now, she needed to choose her words carefully. "I was so exhausted the night of the AMA party I could barely stand up. I had to be in Tokyo for a show the next day. I skipped the party, yes, but I did the awards as per my contract, a photo of which made it to the front page of the *New York Times*. As for Pascal's fittings," she concluded, "we only pushed them a few days."

"Days we do not have with a print and television campaign waiting in the wings. The most expensive in the company's history...in the *industry's* history. There is no room for error here, Ms. Davis, something you don't seem to understand."

She absorbed his impenetrable expression. How immovable he was. "I have other commitments I need to meet, Cristiano. We all need to be flexible here."

His expression darkened into combustible blue fire. "We are five weeks away from the launch of Pascal's collection—a collection the world will be watching. The campaign for which has not yet been finished. *You* are the face of the FV brand—a job I am paying you twenty million dollars a year for. The largest contract of its kind in the business right now. There *are* no other priorities."

She absorbed the fury coming off of him. She got it— she did. She hadn't been prioritizing her FV work of late as much as she should have been. But what could she do? She'd been fighting the impossibility of her schedule for months, a schedule Tatiana had jam-packed, because her agent had made it clear she needed to make hay while the sun shone. Who knew how long she'd be on top? And quite frankly, she needed the money if her mother was to keep her house in Beverly Hills. But, she conceded, the impossibility of it all weighting her limbs, she also needed to keep Francesco Vitale—her marquee client—happy.

"I will talk to Tatiana," she offered in her most conciliatory voice. "We'll come up with a plan."

"Actually, I already have a plan," he dismissed, "one that will extricate us from this mess you've landed us in." He tipped his glass at her, the dark amber liquid glinting in the light. "My PR department has developed a strategy to rehabilitate your image. To do *damage control*. A couple of FV-sponsored charitable events over the next couple of weeks with a global reach that will cast you in a better light. Something for the press to feast on rather than their current diet."

"That's not going to knock them off course," Jensen protested. "It would be naive to think so. It would be better to let this die out like it undoubtedly will." *Eventually.* "And, besides," she tacked on, "I really don't think I can pack anything more into the next couple of weeks. I have multiple assignments to do before I fly to Milan, then a shoot in Cannes, the—"

He waved a hand at her, cutting her off. "Your agent is going to cancel those so you can focus on FV."

Her jaw dropped. *What? Tatiana was doing what?*

She couldn't possibly cancel those assignments. One of them was a show she was headlining in Shanghai for one of her favorite lingerie clients. Not to mention key assignments in Berlin and Cannes—one of them for an up-and-coming swimsuit brand she'd just signed on with. Business she needed to keep.

"That isn't possible," she said in as calm a voice as she could manufacture. "My clients are depending on me. They can't possibly replace me this late in the game."

"Clearly they will have to. You are the one blowing off the assignments, not me." He forged on, as if he hadn't just thrown a grenade at her. "The rest of the plan," he expanded, "is that you will travel back to Milan with me tonight. You will stay on my Lake Como estate where we are shooting the collection, out of the media eye, a level of discretion my security team will ensure. There will not be one more photograph, one more stunt, one more *indiscretion* before this launch, or I will personally cancel your contract so fast it will make your head spin."

Her stomach plunged to the floor. *She couldn't believe he was doing this.* Her rational brain told her he couldn't do it—that he would never do it given everything he'd invested in her. She *was* the brand right now. But another part of her was afraid he would. That challenging Cristiano Vitale in this moment would be a bad idea given the ruthless business-focused decisions he'd been making of late. Another of those career-limiting moves she didn't want to consider.

She set her gaze on his, eyes beseeching. "This isn't necessary. The headlines will stop, Cristiano, I promise. I can make it all work."

"It's already done." His gaze glinted, hard like polished sapphire. "This is the deal, Ms. Davis. Take it or leave it. I would advise," he suggested, a warning note in his voice, "you think very carefully before you reply. Because if you imagine I am bluffing, I can assure you that I am not. You are at the heart of my campaign. At the heart of the brand. I will do whatever I need to do to make sure you are in some kind of reasonable shape to deliver on everything you've promised. Trust me on this."

She stared at him, dismay sinking through her. He had just thrown the one thing at her she couldn't afford to lose—the contract she'd worked her entire career for. Not to mention the knock to her reputation she would suffer if she did lose it, a stain on her track record she could never erase. And then there was the fact that her powerful New York agent had apparently already weighed in—a decision she wished desperately she'd consulted her on. Which left her with no options.

"I clearly have no choice," she said evenly, meeting Cristiano Vitale's vibrant blue gaze.

"No," he said matter-of-factly, "you don't. We leave in an hour. Do what you need to do."

CHAPTER TWO

JENSEN WATCHED THE twinkling lights of London disappear as the sleek, luxurious jet climbed high into the night sky, rendering the world below a miniaturized replica of itself. Her head was still spinning from the events of the night, her equilibrium not so easily restored as the tiny jet had achieved in its quick climb above the clouds. *Freaking out* more accurately described her current state of mind.

They had stayed at the party long enough to make the perfunctory rounds and engage in the requisite small talk she'd needed to do on behalf of her clients, before they'd left via the back exit of the venue, thereby avoiding the throngs of press at the front. From there, they'd made a quick stop at her hotel to retrieve her things before continuing on to Luton airport, where they were to fly out of.

It had all happened with the rapid-fire efficiency the FV CEO was clearly used to. Cristiano had spent the entire ride to the airport on a call with Brazil, Portuguese rolling off his tongue as if it were his mother language, followed by a conversation with someone in LA, in which he'd plowed through a list of issues the subsidiary was facing with a razor-sharp intelligence and problem-solving ability that left her dizzy. When he'd closed off a conversation with China with a few sentences of fluent

Mandarin, she'd observed the exchange with disbelief. Was there any language the man didn't speak?

She would have been impressed if she weren't consumed by the repercussions of his autocratic behavior on her career, and her worry about the impact it would have. She'd called Tatiana from the airport, searching for solutions. But her agent had simply restated the facts at hand. Cristiano Vitale was not happy with her recent headlines. He was her largest client and she had to keep him happy. End of story.

"Do whatever he wants for the next five weeks," her agent had advised, "until the launch. I'll deal with the rest."

Except this was her career. *Her* reputation. Her agent could likely reschedule the shoots she had planned, but Shanghai was another story. She either walked in the show or she forfeited the job to someone else. Not an option when she'd worked so hard to land the assignment. When *reputation*, as her agent was so fond of saying, was everything in this business.

Her chest clenched, her fingers tightening around the mug of tea she held. Her career had always been her anchor—the one thing that had protected her when things fell apart, as they inevitably did in her life. She could not, *would not*, put that in jeopardy. Which meant she had to convince Cristiano she could manage all of this without him resorting to such drastic measures.

Her gaze bounced across the table, to where he sat opposite her in the luxuriously appointed seating area. Eyes on his laptop, his concentration complete, he looked formidably unapproachable, having stripped off his dark suit jacket to reveal the dove-white shirt, shirtsleeves pushed up to expose corded, muscular forearms. An impressive display that didn't end with those amazing arms, the fine material of his dark suit trousers emphasizing the equally powerful muscles of his thighs.

As intimidating as Millie had pegged him to be, he was also undeniably gorgeous, what was more than a five o'clock shadow darkening his lean cheeks, his generous, sensual mouth softening the impossibly hard lines of his face. And then there were those eyes, the darkest, most vivid blue she'd ever seen. A woman could drown in those if she let herself and not ever want to call for help.

Good God, she thought, summoning her rationality as a wave of primal heat coursed through her. So he was *manly* in the way Millie had described, far more attractive than the whipcord-lean male models she worked with, who never did it for her. *This* was not the way to a clear head. To the strategic thinking she clearly needed to possess if she was going to talk her way out of this mess.

She eyed his recently filled coffee cup, searching for a way to break the ice. "You're not afraid that's going to keep you up all night?" she murmured.

He set the coffee cup down, those incredible blue eyes moving to hers. "We *are* going to be up half the night. I might as well be productive with my time."

A state of affairs he clearly interpreted as her fault, she absorbed, surveying the faint traces of irritation creasing the edges of his mouth. He was still furious with her, that was obvious. It had been there in the brusque way he'd treated her ever since they'd left the party, using the minimum number of words necessary to communicate. A wall she needed to get past if she was going to rightside the situation.

"I apologize about the press," she said quietly. "I know this is not the type of coverage you are looking for, Cristiano. But I promise you, there is very little truth to any of it. It's all been exaggerated way out of proportion. It will blow over before long, I'm sure of it."

"You think so?" He picked up a stack of paper and tossed it on the table in front of her. "My evening press clips. *Gaining* steam is more how I'd describe it."

She scanned the headline of the story on top.

Palace Readying a Statement to Deny Playboy Alexandre's Wild Love Life

Read on, through the first paragraph, which detailed an inside source at the palace who'd revealed the royal family would ask for the prince's privacy as he and Juliana "worked through their relationship." The same source who referred to her as a "diversion" for the prince, who couldn't possibly be taken seriously.

That hurt. Her stomach plunged, lodging itself somewhere above her twisting insides. But more than that, it was *ridiculous*. This had gotten out of hand. Completely out of hand. She flipped through the articles beneath, each more ludicrous than the last, earmarking her as the catalyst for the destruction of the rumored royal match. Jensen Davis, modern-day Scarlet Woman. *Man-wrecker extraordinaire*. The woman who would bring the royals down.

She bit her lip, tasting the salty tang of blood. This had gone far enough. She was through being the fall guy for her mother and Alexandre. Not when it came at the expense of her career. Her *reputation*.

She set her cup down and sat up straight, squaring her shoulders, her eyes on Cristiano. "I am not having an affair with Alexandre Santeval. He is a good friend of mine. The episode in the fountain was a stunt for my mother's show—one Alexandre went along with because he and

Juliana had gotten into a fight and he wanted to make her jealous. I had no idea that he was going to take it this far. If I had, I never would have done it."

A skeptical look crossed his face. "So this is all the prince's fault?"

"No," she conceded, her chin dipping. "It was mine as well. I agreed to do the stunt. I bear responsibility for it, too."

His expression darkened. "And it didn't strike you as being *unwise*, given your current commitments? That this type of juvenile schoolyard stunt was a bad idea?"

She swallowed past the bitter taste of regret that stained her mouth. Yes, it *had* occurred to her that it was a bad idea. She'd signed off those stupid stunts when she'd left her mother's show. But she couldn't go that far with the truth. Not without revealing her mother's business, something Veronica Davis would never forgive her for.

She sank her teeth deeper into her lip. Eyed him. "I was exhausted. I don't always make the best decisions when I'm in that state of mind. Clearly," she acknowledged, for good measure, "this was not a good one."

Cristiano regarded her for a long moment, as if he was debating whether or not to believe her. She thought maybe he'd decided it was inconsequential when he finally spoke. "Good thing, then, that we have cleared your schedule and you will now be able to get some rest in Milan. Perhaps it will improve your decision-making skills."

Frustration bubbled up inside her. He was *impossible*. Not budging at all. "Tatiana," she elaborated, "thinks she can reschedule the shoots I have planned. But Shanghai is a live show—one I'm headlining. I was looking at this," she said, picking up the PR plan he'd handed her in the car. "There's no reason why I can't do Shanghai and keep my FV commitments. It's only one day."

"It's not one day," he replied, a hard edge to his voice. "It's two days of travel at a minimum, then the day of the show. Which will leave you jet-lagged and exhausted— the exact opposite of what all this is meant to accomplish. To allow you to focus on your FV work the way you should be. Not to mention the strategy of removing you from the media eye—perhaps my stronger reasoning at the moment."

She eyed the impenetrable terrain of his face. "Cristiano," she murmured, letting her dark lashes flutter down over her eyes in a gesture that always, without fail worked. "I understand that you are angry. I have apologized more than once for my actions. But I cannot miss this show. If I do, my reputation will suffer. Imagine if this were me, reneging on a million-dollar show with FV. How would you feel?"

"Furious," he agreed evenly. "Exactly as I do right now, given you've thrown my entire advertising schedule into chaos." He arched a dark brow at her. "Perhaps the better question is why you keep doing this to yourself. I've seen your schedule… Tatiana reviewed it with me. You would have to be superhuman to pull that off. *I* have a crazy schedule and it far supersedes mine. And for what?" he asked, flicking an elegant, Rolex-clad wrist at her. "So that you can host the entire French Riviera at one of your wild parties?"

Ooh. A bolt of heat moved through her. She was going to kill her mother. She truly was. She hiked her jaw higher. "That was a onetime thing. And the reason I work so hard is not to party, it's to protect myself. A top model only has a few years at her peak, then it's downhill from there. It's only smart business sense to maximize my earning potential."

"While you neglect your responsibilities and put those relationships in jeopardy?" He shook his head, an infuriated look on his face. "If you are so intent on protecting your career, I suggest you get a handle on your schedule. Rethink your current trajectory. Draw some lines between your personal and professional lives. Because I didn't sign up to put a Davis on my payroll. I signed up for the model with the power to transform my brand. *That's* what I want from you over the next few weeks."

A feeling of complete impotence swept over her. She'd attempted to do exactly that when she'd finally walked away from the show—to *not* be a Davis anymore. She'd spent her entire life at the mercy of the show and its scripted plotlines with utterly no power of her own. Yet now, when she'd finally cut those ties, her mother was still pulling her puppet strings from afar, to the detriment of everything Jensen held dear.

Her nails dug into her palms. *This* was the last time she allowed her to do it. The queen of manipulation was no longer going to orchestrate her life, no matter what sob story she threw at her. But first, she acknowledged, she needed to clean up the mess her mother had created. *Again.*

"You know what I've done for the brand," she said quietly, her eyes fixed on his. "That I've made it hip again. *Buzz-worthy.* That I've gone above and beyond the call of duty to do so. You might consider cutting me some slack."

"Give me a reason to do so," he returned in a voice hard as flint, "and I might consider it."

Cristiano observed Jensen as she curled up in the chair opposite him, an embattled look on her beautiful face. She had batted those long, dark lashes at him, fully expecting him to capitulate—the usual reaction she undoubtedly elicited from men—and allow her to jet halfway across the world to China, as if he hadn't already made it clear what her responsibilities were for the next five weeks. How *unhappy* he was with the current situation.

She had chutzpah, that was for certain. And maybe, he conceded, eyeing those luminous dark eyes and impossibly long lashes, she'd had reason to believe it could have worked. He'd have to have been deaf, dumb and blind not to admit she was beautiful. It had been there in that initial flash of attraction between them at the party tonight.

His gaze slid over her, curled up in the seat. She'd removed the dramatic stage makeup she'd been wearing. Without it, she looked about eighteen rather than twenty-six, her high cheekbones and full mouth set off by a flawless honey-hued complexion that made makeup unnecessary. And then there was the perfect voluptuous body beneath the silky material of the soft white T-shirt and black yoga pants she wore. The long legs that went on forever.

He would have to be far less of the man that he was not to imagine them wrapped around him in a hot, no-holds-barred encounter. She'd sold that particular fantasy the first time he'd ever laid eyes on her in that shoot. It was why he'd hired her—because he'd wanted to wrap that all-American sex appeal around his brand. Which didn't mean he was going to allow her to play him like she'd clearly done so many others.

He studied the shadows beneath those glittering, dark eyes. One minute she was the brilliant business-woman he'd seen flashes of, the next the wild child the papers liked to capture her as. And then, there were those glimpses of vulnerability he swore he saw, so fleeting they were there one minute and gone the next.

What must it have been like to grow up as a Davis? In front of America, with your entire life on display? With no buffer from the world. He couldn't actually imagine, given the strict, traditional upbringing he'd had. Perhaps it explained her inability to make good decisions. Not helped by the fact that she'd had two of the greatest stars Hollywood had ever known as parents, notoriously emotional, dramatic personalities who couldn't have made good role models.

Which was all inconsequential, he reminded himself. Even if she hadn't engaged in a very public affair with Alexandre Santeval, she'd still gone along with the stunt, recklessly putting her reputation and the reputation of his brand at risk. Not an option, when he'd spent his entire career at FV attempting to pull his legacy out of the ashes and restore it to its former glory. When his grandfather, who had been both mentor and father to him after he and his sister Ilaria had lost their parents in a boating accident as teenagers, had entrusted him with the future of an Italian legend. When not one piece of his plan to reinvent FV could go wrong without the whole thing tumbling down around him like a house of cards. A pressure he went to bed with every night and woke to every morning.

He set his gaze on the woman opposite him, her dark eyes fixed on the night sky beyond the window. She was on some kind of a spiral—one he was determined to put an end to using whatever methods he deemed necessary. Because there was no way he was going to let her run helter-skelter through his life, causing more of that particular brand of mayhem she engendered. Not with everything he'd built coming to fruition at this very moment, a crucial few weeks in which he couldn't afford to take his eyes off the ball.

She was clearly incapable of taking care of herself. So he was going to have to do it for her. Even if it killed him in the process.

He worked through the next couple of hours before they landed in Milan. Jensen slept through most of the flight, waking up for the transfer to the helicopter that would fly them up to Lake Como before promptly falling asleep again, a Herculean effort given the noise in the aircraft. He let her sleep, because it looked like she hadn't done so in weeks, waking her when they approached Villa Barberini, situated on a hill above the western shore of the lake.

Magnificent in the late-night hour, the lights from the estate spilled out onto the dark, silent water. Built by an Italian count who'd constructed the spectacular thirty-thousand-square-foot showpiece to entertain his many famous guests, it sprawled across the hill from high up in the village of Moltrasio all the way down to the lake's shore.

Constructed of thick layers of ancient stone, the elegant cream-stuccoed villa was surrounded by magnificent gardens preserved exactly as they had been centuries ago, olive trees flourishing alongside ancient date palms and lemon trees. But most sensational of all was the view of the lake and the mountains from every vantage point on the property.

Jensen blinked in the light, rubbing her eyes with her fists. "I must look a sight."

Cristiano eyed the full curve of her mouth, pillowy soft in the filtered light. The darkness of her sleep-softened eyes, her chestnut-colored hair spilling over her shoulders in a tumbled, silken swath. She looked exactly like the type of woman a man would want to wake up to in his bed. In an albeit spectacular fantasy. Although sleep, he conceded, a series of carnal images flashing through his head, would be the last thing on his mind.

His gaze met hers in the dim light, and he was fairly sure he hadn't wiped the erotic images out of his head fast enough, her dark eyes widening as a current of electricity passed between them. It hung there, pulsing on the air in the intimate confines of the space, until his pilot broke the silence, announcing his intention to land.

"You look fine," he murmured, a rough note to his voice. "You should buckle up."

Jensen nodded, ripped her gaze from his and fumbled with the belt around her waist. When her awkward attempts to tighten it proved fruitless in the thick tension between them, he reached over and did it himself, inhaling the tantalizing scent of her perfume as he did.

She was some kind of sorceress, he thought, as the helicopter set itself down on the landing pad near the main house, whipping up the wind in the silver-leafed olive trees. Because no way was this logical thinking. It had clearly been too long since he'd slept himself.

Once it was safely on the ground, he jumped out of the helicopter, its blades still whirring a slowing pattern. Wary about Jensen's ability to navigate the step in the darkness given her fatigue and half-asleep state, he caught her, hands around her waist, and lowered her to the ground when she misjudged the depth of the step, a smothered sound of surprise leaving her lips as she pitched forward.

"Sorry," she breathed, the warmth of her breath skating across his cheek. "I got a bit dizzy. I haven't slept much the past few days."

His hand splayed across her bottom, holding her securely. He didn't let go immediately, afraid from the way she swayed she didn't quite have her legs underneath her. The intimate fit of her lush curves against the hard length of him did something strange to his senses. Heated his blood in a way he hadn't felt in ages. And suddenly, those erotic images he'd envisioned waking up to replayed themselves in his head in vivid Technicolor detail. Except this time, he knew what she felt like, and he wasn't certain it was an image he could get out of his head.

Which was *folle*, he breathed, because she was trouble, and this was the last thing he should be thinking. Moving his hand up to a more respectable position at her waist, he set her away from him. That inconvenient chemistry flared between them, dark eyes fixed on blue, smoking up the air between them for a long, infinitesimal second, before she slicked her tongue over her lips in a nervous movement and stepped back, his arm dropping away from her waist.

"Thank you," she murmured in a husky voice. "That could have been a nasty fall."

He doused the heat snaking through his body with a superhuman effort, because *this* was not happening between them. *He* was here to enforce the rules. Nothing more.

"The last thing I need is you walking down the runway in a cast. It would be bad for business." He picked up her bag along with his own, ignored the way her jaw had dropped open and carried it toward the house, where he introduced her to his housekeeper, Filomena, who had waited up for them. Introductions complete, he sent Filomena off to bed, then showed Jensen the way down the lamplit path toward her accommodations.

Located within walking distance of the main house, the small dwelling sat directly across the vibrant blue depths of a spotlit butterfly-shaped pool, fed by a waterfall that cascaded softly into the far end. Constructed of floor-to-ceiling windows that maximized the view and fully equipped with everything she would need for a multi-week stay, lamplight poured from the windows onto the sparkling surface of the water.

"The pool house," Jensen murmured, surveying its proximity to the main villa. "You truly do mean to babysit me, don't you?"

"Si," he murmured, "You've driven me to it."

She cocked a brow at him. "Aren't you afraid I'll cramp your style? What if you have a hot date?"

"I will manage." He set her bag down on the porch and propped himself up against one of the pillars, which rose gracefully to the roof. "Here are the rules. You will remain on this property, where you will carry out whatever task my marketing team requires of you, which includes following through on the PR plan in its entirety. Someone will be by to brief you on it in the morning. Filomena will be at your disposal for anything you require while you're here. Simply ask her, and it will be done."

"Where is the rest of the crew staying?"

"In the cottages near the lake. If you have free time," he continued, "you are welcome to use any of the facilities on the estate. If you swim, however, please notify a member of the staff so they can keep an eye on you. And," he added with emphasis, "if you could keep your clothes on, it would be much appreciated. For the staff's sake."

And for his, to be honest.

Her full mouth twisted. "I will do my best. Sometimes I just find myself with the *need* to disrobe. I can't always catch myself before it happens."

He eyed the dark glitter in her eyes. She was baiting him. And while a part of him would love to pursue it, considering the Y chromosomes he possessed, another more sensible part of him recognized it for the folly it was. He found nothing about the fountain episode amusing, nor should she, given that *Hollywood Divas* had been fined in excess of a quarter of a million euros for the episode, which had left all Italians unamused. Although he suspected it had been more than worth it from the show's perspective, given the massive ratings it had engendered.

"Make yourself at home," he said, shutting down that very male part of his brain. "Invite a friend or two over. You are free to leave the estate to do an errand, provided you have Saul, my bodyguard, with you. He will make sure you are protected from the photographers. You will not," he underscored, "under any circumstance, throw any parties on the estate or use any illegal drugs. Nor will you go clubbing or undertake any other activity that will put you in the limelight, unless it is specifically outlined in the PR plan. When I said no headlines, I meant *no* headlines." He set a hard gaze on her. *"Capisci?"*

She eyed him. "I don't take drugs."

"I know the scene, Jensen. It's full of them."

"Not with me. *Ever.* It's the quickest way for a model to ruin her looks."

He thought she might be telling the truth, because her dark, lustrous eyes were clear, her thick, wavy hair, the color of darkest cocoa, lustrous, as was the unmarred expanse of perfect, sun-kissed skin that covered every inch of her. Which only brought to mind what she'd look like with nothing on at all.

"Bene," he murmured, refusing to let his mind wander. "Then it won't be a problem."

She crossed her arms over her chest and leaned back against the railing. "What about Pascal and the fittings? Will I travel to FV for those?"

"Pascal is going to come here and do them, starting tomorrow afternoon. It will save him moving the clothing back and forth for the shoot. Which begins on Wednesday," he qualified, "followed by the television commercial, which they expect will take a few days to shoot. We are cutting it close on all of it, so make sure you get some rest. It's going to be a busy few weeks."

Her lips firmed, and he got the impression she barely resisted rolling her eyes. "I'm used to that," she murmured. "Is there anything else you'd like to decree, while you're so clearly on a roll? Anything else that would keep you happy?"

"Si," he returned in a soft, unmistakably commanding tone. "What I would *like* is to hear from my staff that you are going above and beyond to accommodate their needs. That their stress levels have been greatly reduced over the next few days. And *then*, I will be happy."

Fiery dark eyes rested on his, but she wisely abstained from perpetuating this battle between them further. He pushed away from the wall, intent on getting some sleep, before the lack of it made him partake in any other irrational thoughts that were wholly unwise.

"Buona notte, Jensen. Get some sleep. You're going to need it."

CHAPTER THREE

"Santo cielo. You've lost at least ten pounds... What have you been doing? Not eating at all?"

Jensen stood completely still as Pascal Ferrari stuck yet another pin into the midnight-blue gown she was wearing, a dark frown on his expressive face. She knew she'd lost weight. She'd been too stressed and working too much over the past few weeks to eat proper meals, which was revealing itself in the gaping fabric at the back of the dress. A state of affairs that had, unfortunately, meant that quite a few pieces of Pascal's collection had required alteration, not ideal at this stage of the game.

"Mi dispiace," she murmured, flashing him a guilty look. *I'm sorry.* "My schedule has been nuts. I'm too tired to eat when I get home, I have breakfast, and then it starts all over again."

"I guess," the designer exhaled on a pained breath as he affixed yet another pin to the dress, "I should be grateful you didn't blow in at the eleventh hour, expecting me to fix it. I had visions of a week spent pulling the shoot out of the fire."

Jensen sank her teeth into her lip. Absorbed the strain written across Pascal's charismatic features. He'd nearly wept with relief when she'd appeared for the fittings, his happiness at finding a break in her schedule palpable.

Which had made her feel awful. He had the weight of the world on his shoulders with his first collection as the new design chief of FV set to debut in weeks. The shoes he had to fill in Francesco's as big as they got. But she'd been too overbooked and overwhelmed to even consider what this must have been doing to him—one of her absolute favorite designers. The pressure it had put him under. So she'd tried to make it up to him the best way she could.

When they hadn't been shooting the collection in gorgeous lakeside locations on the Vitale estate, they'd been finalizing the lineup piece by piece so it would be perfect for the shoot and show. Which had every muscle and bone in her body aching from the interminably long days spent in front of the camera, followed by these sessions with Pascal.

It had gone some way toward assuaging the guilt she'd felt toward shirking her duties. But it was doing little to alleviate the anxiety eating away at her insides when it came to her career. Tatiana had managed to reschedule her shoot in Paris, but Berlin had to go ahead without her, and Cannes, an assignment for an up-and-coming swimsuit brand, was still a question mark, given the date couldn't be altered and her client didn't want anyone else. Not helped by the fact that her American lingerie client had hired Ariana Lordes, a Brazilian superstar in the making, to take her place headlining the show in Shanghai—a highly visible replacement that had everyone talking.

It was unnerving to lose the job, given how hard she'd worked for it. The buzz about Ariana was immense, and she couldn't help but feel insecure. What if her client, who hadn't been happy at all with her last-minute cancellation, loved Ariana? What if they decided they liked her *better*? Not helped by all the rumor and innuendo over why she'd been replaced, which she hadn't been able to comment on at all.

The only thing she knew for sure was that in the cut-throat, fast-paced world of high fashion modeling, there was always another girl waiting in the wings, ready to take her place, a prospect that had left her with an ever-present knot in her stomach. So she'd decided to do the only thing she could do: throw herself into her work and focus on the things she *could* control—a tactic that was working with limited effect.

"I'm sorry I've been MIA," she told Pascal as he finished with the back of the dress and sat back on his heels to peruse his work. "I've been trying to do too much. I'll do better."

He waved a hand at her. "You're the world's top model. You are busy. *In demand.* Would I like to have more of you? Of course. But you are a consummate professional when I do have you, and you make magic with my dresses. That's what matters."

"I'm not so sure Cristiano would agree," she said drily. "He's not very happy with me."

He shrugged a shoulder. "Cristiano is under a great deal of pressure right now. He's spent the last eighteen months battling his grandfather and then the board on the way forward. Digging the company out of the dark ages. He's taken a big risk on me. Not to mention having the weight of a national legacy resting on his shoulders."

She was intrigued. "What did Cristiano and Francesco disagree about?"

A wry smile curved his mouth. "What *didn't* they butt heads about? Francesco was old-school. He didn't get the new realities. How the fashion world has changed. The markets we need to capture if this company is to survive." He waved a hand at her. "Look at his opinion of you. He didn't value you as the influencer that you are because he didn't understand the current social climate. Cristiano does."

She absorbed the additional perspective. It was the reason she'd signed on with FV, a brand many would have called a fading star. Because she'd believed in the company's current direction. In Cristiano's plans. In his track record as a brilliant thinker and marketer. But she'd always sensed that Francesco, whom she'd worked closely with until his death three months prior, had not been a fan of hers—an opinion she hadn't seemed able to shake.

"And then there was Francesco and me," Pascal continued, a mischievous sparkle in his dark eyes. "We were just as bad. We rattled the rafters some days."

She frowned. "What did you two disagree about? Francesco chose you as his heir apparent, after all."

He threw up an expressive hand. "Francesco was a rose and I am a garden bursting with outrageous color. He had his vision, I had mine. I knew it would be fine when I eventually took over. Meanwhile," he conceded, his wry smile deepening, "Cristiano had to play referee, which couldn't have been easy for him."

Which, in hindsight, made Cristiano's actions more understandable. His autocratic behavior with her had been infuriating, but she could see, given the pressure he was under, why he might have done it. She had backed him into a corner. Given him no choice. Not that it made what he'd done okay. She was still intent on convincing him to allow her to do Cannes, once she'd demonstrated to him he had nothing to worry about. That she would do her job. She intended to knock his socks off.

As for that strange, inexplicable attraction she'd sensed between them the night they'd arrived? Her mind went back to the moment he'd lifted her down from the helicopter. The heat that had pulsed between them. She would almost have believed she'd imagined it she'd been so exhausted, practically hallucinating by the time her face hit the gazillion-thread-count pillow. Except it had been too palpable, too *real* for her to have conjured it up.

The sensation of his tall, hard body plastered against hers was still imprinted in her head. The spicy, intoxicating male scent of him. It didn't take much for her to imagine him without the clothes in an intimate encounter of another kind. How impressive he would look. Which was insane thinking, because just as he'd clearly turned it off that night, it was ridiculous to even think about it.

He thought her *beneath* him. That was clear. A royal pain in his behind. She would do well to put it out of her head and concentrate on what was important here. Impressing him with her work, so she could get back to her other assignments and undo the dents she'd done to her career.

She looked down as a message buzzed on her phone, sitting on the table. *Her mother.* If a silver lining existed in all of this, it was that here, on Cristiano's fortress of an estate, her mother couldn't get to her. Not that she hadn't tried. She'd called, shortly after Jensen had arrived in Milan, over the moon with the royal buzz. Had proposed a follow-up stunt to the Alexandre story to keep the buzz going for next season. Jensen had told her no, absolutely not. And this time, she'd meant it. She was staying on Cristiano's estate and immersing herself in her work, she'd told her mother, which she desperately needed at the moment.

When Veronica Davis had responded to the whole idea of her staying on Cristiano's exclusive estate with the glee of a genie rubbing her hands together, calling him "beyond delicious" with that Machiavellian brain of hers, Jensen had stopped her in her tracks. Made it clear that Cristiano and her FV work were off-limits, not to be touched under any circumstance. Which didn't mean her mother had listened to her, a worry that percolated in the back of her head. But given that was another of those things she had no control over, all she could do was try to make her mother see how serious she was about it, the part of this she *could* control.

She reached down and swiped the message from the screen without reading it. She was done with her mother. The only thing she planned on doing this evening, given she and Pascal were finishing early for once, was to keep her date with the hot tub outside the pool house, its views of the lake legendary. Which might go some way toward easing some of the wickedly sore muscles in her body so she could actually work tomorrow.

She had just stepped out onto the terrace on a hot, sultry night in Moltrasio, intent on a light dinner and an early night after her epic soak in the Jacuzzi, when a shadow fell over the gray stone tile. She looked up, a smile on her face, expecting it to be Filomena who normally stopped by with news of dinner at around this time. Instead, she found herself face-to-face with Cristiano, dressed in dark jeans and a blue T-shirt, his jet-black hair scraped back from his face as if freshly wet from the shower. The designer jeans hugging the powerful muscles of his thighs, the T-shirt defining the impressive line of his abs, dark stubble shading his jaw, he was blatantly male in a way that stole her breath.

Caught off guard, she pressed the book she'd been about to read to her chest, drawing his attention to the flirty neckline of the rose-colored sundress she wore. Which exposed nothing really, except for an expanse of tanned skin and bare shoulders, yet she somehow felt branded by his dark appraisal, which moved slowly over her, missing nothing.

"Checking up on me?" she murmured, to divert her attention from the warm burst of awareness that moved through her. "Making sure I'm not off lighting up the town? Causing a ruckus? Because I can assure you the only plans I have for this evening are a glass of wine and this book. Very exciting, I know."

His hard mouth quirked. "Actually," he drawled, his rich, lightly accented voice sending a shiver of response through her, "I hear you've been working hard. I thought that since I'm home early tonight, we could have dinner together. Talk about the upcoming week. We have some engagements we are doing together it would be good to discuss. Filomena has prepared a fantastic linguine carbonara. I can promise an equally good bottle of wine to go with it."

Have dinner with him? She eyed him silently. He wasn't wearing that combustive look anymore. He looked relaxed and almost approachable. Amiable, even. Was this a peace offering? And if so, would it be wise for her to reject it?

She chewed on her lip. Could one dinner hurt? Surely she could suffer his infuriating arrogance for an hour or so? Ignore how he looked in jeans and a T-shirt, which took his level of attractiveness from superior to some-where approaching drool-worthy.

"All right," she agreed, "that would be lovely. Where will we eat?"

"On the main terrace." He tipped his head in the di-rection of the house. "Shall we?"

She deposited her book on the table beside the lounger and fell into step beside him on the stone path. Even at five foot nine, she was dwarfed by him, the warm palm he held to her back large and masculine, sinking into her skin and warming her all the way through.

She got the distinct impression that, despite his auto-cratic behavior, he was at his core a gentleman. An opin-ion that was confirmed when he pulled out her chair for her on the torchlit patio and ensured she was seated be-fore he sat down opposite her. Resplendent with a glorious mix of primary colors that spilled from the flowerpots and shrubs along its periphery, the terrace offered a mag-nificent view of the glittering, cerulean-blue lake, bathed in a golden pink shimmer as the sun sank below the mountains.

It was a ridiculously romantic setting. Although clearly this was a business dinner, and Cristiano was merely keeping tabs on her, just as he'd promised he would do. Still, it was hard not to enjoy the spectacular setting and the even better Chianti Filomena poured for them both, its fruity, full-bodied flavor exactly what she needed after a ridiculously long day that had begun at the crack of dawn.

They traded small talk about how the shoot was going, presided over by one of the world's top fashion photog-raphers, and the social media posts she'd been doing to tease the campaign. Cristiano was an excellent conver-sationalist, sharing some of his own plans for the company, smart, strategic ideas that revealed more of that razor-sharp brain of his.

Sprawled in the chair opposite her, the hard, angular bones of his face powerful and perfectly put together in the candlelight, his effortless charisma was so imposingly male it was impossible not to be aware of him on a physical level. To wonder what it would be like to be on a real date with him, with all of that intensity focused on her with an end goal of an entirely different nature. Which made her glad for the small talk they exchanged, so she could attempt to avoid that distracted thinking.

"Speaking of partnerships," he murmured, sitting back in his chair and cradling his wineglass in his hand as Filomena cleared away the main course, "I met with Nicholas Zhang this afternoon."

Nicholas Zhang? Jensen knew Nicholas. Few would not. The consumer goods scion was one of the most powerful businessmen in Asia, his empire ranging from household goods to health products to fashion and beauty. It was why Cristiano would be talking to him, when he could be considered a competitor to FV, that intrigued her.

She arched a brow at him. "You are considering a partnership with him?"

He lifted his glass of wine to his mouth and took a sip. Savored it before he set the glass down. "He is buying a one-billion-dollar stake in Francesco Vitale."

Her eyes widened. FV had been a family-controlled company for fifty years—ever since Francesco had founded it as a young window dresser in Milan. It was a revered Italian fashion powerhouse. *Iconic.* The thought of Cristiano ceding any amount of control over it to a foreign entity seemed inconceivable. "Why?" she breathed.

"Because we don't have the financial ability to square off against the mega giants taking over the industry," he said, matter-of-factly. "This will allow us to do so. It will also offer us unparalleled access to the Asian market, which is critical to our success."

Which made complete sense. The fashion show she'd been slated to do in Shanghai had been for an American label. Everyone wanted to plunder the luxury fashion market, and Asia, with its massive growth opportunities, was the most coveted jewel in the crown. It was, however, a huge departure in strategy for the venerable Francesco Vitale, which had always prided itself on being *above* the industry. Untouchable in its prestige.

"That's a big move," she observed.

"Si," he agreed. "But necessary." He tipped his glass at her, his blue gaze intent. "I need you to do me a favor. Zhang mentioned to me that his sixteen-year-old daughter, Ming Li, is accompanying him to Milan next week. She wants to shop. Attend the Associazione Nazionale della Moda Italiana party with him. She is, in Zhang's words, *obsessed* with you. I thought you could dress her for the party. Take her under your wing. Show her a good time. Within reason," he qualified, with a pointed look. "She does not need to be learning bad behavior from you, although I'm sure you can teach her that in abundance."

She ignored the slight and gave him an intrigued look. "So, you need my *help.*"

"Si." He looked a bit pained as the word crossed his lips. Sensuous, beautiful lips it was hard to keep her eyes off of.

Her head flicked to Cannes, looming less than three weeks away—a pressing issue that had yet to be resolved. "What do I get in return?"

"A gold star for good behavior." He said it with a completely deadpan expression. "You are due a few of those, don't you think?"

"I thought I already had a whole scrapbook full of them with all of the work I've done to build the brand." She eyed him in the candlelight. "You do realize I did an entire behind-the-scenes video at the spring launch that has garnered millions of views? That the press office has been besieged with phone calls about the dress I wore to the AMAs, with people wanting to buy it before it's even out? That I've done double the amount of social media posts I'm contracted to do on behalf of FV in order to ensure the brand's success?"

"I had not realized all of that, no," he murmured. "It is much appreciated, however."

She toyed with the stem of her glass. Decided this was her opportunity to get through to him. "This partnership isn't just a business deal to me, Cristiano. I've loved the brand ever since I was a teenager." A whimsical smile touched her lips. "My mother used to wear Francesco's designs, back in the day, when she was doing pictures. They were elegant, *ethereal*. Sophisticated, yet romantic. I was obsessed with them. I used to play dress-up in them with my sisters. Once," she acknowledged, "I spilled grape juice on one of his couture pieces and my mother nearly blew a gasket. I lost my allowance for weeks. But it was worth it to me."

His hard mouth curved in a rather devastating smile. "So it was a goal to model for FV?"

"The *ultimate* goal. I knew I could help revive the brand. Return it to its former glory. I liked your plans—what you were doing with the company. I even went against my agent's advice to go with Denali instead, because I believed in the brand so much. But for me," she explained, "it's always been about my personal style. I couldn't just wear the FV pieces, I had to make them my own. So I styled them with my own fashion sense, made the look signature Jensen, which resonated with my followers. They've started to see the brand as current again. *Fashion forward*."

He inclined his head. "You have delivered on your promises, I don't disagree. I am merely trying to make sure you continue to deliver on those promises in the way I am paying you to do."

She eyed him quietly. "It's been a rough few weeks, Cristiano. I admit it. There's no question about it. But I've worked my butt off for the brand, and will continue to do so to make this launch a success. And yes, I will help you with Ming Li. But in exchange, I need something from you."

He arched a brow. "Which is?"

"A deal," she murmured. "I help you win Nicholas Zhang and his daughter over, and you let me do my shoot in Cannes."

Cristiano sat back in his chair, observing Jensen from over the rim of his glass. She looked fairly angelic this evening dressed in a pastel-colored sundress, her dark hair caught up in a ponytail, her delicate face free of makeup, all of that sun-kissed skin on display. He'd be lying if he didn't admit he was drawn to her. That the vibrancy she exuded did something to him—kicked something alive in him that had long remained dormant. He'd found himself just as caught up in her as everyone else as he'd watched her work this week, making magic with the camera. But he was also aware that she was far from an angel. That she'd raised hell for his brand over the past few weeks, and he wasn't about to give her full rein so that she could do it again.

His gaze rested on the determined set of her lush, full mouth. She didn't give up. It was a quality he admired about her. He needed her, and she knew it. And quite frankly, given how hard she'd worked over the past few days, his staff full of nothing but compliments about her professionalism, along with the fact that he thought he might have been a bit quick to judge, given his anger, he was content to give a little here, particularly if she helped him with Ming Li.

"Bene," he replied. "Prove to me I can trust you over the next three weeks and you can do Cannes."

The tense, watchful lines of her face relaxed. *"Grazie.* I can assure you, you have nothing to worry about."

He wasn't entirely convinced on that point. The last thing he needed was her going off the rails again, particularly when he was involving her with Nicholas Zhang and his daughter—an opportunity he couldn't afford to pass up. Zhang was a cagey customer, a tough negotiator at the best of times, whose signature was far from guaranteed on the deal they were negotiating. Which meant he needed all the aces up his sleeve he could manage. Having Jensen—his resident wild card—mess this deal up for him was not an option. Which meant he needed to figure out what made her tick, given they were going to spend the next few weeks working at each other's side.

She had been reliable at the beginning of her contract, a true professional according to his marketing team. So what had caused her to go off the rails? If it wasn't Alexandre Santeval, which he tended to believe, nor a drug or alcohol habit, which he also believed was not the issue, what had spurred all the wild partying? The outrageous antics? Because she couldn't shake her legacy as a Davis? Because it was her natural inclination to act out? Or was it something else she wasn't sharing?

He thought back to an incident when he and his younger sister Ilaria had been in middle school, his grandparents their de facto parents after they had lost their own. A boy his age had stolen his sister's lunch and left her in tears. Cristiano had wanted to punch him in the face. His grandmother, however, had counseled him not to. Had said that whatever had made the boy steal his sister's lunch had been rooted in far more than mere malice. Which had turned out to be true—the boy's family struggling over a bitter divorce, which had ripped it apart. A boy Cristiano had later become friends with, his best friend Rafe.

The story lingering in his head, he sat back in his chair as Filomena poured their coffee, along with a traditional Italian Amaro, then disappeared back inside. "I do wonder," he said idly, his eyes on Jensen, "what's been going on the past few weeks? What's sent you into this spiral you seem to be on? Because, to your point, this behavior was not an issue over the first year of your contract. So perhaps you can share what it is. Maybe I can help."

Her dark eyes widened, an emotion he couldn't identify flitting across her face. She veiled it just as quickly, her long lashes sweeping down over her cheeks. "Nothing is going on," she said quietly. "I overextended myself. Made some bad decisions, just like I said."

"And the wild partying?"

"Is how the press paints it." She threw up a hand, her ebony eyes glittering in the candlelight. "I didn't stumble out of Zoro after the incident with Juliana, Cristiano. I *tripped* over the sidewalk, there were so many photographers chasing me. I rarely drink much when I go out for the same reason I don't do drugs—because it would mess with my looks. As far as Monaco goes, some of my...*friends* got a little out of hand that night. It was not ideal, I agree, and also my fault, because ultimately, it was my hotel suite. *My responsibility.* I am not, however," she said, her gaze meeting his, "on a spiral, as you put it. On the contrary, if anything, I've been working far too much, which is my biggest problem."

He scoured the frustrated set of her jaw. The very real emotion written across her face. She was either a very good liar, or she was telling the truth. For some reason, he tended to think it was the latter, which either made him a fool or right, that there was something else going on with her she wasn't sharing. Because this type of behavior didn't come out of nowhere. And given his instincts were usually accurate, he went with the second theory.

"Your agent should be managing these things for you," he pointed out. "It's what you pay her for. Tell her it's too much, that you need to cut back."

Her dark gaze slid away from his. "It's not that simple. People depend on me. *Clients* depend on me. I have a reputation to protect."

"Which will only benefit from you pulling back and taking stock." He waved a hand at her. "What's going to happen if you take a step back? Maybe take on a client or two less? Look at Shanghai. The world hasn't come to an end because you didn't walk in the show."

Her chin lifted. "Ariana Lordes took my place in Shanghai. She is a bona fide superstar. Everyone's talking about it."

He studied the vulnerability written across her face,

a fascinating crack in the perfect armor. Remembered what she'd said on the plane about the short duration of a model's career. Her reluctance to give even a little on her insane schedule. "And so you worry that what?" he challenged. "She will take your place? That you will lose your relevance? You can't control what happens in the industry, Jensen. *No one* can control that. All you can do is make the best decisions for your career. For you. For what *you* need."

She was silent for a long moment, her ebony eyes contemplative. "Life is more complicated than that."

He wasn't content with that answer. "How so?"

"It just is." She caught her lip between her teeth. "My career is important to me, Cristiano. It's more than just a job. It's—"

"What?" he pressed, thinking he might finally be getting somewhere.

"It's my grounding force. It's the only solid thing I've ever had in my life. I will not put it in jeopardy."

That kicked him right in the chest. Thudded hard in his inner recesses. His gaze moved over the vibrant, beautiful lines of her face, the fragility he sensed about her in this moment so completely at odds with everything she'd thrown at him thus far.

What must it have been like to grow up like she had? In a world where nothing was real? Where the news value of what she was living ruled the day? Where the solid, grounding existence he'd experienced as a Vitale would never have been even remotely possible for her? How had she handled it? What impact had it had on her? His curiosity resurfaced, stronger than ever.

"What was it like?" he asked quietly. "To be a Davis? To grow up like that?"

She eyed him, an emotion he couldn't read flickering across her face. "That's a fairly broad question," she murmured. "We could be here all night."

"Humor me." He waved a hand at her. "You were on television from when you were very young to just recently, no?"

"From when I was ten to when I was twenty-three." She was silent for a long moment, swirling her wine in her glass, the ruby-red liquid glittering in the candlelight. "It was," she said finally, "the furthest thing from normal you could imagine. When other kids were climbing trees, my sisters and I were memorizing plot lines. We shot ten to twelve hours a day, so we couldn't go to school. We had tutors instead. And a nanny when I was younger. Everyone on the show had to sign an NDA, which meant I rarely got to spend time with my friends whose parents wanted nothing to do with the show. Which was most of them," she acknowledged, her mouth twisting. "I don't blame them at all."

So in essence, he concluded, his heart pulsing for the young girl she'd been, she hadn't *had* a childhood. He could identify, on some level, given he'd lost his own parents at fourteen, when the boat they'd been piloting had crashed head-on into another vessel, killing his father instantly, and his mother days after. He'd been shattered. Annihilated at the loss. But he'd had no choice but to grow up fast, to mourn his parents from a place deep inside, rather than reveal his grief to the world, to give in to it, because his younger sister had needed him.

They'd been lucky enough to be put into his grandparents' care, but in the years following his father's death, Francesco had been heartbroken. Consumed by his grief, his grandmother preoccupied in her efforts to comfort him. They had, however, had the traditional family structure his grandparents had provided for them. The solid base to his life Jensen had never had. And for that, he would be eternally grateful.

"That couldn't have been easy," he observed. "Not having any kind of a normal life. How did you feel about it?" Because she'd always been positioned as the ringleader. The girl who would try anything.

She shrugged a slim shoulder. "In some ways, it was fun—a new adventure every day. We received a lot of attention...what teenage girl wouldn't like that? But then," she continued, a frown creasing her brow, "it all became a bit much in our teenage years. It never stopped. The show...the media coverage. We had no privacy. It was impossible to carry on a real relationship. So my sisters and I decided to get out. Ava and Scarlett started a fashion and design business in Manhattan, and I began modeling."

"Which made sense given your background as a fashion influencer." He tipped his coffee cup at her. "Was it an easy transition?"

Her mouth curved in a rueful smile. "Technically, yes. I had a natural fashion sense. I knew how to act, which is a crucial part of modelling. But few people in the business took me seriously in the beginning. I was an influencer, not a model. My celebrity, my built-in endorsement value, might have gained me access into the upper echelons of modeling, but it was also a strike against me. Brands were wary of hiring me. Other models were resentful when they did. I had to work twice as hard as everyone else to land jobs, and sometimes even that wasn't enough."

He recalled his own skepticism when she'd been presented to him as a candidate for the face of his brand. He'd pretty much dismissed the idea out of hand, based on her reputation alone, even after she'd established herself as a top model. Which was a perfect example of how hard it must have been for her to overcome that prejudice lobbied against her.

"But you persevered," he pointed out. "That took guts."

She shrugged. "It was the only thing I knew. I wasn't afraid of hard work. Of having to prove myself, and people eventually began to see that I was serious. That I was good at my job."

Only for her to put it all in jeopardy with this spiral she'd been on of late. It made no sense. Not when he could see how seriously she took her career. Which made him more mystified than ever.

He hiked a dark brow. "And so, you thought that by frolicking naked in the Trevi Fountain with a playboy prince and setting off an international scandal, it was going to preserve your stellar reputation?"

Her long, sooty lashes swept down to veil her gaze. "No," she said quietly, "I did not. Sometimes my...*impulses* get the better of me. Old habits die hard, I guess."

He eyed the wealth of emotion simmering behind those midnight-dark eyes. He wasn't getting the full truth here. He was getting partial truths. He was sure of it. He had the distinct feeling she'd just thrown him a line—told him what he'd wanted to hear—just to get him off the subject. And why that bothered him, why he wanted to get to the bottom of her, he didn't know.

He could tell himself it was because she was a crucial asset to him and he couldn't have her going sideways during this launch. But he thought it might be more. That there was something about that vulnerable light in her eyes that got to him. That there was so much more to *her* than met the eye. That beneath the brilliant, beautiful packaging lay the real Jensen Davis. And as insane as it was, he wanted to see it. He was *intrigued*.

Which was *irrational*, given she was the exact opposite of the type of woman he normally gravitated to—the self-possessed, stable, dependable females he had always chosen—because that's what his life had required. A woman like Alessandra Grasso, a predictable, *safe* choice, with the breeding and power to unite two family dynasties and create an even stronger whole. Something that would only underscore his revival of FV.

The fact that he'd been unable to pull the trigger on that particular match, that he'd told himself it was better done after he'd right-sided FV, when he had the time to invest in a relationship, that he'd harbored niggling doubts about the match, that she wasn't *the one* for him, that had held him back, was beside the point. Jensen Davis was a wild card better left alone.

She swallowed hard. Dragged her gaze from his, as if the exact same thoughts were going through her own head, and glanced at her watch. Finished the last sip of her coffee and set the cup back down in its saucer. "I have to be up at five," she murmured. "I should get some sleep."

"Bene." He shut down his own thoughts that were sure to get him into trouble. "I will walk you back."

Jensen walked with Cristiano back to the pool house, his large palm at the small of her back to guide her across the uneven stones burning a heated imprint into her skin. What on earth was she doing opening up to him like that? Telling him those things about herself? She'd been so intent on steering him away from the truth about Monaco, about her recent headlines, she'd revealed things about herself she'd never told anyone else. How much her career meant to her. The very real fear she had about losing it.

Everything good she'd ever had in her life had disappeared. Her family, when her father had left. The normal life she'd never known she'd craved until she'd been thrust into the spotlight and lost it for good. Any semblance of a maternal instinct her mother might have possessed with the bitter divorce and her one-track focus on the show. She'd always been afraid that would happen to her modeling career, too. That it would vaporize like everything else good in her life. Fears that had been heightened by the missteps of the past few weeks.

She'd seen what it had done to her mother, to lose her movie career. When the beauty you'd traded on faded and you were ruthlessly cast aside for the next bright star. One minute her mother had been a glittering beacon of light, the ultimate Hollywood icon, the next bemused and lost. It was why she'd signed up to do *Hollywood Divas*—because Jensen's father had left her with nothing and she'd needed to survive.

Jensen had sworn it would never happen to her. That she'd build a career so successful, so indestructible, it could never be shattered. Except now, with her mother's ruinous addictions and financial issues, her bank account was empty and that security she'd been building was gone. It made her feel off-balance and scared, something she was afraid Cristiano had picked up on. When exposing vulnerability was the last thing she'd wanted to do. The last thing she *ever* did.

And then there was the part of her that was frightened of what her mother might do, when she'd just assured Cristiano he had nothing to worry about. That her mother's promises only lasted as long as her need for the next big hit. Which wouldn't take long, given how precariously close the show had come to being canceled and the pressure the producers had put her under. She had no idea what her mother would do. A very real fear that made her stomach churn.

She took a deep breath as they reached the pool house, now cast in darkness.

"Oh," she murmured, "I forgot to turn on a light."

She'd never liked darkness. Not since she'd been a child and she and her sisters had been left on their own in bed, while her parents had fought like gladiators, rattling the roof of their Beverly Hills home and raising goose bumps on her skin.

Cristiano released the hand he held to her back and walked inside, flicking on a lamp in the living room. Jensen followed him inside, where the salon was bathed in a soft, golden glow, her gaze drawn to the hard muscles that flexed and rippled in his back. The amazing arms which she was sure could hold a woman in any position he chose, for as long as he desired. The thought made her throat dry in the dim, intimate confines of the room, mixing with the cavalcade of emotions coursing through her.

He turned around, his azure gaze focusing on her face. On the tumult that raged beneath. He stepped closer, lifted a hand to trace the line of her jaw, sending the most delicate of shivers down her spine. "Jensen," he murmured, "are you okay?"

It might have been the wine, or maybe it was the dark spell that wove itself between them, but she suddenly had the insane urge to tell him everything. To unburden herself of the insanity of the past few months. To explain to Cristiano why her professionalism had suffered of late. But she'd learned from experience that trusting anyone with that kind of knowledge was dangerous, even Cristiano, whom she felt instinctively she could trust. Especially with the secrets her family guarded like the crown jewels. Because they would explode, her mother's secrets, if they ever came to light. It would ruin everything. Not a risk she was prepared to take, no matter how much she wanted to.

"I'm fine," she said huskily. "Just tired."

His blue gaze narrowed. Darkened. She should have thanked him and bid him good-night. Instead, she seemed to gravitate toward him, toward that rock-solid presence he exuded, because even if she couldn't tell him what was eating away at her insides, she could soak up that silent assurance of his. That chemistry that fizzled between them.

His gaze dropped to her mouth, the heat between them banking up into an undeniable force. An instinctual thing, a primal draw that happened every time they came within five feet of each other. A living force that begged to be fulfilled. The wine, which had injected her blood with a heated, sinuous warmth, stripped away her inhibitions, and experiencing what that hard, sensual mouth would feel like on hers became her sole focus. Because she knew it would be amazing. *Life-altering.* And the reckless part of her, the one that always seemed to hold the greatest sway, wanted it. Was only a second away from acting on it.

She heard him mutter a rough oath under his breath, low and thready. It knocked her out of her stupor as effectively as the frigid water she splashed on her face every morning to wake herself up for a shoot.

What was she doing? She knew better than this. They'd just established some sort of rapport between them. Was she really going to mess it up by doing this?

She wasn't sure where her brain had gone, but she needed to find it in a hurry. Because confiding in Cristiano, allowing herself to get involved with him, was stupidity of the highest order when he held her destiny in his hands. When she needed this job more than she'd ever needed one in her life. When opening up to someone else had never been an option for her.

She stepped back. Away from all that hard, muscular warmth. Away from temptation.

"I should get some sleep. *Buona notte,* Cristiano."

CHAPTER FOUR

JENSEN SAT IN the sun-soaked kitchen of the main house, devouring one of Filomena's *cornetto alla crema* along with a cappuccino the housekeeper had made, which were always beyond compare. She'd been working since dawn, her only sustenance an apple for breakfast. Famished, her legs needing a rest, she'd sunk down on one of the kitchen stools when her break had arrived, which, according to most people's schedules, was when they would be leaving for work.

Filomena, busy with her morning duties, had been keeping her company while she baked more *cornetti* and complained about Pedro, the gardener, who had once again overwatered the roses in the garden, which, according to the formidable Italian, looked *tristi e appassiti*, which Jensen had translated loosely with her newly acquired language skills as sad and droopy. She didn't dare disagree with Filomena, because the roses did indeed look unhappy, and furthermore, no one ever disagreed with the housekeeper if they knew what was good for them. Filomena ruled with an iron fist and was proud of it.

Jensen loved these sun-soaked breaks in the kitchen she'd taken to enjoying every morning. Once you got past her outer walls and earned her trust, Filomena was warm and motherly when it came to her charges, which she now considered Jensen to be. Aware of Pascal's complaints his dresses didn't fit, she'd put a fresh tray of pastries in front of Jensen when she'd sat down and ordered her to eat. Which might soon put her in a sugar coma, but it would be well worth it. They were the best thing she'd ever tasted.

It was so nice to have someone take care of her for a change, rather than the other way around—so much of her time spent tracking her mother down and making sure she was on the straight and narrow. A relief to simply sit there and enjoy the sunshine for a few moments while Filomena fussed over her. While the eye of the storm seemed to have passed for the moment.

Alexandre was off in the Caribbean on a whirlwind trip with Juliana working things out, the paparazzi following to capture the drama. The shoot for the collection was going well—one of her favorites ever. The only thing burrowing away at the back of her mind was the conversation she'd had last night with Scarlett.

Her mother, on a high from her record-level ratings, had been blowing off her appointments with her therapist, insisting she had *everything under control*. Which, to Jensen and her sisters, only meant that her mother was going through another of her manic phases. It was making them all nervous. But given she was thousands of miles away and out of reach, this time it was her sisters Ava and Scarlett's responsibility. A fact she was grateful for, given tonight was the Associazione Nazionale della Moda Italiana party, at which she was to host Ming Li Zhang, a night that had to go seamlessly, without incident.

Filomena regaled her with another colorful tale about the gardener, this time about his encounter with a harmless garden snake, which he had mistaken for a *vipera*. His headlong flight into the kitchen, where he'd snatched up the phone and called the state police, who funneled any kind of emergency to the correct authorities. Only to have the animal expert who'd showed up inform him that the gray-green creature he'd spotted was a garden-variety reptile, whose most harmful property was the foul-smelling odor it emitted when frightened.

"Idiota," Filomena snorted. "Surely he should know."

Jensen bit back laughter. "Perhaps he's had some kind of trauma with snakes."

"Trauma to the head," Filomena suggested, tapping her gray-haired temple.

Jensen burst out laughing. She had just recovered and taken a big bite of the melt-in-your-mouth pastry, when a deep male voice broke up the party.

"Sono in ritardo, Filomena. Un caffè da asporto, per favore."

Cristiano swept into the kitchen, a blur of purposeful motion as he informed the housekeeper he was late and needed his coffee to go. His gaze moved from Filomena to Jensen, who sat frozen, her mouth full of *cornetto*, his eyes a sharp, brilliant blue that rivaled the morning sky. "Care to share the joke?"

She shook her head. Attempted to swallow. He looked *incredible*. Like sex poured into a suit, his long, lithe limbs filled out with enough muscle she decided it must be the perfect ratio. That the suit was clearly custom cut to mold every centimeter of his spectacular body didn't hurt. Clearly one of Pascal's, she concluded, reaching for her cappuccino before she choked on the pastry she'd consumed.

Disaster averted, she set the cup down. "You're late leaving today."

"An early conference call. I did it from here." He leaned a hip against the counter as Filomena bustled around, preparing his espresso. Moved his gaze down over the sweep of her cheek, to her full mouth, resting there in a lingering appraisal that made her cheeks heat. "You have chocolate on your face."

She lifted a hand. Scrubbed self-consciously at her mouth. "I was starving. They're so good, I couldn't stop."

His mouth curved in an amused smile. "The breakfast of champions, clearly."

Jensen's stomach flip-flopped. She could ignore the attraction between them when he was being his typical arrogant, slightly insufferable self. It was a whole other ball game when he turned on the charm. Given she'd spent the last few days studiously avoiding him after that *almost-kiss* the other night, in which she'd nearly done something stupid and unwise, as she suspected he himself had been doing, it felt like a minor setback. However, she concluded, inhaling a deep breath, sanity had now prevailed, and she was intent on sticking with it.

"All good?" he probed, his azure gaze speculative, sensing her inner turbulence.

"Perfetto," she replied, plastering a smooth, even-keeled look across her face.

"Bene." He surveyed her a moment longer before accepting the coffee Filomena handed him with a murmured thanks. "I thought," he drawled, "that we could attend the party together tonight. We are meeting the Zhangs at the event. You can occupy Ming Li, show her a good time, while I work through some things with Nicholas."

Spend the entire evening with him? Her heartbeat quickened at the idea, accompanied by an equally strong surge of dismay. Surely that wasn't necessary? But, she conceded, if the plan was for her to show Ming Li a good time while Cristiano schmoozed Nicholas Zhang, she would hardly spend much time at his side. Very little, in fact. *Safe*, in the great scheme of things.

"Fine," she agreed. "Will we leave from here?"

"*Si*. I will pick you up when I get home from the office."

She nodded. He pushed away from the counter and picked up his briefcase. She was halfway out of her chair, plate in hand, when he stopped in the doorway, his broad shoulders filling the frame.

"Jensen?"

She looked up at him.

"Ming Li is an impressionable sixteen-year-old. Keep it PG tonight."

She absorbed the concern written across his face. He really had bought into the headlines about her. Which, until the past few weeks, had been an ancient replica of her that had nothing to do with reality. It dug into her gut, stoked the frustration simmering inside her. Because that wasn't her anymore. But all she could do was swallow it and let him think what he was destined to do.

"I will be on my best behavior," she assured him, hiking her chin. "Strike any worries from your head."

The paparazzi were lined up three rows deep at La Scala as the world's glitterati arrived to celebrate the current innovators of Italian fashion. The cocktail reception, held in the Palazzo La Scala outside the majestic opera house, was in full swing as Jensen and Cristiano stepped from his midnight-blue two-seater on a still-warm, sultry night, black-coated waitstaff serving cocktails in advance of the dinner to follow, a string quartet providing the music.

All eyes were on them as they worked the red carpet, done tonight in Italy's national colors of red, green and white, negotiating the blindingly powerful camera flashes as they stopped to greet the people they knew, the crowd a virtual who's who of global fashion.

They made their way toward the step-and-repeat banner emblazoned with the logos of the famous Italian fashion conglomerates represented that evening. Besieged with questions about Prince Alexandre and the current scandal, Jensen refused to give credence to the tabloid rumors tossed at them from the teeming pack of hungry reporters, focusing instead on presenting the details of Francesco's dress she was wearing.

Together, she and Cristiano worked their way through the crowd. If she could sense the gossip percolating beneath the surface of the aristocratic gathering, with herself and the prince as its focus, perfectly concealed in that cultured, subtle way the Milanese used to dig their way beneath your skin, it was blunted by Cristiano's presence at her side. An absolute refusal by the elite to visibly slight a gilded member of that aristocracy, despite the chatter happening beneath the surface.

A glass of champagne in her hand, Cristiano's palm at her back, she focused on dazzling the crowd. Exchanging the witty repartee she was known for. And if his touch evoked a warm, tingling sensation, a reaction she couldn't seem to avoid, as the man himself did, she ignored it. Because tonight, she was not going to get sidetracked. *Distracted.* Ambushed. Tonight she was going to be *perfect.* Her career depended on it.

Midway through the packed throng, she felt Cristiano's attention shift, his fingers tightening at her back, before he bent his head to hers. "Nicholas Zhang and his daughter are on your right. In the black tux and the fire-engine-red dress."

Jensen took in the distinguished-looking Zhang, known for his cutthroat deal-making. Handsome in the stern, aristocratic sense, with an aquiline nose, the sharp, hard lines of his face seemed to reflect his legendary personality. His daughter, on the other hand, was delicate and lovely, with luminous dark eyes and a perfect oval face, framed by a swath of silky dark hair. She also, clearly, had a formidable fashion sense in the way she wore the gorgeous red silk dress Jensen and the design team had sent over, with a scarf and glittering heels to match.

Cristiano made the introductions. Nicholas Zhang clasped her hand in a firm grip, his sharp gaze assessing. Then he introduced his daughter, Ming Li, who proffered a delicate hand to Jensen, an animated expression on her beautiful face.

"Thank you so much for the dress. It's perfect."

"Thank Pascal," Jensen deferred to the brilliant designer. "You look gorgeous in it."

"*You* are even more beautiful in person. I begged my father to bring me with him, because I wanted to meet you."

"That's very sweet of you to say." She acknowledged the compliment with a smile. "You are quite stunning yourself."

"I want to be a model," said Nicholas's daughter, her chin lifting, "but my father is dead set against it. He wants me to go to business school so I can run the company someday."

"Which you will," her father inserted evenly.

Jensen stifled a smile at the exchange. "It isn't all glamour, you know…modeling. It's a lot of hard work. Long days."

Ming Li rolled her eyes. "So is keeping my four-point-zero GPA."

Jensen noted the very American term. "You go to school in the US?"

Nicholas's daughter nodded. "Father wanted me to have an international view to the world. I go to boarding school in Connecticut."

Jensen wasn't inclined to disagree with her father. Modeling was a viciously competitive world. Few models ever made it to the top. And even when they did, that success could be fleeting. It had always been her biggest regret having begun modeling at sixteen, that she had just a GED designation to her credit through her private tutors, her schedule making it too difficult for her to attend school. Something she'd always felt she'd missed out on.

But she also wasn't in the business of raining on other people's dreams, because she knew what her own had meant to her. How reaching for the seemingly unattainable could push a person past what they thought they were capable of. She flicked her gaze to the two men, intent on giving Cristiano the time with Nicholas Zhang he'd desired. "Perhaps I can introduce Ming Li around? There are scads of famous designers and models here tonight. Some real legends."

Ming Li's eyes lit up. "That would be amazing."

Her father eyed her with a firm look. "If you behave yourself."

"Of course." Ming Li hooked an arm through Jensen's.

"Introduce me to *everyone*. Don't leave anyone out. I want to meet them all."

Cristiano shot her an amused look, his gaze seeming to convey a mixture of gratitude and wariness. She sent him a reassuring look back, ordering her heart not to beat in triple time at how insanely handsome he was in the dark tux. Then she and Ming Li disappeared into the crowd.

"God," the teenager said, exhaling on a sigh, "It is so *stifling* being with him. I need a break." She scooped a glass of champagne off a waiter's tray and laced her arm through Jensen's. "Cristiano, on the other hand, is amazing. I know he's too old for me," she said at the look Jensen threw her. "I'm not totally deluded. However," she added on an airy breath, "I want the full scoop on everything. The prince. The affair. The truth behind all the rumors."

Jensen plucked the glass from her hand and returned it to a passing waiter's tray. "That will not endear me to your father. Secondly," she added, procuring a frothy non-alcoholic cocktail for the teenager, "I hate to burst your bubble, but there is no affair with the prince. I can, however, introduce you to David Swanson. He's here somewhere. Will that do?"

A dazed look crossed the teenager's face at the mention of one of Hollywood's leading men. "You aren't serious."

"Very. He's a personal friend of mine. In fact, I see him now. Let's go say hello."

Cristiano watched as Jensen worked the crowd, Ming Li at her side, the brightest light in a sea of glittering stars. Clad in an ethereal creation of Francesco's, its blush-nude hue the perfect contrast for her dark eyes and olive skin, the bespoke organic silk georgette gown had a flowing,

fairy-tale-like silhouette. But the gown was not all innocence with its plunging neckline that skimmed the curves
of her breasts, its clever cutouts that revealed tantalizing
glimpses of smooth, creamy skin, and elegant crisscross-
ing straps that left her back bare to the waist.

She was shockingly beautiful. There wasn't a man in
the crowd who hadn't had his eyes on her at one point or
another. It was, however, the light that seemed to emanate
from her that captured him. How everyone she talked to
seemed drawn to her in that inevitable way that he was.
There wasn't a sign of the vulnerable, complex creature
he'd witnessed at dinner the other night. Instead, it was
all the glittering glory of Jensen Davis, supremely in
her element. And while he appreciated the perfect show
as the representative of his brand, what he himself had
asked for, he found himself wondering what was going
on in her head as she flitted from group to group, as elu-
sive as the most vibrant butterfly.

What made her tick. Why she refused to let anyone get
too close. Why she spread those delicate wings of hers
and took flight when anyone did. If the truth be known,
he hadn't been able to get her out of his head all week
after that almost-kiss, which had seemed to occupy far
too many of his thoughts. They had a physical chemistry
that couldn't be denied, that was clear. But it was more,
this curiosity of his he couldn't seem to escape.

She had been tireless in her work ethic since she'd arrived, completing every one of her responsibilities with
that vivacious energy she possessed, including a charitable event with young, at-risk girls in which, according to
his staff, she'd shone, her natural warmth and empathy on
full magnetic display. Perhaps, he pondered, it had been

her own chaotic upbringing that had contributed to that sense of connection between her and the other women.

"She is a shining star," Nicholas Zhang murmured, following Cristiano's gaze across the crowd to where Jensen stood. "A masterful play on your part, Vitale. Brands can no longer afford to simply sit on the sidelines and ignore the fact that influence is fast moving to the social space. To marry that strategy with such a legendary brand, to take that risk, was pure genius."

Cristiano had long ago decided the risk was worth the reward. That big gambles were the only way he was going to save his legacy. A play he hoped wouldn't blow up in his face, given the complex, multifaceted plan he'd crafted, the gamble he'd taken on the man standing in front of him the key to it all. It wasn't a vision he could second-guess now, at its most critical juncture.

"I think," he said deliberately, transferring his gaze from Jensen to the cutthroat billionaire, "it's time we take the gloves off and discuss the real issues at hand, don't you? Get this deal done."

Nicholas Zhang's dark gaze gleamed at the challenge. "I never did like doing business with a suite of lawyers in the room. Throw in a '46 Macallan and we can get down to it."

Jensen returned Ming Li to her father after dinner, which gave Cristiano a good deal of time to work through his issues with Nicholas Zhang. She felt lighter than she had in weeks. Buoyed by her success as she and Cristiano waved the Zhangs off. Not only had she shown Ming Li a good time, chock-full of all the biggest celebrities, she'd also had the brilliant idea to take the younger woman backstage at Pascal's debut show. A once-in-a-lifetime opportunity she hoped would help cement Cristiano's deal.

Cristiano frowned as she recounted the offer. "Are you sure you want to take that on? There will be a lot going on that night."

She brushed the objection aside. "It will be brilliant for her. There is no experience like it. Nicholas will be there, the excitement will translate to him and it will be a moment she'll never forget. Plus, if Ming Li is serious about a career in modeling, she will also get to see the pressure, the intensity of it all. If she still wants to do it after that, she will have the full picture. She will *know*."

A reluctant smile curved his mouth. "In that case, I think it's a fantastic idea. I'm hoping to have the deal done by then, but if anything, it will provide a very resounding exclamation point to the night. *Grazie mille*," he murmured, fixing those amazing blue eyes on her, "for everything you've done tonight. Ming Li clearly had a wonderful time."

She tried to ignore how that meltingly slow smile affected her insides. Lit a flush beneath her skin that seemed to spread body-wide. "It was nothing. I had fun. Did you get things ironed out with Nicholas?"

A frown creased his brow. "There are a few things left to finesse. Speaking of which," he said, nodding toward his family, congregated at the bar, "I should give them an update."

She balked when he set a hand to her waist and would have propelled her there, the idea of facing Cristiano's supremely aristocratic family with the rumors about her and Alexandre still circulating distinctly unappealing. Federico, Cristiano's uncle, had always been somewhat aloof; Marcella, his grandmother, the matriarch of the family, was frankly terrifying; Ilaria, Cristiano's sister, who headed up FV's public relations, the only Vitale she had a warm relationship with.

"I have a few people I should say hello to," she protested. "Perhaps I should—"

"Afterward," he interrupted, brushing over her protest and shepherding her toward his family. "This won't take long. Ilaria made me promise to bring you by. She saw the proofs of the collection and is over the moon."

Jensen acquiesced, if reluctantly. She did love Ilaria, and she was equally excited about the shoot. Squaring her shoulders, she allowed Cristiano to guide her to where his family stood assembled at the bar, set up outside on the warm, sultry night. She greeted Federico, Cristiano's uncle and head of the company's Italian operations, first, who offered a cool if polite greeting, then Marcella. If the ice-cold look on the silver-haired matriarch's elegantly lined face was anything to go by, she'd been right in her presumptions. Marcella had heard the gossip about Alexandre and was less than impressed.

She exchanged perfunctory kisses with the matriarch, steeling herself against the icy chill directed her way, then turned and greeted Ilaria, brushing a kiss to the tall, attractive brunette's cheek.

"Don't mind her," Ilaria murmured, pressing a kiss to her other cheek. "She just received an earful from the church about your dip in the fountain. They are all quite scandalized. She is also a personal friend of Queen Sofia, so you're hitting her from all angles. You look amazing, by the way."

Jensen cast a thankful look at Ilaria as she pressed a glass of champagne into her hands. She'd been intent on nursing one glass the entire night in an attempt to keep her head clear, but for *this*, she just might need it.

Ilaria drew her into conversation while Cristiano and Federico talked business. Ilaria's illustrious MBA and whip-smart brain had earned her the director of communications job at FV at age thirty, an impressive feat by anyone's standards. Yet she had always picked Jensen's brain on marketing, recognizing her social influence and her ability to reach the young women who were crucial to the brand.

She and Ilaria talked strategy until Cristiano and Federico concluded their rather heated discussion and joined in, the conversation shifting to the busy fall fashion season ahead and FV's fiftieth anniversary party, which would kick off Milan Fashion Week, highlighting Francesco's historic contributions to Italian fashion. The perfect precursor to Pascal's spectacular debut collection for FV, which would follow at the end of the week.

The anniversary party, which Ilaria was organizing, would be a star-studded event, hosted at a glorious Milanese landmark. Jensen found herself entranced by Ilaria's brilliant idea of ending the evening with an auction of Francesco's most famous dresses, one from every year he'd been designing, with the proceeds donated to the local hospital charity Marcella sat on the board of.

"It will be magical," Jensen murmured, her brain conjuring up all sorts of wonderful images.

"Si." Ilaria sighed. "I love the idea. But I'm afraid I've bitten off more than I can chew. My team is maxed, and it's a logistical beast curating all the gowns."

Jensen was still caught up in the magic of it all. "How are you going to display them?"

"A museum-like retrospective…we have a beautiful open space to do it in."

A vision built itself in Jensen's head, layer building upon layer. "What if you did it live instead? Used some of the original models who wore the dresses… I'm sure there will be quite a few of them attending the party."

A glitter entered Ilaria's eyes. "Oh," she breathed, "that would be incredible. What a story it would be. The original supermodels in the original dresses. It would blow the roof off the night."

"You have no time," Cristiano interjected. "You are already working until midnight every evening."

Whereas she had time, Jensen thought, chewing on her lip. The collection was almost shot, the television commercial the last big piece to come. "I could do it," she offered. "I have the contacts. I could pull in some favors from friends to fill out the lineup. Handle the logistics of the auction for you so it would free up your time. I've done a million charity events like this."

"I don't think that's a good idea." Marcella interjected, directing a pointed look at Jensen. "This is not a publicity stunt to flog the Vitale name. The type of…sensational, headline-grabbing events you are used to. It is a serious charitable endeavor that requires class and commitment. It's the biggest event this company has done in its history. It needs to be done right."

Jensen's fingers tightened around her glass, the insinuation she had no class stinging her skin. She was used to the criticism of her scandalous family and the manufactured celebrity it traded on. And yes, many of the events she'd done as a Davis had been just such high-profile occasions designed to generate headlines. But they had also been rooted in good—her mother a champion of the community. To have Marcella throw it in her face like that, when she'd spent the past year devoting herself to putting FV back on the map again, was just too much to take.

Cristiano, who'd detected the temperature change, set a warm palm to her waist, but she ignored it, too annoyed to heed it. Directed a pointed look at Marcella. "I am well aware of the importance of this event," she said evenly. "And I understand the last few weeks have been a bit rocky—something that I apologize for. I will do better. But if the purpose of this auction is to draw attention to an historic anniversary for the brand as well as generate profile for a good cause, *that* is something I know how to do. I am well aware of what the *tone* should be."

Ilaria flicked a glance from her grandmother to Jensen, clearly attempting to figure out how to navigate this battle. "The photo of Jensen at the AMAs is the most popular post on Instagram this year," she pointed out. "*Fifteen million* people have liked it. The PR department has been deluged with inquiries on where to buy Pascal's dress. I think she could really help us move the needle on this."

Marcella opened her mouth to object, but Cristiano silenced her with a wave of his hand. "I think it's an excellent idea," he weighed in. "The PR department will appreciate another charitable activity on Jensen's part, given the recent headlines. Jensen clearly has the clout to help Ilaria blow this thing out of the water. It makes perfect sense. Of course," he concluded, "she will be wearing the final dress of the evening as the current face of the brand."

Marcella raised a silver brow, as if to ask her grandson if he knew the disaster he was inviting. Cristiano ignored it completely. "It's decided, then. I think it's a fantastic idea."

* * *

Jensen was still fuming when Cristiano separated them from his family and shepherded her through the crowd, the party still going strong as guests enjoyed after-dinner drinks and dancing in the square, champagne flowing from fountains like water, the elegant fairy-tale lighting in the palazzo casting a warm glow over the night. Deciding she needed a few moments to cool down, and done with his quota of small talk for the evening, Cristiano directed her toward the dance floor, set off by a series of twinkling lights.

"I think," he murmured, "we should dance."

A look he couldn't read moved across her face. "I'm fine," she said quickly. "We're pretty much finished now anyway, aren't we? Always best to end these things on a high note."

"You have smoke coming out of your ears. One dance," he insisted, "and then we will go. Also," he added helpfully, nodding at a point over her shoulder, "Beryl Morgan is on her way over." One of Milan's most outrageous gossip bloggers, she was known for her vicious virtual red pen. "Unless you'd like to give her the unadulterated scoop."

Jensen's face telegraphed her horror at the prospect. She followed him onto the dance floor then, taking the hand he extended, a slight flush lighting her high cheekbones as he pulled her closer before placing his other hand at the small of her back, his palm absorbing the warmth of her bare, silky skin revealed by the daring dress. It was even softer than he could have imagined. Lacing his fingers through hers, he pulled her a step closer, until the scent of her delicate floral perfume infiltrated his senses.

It was still a very respectable hold. But with that innate

chemistry between them crackling to life and sensitizing every one of his nerve endings, they might as well have been cheek to cheek in the way that she affected him. *Vastly. Completely.*

His heartbeat quickened in his chest, his blood sliding through his veins on a heady pull, his every sense attuned to her. He was fairly sure she felt it, too, from the way her breath caught in her throat, the way she seemed to focus everywhere but on him, staring at the lapel of his jacket for long moments, before she finally looked up at him. And then there was no mistaking the heat that smoldered between them, the flames in her dark eyes spilling out and licking across his skin.

"I'm sorry," she said, in what seemed like a valiant effort to deflect from it, "about your grandmother. I just get so frustrated when people have these preconceived notions about me."

"Preconceived?" He arched a dark brow at her. "You do stoke the flames, you have to admit. Give her some time," he advised. "Do the job I know you can do with the anniversary party. She will come around."

She didn't look entirely convinced, a battle going on in those luminous ebony eyes of hers. He sought to explain, to calm the turbulence emanating from her. "All she sees are the publicity stunts your family engages in. The headlines surrounding the events your mother puts on, which Marcella then interprets as a less-than-altruistic cause."

"Which might be absolutely true," she agreed, her beautiful face expressive. "She does do sensational things for the media coverage. For the *buzz.* But there is also good in what she does. She has always been a keen supporter of the community. Those causes she supports *mean* something to her. She puts an incredible amount of work into them. As much as Marcella does. Yet look at how she is treated."

Loyalty, he registered. Another facet of her he was discovering. That same loyalty she'd displayed toward his brand, that he hadn't been fully aware of. Her refusal, even now, to criticize her mother, who according to those who knew Veronica Davis was a master strategist, moving her daughters around like chess pieces.

"No doubt," he conceded softly, "she does good work. My grandmother was harsh. She can be that way. She only sees one right way of doing things, and that is based in propriety—what she's been schooled in. It was not, however, fair of her to pass judgment on your family in that way. I apologize for her behavior."

She was silent, whatever was going on behind those darks eyes still festering. He tightened his fingers around hers. *"Che cosa?"* he murmured. *What?* "Talk to me."

"That's the way I used to be," she admitted. "I used to 'stoke the flames.' Be as outrageous as I could possibly be, because that worked for me. It got me the attention I was looking for. It got me star status on the show. But I am not that person anymore." Her mouth twisted on a frustrated curve. "I made the decision to walk away from the show. To be someone different. But it always seems to come back to haunt me."

"Because you are your own worst enemy," he opined. "All my grandmother sees, all the *world* sees, is a vision of you, without your clothes, frolicking in that fountain. Being outrageous for the sake of being outrageous. And," he proposed, "where has it gotten you?"

A myriad of emotions flickered across her face. He thought for a moment she might answer, then he watched her retreat. Slide a veil over those dark eyes, and it irritated him. Perhaps because he'd seen more of her now. Enough to know she was hiding behind this public persona of herself she'd manufactured that he didn't think had anything to do with reality. "Why," he pushed softly, his eyes on hers, "do you do these self-destructive things to yourself?"

She sank her teeth into the plump skin of her lush lower lip. Eyed him. "I don't know," she said finally. "Maybe I get drawn back in sometimes, when I shouldn't. Maybe I make bad decisions in the moment, based on my history." She hiked a shoulder. "Maybe it's easier to be that version of myself, because that's what people expect of me. Which I always regret after the fact."

He absorbed the vulnerable curve of her mouth. The deep internal conflict written across her face. He didn't understand it, because he'd never operated that way himself. He'd always learned from his mistakes and moved on as a more self-aware version of himself. But with Jensen, it was more complex. If a half real, half manufactured world was all she'd ever known, sliding back into it would be far too easy, given the right incentive. Of which there were many.

"You must recognize the folly in that," he murmured. "It will never end. You will keep getting drawn in. It's the nature of that world."

"I know." Her mouth turned down. "It was a moment of weakness. I went against my better judgment, only to have it blow up in my face."

"So you learn from your mistake. Make better decisions next time. You know who you are, Jensen. Who you want to be. You made that decision when you walked away from the show."

She nodded. "I know. You're right."

And that, he concluded from the shuttered look on her face, was all he was going to get. Which was more than what he'd been able to glean from her thus far. It should have been a red flag for him that she was far from a sure bet. That she had a tendency to fall back into old habits. That he should keep his guard up. Instead, it was her vulnerability that got to him. The bizarre urge he felt to protect her from this crazy world she'd been born into. All mixed up with an attraction he couldn't seem to ignore. The way she moved him in a way he couldn't seem to understand.

His hand dropped lower on her hip, the delicate scent of her perfume filling his head. He felt, *heard*, the quickening of her breath as his hold shifted that much closer and his breath skated across her temple. The heat of his palm sinking into the curve of her hip, her soft contours melted into him, fitting perfectly against the hard planes of his body, as if she was made for him. And then, it was only them, the noise of the buzzing crowd receding as the force of their attraction ignited.

It was becoming an almost compulsive urge to know her, to explore the chemistry between them. To harness all of that vibrancy for himself, to hell with his better instincts. Because he knew it would be like nothing else he'd ever felt. That it would light him up in a way he'd never experienced before. As irrational as it was, as unadvisable as it was, it was also undeniable.

The moment hung there, thick and uncharted, neither of them daring to break it, because it was just that powerful. Until the last notes of the music played and the spell was broken. Aware of where they were, of the eyes on them, he stepped back, reluctantly releasing Jensen from his hold.

"It's getting late," he said huskily, his gaze on hers. "You have to get up early for work. Let's say good-night to the organizers and I'll get the car."

Jensen waited near the exit for Cristiano to collect the car, her head reeling from that moment between them on the dance floor. It had felt *real*, tangible, the connection between them. Unmistakable this time. She could have sworn that had been regret in his eyes when he'd released her. That he'd been as loath to break the moment as she had. It had her insides in a tangle, her heart beating far too fast. Because if it was *real*, if there was something between them, what was she going to do about it?

Ignore it. She had promised herself she wasn't going to do this. That she was going to focus on the job at hand and nothing more. And then Marcella had torn a strip off of her and it had all gone sideways. She'd been so stung by the Vitale matriarch's treatment of her, had felt so *humiliated*, so unfairly judged, she'd felt compelled to defend herself to Cristiano.

She'd thrown pieces of the old Jensen at him to justify her behavior. She wasn't sure he'd completely bought it, but it had been the best she could do to steer him away from the truth about her mother. As for the intense connection they shared that seemed to build with every encounter? She blamed it on her vulnerability in the moment. Her uncertainty of what her mother would do in this manic state of hers. Maybe she'd wanted to lean on Cristiano in the midst of the storm. Take refuge. But it was his reaction to their conversation that had thrown her.

Unlike her ex, Daniel, who had walked away from her when her reality show life had proven too much, Cristiano hadn't seemed to judge her for it. Instead, he'd seemed to understand, to *empathize* even. It had her feeling distinctly off-balance and uncertain, because experience had taught her that her past would always be used against her, that *she* would always be judged by it. She'd taught herself it would be naive to think it would ever be any different. To protect herself against future hurt. And yet Cristiano *had* reacted differently.

Her heart beating far too loud in her chest, her legs a little unsteady, she sat down on a low concrete wall while she waited. When several minutes had passed and it seemed to be taking Cristiano a long time to return with the car, she got up and went looking for him, too tired and exhausted to sit still. Found him standing near the valet stand, talking to a tall, leggy blonde.

The woman's honey-colored hair cut into a chic bob that skimmed her shoulders, she had delicate, finely boned features, big blue eyes and effortless style in the sapphire-blue sheath dress she wore. An air of confidence that came from her roots in one of Milan's oldest, most aristocratic families made Alessandra Grasso the perfect choice for Cristiano, according to the models who'd pointed her out earlier. Everything she was not.

It had been the subject of a full-fledged gossip discussion, Ming Li looking on with avid curiosity while the models had engaged in innuendo-fueled speculation. Whether or not Cristiano would finally pull the trigger and marry Alessandra. How, even if they'd had their rocky times, she was still destined for him—the heir to an Italian textile dynasty, who could unite two Italian fashion legends. And Alessandra, according to the models, tended to get what she was after.

Jensen felt as if she'd been socked in the chest as she watched them talk, Cristiano's dark, handsome head bent to Alessandra's, the intimacy of the moment clear. She really had to get over this infatuation she had with him. The belief that there was something between them, when in actual fact, she was the last female he'd ever get involved with, even if there was a blatant attraction between them. Because he would end up with a woman like Alessandra Grasso, not someone like her. It was preordained.

His family had made it clear what they thought of her tonight. That she was the kind of scandalous American reality show trash she was so often billed as. To think Cristiano would think differently, despite his outward empathy, was naive. Which meant she needed to get her head together and fast.

When Cristiano finally returned, car keys dangling from his fingers, her composure was restored. "Are you all right?" He eyed her with a look of concern.

"Perfect," she murmured. "Just tired. Are we ready?"

He gave her a long look, then nodded and held the car door open so she could get in. Then he got behind the wheel of the low-slung sports car. They made the drive home in silence, a palpable tension throbbing between them she made no attempt to address. When they stopped in the circular driveway of the villa, and Cristiano got out to walk around to her side of the car and open the door for her, she slid out and took a step backward, away from his tall, overpowering presence. *"Buona notte,"* she murmured. "Thank you for a lovely night."

Jensen couldn't sleep. Her head was too full, her thoughts too disordered since she'd walked away from Cristiano earlier. Which should have been the right decision. Which *was* the right decision. But she couldn't stop thinking about it. About that moment between them on the dance floor. Couldn't get it out of her head.

She was also hungry. *Starving.* She'd done so much socializing, intent on showing Ming Li a good time, she'd barely eaten anything. Her stomach rumbled, a headache threatened, and a vision of Filomena's delicious homemade bread filled her head, topped with a thick slice of Italian cheese. And once there, she couldn't get rid of it.

She was never going to sleep. And, given she needed a good rest before tomorrow's shoot, waking up with a stormy head wouldn't be an auspicious start. Gathering her hair into a ponytail and pulling on delicate, bejeweled flip-flops, she slipped out the door and headed toward the main house, the interior of the villa cast in darkness in the late hour.

Filomena was off tonight, but she'd told Jensen to help herself if she ever needed anything. Slipping into the warm, inviting kitchen, where a lamp was always left on in case someone needed something, she poured herself a glass of milk and made a sandwich with the thick, delicious bread. Seated on the marble countertop, she absorbed the peace of the night, an army of cicadas singing their song through the big, open bay windows, moonlight flooding the fragrant gardens outside.

She had just finished her sandwich and was reaching for her glass of milk when Cristiano walked into the kitchen, another pair of those dark, sexy denims slung low over his lean hips, a black T-shirt hugging his muscular torso. Distracted and disheveled, as if he'd pushed his hand through his hair a dozen times, he looked up to see her perched on the counter, the glass of milk poised halfway to her mouth.

She wasn't sure what rendered her off-balance more—

how insanely good he looked in the casual clothes, clinging to all of that honed, delicious muscle, or the fact that she was perched on his kitchen counter in a camisole and short pajamas that had seemed perfectly appropriate in the intimate confines of her cottage, but now with his dark perusal raking over her, absorbing every detail, felt far too revealing.

He moved his gaze down, over the long, bare length of her legs, up over the smooth skin of her thighs, then higher, to where the camisole clung to her curves. This time, when he lifted his gaze up to hers, he didn't attempt to hide the dark embers that glimmered there. To deny this crazy attraction between them. Instead, he moved closer, coming to a halt a few inches in front of her.

Jensen set the glass on the counter, her fingers shaking slightly. She could feel the heat that emanated from him, bleeding into her skin. Her bones. She'd never met a man so *male*, in the true sense of the word. So earthily attractive. And she worked with some of the world's most beautiful men.

A flush bloomed in her chest, moving up to consume her cheeks. It felt like she was on fire, but she was fairly certain most of that was the internal combustion they created together.

"I thought," she said haltingly, "that everyone had gone to bed. I haven't eaten much all day. Filomena said to help myself. So I—" she waved a hand at the cupboard "—made a sandwich."

"You were busy with Ming Li. You must be hungry." He thrust his fingers through his hair in an action that only increased his disheveled look. "I had a conference call with Brazil. It ran late."

She absorbed the deep shadows underlining his eyes.

His palpable exhaustion. "You should get some sleep," she murmured, her breath feeling a little trapped in her throat. "You have Zhang in hand. Everything else can wait until the morning, no?"

Cristiano knew he should. Go to bed. He was beyond coherent at this point he was so exhausted. But he couldn't seem to make himself move. Not when she looked like his every fantasy come true in those provocative silk pajamas, which put those long, incredible legs of hers on full, magnificent display. Not when every brain cell he possessed was focused on the voluptuous curve of her breasts the silky material hinted at, making him wonder what she'd feel like in his hands. When beneath the vulnerable curve of her mouth and the wary cast of her eyes lay the same burning fire consuming him.

He tightened his hands into fists at his sides. Unfurled them slowly. Fought it valiantly, because surely this was a bad idea. He'd been telling himself that ever since she'd walked away from him earlier, as if the hounds of hell had been at her heels. Over the past couple of hours, as he'd sought to find a solution to Zhang's aggressive demands that his family and the board could live with, a delicate minefield he had to tread carefully. Which had been the smart thing to do. Was still the smart thing to do.

He exhaled a deep breath. Moved to the water cooler, where he poured himself a tall glass of water, and stood, leaning against the counter as he downed half of it in one go. Inhaled a deep breath to deliver some much-needed oxygen to his brain, which he wasn't sure was going to do much good with the heat smoking through the kitchen. "Zhang threw a few monkey wrenches my way tonight. I've been trying to untangle them."

She cocked a brow. "What kind of monkey wrenches?"

"A larger say in what FV does. Creative input in the brand. A seat on the board, which I had anticipated. The rest not so much."

"Oh." She absorbed the information. "That won't go over well with your family, will it?"

"No. My grandfather was not for giving up any control of FV to outside influences. Neither is Federico. I've convinced him we either make this play, or we dig our own grave as we lapse into irrelevancy. Zhang, however, is driving a hard bargain."

She sank her teeth into her lip, worrying the tender flesh. "Nicholas is undeniably brilliant. He understands the global marketplace and he understands how customers are consuming fashion. Get Ilaria to pull the spring campaign he did for Kyra and show it to Federico. When you dig into it, it's a complete masterpiece. It will demonstrate his worth."

"That's a good idea." He rubbed a palm against his temple. "Maybe I will. Zhang also thinks we should expand our influencer base. Develop some branded lines to target different lifestyle segments. You could be valuable input on this."

She nodded. "Anytime. Just say the word. And I'm sure your family will come around. You haven't made a wrong decision yet." She slid to the edge of the counter, the nervousness of her movement betraying the tension between them. Tension that had been seething between them for days. Tension that had been occupying far too much of his head.

And suddenly, he didn't want to avoid it anymore. He wanted to confront it, because he didn't think it was going anywhere. If anything, it was only getting worse.

"Maybe," he murmured, setting his gaze on hers, "you'd like to tell me why you ran away from me earlier. The car had barely come to a stop and you were hightailing it back to the pool house."

Her ebony eyes widened. Darkened. "I wasn't running away. I was tired."

"And that's why you did the same thing after dinner the other night…because you were tired? Because it seems to me, this attraction between us is clear. What we need to do is decide what to do about it."

"Ignore it," she said instantly. "I work for you, Cristiano. We need to keep a professional relationship."

"You work for yourself," he returned, eyeing the flash of heat that had consumed her creamy cheeks. "The only reason I stepped in in London was because you weren't living up to the terms of your contract. Now that we have that out of the way, I think it's time we faced this thing between us."

"I don't," she said staunchly. "If we were smart, we would shut this down now. Get the sleep we both clearly need."

But neither of them were that smart, clearly, or one of them would have moved. Put an end to the madness. And quite frankly, he was tired of fighting it. Couldn't even, in this moment, as she stared at him with those big brown eyes, her chest moving too quickly up and down, betraying how very affected she was, remember why this wasn't a good idea. Because surely it was not. Because it felt like the most natural thing in the world. Like if he just reached out and touched her, something inside him would be alive again. Which was either his fatigued brain playing tricks on him, or a truth he wasn't willing to admit. And he couldn't, for the life of him, stop himself from taking a step closer.

"I would," he said huskily, "because there is no question I need sleep. That this is, perhaps, not a good idea. But I'm afraid if I did, I would not be able to get this out of my head."

Her eyes widened. Dark, decadent pools of temptation that beckoned him in. "Get what out of your head?"

"This," he breathed, setting both hands on the counter to brace his arms on either side of her. Which only served to send the delicate floral scent of her perfume wafting through his head, intoxicating him on a whole other level. Because it was mixed with *her*—that irresistible, delectable, heady scent that was hers alone.

He stayed there, resisting the urge to move, waiting for a sign from her that she did not want this, because then he could have walked away. *Would* have walked away. Waited for some glimpse of sanity from either of them. Instead, she tipped her head back, her silky hair falling over the bare skin of her shoulder, her dark eyes stormy. He was fairly sure she wasn't breathing, or barely if she was, the pulse at the base of her throat throbbing in a sign he could not have missed.

It was all the invitation he needed. Shifting his weight to one hand, he reached up and set his thumb to the mad beat at the juncture of her neck and throat. Absorbed the frantic pulse that pounded there. It satisfied him in a way he could not begin to describe.

Sliding his fingers up to the curve of her jaw, he held her where he wanted her, bending his head to slide his mouth against the velvety surface of her cheek. Against the delicate curve of her mouth. She sucked in a breath as he took his time, exploring the contours of her mouth, learning every soft facet of her, every centimeter of her lush skin, the mouth of a siren, designed to drive a man wild. When he had prolonged the anticipation, when his name was a barely audible whisper on the air, ripped from her lips, he covered the vulnerable curve of her mouth with his.

Slow, deliberate, *thorough,* he explored every dip and valley of her mouth, satisfying every curiosity he'd ever had about what she felt like. What she tasted like. What it would *be* like to touch her. And if he were being honest, the fantasies he'd indulged in far too frequently of late. When she lifted a delicate hand to tangle her fingers into the hair at the base of his skull and pulled him closer, her breath mingling with his, he deepened the kiss into a more sensual exploration, his fingers curving around her jaw to hold her still.

When she moaned, a low, needy sound that came from deep in her throat, it was an intoxicating admission that electrified him. Pulled him in deeper. Sliding his hands down to her hips, he pulled her closer, her lush, full bottom filling his palms. Which only intoxicated him further, because she was silky soft beneath his hands. Even better than he'd imagined.

Hotter, brighter, the kiss burned, until it was no longer enough to satisfy either of them. His hands guiding her closer to the edge of the counter, he slid his fingers underneath the straps of her camisole, any common sense he might have possessed dissipating on a surge of lust. He dragged the thin straps of the negligible piece of silk down, exposing the full, ripe curves of her breasts. Taut, perfectly shaped and rose-crested, she was jaw-droppingly beautiful. Temptation personified.

Liquid brown eyes met his for a hot, heart-stopping

moment before he dipped his head and explored the voluptuous curve of her breast with his mouth. The velvety skin that heated beneath his touch. Cupping her in his hand, he absorbed the contrast of her creamy skin against his darker olive complexion, fascinated by the play of dark and light, before he lowered his head to take the rosy peak into his mouth. Her back arched, her hands planting into the marble counter behind her, as she gave herself up to his exploration. Which only inflamed him further.

A whisper of a breeze floating over them, the hot, sultry air a teasing caress across his skin, he took her deeper into the heat of his mouth. Sucked the rosy nub into a hard, sensitized peak, while he rolled her other nipple between his fingers. When he was satisfied he'd given her maximum pleasure, he devoted his attention to the other firm peak, the light scrape of his teeth across the engorged flesh pulling a low, thready sound from her throat that fired his blood.

Every ounce of his blood fled south, hardening him like rock. She was the sexiest, most responsive woman he'd ever touched. Voluptuous and perfect. Needing to have her closer, driven to explore more of her perfect, silky skin, he ran his hands up the insides of her whisper-soft thighs. Dipped his palms beneath the hem of her shorts and cupped her bottom in his hands, pulling her even closer. Held her there while he dropped his mouth back to hers and devoured her in a hot, all-consuming kiss that telegraphed his hunger for her.

He was burning up for her. Somehow it penetrated his lust-soaked brain that if they kept this up, they would be having sex on the counter, consummating this insanity between them, where anyone in the household could walk in on them at any moment. The utter lapse of rationality leached into his brain, as unwelcome as it was unbidden. "Jensen—" he murmured, dragging his mouth from hers. "I don't think this is—"

Her hot, passion-soaked gaze was cloudy with desire as she struggled to understand his words. She blinked long, velvety lashes, her hands pressing against his chest to steady herself as she sought equilibrium. Liquid desire morphed into realization in those luminous, dark eyes. At what they had been about to do—ruddy color staining her cheeks. She went stiff beneath his hands, inhaling a visible breath. Then she pressed her palms harder against his chest to put distance between them.

"Jensen," he said softly, reading the regret on her face. *"Cara—"*

Jensen slid off the counter and took an unsteady step backward. Pressed her fingers to her mouth. What *was* she doing? She had nearly given herself to Cristiano on the kitchen counter. Had been so caught up in him she'd literally thrown herself at him. *Fallen into him.* She wasn't sure what was worse, her completely uninhibited response or the fact that he'd had the sense to put a stop to it and she hadn't.

What had she been thinking? How had she stepped so completely across the line? She would blame it on the late-night hour, on the intimacy of the situation, but she couldn't spin that lie even to herself. This had been building between them all week. He had simply made her go up in flames. Which was everything she'd promised herself she wouldn't do with her reputation, with her career on the line.

"This was a mistake," she bit out. "It shouldn't have happened."

"But it did," he murmured, taking a step closer. "I think both of us knew it was inevitable. I wasn't pushing you away, Jensen, I was instilling some rationality into the situation."

Inevitable? Her reckless, careless side might agree with that assessment, but the sensible, cautionary side that needed to take precedence at the moment rejected that assessment wholeheartedly. He probably thought this was normal for her, seducing a man in his kitchen. That she'd left a list of castoffs around the globe—Mata Hari incarnate. When in reality, it couldn't be further from the truth.

She hadn't had a serious relationship since Daniel, who'd unceremoniously dumped her three years ago and broken her heart. Hadn't dated anyone in Lord knew how long. Cristiano, however, had made it clear he'd bought into her headlines. And really, that wasn't such a bad thing at this point, because the smartest thing to do would be to declare this the insanity it had been and forget it had ever happened.

She was stronger than this. She *would* be stronger than this. Because everything depended on it.

"It won't happen again," she stated, in a voice filled with conviction.

"Jensen." Cristiano's gaze darkened as he stepped toward her.

She held up a hand. Stopped him in his tracks. "We both know this is a bad idea. Better to end it right here. Because tomorrow we *will* regret it."

Turning on her heel, she walked out of the kitchen and into the warm summer night.

CHAPTER FIVE

"OH MY GOODNESS." The words slipped from Jensen's mouth, half gasp, half sigh, as she and Ilaria found themselves standing in front of *the* dress—the one that had made Francesco famous, worn in the seventies by one of the original supermodels, Isabella Müller.

They'd been cataloging the designs for the anniversary party dress auction in an afternoon that had been a bit like a dream for Jensen. Never had she imagined she would ever be in the same room as Isabella—her idol—let alone walk a runway with her. That she would be closing the show in Francesco's stunning midnight-blue couture gown he'd created for her before he'd died, which might be more beautiful than all of them.

Ilaria smiled and ran a finger down the gossamer fabric of the stunning metallic silk dress. "It's gorgeous," she murmured. "*She's* still gorgeous. I couldn't believe it when she walked into the room. It's as if she's sailed through time, unscathed, except for a fine line or two."

Jensen attempted to quell the butterflies fluttering in her stomach. She hoped her own career would prove as resilient as Isabella's.

But right now, her only focus was on delivering for Francesco Vitale, as she'd promised she would. Justifying the trust Cristiano had placed in her. Which had involved *not* thinking about that kiss they'd shared in the kitchen, as she'd navigated the various public appearances and meetings they'd done together since, necessary collisions she'd treated with a fearsome determination to ignore it all. How *unwise* the whole thing had been. How unbalanced it had made her feel. How unforgettable it was proving to be—no matter how hard she tried.

Cristiano, apparently, had decided the same thing. Not once had he addressed the chemistry still pulsing between them. The palpable tension. He'd simply focused on business, polite in his usual, cordial way during the interactions they'd had. Which might sting a little, given what had taken place between them. Which was simply lust, she lectured herself sternly.

And wasn't she used to that anyway? Men desiring her, then deciding they didn't want her after all? She'd taught herself not to care. To protect herself against that hurt. This time would be no different. Except, she acknowledged, it did hurt that he'd seemingly turned things off between them. Which was ridiculous, because she'd asked for it.

She made a note of the gown Isabella would wear in her notebook, and they walked back to the front of the studio to chat through the following night's wrap party, designed to thank everyone who'd worked on the shoot and commercial for their hard work. They were just about through when Cristiano walked into the room, a distracted look on his face, a sheaf of papers in his hand, his sister's name on his lips.

His gaze flicked to Jensen, perched on a table with her notebook in hand, then back to his sister. *"Mi dispiace,"* he murmured. "I didn't realize you were busy."

"We're just finalizing some details for tomorrow

night." Ilaria said. "Are you joining us? It will be nice for everyone to blow off some steam. Get some appreciation for their efforts."

A frown twisted his dark brow. "I'm going to try. I have a dinner thing. Maybe afterward." He shifted his attention to Jensen, his sapphire gaze moving over her face, taking in the pencil she had perched between her teeth, her thinking cap on. His perusal lingered on the lush, full line of her mouth for a moment longer than it should have, that electric attraction sparking between them on a wave of powerful energy, before he seemed to catch himself and moved on, scrutinizing the lines of fatigue dug into the sides of her mouth and eyes. "You look tired," he said. "Have you taken on too much?"

She shook her head, absorbing the air of intensity that emanated from him. The barely leashed energy he seemed to wear like a glove. "I'm having fun. I think you're going to be very happy with how this turns out."

"She's being modest," Ilaria interjected. "She's a genius. She has all the models doing teaser videos with clues in them that hint at Isabella's appearance. It's creating a ton of buzz online."

"Bene," he murmured, a tired smile twisting his mouth. "I like it when things fall into place. That's good to hear."

His cell phone pealed from his jacket pocket, commanding his attention. Muttering a goodbye to both of them, he left the room, a blur of dark, purposeful motion. Ilaria moved her gaze from the door back to Jensen, a curious look on her face. "Is there something going on between the two of you?"

Jensen dug her teeth into her lip. "No, why?" she said

as casually as she could manage, because there wasn't, was there, really?

"Because the tension between you two is palpable every time you're in a room together. And that dance at the Associazione Nazionale della Moda Italiana party?" She hiked a brow. "I wasn't the only one who noticed. It was fairly electric."

Jensen shrugged a shoulder. "We strike sparks off each other, that's all. Besides," she added, unable to help herself, "he belongs to Alessandra, doesn't he?"

Ilaria's azure gaze turned speculative, making Jensen instantly regret her words. "To be honest, I thought he'd have already pulled the trigger on that one. She's a perfect fit for him. Our families go way back. But," she said, hiking a shoulder, "something seems to be holding him back. Maybe he's too busy. Or maybe he's decided it isn't going to work. Which would throw off a lot of people's plans," she conceded with a wry smile. "My family has its heart set on it."

Yet another reminder that the decision she'd made to walk away from him had been the right one. That she would be setting herself up for a fall if she perpetuated this thing with Cristiano—this fairly wild attraction they shared. That the best thing she could do was pretend that kiss had never happened.

She pushed her attention back to the plans for the following evening, intent on avoiding the subject entirely. "Right," she said crisply. "So, what do we have left?"

Cristiano arrived at the wrap party when it was well under way, the crew who'd shot the campaign and commercial, as well as the cast and models, enjoying drinks and hors d'oeuvres in the gardens surrounding the villa.

His dinner meeting having wrapped at a reasonable hour, his mind and body tapped out with the exhaustion searing his bones, his deal with Zhang well in hand, he'd decided to take his sister's advice and put in an appearance at the party. Demonstrate leadership at a crucial time for the company.

He stripped off his jacket and slipped into the crowd, where drink and laughter flowed liberally, a buoyant mood to the festivities, and found Antonio Braga standing beside the director of the commercial, famed Italian filmmaker Claudio Uberti.

"Perfect timing," his CMO murmured. "We've put together a rough cut of the spot. It's brilliant." An amused glitter lit his dark expression. "We couldn't have written the script any better given the current headlines. She's amazing."

Cristiano would gladly have sacrificed the sensational headlines Jensen had been generating in lieu of a more stable brand image, but he couldn't deny the synergy between the plotline of the commercial they'd developed and the real-life drama of the face of his brand. The concept for the spot a house party being thrown by Jensen at her parents' luxurious villa while they were out of town for the weekend. The Vitale villa, with its sumptuous, elegant interior and massive chandeliers, had been, much to Filomena's dismay, used to film the spot.

As the sun slipped in a fiery ball behind the mountains, the director rolled the spot, which began with the after-effects of the party filmed from outside the villa, with Jensen's come-hither red dress strewn across one of the manicured hedges that lined the front walkway. As the camera panned inside the villa, partygoers were sprawled asleep on every available surface—chaise longues, reading chairs, the gleaming *seminato alla veneziana* marble floors—streamers and confetti covering everything, a partygoer even asleep in the historic fountain in the backyard.

As the camera panned through the elegant splendor of the villa, various guests began to wake up in a stupor. Then came a scene of Jensen passed out in a king-size bed in the master bedroom, her current *amante* beside her, a dream she was having playing in her head—her father advising her that they would be back on Sunday afternoon. *No parties allowed.*

At that moment, Jensen's big dog, asleep beside them on the bed, nosed her awake, and she awoke in terror. Down the stairs she ran, clad in a flimsy piece of coffee-colored FV lingerie, over the gleaming marble, waking all of the partygoers in a frantic attempt to put the house back in order before her parents returned. Confetti and streamers were plucked from every available surface and tossed into bags, bottles swept into the trash and furniture shifted back to its customary position, just in time for her parents return in a sleek black helicopter.

It seemed as if she had actually managed to pull it off when her parents stepped through the Venetian glass front doors, her mother resplendent in a Pascal Ferrari suit. Until her eagle-eyed father spied a piece of confetti streaming from the massive chandelier in the entrance-way, his eyes going black, and Jensen's partygoing ways were revealed.

Laughter filled the crowd at the spot's understated brilliance, a series of cheers going up for the director. Claudio took a bow, a beaming smile on his face. "Your idea to bring Jensen here was brilliant," Antonio murmured, as the crowd held up a glass for Claudio. "She is focused. At her best. Everything I imagined she could be. *Grazie mille,* Cristiano."

He wished he could say he felt the same. That he thought bringing Jensen here had been a good idea. Instead, he seemed to be more distracted with his wayward charge with every moment that passed. Watching her this past couple of weeks, he could see the consummate professional she was, completely at odds with her reckless behavior of late. The brilliant business brain she possessed. The dedication for the brand she exuded. Which had, apparently, been sideswiped by her insane schedule he'd taken charge of.

And perhaps that was all it had been. Perhaps she had simply been overwhelmed with everything on her plate, just as she'd said, and fallen back into old habits. Made some bad decisions. And perhaps, he conceded, that was simply what he wanted to believe, because he was starting to feel something for her. Something he didn't want to admit. Something he'd wanted to pursue ever since that night in the kitchen.

He spotted her at the center of a group of models, dressed in Pascal's outrageous, reckless glittering red dress. Halter-neck in style, it hugged her sensational body like a second skin, ending a few inches above the knee to show off her incredible legs. Done in a gauzy, semi-transparent material, it did not take much of his imagination to envision her without it. Those decadent curves he'd explored in the kitchen.

They haunted him in his dreams. Visited him in his waking moments, too. He had the fatalistic realization they weren't going anywhere. That whatever attraction had sparked between them that night in London, whatever he had told himself about ignoring it, fighting it wasn't working. It was only making it worse. Because as unwise as it was, as irrational as he knew it to be, he wanted to know more of her. He wanted *her*.

His gaze met hers across the crowded garden, her hair a dark velvet curtain in the muted lighting, her eyes exotic ebony orbs framed by decadently long lashes, her honey-hued skin vibrant, as if lit from within. She was every bit the sparkling party girl depicted in the commercial. Every bit the wild card he'd pegged her. But she had far greater depth than anyone gave her credit for, complex, vulnerable depths that went way beneath the dazzling packaging to the intelligent, whip-sharp woman beneath. It intrigued him in a way that was approaching irresistible.

A moment passed between them, shocking in its intensity, a transfer of energy that rocked him back on his heels, it was so much bigger than both of them. He watched her almond-shaped eyes widen, before she swallowed hard, her slim throat constricting. And then her attention was claimed by someone in the crowd, and she turned and severed the connection, the regret that lanced through him tangible.

Jensen swallowed hard, attempting to absorb the energy that had passed between her and Cristiano, that had literally frozen her to the spot where she'd been standing, but the constriction in her throat was so seemingly immovable, she took a sip of her drink instead, the sparkling soda water infused with a splash of lime moistening her parched throat so that she could actually swallow.

She was exhausted from a sixteen-hour day on her feet. Back-to-back days of the same. It had taken them three hours to nail that final shot on the terrace, working against the clock as the light had faded, everything that could go wrong having gone wrong, blowing the schedule completely. Her feet were hurting in the killer five-inch heels and all she wanted to do was get out of the close-fitting dress and into her bikini, then head straight for the pool for a refreshing swim, which would make everything feel better.

Despite her mythical reputation, she was not in the business of stealing anyone's future husband, of breaking up Italian dynasties or challenging Cristiano's honor, not when the world already believed the worst of her. That she had been the catalyst behind Alexandre and Juliana's royal breakup and the resulting calamity which had ensued. Destroying one national fantasy was enough for the calendar year. This one she would leave alone.

Making the requisite rounds of the party, thanking everyone who'd done their part to make the commercial a success, she slipped quietly out of the crowd as the party was beginning to break up and down to the pool house, where she changed into an orchid-pink bikini. Securing her hair in a high ponytail, she scoured her face clean of her camera makeup before padding outside to the spotlit pool, glittering a deep cerulean blue on a perfect Italian night, the only sound on the still evening air the peaceful trickle of the waterfall at the far end of the butterfly-shaped pool.

Dipping a toe into the cool, refreshing water, she tested the temperature before wading in, allowing the water to carry away the grime and hard work of the day and ease her sore muscles. Floating silently on her back, soaking up the paradise she was in, the scent of jasmine and peony filled her head, the sky a blanket of sparkling gold stars overhead. She was in a dreamlike, half-awake, half-asleep state when the sound of clinking crystal broke the silence.

Flipping over, she tread water, her gaze widening at the figure standing on the pool deck. Cristiano, clad in navy-blue-and-green-striped swim trunks, set a bottle of champagne and two glasses he was carrying down on the tiled surface of the pool deck. Her throat, already dry from the blazing heat, went to desert dust.

She'd worked all day with a famous male model who'd been sashaying around half-naked during the out-of-control house party they'd thrown, and not once had she looked twice at his lean, well-built body. Cristiano, however, was a whole different story. All hard-packed muscle, underscored by the perfectly cut walls of his abs, a delicious vee forged a descent to his lean, powerful hips. Which were accented by muscular, trim legs that had clearly logged a great deal of miles on the cross-estate run he did every morning. The ideal combination of brawn and stealth, innate grace, which allowed him to wear his beautifully cut clothes so perfectly.

Except he didn't have many clothes on right now, she registered, her throat going even drier as she took in the low-slung dark swim trunks, which rode his lean, graceful hips. He was *insane. Spectacular.* Millie would be having a coronary right about now.

"You don't usually swim at this time of night," she managed, the words coming out as half sentence, half croak.

"You are supposed to alert someone when you are using the pool," he stated in that low, husky, accent-affecting tone that sent goose bumps to every inch of her skin.

"Yes, well," she prevaricated, "everyone was busy cleaning up from the party. I was just taking a quick dip."

"It doesn't change the rules." She could see from the

stern look on his face that he wasn't kidding. And, given the rumors she'd heard about his parents' untimely death on the famous lake a few hundred feet below them, she could understand the reasoning behind the autocratic set of rules he'd thrown at her upon their arrival.

Which left only his supreme arrogance as her source of antagonism between them, and that wasn't holding up very well as the days had passed and she'd watched how hard he'd been working to make his dream for FV a reality. To systematically bring the vision he'd promised the world to life, all of the responsibility he bore to his family sitting squarely on his broad shoulders.

"Your parents died in a boating accident," she observed quietly, as he uncorked the champagne and poured it into two glasses, the froth reaching up to the rims.

"When I was fourteen, *si*." He carried the glasses to the edge of the pool, set them on the edge, then stepped down into the water, rivulets of moisture rolling off his hard-packed abs. What might have been a humiliating form of drool moistened her mouth. *Good God*. She swallowed it back. Lifted her gaze to his sapphire-blue one as he lounged back against the side of the pool opposite her. Which didn't necessarily help, as she read the banked heat gleaming there, mirroring what was bubbling up inside of her at an alarming rate.

"That must have been very traumatic," she murmured, determined to ignore it. *Desperate* to ignore it. To focus on more sobering things, such as the loss of his parents at such a young age, which must have had such an impact on him.

"It was...*difficult*." A dark light flickered in his blue gaze. "But you weather it and move on. My grandparents needed me. My sister needed me. You do what you need to do."

Which had been to protect his vulnerable young sister and eventually, to save the company his grandfather had founded. His legacy. Which once more underscored the impenetrable stuff this man was made of. Explained the rigid control with which he exerted that authority. The loyalty and duty that drove him.

She'd never met a man like him before. Her own father was so far from that type of man it was laughable, the way he'd abandoned their family without a backward glance, leaving her mother devastated and in tatters. It made her wonder, just for a second, what it would be like to be wanted by someone like him—someone so strong and honorable. Not just physically, because she knew they shared that devastating chemistry. But *emotionally*. Unconditionally.

How safe you would feel. How buffeted against the world. She imagined it would feel...*life-changing*.

But he wasn't hers to have. He would eventually be someone else's. And that, she had to keep reminding herself of.

He picked up the two glasses and handed her one.

She wrapped her fingers around the glass. Cocked a brow. "Champagne?"

"I thought we could celebrate wrapping the campaign. You did a spectacular job on it. *Grazie mille*, Jensen."

His rich, deep voice, laced with that undeniably sexy, husky accent warmed something deep inside her. And it wasn't all professional pride, because she was sure he didn't celebrate like this with all his employees. *This* was something else entirely.

She shrugged a shoulder, attempting a nonchalance she

didn't remotely feel. "I was just doing my job. Working with Pascal and Claudio was a dream. I'm the lucky one."

"Well, you were brilliant," he murmured. "The marketing team is over the moon. Not to mention the assistance you've been with Federico. We pulled the Kyra campaign and showed it to him. He was very impressed. So much so that he is warming to the idea of allowing Nicholas some creative control. Which is a much more flexible stance than he's had thus far."

"That's great." She was happy her advice had helped. "I knew he would like that campaign."

"He did. Ilaria," he added, "is also ecstatic with your buzz campaign for the anniversary party. *Saluti*," he murmured, lifting his glass. "To all of your hard work."

She raised her glass, attempting to control the wild butterflies beating circular tracks through her stomach. "Aren't you afraid I might get wild?" she quipped, in an attempt to break the intensity between them. "Out of *control*?"

His sapphire gaze darkened with amusement. "I'm not so sure about that depiction of you anymore. You were drinking soda water at the party. Nor have you drunk much of anything on any social occasion we've attended since you've been here. Which leads me to believe that *partying* might not be your natural state of existence."

Her lashes drifted down, shielding her from his inscrutable assessment. "And what do you think is?"

"I don't know," he said quietly. "I think it's buried somewhere beneath those numerous impenetrable layers of yours. Those pieces of you that you refuse to show the world. You are so much more than that, Jensen."

"Perhaps," she agreed with a self-conscious shrug. "And perhaps there isn't that much more to tell."

"I think there is." He levered himself away from the wall with the push of a powerful bicep, propelling himself to within an inch or two of her. She felt a rush of blood in her ears as the force of the attraction between them roared to life, the heat of his muscular body so close she could feel it emanating from him.

"You are a brilliant marketer," he observed, his eyes on hers. "You have an innate talent. *Incredible instincts.* You could run my marketing department with the tip of your baby finger. And yet to my knowledge, you have no formal education in business."

She shook her head. "I am self-taught. Marketing always fascinated me, right from the beginning. I would study how people reacted to the things I would post. Pinpoint the best ones, study the messaging and learn how to replicate that success." She hiked a shoulder. "It came from a genuine place within me, I think that was the key. I loved fashion. I loved helping other people find their own. People picked up on that and followed me."

He cocked a dark brow at her. "And yet you persist in allowing the world to believe that you are a glamorous party girl and nothing more."

"That's my brand," she corrected. "It sells your clothes, Cristiano. Young girls want to be that glamorous icon."

"Yet we have no idea what's underneath," he said softly. "Who the real Jensen is. I wonder what the truth is?"

"A mixture of both," she answered honestly. "I'm not so difficult to figure out. I wouldn't overthink it."

His mouth curved. "There you go again, avoiding the subject." He pointed his glass at her. "Perhaps we can try another."

"Which is?"

"I would like to discuss what happened in the kitchen."

Oh no. No. They did *not* need to do that. "I think we should ignore it," she proposed firmly. "It's been working great so far."

"No, it hasn't," he murmured. "I think we both know that. I think we need to address it, Jensen."

Her throat seized. "A-address it?" she stammered, when she'd finally yanked in some air. "What do you mean?"

"Confront it," he said softly. "Face it. Deal with it. This thing between us isn't going away. It's only getting worse. And I, for one, am done fighting it."

She swallowed hard, past the flock of butterflies in her throat. He was close, too close, and her heart was beating so hard in her chest, it was difficult to function. So she grappled for the most pressing piece of information she could find to avoid what seemed like the inevitable. "Alessandra," she breathed, her eyes on his. "I am not stepping into the middle of a relationship between you two, Cristiano. It isn't my style, as much as the media likes to paint me as Mata Hari incarnate."

He frowned, a furrow marring his handsome brow. "Alessandra? We are not together."

"But you will be," she countered, far more out of breath than she would have liked. "Everyone knows it."

"Except me," he responded silkily. "Perhaps you will provide me with the benefit of the doubt on this, *bellissima*, because I am sure I am correct. Alessandra and I broke up months ago."

She caught her lip between her teeth. "I saw you together at the party. When you went to get the car. It looked intimate, Cristiano."

The furrow in his brow deepened. "So you thought

there is still something between us? That's why you walked away from me in the kitchen?"

"No." She shook her head vehemently. "I walked away from you because it was a bad idea. Which it *is*," she added quickly at the dark glitter that entered his sapphire eyes. "Alessandra is only a secondary reason."

He raked a hand through his rumpled hair. "Alessandra," he said, after a moment, "was…*emotional* the night of the party. We have tried to make things work multiple times, and yet they are not working. She seems determined to make it happen. I have my doubts it ever will."

So what was he doing with her? Entertaining himself in the meantime? *Blowing off some steam?* Because surely he would never be serious about her. She wasn't about to do that with Cristiano. Not with the depth of the feelings she already had for him, feelings that seemed to be growing exponentially stronger by the moment.

"I'm not interested in being your *plaything*," she murmured. "Someone you blow off some steam with when you feel like it, Cristiano."

An offended look moved across his aristocratic face. "Is that what you think I'm doing? *Blowing off some steam?*"

"Yes," she said staunchly, "I do. We are attracted to each other. That's clear. Both of us are having a difficult time controlling it. Also true. But I won't put my career in jeopardy so I can have a dalliance with you, Cristiano. It's not happening."

His brow hiked higher, the offended look on his face deepening. Setting his glass down on the side of the pool, he moved until he was so close the heat emanating from him seared her skin. "Although I am a fan of *blowing off some steam* at this very moment," he murmured darkly, "because I think we both need it, my interest in you is more than surface deep, Jensen. I *like* you. I desire you. I would like to get to know you on a deeper level, *if* you will let me in. As for your career," he tacked on evenly, "I made it clear that night in the kitchen I am capable of separating it from any personal relationship we might have."

He said that, but did he mean it, when the two were so inexplicably intertwined? Which wasn't at all an effective deterrent when she was already melting inside at his words. Dissolving into a simmering inferno of emotions she had no idea how to manage. Because Cristiano announcing his intentions toward her—serious, unapologetically stated intentions of his desire to get to know her—was as terrifying as it was beguiling. Because the last time she'd done that, the last time she'd opened herself up to someone, *trusted* someone, she'd had her heart broken. And that she could never stand. Not from Cristiano.

"I'm sorry," she said quietly, her heart hammering louder than the quietly trickling waterfall. "I didn't mean to offend you. It's just—" She raked a hand over her sleek ponytail, searching for the right words. "I'm used to men viewing me as a...*prize*. As a distraction, until they move on to something better. *Serious*. It's a lot for me to put myself out there, when it's happened so many times before."

His gaze darkened to a deep midnight blue. He reached a hand out and tugged her closer, his palm settling on the lower curve of her back. Held this close to him, against the hard, hot length of him, she felt as if she'd been zapped by an electrical wire. "Do you think," he murmured, his sapphire eyes on hers, "that I would be stepping across the line if I didn't think there was something here? Because I wouldn't, *bellissima*. Trust me."

The languid warmth spreading through her melted her bones completely. His sincerity, the heat in his blue gaze, doing something strange to her insides. "I didn't put a halt to things in the kitchen because I'd regretted what I'd done," he said huskily. "I stopped things because it was insanity to be doing what we were doing in the kitchen, where any of the staff could have come in at any moment and found us. Not because I wanted to stop, Jensen."

But now they were alone. Her frantically beating heart tattooed the message on her overstimulated senses. There wasn't a soul who would be around at this time of night.

She wanted to take a leap, to trust him, to give in to this thing between them so badly, it was a living, breathing entity inside her. Obliterated her common sense. Stripped away all her barriers, until it was only them, the heat between them and the moonlight. What seemed so utterly and completely right.

Reading her thoughts, Cristiano removed the glass from her hand, set it on the side of the pool, then cupped her jaw, lowering his dark head to hers. She whispered his name, right before he captured her mouth with his in a sensual, devastating kiss designed to seduce. And this time, she gave him full permission to do so.

Her fingers curled into the thick, coarse hair at the base of his neck, anchoring her as she met his kiss. As meltingly slow and thorough as their first kiss had been, this was even more sensual with the warm play of the water across their skin, as hands slid against warm flesh and body parts settled against each other, the rock-solid breadth of his chest an impenetrable wall that held her steady.

When he moved his mouth to the sensitive skin at the base of her ear and sank his teeth into the tender lobe, she shivered. When he traced a fiery path lower and explored the vulnerable skin at the juncture of her neck and shoulder, she shuddered, her pulse racing beneath the intimate exploration. And when he traveled even lower and brushed the callused pads of his thumbs over the peaks of her nipples, jutting through the silky material of her swimsuit, she gasped low in her throat.

Back and forth he played her, until her nipples were hard, painful peaks, aroused by his sensual touch. Until she felt it deep inside her, stirring an aching, insistent warmth. Anxious for more, she moved closer. She felt his hands move to the tie at the base of her neck, releasing the bow, and then the fabric fell away from her heated flesh, her lush curves filling his hands. She arched back in his arms to watch him, registering the dark arousal in his gaze. The reverent way he cupped her paler flesh in his hands. The way he teased the taut, rosy peaks with his fingers, igniting a firestorm of want deep inside.

"Cristiano." The need in her voice that rang out on the still night air shocked even her. Her stomach muscles went taut, clenched with need as he slid his palm down the flat surface of her abdomen to the edge of her bikini bottoms. Toyed with the flimsy edge as he took her mouth in another hot, mind-bending kiss. And then he was sliding his hand beneath the silky material and down to the tender, soft flesh at the apex of her thighs.

She moved her thighs apart on a low moan, his knowing, expert touch finding the hot, wet flesh that ached for him. His mouth on hers, he whispered sexy things to her in Italian as he stroked her from top to bottom, exploring her soft femininity, every breathy moan she made guiding his journey. And when he'd completed his survey, he set his thumb to the soft nub at the heart of her and played her in a soft, seductive motion that tore low sounds from her throat.

His name falling from her lips, she moved her hips against his hand, urging him on. And when she was writhing against him, begging for release, he slid his fingers lower and sank one inside her, sliding slow and deep. She broke the kiss, too breathless, needing air, her hips arching into the sensual, knowing caress, which went deeper with every slide, until he hit a place inside her she didn't even know existed.

Sweet, all-encompassing pleasure coursed through her, deeper than before. Even better. And when she moaned and pleaded desperately for more, he slid two of his fingers deep inside her and took the pleasure to a whole other level.

Shaking in his arms, needing release, but afraid to go there because the pleasure was so intense and she'd never felt anything so good, she rested her mouth against his cheek, gasping in a deep breath. His sensual mouth moved to her ear, his husky, accented voice a reassuring, firm command. "Let go, *cara mia*. I've got you."

Closing her eyes, her head anchored against the strong wall of his cheek, she gave in to the pleasure. Allowed the deep stroke of his big, knowing hands to catapult her over the edge into a pleasure so searing, so exquisite, she lost her breath completely. He held her through it, his fingers continuing their sensual caress until the tremors inside her had subsided.

She had barely recovered when he lifted her out of the water and placed her on the edge of the pool, his hands sweeping aside the silky material of her bikini, while his mouth found the sweet, hot flesh still reverberating from her orgasm.

His other hand tightening around the soft flesh of her hip, he held her still while he devoured her with his mouth, his intimate caresses so shockingly good, she couldn't even muster a protest. Her hands in his thick, dark hair, she rode out her release, his hot, insistent exploration sending her spiraling up the ladder of need once again, until she came apart again, her orgasm tearing through her.

So shattered she could barely breathe, she was limp and spent as he lifted her down off the ledge of the pool and into his arms, guiding her mouth back to his for a hot openmouthed kiss that shook her to her core, because she could taste herself on him, and it was the most intimate thing she'd ever experienced.

"Let's go inside," he said huskily.

She murmured her assent, unable to muster anything more coherent.

Scooping up her bikini top with his free hand, he held her against him with that awesome physical strength of his that held her in its thrall, her arms and legs wrapped around his muscular body, as he carried her out of the pool. Acquiring one of the thick towels they'd left on a lounger, he dried her off, moving the fabric over the smooth skin of her shoulders, then the rounded curves of her breasts, paying reverent attention to the rosy peaks, hard and aroused in the moonlight.

"Bellissima," he murmured.

She melted. He wrapped the towel around her, drawing her toward him, his palm splayed over the curve of her buttock as they shared a passionate, sensual kiss. It took her a full second to register the flash of light that exploded behind her head, she was so caught up in him. Cristiano, however, was faster, a dark curse leaving his mouth as he released her and set her behind him, his broad shoulders blocking her from the blinding series of lights that exploded on the night air.

Camera flashes, she registered belatedly, her stomach plunging to the ground. *Oh God.* Shoving her bikini top behind his back, Cristiano barked at her to put it on. Her hands shaking, she fumbled in her efforts, cursing herself weakly as her fingers refused to cooperate. Finally, she managed to get it on, tying it clumsily behind her back and neck. By that time, Cristiano was on his phone, issuing terse instructions to his security staff, an infuriated note to his voice.

How they had ever penetrated the ironclad perimeter of the estate, she had no clue. Unless, she registered numbly, they had somehow taken advantage of the activity surrounding the wrap party, and the various suppliers who had worked it, to slip in undetected. Which would take a sophisticated, experienced paparazzo with extensive connections.

A feeling of dread wove its way up her spine. This bore all the hallmarks of one of her mother's operations. She had the means to do it and stupidly, perhaps, even the motivation after Jensen had texted her back earlier that she was happy the campaign had wrapped and looking forward to the party to celebrate. A carrot she'd offered her mother after not replying to dozens of her texts in an attempt to stay focused. And, she conceded, a part of her had been worried about how she was doing, anticipating another one of her vicious plunges.

Oh no. Please, God, no.

Cristiano barked a final order into his phone, then slid

the device into his pocket. The camera flashes had sub-sided, his security crew undoubtedly hot on their heels. But she knew the damage was done. The intimate sort of photos they could have taken. How disastrous this was going to be.

"I need to sort this out," he murmured, a furious look on his face. "Go inside."

"Cristiano," she murmured, desperate to say some-thing, *anything* that would rescue this situation before it spun out of control.

He set a palm to her back and moved her bodily inside. "Stay here. I'll find you later."

CHAPTER SIX

BUT CRISTIANO DIDN'T find her later. Jensen waited until
after midnight for him to return, and when there was still
no sign of him, she finally went to bed and fell into an exhausted, restless sleep. When she woke, she was shocked
to find it was eight o'clock, the sun blazing a path into the
sky, and remembered she hadn't set her alarm because
they'd finished shooting and she was free for the day.
Which would have been lovely, if not for the disaster of
the night before. What she had to face.

She picked up her phone. Checked her notifications.
There were dozens. A brief scan of the headlines revealed
it couldn't be good. Her heart plunged, resting somewhere
above her churning, misplaced insides.

Davis Drops Prince for Fashion Magnate, read the
headline of a British daily newspaper. *Caught in the Act!*
blared a spicier UK tabloid. *The CEO and the Supermodel,* the clever title for an Italian tabloid, known for
its juicy stories.

Oh my God. Her heart dropped further, if that was possible. She clicked on the first story, from the gossip page
of one of Britain's daily newspapers. Below the headline
was a story suggesting she'd left Alexandre for Cristiano,
in a fortuitous swap, alongside an intimate shot of them

in the pool together, her wrapped in his arms, locked in a passionate kiss. Which was likely as racy as the newspaper had been willing to go. The tabloids, on the other hand, had no such scruples.

She opened the British tabloid, known for its scandalous coverage, terrified at what she'd read. Under the headline *Caught in the Act!* were two photos, one of her and Cristiano on the dance floor from the Associazione Nazionale della Moda Italiana party, suggesting speculation had been rife about their relationship ever since the intimate dance at the party. Beside it was a photo of Cristiano carrying her out of the pool the night before, minus her bikini top. His arm was shielding her nudity from the camera, but her half-clothed state was apparent, as was the fact that they only had eyes for each other.

Her heart went into a free fall. This couldn't be happening. Not now. Not when everything had been going so well. When she'd been doing her job exactly as Cristiano had mandated, when the scandalous headlines about Alexandre had dissipated and the campaign was set to be a brilliant success. When Cristiano had said those monumental things to her last night about wanting to get to know her. About wanting *her*.

Her stomach churned, bile rising hot and insistent in her throat. Her mother had done this. She was sure of it. That she would do this to her, take advantage of her like this, despite her explicit instructions to leave her alone, was a betrayal that rose above all others. She couldn't believe she'd done it. But she was more angry at herself for being naive enough to think her mother could employ that type of rationality when she was in such a desperate state. It had been a massive mistake.

She read everything so that she knew the damage

that had been done, then dressed in a T-shirt and shorts, shoved her hair into a ponytail, and slipped on running shoes. Then she headed up to the villa, dread in her every step. Filomena was in the kitchen, making coffee, a delicious aroma permeating the sunny space.

"Buongiorno." She murmured a greeting. "Has he gone to the office?" she asked, not even attempting to avoid the subject, because she knew Filomena would know. Would have gotten the full report from the staff.

"He's here, in his office, on a call," the housekeeper replied. "You look like you need some coffee. Sit."

She sank down on a stool, eyes bleary. Filomena handed her a steaming cup of coffee and a pastry, but Jensen refused the croissant, her stomach churning too violently to entertain the idea of eating. She took a sip of the coffee. Eyed the housekeeper. "Has everyone seen the photos?"

"Si." Filomena leaned a generous hip against the island. "It's the talk of the estate. They weren't able to catch them. They must have escaped via the water. There was so much coming and going last night, things weren't as strict as they normally are."

Jensen's head began to throb in earnest. She pressed her fingers to her temples and willed it away.

"Let's be honest," the housekeeper said quietly. "It was only a matter of time before this happened between you two."

Jensen's eyes widened. "Alessandra is not the right woman for him," the housekeeper continued, in her patented, matter-of-fact tone. "She is selfish and focused on what he can give her. You are different. He seems happy when he is around you. Which," she added, "he deserves to be."

And how was he going to feel this morning with everything blowing up in his face? Jensen's insides twisted into a ball. Because this wasn't just another scandal. This one had him at the heart of it.

"It will blow over, *piccolo mio*," Filomena said quietly. "Don't fret." She walked over to the cupboard and retrieved a bottle of painkillers and set them in front of Jensen.

Jensen had taken the painkillers and was stewing over her coffee when Cristiano walked into the kitchen a few minutes later, dressed in a crisp navy-blue suit, gingham-checked white-and-blue shirt and purple tie. Looking crisp and beautiful, in high-alert business mode, the lines of fatigue etched around his eyes and mouth were the only sign that anything was off-kilter.

His gaze moved from her to Filomena. "Give us a moment, *per favore*?"

Filomena nodded and vanished inside the massive pantry. Cristiano leaned a hip against the island. Surveyed her pallor. The bottle of painkillers in front of her. "Are you all right?"

She nodded. "Just a headache."

He rubbed his palms against his eyes. "*Mi dispiace.* I was up half the night with my communications team, attempting to stop them from publishing the photos. But we couldn't track them in time, given we didn't know who it was who took them."

Her stomach roiled. She didn't want to tell him. Would rather do anything but. But she knew who it had been. Almost assuredly.

"It was my mother, Cristiano."

He frowned. "How do you know? It could have been anyone."

"Because it has her MO written all over it." She drew

in a breath. "I hadn't talked to her in a while. I'd been ignoring her texts, because I needed to stay focused and she was pressuring me into doing a follow-up stunt to the Alexandre thing and I wanted nothing to do with it. Yesterday, I texted her and checked in. Told her the campaign was wrapped and I was looking forward to the party. She clearly saw an opportunity and took it."

An incredulous look moved across his face. "She would do that to you? Hurt you in that way?"

She absorbed his disbelief. The shock written across his face. She didn't expect him to understand the way her mother's mind worked. How messed up her family was. It continued to astonish even her. Nor could she explain how desperate her mother was, because that would lead to her current addiction issues and mental health challenges and that was a place she couldn't go.

She fidgeted with the handle on her cup. "She destroyed my sister Ava's life when she convinced her to get married for the season finale of the show, when all of us knew Dimitrio was an unfaithful piece of dirt who wasn't good enough to grace the ground she walked on. But Ava loved him, it generated the highest ratings of any network reality show in the history of television, so who cared?" She threw up a hand. "The show must go on."

Cristiano stared at her, wide-eyed. Her shoulders slumped. "She thinks about it for about ten seconds, then decides we'll forgive her. I'm so sorry, Cristiano. It was a gross miscalculation on my part to trust her. It was my fault."

His gaze darkened. "It wasn't your fault. My security should have caught them. Not to mention the fact that I was the one who came down there last night with the champagne, intent on pursuing things with you. If anyone offered them the opportunity, it was me."

She scoured his face, attempting to figure out how he felt about it all, but his phone was buzzing, his attention diverted as he glanced down at it, then back up at her. "The communications team is advising we let this blow over. Let it run its course. There's no point in chasing after a horse that's already left the barn."

She knew that to be the truth.

He glanced at his watch. "I have a meeting in forty-five minutes. A crisis brewing in LA with my supply chain. I have to go."

She nodded, wishing desperately for some reassurance, for some indication of where they stood, but he merely bent his head and brushed a kiss to her cheek, then picked up his briefcase and left.

She stared down at her coffee. He had so much on his plate. So much pressure and stress, and she had only added to it with this. Done the one thing he'd asked her not to do in creating another scandal.

She knew that shuttered, aloof look. Daniel had worn it before he'd ended things between them. When he'd arrived home at their apartment, only to find a horde of paparazzi waiting, hot on another story. She couldn't even remember what it had been. She only remembered the look of finality on Daniel's face when he'd told her they were done. To pack her things and go.

She sank her teeth into her lip. Had she ruined any chance of a relationship with Cristiano? Of pursuing this fledgling connection between them, one that seemed so very monumental and different? Surely he wouldn't want anything to do with her after this?

* * *

Cristiano got into his sports car and drove the winding highway to Milan. He was cutting it close for his meeting, traffic thick on the early-morning commute, and he had a full-on crisis to navigate in LA, one he thought he'd put to bed weeks ago. Not helped by the couple of hours' sleep he was operating on, which had put him in a combustible mood. Exacerbated by the information Jensen had just given him.

Veronica Davis had sent that photographer to scale his defenses and take lurid, intimate photos of her daughter to satisfy the gossip mill of a television show she subsisted on. He was angry, *furious* about it. At Jensen's mother for abusing her daughter's confidence. For invading his privacy. At the Davis matriarch's absolute refusal to acknowledge the damage she was inflicting on her daughter and her career.

He couldn't believe she would do that to Jensen. But then again, she'd been doing it her entire life. Why stop now? It made him so angry he wanted to slap a restraining order on Veronica Davis and sue her for invading his privacy. But that wasn't going to help the situation. Not aided by the fact that he had known exactly what he was doing when he'd taken that champagne down to the pool last night to seduce Jensen. He'd chosen to complicate things by getting involved with her. By giving in to the madness that consumed him every time he was within touching distance of her.

He was the one who had provided the fodder for her mother's cameras, the photos of Jensen and the prince in the Trevi Fountain downright innocent compared to the intimate photos of them in the pool the night before.

He'd barely been awake, without even a cup of coffee in hand, when he'd received a tearful phone call from his ex-fiancée. Which shouldn't have damn well been a thing, because he'd ended that relationship on as clear a note as he'd thought humanly possible. But Alessandra had been wrecked, *distraught*, which made him wonder if his family had been stepping in, massaging that relationship, planting the seed that he would come around eventually. Which had left him somewhere close to incendiary.

He knew the political value Alessandra brought to the company. The strategic asset she was. He'd spent his entire life devoting himself to FV and what the company needed. Alessandra would no doubt make someone the perfect wife. Just not him. Because after the passion he and Jensen had shared, he knew a marriage to Alessandra would never be enough. His head wanted her to be the one, but his heart did not. It was a truth he was finally willing to admit. His heart was in another place entirely. Which was a problem.

Jensen spent the next few days working long hours to make sure every model who was to appear in the anniversary party show knew their role, right down to the last detail. She knew how frantic the final minutes before a show could be and wanted to make sure they got it right, particularly when she'd asked each model to share a memory of her work with Francesco during the backstage video they were shooting, which she hoped would be a wonderful retrospective of his career. Not to mention the fact that if she was busy, she didn't have to think about her mother and how furious she was with her.

She'd received a text from Veronica late the day the photos had appeared, a response that had made her so angry she hadn't talked to her since.

Of course it was me, darling. It was too good an opportunity to pass up. The Alexandre story was dying out and this gives it fresh legs. Apologies, I know you wanted to keep things quiet, but the producers are ecstatic.

She'd called her sisters, smoke coming out of her ears. Strategized an intervention for when she returned to New York in a few weeks. Obviously, Veronica needed more help than she'd been getting. No longer was Jensen going to bankroll her while sacrificing her own future. Cristiano had been right. She did know herself. Knew who she wanted to be. And she was done enabling her mother to her own detriment.

But first, she acknowledged, her hair and makeup done as the preshow buzz reached a fever-pitch backstage at the party, held at a magnificent seventeenth-century palace in the heart of Milan, she had a promise to Cristiano to keep. She had promised him tonight would be one for the history books. That she would make it the most-talked-about event of the fashion calendar, less Pascal's spectacular debut in a few days' time.

Picking up her bejeweled pink phone, she wound her way through the models, all in various states of readiness, warning them she was about to start filming.

Assured that all the models were at least partially attired in the short Vitale blue robes as she herself was, she started filming with her phone, introducing the backstage video and making her way through the buzzing crowd, stopping to speak with each notable model as they shared a reminiscence about Francesco and his career. By the time she made it to Isabella Müller, who offered a great story about the young designer's genius and his subsequent rise to stardom, it was time to sign off the video, put her phone down and change into her dress, with the show having just begun.

Her heart pumping with blood, her skin flushed with excitement, she slipped on Francesco's bold one-shoulder midnight-blue gown, with its spectacular bedazzled cutout detailing across the back, accentuated with crystal paisley embellishments. A thigh-high slit showed off her endless legs, the figure-hugging design of the dress and the silky, rich material highlighting her pert posterior, perhaps her best asset.

Her dresser adjusted the single strap of the gown so the material lay perfectly flat against her skin, like a glove. She added sparkling diamond drop earrings and a matching cuff bracelet, the perfect accompaniment to the glamorous dress. Her chestnut tresses caught up in a high ponytail, curled, sophisticated ends gave her an effortlessly chic look, highlighting her naturally striking features, set off by a hint of bronzer that dusted her impressive cheekbones.

"Are you ready?" Isabella murmured, appearing at her side, her still-strong accent giving the words an exotic flavor, her calm composure born of thousands of hours on the runway.

Jensen nodded. Wiggled her toes in the silver stilettos she'd donned in an attempt to convince herself this was really happening. That she was about to walk the runway behind her idol. It brought all of her teenage fantasies full circle, and she thought she might burst from the wonder of it all.

Tempering her unusual nerves, she followed Isabella to the wings, created tonight in the ornate anteroom of the palace gallery. The beautiful gilded room was packed with every notable face in fashion, along with every kind of celebrity imaginable, from film to music to theater to the literary world. Given the buzz she'd generated with her social media campaign, she knew it had provided an extra push, intense visibility around the night, but even she was shocked by some of the faces in attendance.

Her gaze found Cristiano, standing in the audience, leaning against a pillar that rose to the majestic second-floor balcony. Dressed in a superbly cut black suit tonight, with a snow-white shirt and a Vitale blue tie, he looked so insanely handsome, her heart skipped a beat, then galloped forward at an unsustainably quick pace.

She'd only seen him in passing since that morning in the kitchen, learning from Ilaria that he'd been embroiled in a supply chain crisis in LA that was causing serious difficulties in the manufacturing process. She'd been worrying about him, about the pressure he'd been under, about everything on his shoulders right now. But according to an earlier conversation with Ilaria, they'd had a breakthrough last night, and a temporary solution was now in place. Which was a massive relief.

"He is ridiculously handsome," Isabella murmured, following her gaze to Cristiano. "Not such a bad subject to play to, is he?"

Jensen's stomach dropped, swirling in a crazy, off-beat rhythm. She had no idea where they stood. Whether he'd changed his mind about her after the paparazzi debacle. She'd convinced herself that if he had, it would be fine. It was always fine. She would bury herself in her work and pretend she didn't care, because that's what she always did. Ignore how she felt, retreat into herself, refuse to acknowledge her feelings. Because then, she'd never have to feel the pain of rejection. Of him deciding he didn't want her after all.

But she knew she was lying to herself. Knew why she'd been running from him the past few weeks. Because of the wild, uncontrollable longing he unearthed in her. Because she wanted *him*. The strong, honorable, impenetrable man that he was, one a woman might desperately want at her back. The kind of man she never even knew existed. She wanted the headlines to be true—that she could be the woman at his side. And she thought she might be fooling herself into thinking that could ever happen. Because surely, he'd never choose someone like her.

The show director announced her cue. Drawing in a deep breath, she pushed her shoulders back and stepped into the lights at the head of the runway.

Cristiano watched Jensen step into the spotlight in Francesco's magnificent midnight-blue dress, so spectacularly beautiful, she hurt his eyes. She was the brightest star by far on a night that had featured a cavalcade of them. A spectacular celestial event you saw once in a lifetime. From her gleaming mahogany hair, swept back from her face in a high ponytail, to her ebony eyes that shone with exotic promise, to her incredible, curvaceous body set off to perfection in the stunning dress, she was a vision.

She had promised him she would deliver, and she had. Social media was ablaze with photos and posts about tonight's show, making it unlikely any moment in fashion would top it this year. She had been dedicated and brilliant these past few weeks, everything he'd needed her to be. But she'd also gone above and beyond the call of duty to make sure everything fell into place for tonight.

The relief he felt was palpable. A massive weight off

his shoulders. He'd needed tonight to go perfectly and it had. A fitting tribute to his grandfather's brilliant legacy. But he knew it meant more to him than that. He'd needed to know he could depend on Jensen. That he was right about her. That his instincts had been correct. Because if he'd thought the last few days might have cooled his ardour, might somehow have imprinted some last vestige of sanity on his brain, they had instead only underscored his feelings for her. Intensified those emotions.

He had missed her. Missed her company. Missed talking to her—the escape she provided from the endless weight on his shoulders. And he wasn't in the mood to hold back. Not any longer.

She stepped back with the other models, her breathtaking trip down the runway complete, applauding the historic moment as his grandmother stepped onto the stage. Seemed utterly flustered when Marcella caught her and pressed a kiss to both of her cheeks, murmuring something in her ear that unearthed a flush across her high-boned cheeks. He hoped to hell it was the credit she deserved for her efforts.

"She is spectacular tonight," Ilaria murmured, from her position by his side. "Our brand ratings have skyrocketed since the photos of you two went public."

"I thought the Italian people were furious with her for violating the sanctity of the Trevi Fountain."

Ilaria smiled. "The Italian press is fickle. They have decided you are far too glamorous a couple for them to resist."

Cristiano wasn't in a mood to disagree. He'd decided he wanted Jensen a long time ago. He was all in. And he didn't much care what anyone thought about it.

He bided his time. Through the three-course dinner that followed. Through the speech he made to mark his grandfather's legacy and the others that followed. Through the formal passing of the baton to Pascal, to the prescribed post-dinner chitchat Milanese society required on a gorgeous, late-summer evening. Through the results of the auction, which raised millions for charity, a mind-numbing blur of voices and niceties he abided rather than actually listened to, he was so physically exhausted, he could barely stand on two feet.

He watched Jensen flit from group to group, spreading that inexorable, undeniable charm of hers, casting everything and everyone she touched in a golden glow. Really, he had no interest in dancing when the time came, but the prospect of holding her in his arms held too great a sway. As the band swung into a slow, sultry number, the majestic frescoes of the ballroom a stunning backdrop, he moved purposefully, locating her in a group of people near the bar, giving in to the fiery need that burned in his veins.

Her back turned to him, she was cast in candlelight, the midnight-blue gown following every line of her voluptuous body in a loving, sensual caress. He thought he might be a little obsessed with her perfect backside, which undoubtedly held the entire male population in its thrall. It made him think very improper thoughts, with only her, that dress and himself starring in those particular fantasies. And maybe that was because he hadn't been able to get that night in the pool out of his head and everything in him was clamoring for them to finish what they'd started.

"Dance?" he requested huskily, tapping a finger on her shoulder and holding out a hand. Eyes smoldering with the same banked need he felt, she voiced her excuses to the group and placed her hand in his, following him to the dance floor, which was teeming with partygoers enjoying the live music under a massive twinkling chandelier.

She moved into his arms, one hand clasped in his, the other on his shoulder. He settled his palm to the curve of her hip, just beneath the enticing cutouts that exposed her bare, silky flesh, his other hand wrapping around hers. She was warm, he registered, a flush dusting the creamy perfection of her cheeks, her décolletage, above the sophisticated asymmetrical neckline of her dress.

Luminous brown eyes met blue in a gaze that lasted more than a heartbeat. "Aren't you afraid this will stoke the rumor mill? Make people talk?"

"Let them." The low timbre of his voice sent a shiver through Jensen, as Cristiano rested his sapphire gaze on hers. "Thank you for everything you've done to make tonight a success. It is everything I'd imagined it would be and more."

Jensen absorbed the dark flicker of emotion in his gaze. "You miss him."

He inclined his head. "He was everything. I wish he could have been here tonight to see this. His biggest fear was that he would be forgotten. Tonight would have obliterated that thought."

"He had no need to worry about that," she murmured. "He's one of the greatest designers of all time. *Irreplaceable*."

"*Si*. But he was human, like everyone else. He worried Pascal's legacy would supersede his."

Jensen absorbed that surprising revelation. She'd never thought of the brutally intimidating Francesco as in any way human. He had always seemed so much larger than life. And yet she could see how hard that would be, hand-picking your successor. Finding someone who could carry out your vision, who was successful enough on his own two feet to command the respect of the fashion world, and yet being equally afraid he could overshadow you. She had felt that fear with Ariana.

"Marcella said some very nice things to me on the runway. About tonight."

"It's about time. You've been spectacular." Cristiano's fingers tightened around her waist, drawing her closer, the tantalizing scent of his sophisticated cologne filling her head, annihilating her brain cells. "What was it like to close the show? To walk alongside Isabella?"

"Incredible," she breathed. "She is such an icon. I'm in awe of everything she's done. Both as a model and a businesswoman."

He inclined his head. "Her activewear line has been very successful."

She dug her teeth into her lip. "We had a really good conversation about the pressures of modeling. How she handled it. She knew it wasn't going to last forever, so she put a contingency plan in place. Developed the idea for the activewear line while she was still modeling. Leveraged her influencer status to do it. Someday—" she said, her teeth sinking deeper into her lip "—I'd like to follow in her footsteps."

Cristiano cocked a dark brow at her. "How so?"

"I've always been good at makeup. I helped the team with the shoot when we were down a person and they loved the work I did. I'm always doing experimental videos on social media that get lots of views. I thought," she said, feeling more than a little awkward at exposing her inner musings, because she'd always been afraid they would be shot down given the criticism she'd faced, "I would like to create my own makeup line. If I could find the right partner."

He must have heard the self-consciousness in her voice, because his sapphire gaze softened to a deep midnight blue. "I think that could only be a rip-roaring success. Not only do you have the sharpest business brain of anyone I know, but you have the personality and charm to sell sunshine to a Sicilian, *cara*. Ilaria showed me one of your how-to videos. I think it had garnered about three million views."

A dark flush lit her cheeks. Both at the compliment and the endearment he'd thrown so casually at her. Except Cristiano never did anything carelessly; he did it with thought and *intention*, and the realization sent a full-body shiver through her.

"If you like," he murmured, drawing her closer still, his eyes on hers, "I will put you in contact with a friend who runs a global cosmetics brand. You can decide if it's something you want to pursue. But for now," he said, his mouth moving to her ear, "I am done talking business. I am done solving global supply chain crises, and I am definitely done pretending I don't want you, when I so clearly do."

Jensen's knees sagged, zapped by that definitive promise. "Cristiano," she breathed.

He didn't reply. Just slid his palm lower, until it was resting against the bare skin of her lower back, his fingertips burning her flesh like a brand. A promise. They stopped talking then, just danced, the way they moved together an instinctive thing now. As if their bodies recognized each other in some primal, perfect connection that defied reason. Definition.

"I meant what I said in that pool, Jensen. I'm not walking away from you. I want to know you," he murmured. "All of you. But if I am going to do that, you have to let me in. You have to let me know all of you. You have to trust me."

Her heart raced in her chest. Because hadn't that always been her biggest fear? That if she shared herself with someone, *truly* shared herself with someone, if she let them beneath the sparkly outer packaging she had always hidden behind, they wouldn't want her anymore? They might reject her like everyone else had done in her life. Declare her as superficial as the world believed her to be. And that she could not bear, not from Cristiano.

But if she never learned to open up, to make herself vulnerable, how would she ever know what she could have with him? What she was capable of? If she could have that relationship with him she wanted so desperately? Because she did. There was no point in denying it anymore.

"I am scared," she murmured breathlessly. "I don't know if I can do it, Cristiano. I've never opened up to anyone like that. I've never *allowed* myself to open up like that, because for me, it's always meant getting hurt."

His eyes glittered a deep sapphire blue. "I won't hurt you, *mia cara*. I promise you that."

He bent his head and kissed her, a deep, soul-affirming caress that stole her breath. As if they weren't in the middle of a room full of people. As if he didn't care who knew how he felt about her. It disassembled something deep inside her. Broke down her walls. *Shattered* them.

She kissed him back, her fingers tangling in the coarse hair at the base of his nape. Moved closer still, until she could feel the steady beat of his heart against hers. The heat of his tall, strong body transferring itself to her.

Dimly aware of flashbulbs going off around them, she couldn't bring herself to care, she was so lost in him. In how he made her feel.

They danced like that for a while, reveling in the heat. The anticipation. His hand on her hip moved lower, bringing her into closer contact with the lower half of his body. A gasp left her throat. He was hard and aroused and oh so impressive and it made her heart pound in her chest.

"I think it's time to leave. *Sei d'accordo?*"

She nodded her head, wordlessly. Somehow fumbled her way through the good-nights they quickly made before heading for the exit, where Cristiano's driver was waiting. Climbing into the back of the luxurious vehicle, she had barely registered the click of the door before he was reaching for her, the privacy panel shielding them from view.

Straddling his hard, sinewy thighs, she framed his face with her palms. Lowered her mouth to his. The kiss they shared was passionate and urgent. Long, leisurely slides of her mouth against his hard, sensual one, exchanging breath on heady murmurs that devolved into a more intimate exploration of each other involving a delicate slide of her tongue against his, then his against hers, his knowing expertise lighting her body on fire.

Unable or unwilling to call a halt to the passionate exchange, she dug her fingers into the knot of his tie, breaking the kiss for a moment of air while she stripped it off and tossed it on the seat of the car. Fingers stumbling over the buttons of his snow-white shirt, she managed to get it open, her mouth sliding down over his jaw to explore his salty, masculine skin, dusted with a light covering of coarse dark hair. Slid her hands over the magnificent definition of his muscles as they converged at the center of his hot, hard abdomen, not an ounce of additional flesh on him.

He was so masculine, so intoxicating to her senses, that her brain was overwhelmed. Overstimulated. *Overcome*. He muttered something in Italian, his palms cupping her bottom in the glittery dress. Dragging her closer, so she was straddling the hard jut of his erection. So she could feel every impressive inch of him imprinted beneath the fine material of his trousers, branding her, promising heaven.

Her hands dropped, fumbling with the button on his trousers. She wanted, *needed* him inside her. Needed to feel him filling her with that awesome power of his. To finally consummate this wild thing between them. But he clamped his fingers over hers and dragged her hand away.

"Not here," he rasped.

She yanked in a centering breath as he set her back on the seat, composed himself, his hands dealing with the buttons on his shirt, then depressed the privacy screen enough to tell the driver to step on it, before they lapsed into an anticipation-fueled silence that stoked her nerves to a fever pitch.

The villa was cast in a muted glow when they pulled up in the circular drive. Cristiano issued a curt thank-you to his driver, set his palm to her back and ushered her inside and up the magnificent staircase to the master suite.

With its warm Lombardy cotto stone floors, antique Venetian chandeliers and glorious views of the mountains beyond the open French doors, it was heavenly. She'd fallen in love with the space when they'd shot the television commercial, drawn to its sumptuous elegance and warmth. But now, with the elegant sconces on the wall casting a golden glow throughout the space, the harvest moon gleaming a glorious pink and orange through the open windows, she felt as if she didn't have enough air in her lungs.

Or maybe it was Cristiano, his jacket discarded, in the dove-white shirt, open at the throat to reveal his deep olive skin, his hands tossing his gold cuff links on a dresser. He made her heart flutter in her chest.

"Take the dress off," he murmured, his huskily issued command singeing her blood.

With anyone else, she might have hesitated, felt self-conscious. But not with Cristiano. She moved her shaking fingers to the side zipper of the dress, sliding it down, until it reached its mooring, his hot gaze following every movement. Sinking her fingers into the shimmery fabric, she pulled the dress up and over her head and threw it on a chair, standing in front of him, clad in a wispy cream thong and matching bra.

"Come here." His deep midnight-blue gaze seared her skin. Heart slamming in her chest, her breath coming in short, uneven pulls of air, she closed the distance between them. Stopped when she was mere centimeters from him. He raised his hand, ran his thumb along the smooth skin beneath the clasp of her bra and unhooked it with an expertise that stoked the nerves raging inside her.

When he was done, he sat down on the edge of the massive king-size bed, caught her hand in his and drew her forward, until she was kneeling on the bed, straddling his hard thighs, his palm at her back steadying her. His slumberous gaze fixed on her pert, uplifted breasts, the hazy desire shimmering in his dark blue eyes igniting a confidence she sorely needed.

Closing her eyes, she absorbed the searing pleasure as he took one rosy peak inside his mouth and caressed her, bolts of sensation arcing from the sensitive tip to some-where deep inside, lighting her on fire. It was so good, so intense, it made her moan, dig her fingernails into the skin at the nape of his neck and move needily against the hard ridge of him beneath his trousers, her thin pant-ies little barrier as she rocked against him, each breathy movement pushing the tension between them higher.

His blue gaze tangled with hers as anticipation tore the air between them. Then he took the other throbbing peak inside the heat of his mouth, taking his time, mak-ing sure she felt all of it, making sure she was molten for him inside, ready to internally combust, before he rolled her beneath him, sank his fingers into the delicate strings of her panties and stripped them off of her, so she was bare beneath him. Vulnerable. Aching. Wanting.

She reached for him, attempting to relieve him of his clothes, because he still had far too many on, but his knees on the inside of her thighs spread her open instead, the extreme vulnerability of her position halting her pro-test in her throat. Dipping his head, he trailed his mouth and tongue from the dip of her belly button to the jut of her hip bone, then lower, until she could feel the warm heat of his breath on her aroused flesh seconds before he consumed her with one possessive lap of his tongue, his palm on her belly, holding her where he wanted her when she bucked up from the pleasure of it. Eyes on hers, his gaze hot, he murmured sexy Italian words to her while he consumed her, words she had no idea of the meaning of, except that she wanted more of what he was giving her.

Sinking her fingers into his thick, coarse hair, she held him there while he feasted on her, driving her higher with every expert caress designed to make her mad. Until she was shaking, quivering, her entire body poised on an earth-shattering precipice. Then he kicked her over it with ruthless precision, the hard lash of his tongue against the trembling, tender nub at the heart of her sending a violent wave of pleasure to every nerve ending in her body, in a release that seemed to go on forever.

Cristiano stripped off his clothes, his eyes never leaving the woman in his bed, her chestnut-colored hair a dark flame against the ivory sheets, her long, golden limbs splayed out, his for the taking. She watched as he shrugged the shirt off his broad shoulders, pushed his trousers and boxers over his hips, sheathed himself, then prowled back to the bed to join her.

He was hard, aching for her. He was fairly sure he'd never wanted anything this much in his life. He was also fairly sure she felt the same. Although she was doing her best to maintain her cool, those liquid ebony eyes of hers flashing with heat and humor as he set a knee on the bed and came down over her.

"I will say, that might have been worth the wait," she murmured, her teeth lodging in her full bottom lip.

He slid a palm down the velvety surface of her thigh and urged it around his waist. Slid his other hand to the silky, slick flesh at the apex of her thighs, his thumb finding the tiny nub that gave her pleasure. A moan left her throat, her even white teeth sinking deeper into her lush lip at his slow, sensual caress, her ebony eyes darkening to black.

"Might?" he murmured softly, "I think we're going to need a more resounding response on that one."

Jensen would have told him just about anything if he'd keep touching her like he was, his teasing, circular caresses winding her up all over again, as if he hadn't just given her one of the best orgasms of her life, still pulsing through her nerve endings. But then he slid his middle finger, slick from touching her, inside her pulsing flesh in a smooth, velvet stroke and she arched into the caress, another low moan escaping her mouth. A few deep, even plunges that felt like heaven, then that teasing circular motion of his thumb against her clitoris again, a ghostly sweet caress, and then a second finger sliding inside her, stretching her velvet heat.

"Cristiano..." she breathed, eyes on his. "Please."

"Please, what?"

"Please—I need you. I need—"

He brought his mouth down to hers. *"Tell me."*

"There is no...*might*. It's so good. Please—"

He slid his palm under the satiny smooth skin of her buttocks. Raised her up so he could enter her on a swift, firm thrust. She gasped as he pushed his way inside her, filling her inch by inch with his thick, hard length, his hand at her hip controlling the movement with a sensual expertise that stole her breath. He was so big, so *overwhelming*, her body had to adjust, softening with each lazy stroke to accommodate him, until finally, he was buried inside her and she was struggling for air.

"Breathe," he murmured, his gaze on hers.

Erotic whispers shivered across her skin as she did as he commanded. Felt the pulse of his heartbeat buried deep inside of her, an achingly intimate connection she felt all the way to her soul. Slowly, inexorably, her body adjusted to his. Melted around his possession. And when his hands tightened around her hips and he started to move, holding her still as he stroked up deep inside her, so thick and masculine he stretched her completely, she knew it would never be like this with anyone else. This mind-numbingly good. This soul-shattering.

Drawing his mouth down to hers, she kissed him, her nails scraping down the hard muscles of his back, each hard stroke melting her insides to liquid and deepening his dominant possession. Until she was completely his. And when he curved his fingers around her thigh and wrapped it around his waist, his palm raising her bottom so he could hit a sweet spot, an angle that promised ecstasy, a scream ripped from her throat and shattered the night air as they came together in a hot rush of pleasure that made the whole room go black.

CHAPTER SEVEN

CRISTIANO ARRIVED HOME well after seven, exhausted from an hours-long meeting with his lawyers in which they'd attempted to work through the red tape surrounding his deal with Nicholas Zhang, set to close as soon as they'd manage to do so. It was a relief, given the stakes he was gambling with. But it still didn't mean he hadn't pushed the company to the brink, that every piece of his complex, multifaceted plan had to go as envisioned or it could and would come tumbling down around him. A pressure that coiled around his neck like a golden noose.

With hours of work still left to do, he retreated to his office, requested more strong coffee from Filomena, and attempted to revive his brain, which refused to work on the few hours' sleep he'd had over the past week. Avoided the fact that Jensen was home this evening, and just a stone's throw away, a respite he had allowed himself far too many times this past week, because it felt like the actions of a drowning man, grabbing hold of a lifeline. A foreign vulnerability he had no idea how to process, because it felt like weakness—a state of affairs he avoided like the plague.

He'd never allowed himself to feel this depth of emotion for a woman before. He'd always dated women like Alessandra, safe, predictable choices who wouldn't cause waves in his life, because it hadn't been a luxury he could afford. But maybe, he acknowledged, it went deeper than that.

His parents had loved each other to distraction. Too much so, in his opinion, because in the days following the boating accident which had killed his father, his mother had been so heartbroken, she hadn't had the will to fight for her own life, a critical factor that had determined her survival. She had died days later, leaving him and Ilaria with their own heartbreak.

Maybe he had decided that that level of emotion just wasn't worth it. That he would build a world so impenetrable, so shatterproof, that it could never come crashing down on him like it had that hot afternoon in July. Had built impenetrable walls around his heart to protect himself, walls Jensen had decimated with her intense vulnerability and beautiful smile. And now he didn't know what to do with what he'd been handed. Was navigating uncharted territory—territory he couldn't contemplate negotiating with everything he had resting on his shoulders.

Before his wayward thoughts derailed him completely, he rolled up his sleeves and got to work. It was close to nine when a light knock sounded on the door and Jensen walked in, dressed in an olive-green dress. She closed the door behind her and took up a position leaning against his desk, her concerned gaze resting on his fatigued face.

"Cristiano," she said quietly, "you are exhausted. You've hardly slept this week. If you keep going like this, you won't make it through the rest of the week."

"I'm fine," he murmured, attempting to put up some kind of a fight against the pull he felt toward her, which had never been in doubt, but seemed ten times stronger now. "I'm almost done."

"And what will you have for tomorrow?" She didn't attempt to question why he hadn't come to her, or why he was holding back. He almost thought he read the same elemental wariness in her rich ebony gaze, as if she, too, knew the power of what they shared and its ability to decimate them both. Instead, she cocked her head to the side. "You once gave me a speech about knowing my limits, yet it's clear you don't know yours. Every person at that company is depending on you to pull this off, Cristiano. You need to pace yourself."

He threw down the pen. Raked a hand through his hair. Maybe she was right. His head would likely be much clearer in the morning.

He took her in. The dress she was wearing, one of those deceptively innocent, flirtatious short dresses of hers, that made the most of her undeniably perfect backside. How the olive hue, embroidered with little white daisies, enhanced her sun-kissed skin and devastatingly dark eyes.

"How was the luncheon today?" he murmured, feeling the visceral heat rise between them.

"Good," she replied quietly. "Uneventful. It will play well in the media."

"*Bene*. And the shoot in Cannes. Did you get it straightened out with Tatiana?"

"Yes." She hesitated for a moment, disquiet glittering in her eyes, then plunged on. "I have to be there for another day. Until Thursday. But I will fly back right after that. It's not a problem."

"*Cristo*, Jensen." He blew out a breath. "This timing makes me very uncomfortable. Reschedule the shoot. Let someone else do it. It's not worth the risk."

"It's fine," she insisted. "I will have the jet. I can make it work, Cristiano. *Trust me.*"

He did. She had proven herself to him over and over again. And he wanted what was best for her, because he cared about her that much. *"Bene,"* he agreed. "Do it, then."

"Thank you." She dug her teeth into her lip. Looked loath to speak, but did anyway. "I missed you last night," she admitted huskily. "I didn't sleep well at all."

He crumbled then. Melted completely. Pushed back his chair and beckoned to her. She came to him, slid onto his lap, cupped his face in her hands and kissed him in that way that had always seemed holy between them. He should have stopped it, *would* have stopped it, given there was still a handful of staff roaming the villa, but he didn't have the willpower to deny himself her. Not when she ran her palms over the hard muscles of his thighs under the fine material of his trousers and found the hot, hard length of him aching for her. *Craving* her as he always did.

On the kiss went, burned brighter and hotter. Her name left his throat, raspy and broken. She unzipped him and pushed the skirt of her dress aside. It took him a moment to realize she had nothing on underneath, a fact that made his head want to explode with need, until he realized he had no protection and a smothered oath left his lips.

"It's okay," she murmured against his mouth, "I'm protected." Which had never been a promise he'd elected to accept in the past, given the responsibilities that lay on his shoulders, but in that moment, he could not deny himself what his body was screaming for. And when she took him inside her with a languid tilt of her voluptuous hips, and he was buried in tight, hot, wet velvet, he thought he might lose it, right there and right then, from the pure sensation of it all, because she felt like salvation.

Somehow, he kept his composure, hanging on by a thread, counting backward in his head to maintain some type of control, the connection between them unparalleled as she rode him slow and deep, her eyes on his, his fingers clenched tightly around the arms of the chair. And then she punctuated those slow, sensual, maddening circles with sweet kisses that undid him completely. He held out as long as he could, his body desperate to find release, until the flames threatened to suck him under.

Releasing his death grip on the chair, he found the swollen, slick flesh between her thighs, intent on giving her pleasure. His thumb on the tiny, hot nub he'd come to know intimately, he watched her face as he took her apart with a slow, lazy touch, her beautiful brown eyes glazed with passion, a muffled scream leaving her mouth before he allowed himself his own release, sinking his teeth into the satiny curve of her shoulder as he spilled himself deep inside of her, claiming her in a way he'd never done before. Breaking his last rule.

When they were done, spent and wrapped around each other, when the shudders rippling through their bodies had subsided, he picked her up, her legs wrapped around his waist, and carried her to his bedroom. Once there, he fell into a deep, dreamless sleep, Jensen curved against him, his arm around her waist, his surrender complete.

Jensen woke as the first filtered light of day entered the room, arcing across the massive canopied bed and bathing her in a warm, golden glow. Cristiano had left for the office hours before, intent on finishing the work he'd left undone the night before. She closed her eyes and reveled in the rightness of it all. How adored and protected she felt. How, for once in her life, she felt whole, as if the pieces that had always seemed misplaced inside of her had right-sided themselves. As if she was *enough*.

She snuggled deeper into the silk sheets, basking in the glow. She was terrified to admit she needed him. *Wanted* him. That she was feeling as vulnerable as she was. Had been scared to ask him to give her another day in Cannes, lest she somehow ruin it all. Because she couldn't miss that assignment. Needed to get her career back on track. Dispel the rumors that had been circulating ever since Ariana Lordes had walked in her place in Shanghai and stolen the show. The job *she* had earned. It was a burr that dug itself deep beneath her skin. The need to prove she was still on top. That she was still the *best*. That no one could outshine her in front of the camera.

Feeling lazy and sated from her and Cristiano's passionate lovemaking, which they'd indulged in once more before he'd left, slow and sweet and breathtakingly perfect, Jensen finally got out of bed. Electing not to put on her dress before she showered, and needing java desperately, she padded to the wardrobe and found a white shirt of Cristiano's to slip on. Securing her hair in a ponytail, she went downstairs to the sunny, bright kitchen and opened the cupboard to find her favorite mug, which had somehow made its way to a higher shelf. She stood on tiptoe to retrieve it. Then she poured herself a cup of coffee and was adding a dollop of milk when a hushed gasp sounded behind her.

She spun on her heel, her heart slamming in her chest as she recognized the small, slender, exquisitely dressed female standing in the doorway of the kitchen, her big blue eyes wide. Mouth gaping open, she surveyed Jensen, from the top of her tousled head, down over Cristiano's crisp white shirt, which reached to mid-thigh, to her candy-apple-red-painted toes, glimmering against the dark wood floor.

Jensen wasn't sure who recovered first, her or Alessandra. All she knew was that she somehow had the sense to shove the full cup of coffee onto the counter before she spilled it with her shaking hands. Then decided it must be her, when Alessandra's red-tinted mouth continued to open and close, as if she meant to say something, then stopped to reformulate.

"Dio mio," she finally breathed. "It's true. You *are* sleeping with him. And in his shirt…" She shook her head, china-blue eyes glazed. "You are wearing his *shirt. Santo cielo.* What is happening?"

Jensen curled her fingers around the counter, inordinately aware that Cristiano's shirt only came to mid-thigh, exposing the long, golden length of her legs. That her tousled hair must look like she'd come directly from bed, *his* bed, and her mouth, swollen from the sensual kisses they'd shared, looked vulnerable and well used. Not to mention the bite mark on her shoulder she'd acquired in the height of passion, the too-large shirt gaping at the neckline.

She crossed her arms over her chest and sank back against the counter. Attempted as much composure as she could manage when Alessandra was clearly clad head to toe in designer fabric, her makeup immaculate, her critical gaze assessing. "Alessandra," she murmured, "how lovely to meet you. We haven't had a chance to meet properly in person yet."

The petite blonde's glossed mouth curled. "Perhaps you are too busy making headlines to engage in normal social behavior like the rest of us." She shook her head, her honey-blond curls bouncing, her mouth a hard line. "I have no idea what he sees in you. He must have gone temporarily blind."

Jensen's back stiffened. So it was going to be like that. She'd tried for civil, but clearly civil was not the mood of the day. In the same moment, she wondered if it was the Milanese woman's usual behavior to march into Cristiano's home uninvited. Whether she carried with her such a deeply engrained sense of ownership over Cristiano's life and home, she felt it was within her purvey to do so. Which would have been unnerving, given what she and Cristiano had shared last night, if he hadn't made it clear to her that he and Alessandra were over.

So what was this? A social call?

She set a steady, unwavering gaze on the other woman. "Cristiano is not home. He went into the office."

Alessandra's chin dipped, a visible hint of disappointment glittering in her eyes. 'I was hoping to find him in. I wanted to speak with him."

"Perhaps you can try the office." *Anywhere but here.* She might be assuming a confident demeanour, but nothing about her felt assured when it came to this woman. She reeked of aristocratic authority. It was written across her cultured face. While Jensen felt every inch the scandalous reality show trash Alessandra so clearly believed her to be. "Unless," she offered, "there is something I or Filomena can help you with."

That felt like a stretch, but she tried to keep it cordial. Unfortunately, her words lit a fire under the woman opposite her, her blue eyes flashing against her delicate, finely boned face. "I wouldn't get too comfortable if I were you," she bit out. "Do you really think he's going to take a relationship with you seriously? Cristiano might be having a little fun with you. *Sowing his wild oats* as his grandmother believes he is doing. Perhaps you have seduced him into this—" she waved a hand at her, her face contemptuous "—*fling* with you. But that is all it will ever be. Cristiano will make the right match for himself and for the company, and trust me, that choice will not be you."

Oh my God. The color drained from Jensen's face, until she was sure she was chalk white, the blow the other woman had lobbed at her landing squarely in her solar plexus, stealing her breath. She could not believe she'd just said that. But perhaps what hurt more was Marcella's assessment of the situation. That Cristiano was *sowing his wild oats,* exactly as she'd feared. That no one except him seemed to think this relationship was going to last, and she wondered if that, in itself, was wishful thinking.

It stirred up every fear, every insecurity she'd ever had, anxiety sliding through her blood like a red tide, heating her skin. Because she knew he'd been holding back this last couple of days, fighting his feelings. She'd seen it in his eyes. Watched him battle it. Why it had taken all her courage to seek him out like she had. To put herself out there like that.

Forcing herself to remain calm, she hauled in a deep breath, pulling oxygen into her lungs. "I don't think you have any idea what Cristiano and I share," she finally said quietly. "But thank you for the warning. I will take it into consideration. Now, if you'll excuse me, I have packing to do."

Jensen flew to Cannes the next day, still reeling from her confrontation with Alessandra, which had severely eaten away at the confidence she'd had in her and Cristiano. She was afraid that Alessandra was right. That Cristiano might desire her, might want her, that had never been in doubt, maybe he'd even convinced himself that she was what he wanted. But how could that ever be enough for him? He loved his family. *Adored* them. And Marcella disliked her, despite her latent praise. Cristiano would always do the right thing, just as Alessandra had said he would. How could she ever think he would do otherwise?

How long would it take for Cristiano to realize his mistake? For him to discover she wasn't at all a suitable woman to have at his side? She wasn't stupid enough to think the headlines would stop overnight. That she could control them, when the tabloids would just make something up in the absence of any real news. It had been an omnipresent force in her life.

She and Cristiano had amazing chemistry. But what happened when that passion faded and they entered the reality stage of their relationship? She'd seen what had happened to her parents' marriage when that kind of passion faded. Her mother and father had been completely incompatible. What had happened to Ava's marriage when the glitz and glamour had dissipated and the reality of who she'd married had set in. Everything had fallen apart. Everything always fell apart.

She'd insisted Filomena not tell Cristiano about Alessandra's visit, because it was the last thing he needed on his mind with everything else he had on his plate. A similar promise she made to herself, as she slid into the car her client had sent to the Nice airport, and traveled to the luxury hotel on the beach in Cannes, where she'd been reserved a lovely suite with a gorgeous view of the

Mediterranean Sea. She was going to focus on work and work only, and not let her insecurities rule.

The shoot began at the crack of dawn the following morning on one of the Riviera's most beautiful beaches. Hidden away from the masses of tourists and accessible only via a steep set of steps that numbered in the hundreds, it was a trek to get to the spot the photographer had chosen, a spectacular locale set between two scenic cliffs. She was exhausted by the end of the first day, with the unrelenting heat beating down on her, the weather unseasonably hot for early September.

She collapsed into bed at nine in her air-conditioned suite, only to wake to a second day with more of the same. The end in sight, she marshaled her reserves and fought through the day, which didn't end until well after sunset. Beyond relieved the shoot was over, she returned to her hotel and packed her things, intent on getting to the airport early. She had just slipped the last couple of things into her bag when her cell phone rang. Glancing at it, she absorbed the name of her mother's agent flashing across the screen.

Wondering why Natalia would be calling her, she almost ignored it, given the car waiting downstairs. But something told her to pick up the call. The panic in Natalia's voice chilled her blood. "I heard you are in Cannes shooting. I need your help. Your mother is on a bender and I'm afraid of what she might do. The producer just called and said it's a mess. Your father announced he is marrying some young Hollywood starlet half his age, and she has completely lost it."

Jensen absorbed the somewhat familiar scenario, which had played out far too frequently in her life, her father and the cavalcade of young actresses he'd gone through. That he was remarrying was new and rather startling. She was sure her mother was devastated, because it hadn't been her decision to end things. She still loved him. But that couldn't be her problem right now. Right now, she had to get back to Milan.

She rubbed a palm against her temple. "She is *here?* In Cannes?"

"Yes. They announced next year's jury. Your mother is on it. There was a party afterward. I don't know if she's off her meds or what, Jensen. But it's messy."

Her mind raced, searching for solutions. "Natalia," she murmured, "I can't get caught up in this. I'm about to catch a flight back to Milan. FV is closing Fashion Week tomorrow night and I am headlining the show. You're going to need to handle this one."

"I wish I could, but I'm in New York in meetings and no one there is capable of getting through to her. The usual producer is off, and Veronica doesn't know the new one." The agent paused, swallowed hard. "She is out of it, Jensen. I mean *out of it*. I don't know what's wrong with her. What she's going to do. I've never seen her like this. I'm afraid she's going to destroy her reputation."

Her stomach sank. This could *not* be happening. Tonight, of all nights. But now, she was scared, too, her heart racing in her chest. "Why don't you get Nancy, the assistant producer, to talk to her? She likes her. She may listen to reason if she knows it will affect the show."

"They stopped filming an hour ago. Someone decided it might be inflaming the situation."

Jensen's blood ran cold. They never stopped filming. *Ever*. Drama was great TV.

She frowned. "What do you mean, destroying her reputation? What is she doing?"

"Apparently, she's had a lot to drink on top of the lack or excess of medication. She told Umberto Riccetti he is a misogynistic pig who never knew how to pick his actresses. Riccetti then told everyone she never had any talent and blacklisted her from his events. It's like she's blazing a trail of destruction through the entire party."

Oh God. Jensen wiped a palm over her brow. She could not let her mother disintegrate in front of half of the French Riviera. She would never recover from it. Nor would it aid her efforts to get her mother back on her own two feet.

She didn't have a choice. She had to get her mother out of there. She glanced at her watch. She was early for her flight. With luck, she could make it to the party, retrieve her mother and still get to the airport on time. The key thing was to remove her from the situation before she did any more damage.

"Okay," she murmured. "I'm on my way. Where's the party?"

Cristiano exited his last media interview, the business reporter having peppered him with hard-edged questions that had flayed an inch off his skin by the time she'd concluded. Which had not been unfounded. Francesco Vitale had lost ground to its competitors in the lead-up to Pascal's launch, and his deal with Nicholas Zhang, which would have shored up skepticism about the company's ability to compete on a global scale, was still mired in red tape. Everything, it seemed, was dependent on how Pascal Ferrari's debut collection for FV was received tonight.

Key to which was Jensen, who would wear the most dazzling creations of the evening. Out with Nicholas Zhang and his family for dinner the previous night, he'd missed her call to tell him she had altered her plans because of an issue with the shoot, and would travel back to Milan with Giselle, her client, the following morning. Which had been infuriating enough, given her promises. Then had come the photos of her partying it up on the Riviera with her friends, blowing up his stack of daily clips this morning, which had sent his blood pressure soaring.

He never should have given in to her demands to do that shoot. Should have listened to his instincts, given everything that could go wrong. Given this was the night that could make or break his company. *Santo cielo.*

Lengthening his stride, he strode from the media center to the tent that housed the models and designers as they prepared for the show in the historic Piazza del Duomo, a legendary Fashion Week setting. Featuring the stunning, sparkling Gothic Duomo di Milano cathedral as a backdrop on a perfect Milanese night, the tent was buzzing with activity. Sofia, his assistant, materialized the moment he walked in, the look on her face sending a wave of foreboding through him.

"Where is she?" he bit out.

"She was grounded in Nice until twenty minutes ago, because of the weather. She left you a voice mail."

A dark curl of fury unfurled inside him, twisting itself around his insides, along with a soul-deep, bitter disappointment, because he'd believed in her. He'd truly thought she wouldn't let him down. That she would prioritize him over everything else, particularly given the bond they had created—one he'd thought was special and real. Instead, she had gone out partying the night before, to hell with the responsibilities that lay ahead, had *lied* to him about what she was doing, and now she was going to miss the show.

He listened to the voice mail, heat blanketing his skin. Jensen's voice was husky and halting,

"Cristiano... I'm so sorry. We've been grounded all afternoon. I don't think I'm going to make it. I will call you as soon as I land." Another drawn-out silence, then she whispered, "I don't know what to say."

He didn't either, to be honest. The fury pulsing through him threatened to make his head explode. His twenty-million-dollar bet, the bet he'd fought Francesco tooth and nail for, the bet he'd staked his reputation on, the face of his brand, was MIA. For the biggest show in FV's history. He wanted to lose his shit. But now was not the time, with forty-five minutes left to the show. They had to replace her.

Pascal and his assistant were up to their ears in models and last-minute fittings in the frenetic dressing area, when Cristiano pulled the designer aside with a curt nod of his head. "Jensen's flight just got out," he relayed tersely. "The storms lasted all afternoon. You need to replace her."

Pascal whitened beneath his deep olive skin. "You are sure? There is no chance she'll make it?"

"It's doubtful. You have a contingency plan?"

The designer nodded, his dark eyes troubled. "*Si.* I was holding on for her with the last couple of dresses. I'll make those alterations now. Serafina Bianchi can take her place."

Cristiano nodded. "Do it."

Jensen arrived at the Piazza del Duomo as the FV after-party shifted into full swing. Sick to her stomach about everything that had happened, concerned about her mother, who was still out of it and with a doctor, not to mention the couple of hours' sleep she'd had, curled in a chair by her mother's bed while she watched over her, she felt like a zombie. She wound her way past security and checked in with Pascal. He looked so bitterly disappointed in her, she followed his instructions to don a backless bronze sequined gown he'd designed for the party, without uttering another word.

She peered in the mirror as Stella, her makeup artist, did a superhumanly quick application of color. Registered her unhealthy pallor. She looked downright haggard. It wasn't something Stella could fix, however magical her work, though she did her best as she filled Jensen in on the rumor mill working itself into a frenzy about her absence tonight.

Photos were circulating from the Riviera party the night before, as she'd attempted to blend in and extract her mother while drawing the least attention of the crowd. A photo of her sitting on a not-so-gentlemanly man's knee, his status as a friend of her client's necessitating a polite if firm response from a sharp-toed stiletto, particularly damning. And another from this morning as she'd left the hotel, shattered, a baseball cap pulled down over her eyes.

Oh my God. A buzzing sound filled Jensen's ears. What must Cristiano think? Pascal? She hadn't been able to physically talk to Cristiano to explain anything, and she could only imagine how it looked. Even Stella was eyeing her speculatively, a curiosity she couldn't satisfy. Her mother needed help, but it needed to be private, discreet assistance, not headlines that would ruin her career.

On what might be the only positive note, Stella informed her the response to Pascal's collection had been fantastic, thunderous applause following the designer down the runway, an American fashion guru who ran one of the industry's most prestigious magazines, calling the collection "pure modern genius." Which seemed to be the prevailing opinion.

After Stella pronounced her "as good as it gets," she left the tent and joined the buzzing crowd of glitterati, winding her way through the throngs of people to the VIP group Cristiano stood at the center of, which consisted of Nicholas Zhang, his wife, Claudia, and Ming Li, as well as Marcella, Ilaria and the director of Milan Fashion Week.

Cristiano, his sapphire eyes piercing, stood back as she arrived and held out his arm. Not one physical signal gave away his current frame of mind, except the fury glittering in his eyes. And she knew, as he pressed a kiss to both of her cheeks, that he was going to pretend that everything was fine in an effort to salvage something from the evening, and she couldn't say she minded because she'd never seen him so furious.

She did her job, despite the ice-cold reception from Marcella and Ilaria's clear confusion over her actions, and spent the night attempting to dazzle the Zhang women and make up for her botched promise. The evening seemed to drag on for an eternity as the attendees toasted Pascal's success, one she had always known was predetermined. Her nerves built with every moment Cristiano stayed silent in that supremely controlled, utterly furious way of his that sank into her bones and raised goose bumps on her skin.

Finally, as the party ended, well into the early hours of the morning, the sun starting to rise in the sky, she could stand the nerves no longer. "Cristiano—"

"Not one word," he bit out, his fingers sinking into her forearm. "We will discuss this when we get home."

Back in the quiet, deadly silent confines of the villa, Jensen deposited her bronze clutch on the front entryway table and followed Cristiano into the salon. Pouring himself a glass of water, he turned and leaned against the bar, fury lighting his eyes. "I only asked one thing of you," he rasped. "That you deliver on your promises to me, Jensen. That you *come through* on this for me. But you couldn't even do that. Instead, it was more important for you to party on the Riviera and drink yourself into a stupor."

Her heart sank, ending up somewhere above her churning insides. "I didn't drink myself into a stupor. I wasn't drinking at all. I was at that party because the shoot had run late and Giselle, who'd offered to get me home in the morning, was attending. I never would have stayed if I'd known this would happen."

Cristiano stared at Jensen, sure she was lying. A shoot only ran so late before the light faded. She should have been on that jet, not at that party. As for not drinking, he'd seen the champagne glass in her hand in those paparazzi photos. Her sitting on another man's lap, which might be enraging him the most, because he cared about her on a level that was unprecedented for him, one he refused to admit even to himself. And then, if that hadn't been enough, there had been the photos from this morning, in which she'd looked gray and hungover.

She looked uncertain and guilty. He knew her intimately enough now to read those emotions. Although to be honest, he wasn't sure he knew her at all. Not if she'd do this to him. "That's why you *plan* for things to happen," he bit out. "That's why I made those rules you thought were so silly. Because this was the one thing that *could not* happen." He raked his fingers through his

hair, struggling to focus through bleary eyes. "You humiliated me in front of the media, in front of my inves-
tors, in front of the *Zhangs*. You've stirred up a hornets'
nest of gossip the company does not need, when Pascal's
success needs to rule the day. And for what? So you can
party on the Riviera? *Dio mio*, Jensen. Has what we've
shared not meant anything to you?"

She stared at him with those wide, beautiful ebony
eyes. "Cristiano—you have to let me explain."

"Explain what?" He spread his hands wide. "Give me
one reason, *one reason* why you would have done this
to me. And maybe I can understand."

She sank her teeth into her bottom lip. Looked to be
searching for an answer, perhaps one that would satisfy
him. Which sent the fury blanketing him surging through
his veins. "Funnily enough," he growled, "the network
has been tweeting pictures of you all day. I assume this
is going to make it into a storyline for the show?"

"It might, yes, but—"

That made something inside him snap, his low growl
cutting her off. He could not handle one more lie. Not
one more thing in this moment that disillusioned him
even more about her, because he was in *love* with her.
Had been for a while. Had taken a chance for once in his
life, at having something more, only to have it blow up
in his face. Because really, he should have known better.

He couldn't believe he'd allowed it to happen. That he'd
allowed himself to be seduced by her beautiful smile and
body, by that delicate vulnerability about her that had
made him lose his head when he'd needed it the most.
Because clearly, he had not been thinking rationally. He
hadn't been thinking at all.

Maybe she couldn't help herself. Maybe he'd always

known it was her Achilles' heel. But he'd hoped it could be the alternative. That he'd known where her heart was. Which clearly, he hadn't.

He held up a hand. "I don't want to hear it. I am exhausted and I am *done*."

Her eyes widened. "Done? What do you mean?"

He inserted a hard edge to his voice, because it was the only way he could get the words out of his mouth with conviction. "Done with us, Jensen. I thought that maybe you could be what I needed, but clearly, I was mistaken. You aren't even remotely capable of filling that role. Clearly, I was delusional to think so."

Her delicate face crumpled. She stepped toward him, her fingers resting on his arm. "Cristiano—"

He took a step back, away from all that gilded temptation. "Get some sleep. Do your job, Jensen. That's the only thing I want from you."

CHAPTER EIGHT

JENSEN ARRIVED BACK in New York on a steamy, late-summer evening, in a brief few days' respite from her schedule, after which she was due to close Fashion Week in Paris for FV at the end of the week. It had been too difficult to remain in Milan, on the estate, after everything that had happened, with even Filomena giving her the cold shoulder, as if she'd let her down, too, in the worst way possible.

She was heartsick. *Heartsore,* about the spectacular collapse of her relationship with Cristiano. She knew she should have prioritized him and the show over her mother, but she wasn't sure what else she could have done. Allowed her mother to self-destruct in front of half of the French Riviera, decimating what remained of her career, or step in and try and salvage the situation. Either decision had been impossible.

The car drew to a halt in front of her Upper East Side apartment. The sight of the elegant cream-stuccoed town house might have given her some degree of comfort after months on the road had there not been half a dozen paparazzi clustered outside of it, lying in wait.

Salvador, her driver and bodyguard, turned to look at her from his position in the driver's seat. "Do you want me to circle back around? See if we can shake them?"

Jensen shook her head. It was fruitless to even try. And even though the thought of negotiating that gauntlet in her present state of mind was daunting, she had no choice. The photographers had already spotted her, and her sisters were waiting for her inside.

She jammed a baseball hat on her head and pulled it down over her eyes. Braced herself for the impending fracas. Salvador slid out of the car, opened her door and positioned himself between her and the photographers as they walked quickly up the walkway, his hulky, menacing bulk shielding her from the flashbulbs that exploded in her face.

Forced to keep their distance, the paparazzi fired their questions at her, exploding like stray bullets on the night air.

"Why didn't you walk in the show, Jensen?"

"Are you checking yourself into rehab?"

"What's the status of you and Cristiano Vitale? Are you still together?"

The last one physically hurt. Murmuring her thanks to Salvador, she pushed through the front door of her apartment, closing it on a hail of flashbulbs. Ava, her eldest sister, dark-haired and elegant, and Scarlett, her youngest, blonde and rebellious, were waiting in the foyer.

"Can't they leave you alone for one minute?" Ava asked, frowning. "They are like a pack of hyenas."

"There is nothing as scintillating as when a Davis screws up," Scarlett inserted, cynicism staining her voice. "They can't help themselves. It's a national pastime."

Which she'd done more than once over the past few weeks. Jensen threw her purse on the foyer table, too exhausted to move. Ava hooked an arm through hers and drew her into the salon. "You need a glass of wine, and it will all feel better."

She was afraid it was never going to feel better. That Cristiano had torn her from end to end and nothing was ever going to fix it.

She sank down on the white brocade sofa in her favorite room with its beautiful antique fireplace and elegant wood paneling. Ava poured her a glass of wine and pressed it into her hand before leaning back against the fireplace. "Are you okay?"

Scarlett gave Ava a withering look. "Does she look okay? She's been drying mother out again, while her career goes up in flames." She flicked her gaze to Jensen. "What happened with Cristiano?"

"He is furious. I let him down. I let them all down. He told me we are done. That I am not what he wants or needs."

Scarlett sank down on the sofa beside her, her face resolute. "You're done covering for her, Jensen. Destroying yourself for the sake of her, when she doesn't even appreciate it. She just keeps doing it, again and again, because she knows you'll clean up the mess. And Ava and I have let you carry far too much of the load."

"What choice do we have?" Jensen asked wearily. "We can't abandon her."

"Force her to stand on her own two feet. Act like the grown-up she is." Scarlett waved her phone at her. "We have researched a very discreet rehab center in Arizona. They have some of the top specialists in the country. Mom either decides to complete the program during the hiatus, or she doesn't. But the money stops there. You are not putting one more penny of your savings into her, Jensen."

Jensen swallowed hard, because leaving her mother hanging out to dry was a difficult concept to get her head around.

"It's time for you to focus on yourself," said Scarlett. "On your career and, more importantly, on your love life. Surely, things are repairable with Cristiano?"

Jensen's heart pulsed, her misery bubbling over. She told her sisters the whole story then, everything she'd been holding tight to herself these past few weeks, afraid to break what she and Cristiano had. Worried it would somehow vaporize. The home she'd found on the estate with him and Filomena. The stability and grounding she'd discovered with him. The best version of herself she'd allowed herself to be.

"I miss him," she murmured. "I love him. He's everything I never knew I wanted or needed. But I'm afraid I've messed it up too badly to fix it. I lied to him. I didn't prioritize him, and I put the company's reputation in jeopardy. And," she added, her insides still singed, "he made it clear I am not what he wants or needs."

"Because he isn't operating with all the information," Scarlett reproached. "Why didn't you tell him the truth?"

They'd never told *anyone* the truth. It had been far too risky. "We've signed an NDA. The show could sue us."

"Screw the show," Scarlett said baldly. "I'm done letting it ruin our lives."

Jensen sank her teeth into her lip. What if she told Cristiano the truth and he decided it was just another reason he should have nothing to do with her? Because he might, and she wasn't sure she could take another rejection from him, because the last one had been devastating enough. But she wondered if the truth also went deeper than that. To how intensely vulnerable she'd been with him. How much she'd come to need and depend on him. His demands that she trust him and open up to him. How much that had scared her.

Yes, her mother had been in a precarious situation, but it had been *her* choice to protect her, rather than fulfil her obligations to Cristiano. She could say that she'd been putting the bonds of family first, which she had, but she wondered if it had been more than that. That she'd felt so scared about her growing feelings for Cristiano, so afraid to put herself out there, so afraid of being rejected again, she had subconsciously decided to sabotage her relationship with him rather than have him end it first. That she'd told herself she was protecting her mother, when in fact, she had been protecting herself.

The visit from Alessandra had shaken her. Unearthed every insecurity she'd ever had about herself and her relationship with Cristiano. That even if he wanted her, needed her, he would never end up with someone like her, a message he'd driven home in that final conversation they'd shared, in which he'd assumed so much and hadn't given her a chance to explain.

Even if she told him the truth, as Scarlett was urging her to, and he did forgive her, it still didn't change the facts at hand. That Cristiano needed something other than her, and she couldn't live her life waiting for the other shoe to drop.

Cristiano stood looking out at a breathtaking view of the lake from the terrace of the villa on a picture-perfect Milanese night. Nicholas Zhang's signature was on the contract his lawyers had drawn up, his manufacturing issues had been ironed out, and Pascal's collection was garnering rave reviews from every corner of the globe, ensuring the rebirth of the company he had spent a decade rebuilding. Everything he'd worked so hard for, there in the blink of an eye.

He should feel some deeply ingrained sense of vindication. A weight lifted off his shoulders. The chance to perhaps sleep again at night. Instead, his dreams were haunted by a mahogany-haired siren. And she was everywhere. Sitting on the counter in his kitchen, laughing at him with those beautiful dark eyes. Perched on his desk, offering some uncannily sharp observation from that whip-smart brain of hers. In his bed, her long golden limbs splayed out for his delectation, his every fantasy come true.

He knew he looked haunted. He had caught himself staring off into space more than once this week. But he was so disappointed in Jensen, so bitterly disappointed, he wasn't sure he could get past it. He'd been clear he needed honesty from her. Reliability. *Transparency.* It was the only way he could live his life, given his backstory. And yet she hadn't given it to him—she'd given him the opposite.

His fingers tightened around the railing as he took in the sunset setting the sky on fire. He'd broken every rule for her—shattered those carefully delineated lines he drew between business and pleasure. Had gone off script for the first time in his life. She'd been the absolute riskiest choice for him, but he'd done it anyway, because the way he'd felt when he'd been with her had been like nothing else he'd ever experienced. A hedonistic side of himself he'd never tapped into.

He'd known he should listen to his rational self—that she was too much trouble, too young, too *flighty* for him. Had told himself more than once over the past few weeks that he should walk away. Instead, he'd gotten so wrapped up in her, been so mad about her, he hadn't wanted to let her go. Had wanted to keep that piece of himself he'd discovered. To hell with the consequences.

And now she was gone. Restless, unsure of how to handle the unfamiliar emotion bubbling up inside him, how to *shake* it, he carried the glass of scotch to his mouth and swallowed a long draw. The clatter of Filomena's heels on the terrace pulled him out of his reverie. Turning, he absorbed the grimace written across her lined, aged face.

"The *biondina* is here," she said, sottovoce. "I have tried to get her to use the front door, but it doesn't seem to be in her vocabulary."

Cristiano would have smiled at her description of his ex as the *blonde bombshell*, Filomena's feelings for Alessandra long apparent, but he didn't have the heart for it tonight. He wasn't sure he had the patience for it either, but given that Alessandra had already penetrated his inner defenses and was walking out onto the terrace, clad in a chic white pantsuit, he clearly had no choice.

"Va bene," he murmured to Filomena. "Finish up. Enjoy your night."

His housekeeper nodded and vanished inside. Alessandra, an ocean's worth of confidence in her stride, walked across the terrace to greet him. Given their close personal relationship since childhood, a friendship that had eventually turned into a relationship that had been more mutually beneficial than anything, he pressed a kiss to both of her cheeks and summoned a patience he did not possess.

"To what do I owe the pleasure?" he drawled, sinking back against the railing, arms crossed over his chest, drink pressed to his side. "I thought we were going to see each other at the benefit next week."

Her scarlet mouth firmed. "I thought we should talk, given the events of the past couple of weeks."

His instincts told him to cut it off right there, because this was a path they definitely didn't need to go down, but Alessandra looked as if she had something to say and wasn't about to be derailed.

"Bene," he murmured. "About what in particular?"

"Us." She fixed her china-blue gaze on his. "It is clear that you needed a break, Cristiano. That you've been on a—" she paused, flicking her wrist at him "—how do I say it? A walk on the *wild side*. But it's time we worked things out. You and I both know we are perfectly suited for each other."

Cristiano's mind was boggled. What part of *we are done* had she not understood? How much clearer did he need to be? "We are not getting back together, Alessandra. *Ever*. I thought I made that clear."

She shrugged a shoulder. "You've been under a great deal of pressure. You will change your mind, I'm sure, once you get over this brief lapse of sanity."

Brief lapse of sanity? He eyed her. "You're referring to Jensen, I take it?"

"Si." She crossed a slim leg over the other and rested back against the railing. "I met her. Last week, before Pascal's show. I came to see you, but you weren't here. She came into the kitchen as I was leaving, dressed in one of your shirts, acting as if she owned the place. Honestly, Cristiano, I don't know what you see in her. She is pretty, I will admit, if you are focused on sex appeal. Which is exactly where Marcella thinks the attraction lies. She thinks you are 'sowing your wild oats' with her."

Blood pulsed through Cristiano's head. He couldn't believe his grandmother had said that. But he was more concerned with what Alessandra had said to Jensen. "You talked to Jensen?"

A tiny shrug. "A brief conversation."

"What did you say to her?" he gritted out.

"The truth. That you will never end up with someone like her. That she is just a temporary thing for you while you work your way through whatever it is you are working through. And good that I did, because she has now clearly revealed her true colors." Her voice softened. "I wanted to let you know that I forgive you. I understand that I have been selfish and demanding, and that has been an issue for you. I will work on it. But I think we should choose a wedding date and truly commit, Cristiano. I'm not getting any younger and I know you want to have lots of *bambini*, so we need to do it soon."

Cristiano's head threatened to explode. He could not believe she'd said that to Jensen. That she was so severely deluded. Maybe he'd strung it on too long, maybe part of this was his fault for giving in to the pressure his family had been applying around the match, because in some ways, it had made sense. But *this*, this was so far over the top, he couldn't even comprehend it.

His brain flashed back to the morning Jensen had left for Cannes. She hadn't looked right. She'd looked *off*. He'd brushed it off as stress about the trip, but now, he wondered if it had been more. How must it have felt to hear Alessandra say those things? Given what she'd shared about never being taken seriously by men? How sensitive she was about her family's reputation? Exacerbated by the harsh words he'd uttered when he'd ended things between them, without even giving her a chance to explain. Words he hadn't meant. Words he'd wished he could take back the minute they'd left his mouth.

She must have been devastated. His heart sank deep into his chest. And what had he done to reassure Jensen about his feelings for her? About his intentions? He'd been so focused on work, on getting through the crunch he'd been in, he'd refused to address his emotions for her. Had been terrified to, because of what that admission might mean. That he was in love with her. Had thought his actions spoke louder than words.

"You can't marry her," Alessandra said dismissively, clearly reading his face. "Honestly, Cristiano. With that video floating around with her mother melting down in France? That family is a disaster waiting to happen."

Cristiano blinked. "What video?"

"Non lo so." I don't know. She waved a hand at him. "Some tacky video someone shot with a cell phone. Veronica Davis was apparently out of it at a party. Drugs, alcohol...who knows? Apparently, she also has massive gambling debt. Jensen had to step in and clean up the whole mess. Can you imagine taking that on?"

No, he couldn't. An unsettled feeling moved through him. Jensen had looked worried, *decimated*, on her return from Cannes. He'd marked it as the guilt she'd felt from letting him down. But now, the pieces of the puzzle he'd been attempting to decipher ever since that first night in London, about Jensen's erratic, contradictory behavior, slotted themselves into discomfiting place. The thirty-thousand-euro bar tab and wrecked hotel rooms in Monaco she had said were some *out-of-control friends*. Her frenetic schedule she wouldn't cut back on. The fear in her voice when she'd called him from France, and said something had come up.

The anxiety he'd sensed in her in the in-between moments when she'd thought no one was watching. She had been and was still covering for her mother, who was, apparently, not only an alcoholic, but a drug and gambling addict as well. Which explained Jensen's insane schedule and need for endless money. She couldn't stop working or the whole thing would fall apart.

He raked a hand through his hair. He'd been so sure he *knew* her. Where her heart was. That he could trust her. And yet what had he done? Believed the worst of her without even giving her a chance to explain. And why would she really? All he had done was throw his autocratic rules at her from day one, dictating what she could and could not do, because she'd led him to believe what he had, clearly to protect her mother. Made it clear where his priorities lay in FV. Nor had he given her any indication she would have his support if she did come to him. That he would have protected her. Because he would have.

She'd told him she found it hard to trust. He had known that. And yet he'd missed all the signs. Every clue he should have caught.

Jensen had never been on a spiral. Her mother had.

Jensen stood backstage at the Palais Garnier in Paris, the historic Fashion Week setting raising goose bumps on her skin with its gorgeous, gilded interior and ceiling painted by Marc Chagall. Never in her life had she felt this nervous before a show. Anxious, yes, in her first few appearances for big designers, but not this kind of debilitating, bone-deep fear. Her life had exploded around her in the last week, every Davis secret she'd ever harbored on display for the world to see. Lurid, embarrassing details about her mother's descent into gambling and addiction and her decision to enter rehab earlier that week.

Everyone, it seemed, had an opinion about her family's manufactured stardom and their very public fall from grace. But amidst it all, despite her position at the center of the storm, she had a job to do. A promise to keep. And this time, there was nothing to shield her from it. For once in her life, she had to put herself out there. Lay herself bare to the world. Show herself in all of her flaws. And hope she was forgiven.

She took her place at the top of the grand double staircase, Millie on her opposite side, where she would descend, lit by candelabra, to the opulent foyer, and walk the gilded runway. Her knees practically knocking together because she wanted this to be so perfect, to somehow make up for everything she'd done, she drew in a deep breath, waited for her cue, then started down the stairs, flanked by the stunning chandeliers and exquisite bronze sculptures.

The train of the dress in her hand, her concentration complete, so she didn't take a disastrous tumble down the stairs, she absorbed the exquisitely dressed crowd, waiting at the bottom of the staircase. The buzz in the room for Pascal's incredible collection, which was taking the fashion world by storm. But it was the man leaning against one of the massive gold pillars who stole her attention. Dark and insanely good-looking in the tailored navy suit he wore, accented by a pale lavender shirt, he stopped her heart in her chest.

He was not supposed to be here.

Had, according to Pascal, elected to tend to other business, rather than attend the show. Her gaze locked with Cristiano's sapphire-blue one, emotion clogging her throat. What was he doing here, just when she'd finally gotten a hold of herself?

Cristiano's unfathomable gaze slid over the sheer, nearly transparent silver dress she wore, lined only where it absolutely needed to be lined, the slit that began high on her thigh exposing the sweep of her long legs. Over the artfully wild tumble of her dark hair, cascading over her shoulders and down her back. She swallowed hard at the energy that passed between them, the muscles in her throat contracting.

It was undeniable the heat between them. It froze her in her tracks. Sucked the air from her lungs, because that part of them had never been in question. It was everything else that threatened their connection. That her past would always be a barrier for them, no matter how hard, how resolutely, she tried to leave it behind. That being a Davis was a stain on her soul that would forever be a part of her, destroying everything in its wake.

She hiked her chin, holding her head high. She couldn't be anything but who she was. She had finally learned that lesson. But she could define who she was from here on out. And she intended to do just that.

Forcing herself to move, she descended the rest of the stairs. By the time she made it to the bottom, she was shaking in her shoes. It was all she could do to focus for the rest of the show. At the after-party, held in the spectacular Grand Foyer.

She located Cristiano immediately, standing in a group of VIPs, looking immaculately self-possessed as always. Maybe he was here on business, she thought nervously, and it had nothing to do with her at all. Except, why was he looking at her like that, like she was the only person in the room?

Needing something to do, she plucked a glass of sparkling wine from a passing waiter's tray to occupy herself, but Cristiano was already murmuring his regrets to the group he was in and heading toward her, eating up the ground with a purposeful stride.

"Mon Dieu," Millie murmured, her gaze on Cristiano. "I wish a man would look at me like that. Just once."

"He's furious with me," Jensen replied quietly. "I'm not sure you would."

"If that's how he looks at you when he's angry," Millie offered, "sign me up."

Cristiano stopped and greeted them both, the tantalizing citrus scent of his expensive aftershave assailing her senses as he bent his head and pressed his sensuous mouth against her cheek in a whisper-soft caress. It slammed into the protective layers she'd encased herself in, unearthing emotions she didn't want to feel. Memories that held the power to disassemble her completely. She sucked in a breath as he did the same with the other cheek and stepped back, his sapphire gaze fixed on hers, penetrating and unyielding.

"A moment," he murmured, "if you wouldn't mind."

She followed him, knees shaking, as he guided her through the crowd, out to one of the stately balconies, with its superb view of the Place de l'Opéra, deserted as the guests enjoyed a first cocktail inside.

She leaned against a pillar, crossing her arms over her chest as a warm breeze wafted over her, attempting to corral the emotion vibrating her insides. The hurt still bubbling up inside of her like an irrepressible force. Cristiano took up a position opposite her, his gaze trained on her face.

"You aren't supposed to be here," she murmured, bereft as to what to say. Unsure which of the emotions coursing through her it was appropriate to feel. Hope. Fear. Uncertainty. They all seemed relevant.

"I wanted to see you," he said quietly. "And apologize for the way I handled things that night in Milan. I was angry. I said things I shouldn't have. Things I didn't mean. Things I never would have said if I'd known the truth. Which you didn't tell me."

Her lashes lowered, shading her cheeks. "I was protecting my mother."

"Jensen," he murmured on a low note, a banked level of emotion edging his voice that tightened her insides, "we were lovers. As intimate as two people can be. I asked you, *begged* you to tell me the truth. What was going on. I wanted to help. Instead, you allowed me to believe that you had cavalierly broken the terms of your contract, that you didn't care enough to make the show, that you had let all of us down, when in fact, you were cleaning up after your mother, who is an *addict* you have been covering for your entire life. Who is the reason you work yourself into the ground at the expense of your own career." His mouth flattened, a dark brow winging to the sky. "Do I have that right, *cara*?"

"Pretty much." She pushed a hand through the tumbled length of her hair, her stomach clenching. "You were so angry, Cristiano. I didn't think explaining would help. You had made it clear I was not to put a foot out of line or I would lose my contract. I was terrified if I told you the truth about my mother, you would drop me like a hot potato. That you would consider me more trouble than I am worth."

His sapphire gaze darkened. "I *cared* about you, Jensen. If I was autocratic in the beginning, it was because I was protecting my investment. Because I didn't understand what was going on, and you didn't tell me. All that changed when we became lovers. Surely you knew that? Why wouldn't you tell me?"

She drew in a deep breath. "My mother's addictions are a secret we've guarded for years—since early on in the show. She was never quite right after my father left. She was destroyed by it. But she needed the show to survive. The producers were adamant her issues not become public knowledge, because they felt it would ruin the show. Which would have been devastating for her." She sank her teeth into her lip. "My mother is in debt. A great deal of debt. I have been bankrolling her expenses for the past couple of years, attempting to get her back on her feet, yet it never seems to happen."

"Which is why you were so desperate to work. Why you wouldn't take a step back."

"Yes." She inclined her head.

"And the party in Cannes in which you purportedly spent thirty thousand euros on gambling and drinks and trashed hotel rooms… That was not you, but your mother?"

She nodded. "It was easier to let the press think it was me. To draw the attention away from her. Before," she elaborated, "she was more discreet. In control. But these past few months, it all began to spiral. The show was on the ratings bubble. The producers were threatening to cancel if she didn't deliver the numbers for the season finale. It was the only reason I did the fountain stunt. Because she begged me to do it. Her fears about money, the pressure the producers were putting her under. It was crushing. That night in Cannes was a breaking point for her. My father had announced he was remarrying—some Hollywood starlet half his age. She was shattered."

He frowned. "And your sisters? Could they not have helped? Where are they in all of this?"

"They help when they can, but they are managing a fledgling business. There was no money to spare in the early years, nor much time, for that matter. So a lot has fallen on me. Which will hopefully change now that they are more established. We worked out a plan in New York on how to handle things once my mother is out of rehab."

"You should have come to me," he said quietly. "I could have been there for you. I *would* have been there for you. But I can't solve a problem I don't know exists."

She sank her teeth deeper in her lip. "You were in the middle of a tsunami, Cristiano. *Drowning.* I wasn't going to add something else to your plate."

He pushed away from the wall and closed the distance between them, his familiar, delicious scent infiltrating her senses, weakening her knees. "I am in *love* with you, *cara*," he murmured, lifting a hand and brushing his thumb across her cheek. "That's what people do when they care about someone. They put them first. Which is why it hurt so much when you didn't show up for me that night. When you let me down so badly. I couldn't understand why you would do something like that. And you refused to trust me enough to tell me the truth."

Her brain froze at the part where he'd said he loved her. *Loved her.* It was a little too earth-shattering to process. Her gaze locked with his, her heart crawling up her throat. "I have trouble with trust. I told you that. It's something I struggle with."

His gaze softened. "Well, you're going to have to get used to it, because I'm not going anywhere, *cara*."

Her heart started to race like a runaway train. "You told me I'd never be what you needed that night in Milan,

Cristiano. You were fighting your feelings for me. I watched you do it night after night."

"Because I was trying to sort out my feelings. *Process* them. Not because I didn't love you." He raked a hand through his thick dark hair, stark emotion written across his hard-boned face. "My parents loved each other deeply. Ilaria and I were shattered when we lost them. Maybe I decided I was never going to put myself through that pain again. So I chose a woman like Alessandra, who seemed a safe, logical choice. But I couldn't pull the trigger on it."

A glint of humor entered his sapphire gaze. "And then I met you and you whirled through my life like a hurricane, and I discovered a depth of emotion I'd never felt before. A *part* of myself I'd never known. And I knew I could never settle for anything less."

Her knees were feeling weaker with every word that came out of his mouth, dangerously close to giving way beneath her. "I'm so sorry," she whispered. "I know how much that night meant to you. It killed me inside. If I could do it over, find a way to make it right, I would. But I can't."

"I don't need you to do it over," he said softly. "That's one of the things I love so much about you, Jensen—that you love so deeply. That you are still hanging in there with your crazy, misguided mother, when she's given you a million reasons to walk away. Because you value family that much. But there is," he qualified, "one thing I need from you, *cara mia,* if we are to make this work. Honesty. *Full disclosure.* Trust. It's a nonnegotiable for me given my past. I have to know I can depend on you, no matter what."

He was talking about the future. Her brain couldn't seem to process it all, because it felt like a promise. "In exchange," he continued, a solemn expression on his face, "I want to be the man you can always count on. Who will always be there for you. Who will protect you, no matter what. I have broad shoulders, *tesoro*. I can take it."

Her heart thudded in her chest, like it might burst. And then, she thought it might have, when he dropped to one knee right there on the balcony in front of her, in his beautiful dark suit, so handsome he stole her breath, and pulled a satin box out of his jacket pocket.

Oh my God. She sagged against the pillar, knees weak, as he flipped open the box to reveal a sparkling sapphire ring surrounded by diamonds in what appeared to be a deep Vitale blue.

"It seemed fitting," he murmured, capturing her hand in his. "Marry me, Jensen. I'm like a ghost in that damn villa, it's so empty without you. I need you back."

It seemed impossible to get the word out, past the lump in her throat, because he was all she'd never known she could have. And she was afraid he would vaporize like everything else good had done in her life. Except he was so very real as he slid the platinum band over her finger and the beautiful sapphire glittered in the moonlight. And she knew in her heart, it was forever.

"Yes," she finally breathed, acquiring enough air to speak. And then she was in his arms, her fingers buried in his thick dark hair, and he was kissing her.

Neither of them heard Millie and Lucy traipse along a few moments later, stilettos clicking the stone beneath their feet. Until Millie's audible gasp filled the air. "Oh my God. *Oh my God.* Look at that ring. That is so completely unfair."

Jensen stirred out of Cristiano's soul-searing kiss and

smiled against his lips. She liked to think of it as meant to be.

"Go find your own," she tossed over her shoulder. "This one is taken."

"Sure, sure," Millie grumbled. "Tell me where I can find one like that and I will."

* * * * *

COMING SOON!

We really hope you enjoyed reading this book. If you're looking for more romance be sure to head to the shops when new books are available on

Thursday 12th October

To see which titles are coming soon, please visit

millsandboon.co.uk/nextmonth

MILLS & BOON

MILLS & BOON ®

Coming next month

PREGNANT AND STOLEN BY THE TYCOON
Maya Blake

One night. It was only meant to be one night.

Genie only realized she'd said it out loud when Seve's whole body tightened, turning even more marble-like than before.

"Why are you doing this? You don't want even want a child. You said as much when we had dinner."

His eyes glinted, his incisive gaze tracking her as she paced in the small cabin. "What I felt a few weeks ago no longer matters."

"That's absurd. Of course it does."

He gritted his teeth. "Let me rephrase. The child you're carrying—*my* child—is now my number one priority. I'm not taking my eyes off you until he or she is born."

Continue reading
PREGNANT AND STOLEN BY THE TYCOON
Maya Blake

Available next month
www.millsandboon.co.uk

LET'S TALK

Romance

For exclusive extracts, competitions and special offers, find us online:

- **f** MillsandBoon
- **𝕏** @MillsandBoon
- **◉** @MillsandBoonUK
- **♪** @MillsandBoonUK

Get in touch on 01413 063 232

MILLS & BOON

THE HEART OF ROMANCE

A ROMANCE FOR EVERY READER

MODERN
Prepare to be swept off your feet by sophisticated, sexy and seductive heroes, in some of the world's most glamourous and romantic locations, where power and passion collide.

HISTORICAL
Escape with historical heroes from time gone by. Whether your passion is for wicked Regency Rakes, muscled Vikings or rugged Highlanders, awaken the romance of the past.

MEDICAL
Set your pulse racing with dedicated, delectable doctors in the high-pressure world of medicine, where emotions run high and passion, comfort and love are the best medicine.

True Love
Celebrate true love with tender stories of heartfelt romance, from the rush of falling in love to the joy a new baby can bring, and a focus on the emotional heart of a relationship.

Desire
Indulge in secrets and scandal, intense drama and sizzling hot action with heroes who have it all: wealth, status, good looks…everything but the right woman.

HEROES
The excitement of a gripping thriller, with intense romance at its heart. Resourceful, true-to-life women and strong, fearless men face danger and desire - a killer combination!

To see which titles are coming soon, please visit

millsandboon.co.uk/nextmonth

MILLS & BOON
MEDICAL
Pulse-Racing Passion

Set your pulse racing with dedicated, delectable doctors in the high-pressure world of medicine, where emotions run high and passion, comfort and love are the best medicine.

Six Medical stories published every month, find them all at:

millsandboon.co.uk

MILLS & BOON

Desire

Indulge in secrets and scandal, intense drama and plenty of sizzling hot action with powerful and passionate heroes who have it all: wealth, status, good looks…everything but the right woman.

GET YOUR ROMANCE FIX!

Get the latest romance news, exclusive author interviews, story extracts and much more!